LINDSAY BUROKER

STAR KINGDOM

CROSSFIRE

BOOK FOUR

Crossfire

Star Kingdom, Book 4

by Lindsay Buroker

ACKNOWLEDGMENTS

THANK YOU FOR PICKING UP THIS NEXT INSTALLMENT in my Star Kingdom series. I'm not sure yet how many books there will be in the series, but I'm having a lot of fun writing these characters, and I have at least a few more planned after this one. I hope you continue to enjoy the quirky characters and their equally quirky adventures. No spoilers, but Zee gets a new buddy in this one.

Before you jump in, please let me thank my editor, Shelley Holloway, for the help with this series, and also my beta readers, Rue Silver, Sarah Engelke, and Cindy Wilkinson for chiming in with helpful suggestions. Also, thank you to Jeff Brown for the fun spaceship cover art.

Please enjoy the story!

CHAPTER 1

THE SQUIRREL CHATTERED MENACING WARNINGS TOWARD A NESTING tiktik bird as it scampered across the thick branch of the native zindi tree with a peanut in its mouth. Kim Sato scattered a few more nuts on top of the fence post before padding to the small patio table to sit and enjoy her coffee.

While she and Casmir had been away in space, the weather had turned warm, and even though the sun wasn't high enough to shine on her face yet, she sat back and enjoyed the peace of being home again. She wished life were getting completely back to normal, but today, Casmir had to finish packing and get a ride to the launch loop where a shuttle would take him up to the Kingdom Fleet warship the *Osprey*, commanded by his old robotics camp nemesis, Captain Ishii. They would head off to who knew where—another system entirely, most likely—and if Casmir couldn't help Ishii find and reclaim the ancient wormhole gate for the king… Kim didn't know what would happen.

The sliding door opened, and Casmir walked out in his socks and Robot Remstar pajamas, while holding a huge mug of steaming coffee in his hands. His hair was an unbrushed tangle that the tiktik bird might consider a suitable nesting spot if he wasn't careful.

Kim almost shared the thought aloud, but Casmir's eyes were bloodshot, and the coffee was an atypical choice for him. He looked like he needed it. Badly.

"You all right?" she asked as he approached the table.

Casmir paused in the middle of pulling out a chair to stare at her. "I must look wrecked. You never ask me that."

"Only because I'm not good at reading faces. The coffee was my main clue that something's up."

"Ah. Yes." Casmir finished sitting, took a gulp, and made a face. "Rough night."

She waited for him to explain further, assuming he would. Casmir was the chatty one. He loved talking. If there was something he didn't want to speak about, he would simply find something else to burble about, redirecting the listener's interest elsewhere. But for once, he didn't do that. He took another gulp of the coffee.

"Because of the vault?" Kim finally prompted.

The night before, they had slipped into the Royal Zamek Seed Bank, descended to a storage vault in the basement, and verified what Kim had guessed earlier and what Casmir had apparently never guessed.

Three hundred years ago, someone had taken cells from the legendary Admiral Tariq Mikita, and they had been kept safe and viable all that time. Thirty-three years ago, King Jager and Queen Iku had used the sample to have two clones made, one who grew up to become notorious criminal and mercenary Captain Tenebris Rache, and one who'd become robotics professor Casmir Dabrowski.

Casmir shook his head. "No. That was stunning—to me, at least—" he gave her a quick puzzled look, still seeming to find it odd that she hadn't been surprised, "—but not horrifying. I'm feeling…" He blew out a slow breath. "I wish I had time to go to the synagogue and pray this morning."

Kim arched her eyebrows. She knew he was religious and observed all the holidays—when not locked in a dungeon or being chased by bad guys in space—but for him, it always seemed to be about spending time with his friends and family, rather than sitting alone and seeking divine guidance.

"I keep having this nightmare." Casmir took another sip, still holding the mug in both hands, as if for warmth. Or maybe support. It wasn't that cold. "Technically, it's not a nightmare since it's something that really happened. But that makes it worse. And sometimes it morphs into things that didn't happen, but mostly, I keep seeing this… thing over and over."

"You haven't told me exactly what happened when you were in King Jager's dungeon." She considered that Casmir was more likely to be distressed about things that happened to other people than to himself and added, "Or in that terrorist base."

Casmir shuddered, and she believed she had guessed right, that something there had disturbed him.

"Not something Rache did, I hope." Kim knew he was a criminal and had killed countless Kingdom men, but she wanted to believe… she didn't know what, exactly. That he wouldn't have done anything terrible while fulfilling a favor for her. It had meant something to her that he had been willing to risk himself on her behalf—even if it shouldn't have.

"Rache *did* mow down a bunch of people, but there's not much else he could have done at that point. The terrorists knew we were there, and they were trying to kill us. While he went in the front and fought them straight on, I dragged myself through a crawlspace and knocked out the stealth generator. After I did that, I went looking for him—and my parents, because that was right after you'd messaged me that they had been kidnapped. I was worried they might be inside." He gazed at the coffee in the mug, not batting an eye as the chubby squirrel returned, jumping from the branch to the fence post, then back to the branch with a new treasure purloined. "Rache had gotten captured—or allowed himself to get captured so he would be taken to the leader."

Kim nodded, well aware of the great risk Rache had taken in helping, especially since he loathed King Jager and probably hadn't been that bothered by the terrorist attacks on a planet he'd abandoned long ago. Or so she assumed. Now that she knew Rache's real first name, maybe she would dig up more information and figure out what happened to him, how he'd been raised and what had caused him to take up arms against Jager. Or maybe she *wouldn't* dig up that information. He was gone now, and she was back on Odin where she belonged. It would be best for her career if she never had anything to do with Rache again.

"I crawled up to where he was being questioned about me—heard some interesting things about his past if you're ever curious." Casmir's eyebrows rose.

Kim hesitated. She *was* curious, but… "No."

"Good." Casmir smiled faintly, but the haunted look never left his eyes. "The men around Rache weren't in armor so I threw the vials, and that distracted them."

Kim almost said that she'd heard about that from Rache but was reluctant to admit they had communicated after the event. She only nodded.

"Those worked very well. Thank you. The leader *was* in armor. Alexandre Bernard. I looked him up after the battle. He was a Kingdom man and the former chief superintendent of Royal Intelligence, but something obviously happened to make him change sides big time. He had some implants and seemed to be committed to working with the astroshamans—there were a bunch of them in that base, so the working assumption is that they've been behind the terrorist group from the beginning. I need to do some research en route, figure out if the terrorist activity started before or after they could have learned about the gate. I'd assumed the gate was found very recently, but maybe they suspected it was in our system and wanted us distracted at home? Or maybe they wanted us distracted for *other* reasons and just happened to be in the system when the gate was discovered. I am guessing Royal Intelligence has a mole, maybe someone who used to be loyal to Bernard. Remember how we were given coordinates to land at, and then surprise, we were attacked there?"

Kim nodded and sipped from her own mug, aware that Casmir was doing what she'd been thinking about earlier, talking about something else to distract his listener from the uncomfortable thing he didn't want to discuss. Maybe she should let it pass without comment. If he didn't want to talk about his nightmares, who was she to pry? He was a grown man, two years older than she, even, Robot Remstar pajamas notwithstanding.

"I hope I'm left alone, preferably in a cabin and not a brig cell, and allowed to do a lot of research on the way to… wherever they take me first. Probably Modi Moon, where I originally hid the cargo ship, so we can double-check to make sure it isn't there and to see if we can find any clues about where it went. I'm also hoping I can get someone to give me access to the government network. I've thought about trying to hack my way in a few times, but if I were caught… I'm already in enough trouble with Jager."

"I think," Kim said, "for the sake of your life, your career, and your friends and family, you should go along meekly with the Fleet on this mission and do exactly what Jager wants. Even if he's done things of questionable morality, that's true of almost every political leader that's ever existed. This is our home, and we can't do anything about the leadership, not without starting a war. We're not in the nobility and couldn't get a seat on the Senate, even if we wished, and there's only been one king in all of Odin's history who was so loathsome that the Senate acted to get rid of him."

"I know."

"Although…" She tilted her head as a new thought stirred. "*Are* you of the nobility? I'm not sure how much of the Kingdom's revisionist history to trust when it comes to Admiral Mikita—as you pointed out, that's not your face in the history books, not in the digital ones, anyway—but he supposedly was born common and through deeds was granted noble status during his military career. We might have to hunt through the legal records to see if there's a precedent for people cloned from noblemen being granted the rights and status of noblemen. Cloning people hasn't been going on for long, not here on Odin, and there's a stigma against it, at least for people."

Casmir twitched a shoulder. "Rache seemed to think we would be considered noble, but he also said there wasn't much, if any, of a precedent. He was probably raised to believe he was noble—I remember Asger making a comment about how he knew how to fight knights. Like maybe he'd been trained to fight as one himself. I don't care about him, though. He's blown up his chances to ever have a place here on Odin or in any of the Kingdom habitats."

It was silly, but Kim found that thought bleak. Was Rache destined to live and die in the cold of space? Killing for a living and one day meeting a violent end himself? Could a man like that ever change? He'd have to *want* to change, and Kim had a hard time imagining that.

"I better finish packing." Casmir pushed back his chair. "I promised my mother I'd take changes of underwear this time."

"I'm sure she's vastly relieved."

As he headed for the door, Kim heard herself ask, "Casmir?"

"Yeah?" He turned, a hint of wariness in his eyes.

He had to know she was going to ask about the dream. Even if she shouldn't pry if he was reluctant to speak of it, she had a hard time setting aside her curiosity. And if it was possible she could offer some advice or say something comforting that might help him, she wanted to do that. She hated to think about it, but there was a possibility this mission would be so dangerous that he wouldn't survive it, and she would never see him again.

"What happened after you threw the vials and everyone except Rache and the leader—and you—were exposed?"

Casmir leaned against the door jamb. "Actually, Rache's armor had been damaged and his helmet was off, so he was exposed too."

Ah, yes. Rache had admitted that in his letter.

"Probably the only time I'll ever see him with tears in his eyes." Casmir looked at the patio, one socked toe prodding a seam where moss grew. "He got some weapons from the sick guards, including a grenade. The other guy—Bernard—had a grenade too. Rache was going to throw his, and I could see it bouncing off Bernard's armor and not being as effective as if…" Casmir swallowed. "Well, my brain was just trying to solve the problem of something not being effective. I had this duct tape I'd grabbed, and I threw it to Rache and told him to stick it *to* our enemy."

"Oh." Kim could imagine where this was going.

"They grappled, and I didn't see everything, but then the grenades went off. Rache had stuck it to the back of Bernard's helmet. And when it blew, it was graphic." Casmir rested a hand on his stomach. "There wasn't much time to parse it then, since the explosions started a rockfall and I was just trying to stay alive, but that's the moment I keep seeing again and again. I suggested something—and provided the tool to make it happen—that resulted in a man's head being blown off."

He eyed her warily again, and she realized she might have misread the first look like that he'd given her. Maybe it wasn't that he hadn't wanted to talk about it, but that he had feared she would judge him.

Kim shook her head. She was more likely to judge herself, because she felt he'd done the logical thing. Sometimes, it disturbed her how easy it was for her to rule in favor of logic over emotion.

"I can see where that would be extremely disturbing, especially for someone like you, but I'm sure Rache was going to kill that man anyway. It was probably a relatively quick and painless way to go. And I assume he was trying to kill *you*."

"Yes, and I know those things, but you arrest criminals, Kim. You don't blow their heads off. Other people died in there too. All those guys who weren't armored and were puking on the floor when the ceiling collapsed… They didn't have a Zee to protect them. Thank you for sending him, by the way."

"You're welcome." The last she'd seen Zee, he had been standing in the living room next to the coat rack, observing the neighborhood for potential threats. She hoped the Fleet soldiers would allow Casmir to take his stoic bodyguard along on his mission. "And those are the people who were setting bombs, kidnapping your parents, and killing Kingdom citizens. I'm afraid I can't share your distress at their deaths. If they'd been arrested, Jager would have had them executed or sent to one of the prison asteroid mines. Rehabilitation laws are for citizens, not enemies from another system."

"Enemies from another system are supposed to be extradited for their own governments to deal with."

Kim waved her hand. She knew the law, but when she'd been doing research for her thriller novel, she'd learned that those laws were usually only obeyed if the prisoners in question were prominent enough in the other nation's society that returning them might be used as a bargaining chip at a future date. Maybe it hadn't always been like that, but it was like that under Jager's rule.

Casmir started to turn again to go inside, but he paused, his face scrunching in an odd expression. "Someone like me?"

"I didn't mean that as an insult. You have a gentle soul, Casmir." She knew how much it bothered him that the crushers, which he'd helped make out of some notion that they would be deployed as guardians for the planet, were being used to kill people.

"Well, my parents wouldn't let me play violent network games as a kid." The faint smile returned, however fleeting. "My father even lectured me if I slammed the checkers pieces down too hard on the board."

"Your parents are good people."

"Yeah. I'd hate to turn into someone they were disappointed in."

"You won't. I promise."

He gave her another quick smile, but his eyes still looked haunted.

Kim leaned back in her chair, wondering if she'd helped him at all.

She also wondered who had raised Rache. Not Jager and Iku, she was fairly certain. If Rache had been a fixture in the castle, she couldn't imagine that the media would have been unaware of him. Unless he'd been locked in some cell and forbidden to go out where anyone might see him. She doubted that. If Jager had wanted his future war hero to be loyal to him, he wouldn't have been too much of an ass. At least not initially.

She drummed her fingers, wishing she'd asked Casmir to tell her what he'd overheard.

The doorbell rang. Since Casmir had gone inside, she assumed he would answer it. It was probably some Fleet soldier, making sure he didn't decide at the last minute to flee the city. Poor Casmir. He'd gotten himself into this situation, but only because he was skeptical about Jager's intentions. Most people wouldn't put their necks out in front of the king's carriage—or air bike—but Casmir wasn't most people.

"Uhm, Kim?" Casmir stuck his head outside again. "You have visitors." He winced and mouthed "I'm sorry" before backing into the kitchen.

Chief Superintendent Van Dijk walked out, trailed by two soldiers. "Scholar Sato? King Jager has decided that you need to personally go on the mission, in case any adjustments to your bacteria are needed to ensure our people can deal with the gate once they find it."

Kim slumped back in her chair. So much for life getting back to normal.

CHAPTER 2

CASMIR'S STOMACH DIDN'T LIKE HIS SECOND TRIP INTO space any more than his first.

He was pressed back into a pod in Sir William Asger's gleaming purple knight shuttle, with Kim engulfed in the seat beside him. The pods reduced the effects of acceleration as they shot away from the launch loop and into space, where they would rendezvous with the *Osprey*, so Casmir's eyes didn't feel like they were visiting the back of his skull, but his stomach found the whole experience highly suspect.

He'd taken two kinds of anti-nausea medication. Unfortunately, the combined effect was making him nauseated. The legendary Admiral Mikita had reputedly spent half his life in space, battling enemy ships and winning systems for the Kingdom. Had *his* stomach protested against every shift in gravity?

"I may have to take you up on your offer, Kim," Casmir said.

Asger, who sat in the pilot's seat up front, rotated his pod enough to glance back at Casmir. But he didn't comment. Zee, who gripped a handhold on a bulkhead, also did not comment. He was the only robot helper Casmir had been allowed to bring along. Most of the ones he'd created to raid the terrorist base had been too damaged to travel, anyway, but he was finding that he liked having an army of robots he could hide behind when he faced enemies.

"Which offer is that?" Kim sounded completely normal, unaffected by space-sickness.

"To put weird bugs in my stomach to help with my nausea. And high histamine levels." Casmir's left eye blinked, and he sneezed. His nostrils hadn't yet realized that he'd left pollen season behind and that the shuttle's air was highly filtered. "Didn't you say you had some that could do that?"

"My bacteria are not *weird.*"

Kim couldn't look at him over the side of her pod, but Casmir had no doubt he was receiving a glower. Someone in one of the rear seats laughed. A number of large hulking soldiers in combat armor were also on the shuttle. Casmir didn't know if they were there to defend him or to make sure he didn't try to escape his fate.

As if there was anywhere he could go. The blanket of stars on the large forward display was beautiful but also a stark reminder that he was surrounded by a frozen vacuum. Space was a far more effective deterrent to escape than bars on a cell.

"As I've stated before," Kim said, "I have numerous beneficial bacteria that could help you more efficiently clear histamine from your body, which has been linked to motion-sickness. My bacteria have been tested in many randomized double-blind, placebo-controlled studies, and the efficacy is undeniable. Few side effects were reported, even among patients with intestinal dysbiosis, so I don't see why you're hesitant to let me give you some. It's very likely that I could not only fix your tendency toward motion-sickness but also cure your food and drug allergies with the right immune-regulating mix."

"There aren't any cashews trying to ram themselves down my throat at the moment. I'm only concerned about…" Casmir swallowed and grimaced as the shuttle adjusted course, prompting his nausea also to adjust itself to a higher level. "Puking."

"Since I had the leisure to pack this time, I have numerous microorganisms along with me that I thought would prove useful on the mission. Simply let me know when you're ready and if you'd prefer daily capsules or a more permanent solution."

"Who *wouldn't* choose the permanent solution?"

"The capsules contain transitory strains. The permanent solution involves a rectal insertion."

Casmir made a face.

One of the fearsome soldiers behind him said, "Ewww."

"Maybe I'll think about it a bit more first," Casmir said, grimacing again, for the *Osprey* had come into view, the great warship large enough to create artificial spin gravity.

"You should embrace advances in medicine," Kim said, "not shy away from them. I can see shying away from having your skull opened up and a responsive neurostimulation system installed to rectify your seizures, but there's no reason to fear such simple and non-invasive work when there's potential for dramatic health improvements."

"The permanent solution sounded somewhat invasive."

"Less so than a hole in the skull."

"I'm not entirely positive that's true."

One of the soldiers grunted in what might have been agreement.

Another warship came into view as Asger adjusted their course again. And another. And another.

Four? Casmir frowned. Just how many warships were coming along on this mission?

"Asger," Casmir said. "Are those ships all coming with us, or are they simply here for shore leave?"

"Nobody's going on shore leave right now." Asger glanced back. "Have you been watching the news? Tensions are escalating in the other systems. There have been more attacks on stations and mining facilities, and even though I'm fairly certain the Kingdom wasn't behind them, we're being blamed."

"So those warships are here to guard Odin?"

"Others in the system are strategically placed to guard System Lion. Those are going with us."

"If we barrel through another system's gate with so many warships," Casmir said, "won't the inhabitants see that as a hostile and aggressive action? If not a threat of invasion?"

"King Jager is making sure we have the firepower necessary to get the gate back. Further, he may be making a statement. Better to be with the Kingdom than against it."

"Oh, yes. Let's strut around the systems like galactic bullies. That'll have positive long-term results."

Asger slanted him a long look over his shoulder. "I'm sure it's what Admiral Mikita did."

And thus Asger proved something Casmir had suspected, that he knew who Casmir had been cloned from. Asger had once said he'd had a hunch, but at some point, that hunch had turned into a certainty.

Had Princess Oku told him that she'd helped Casmir get into the Royal Zamek Seed Bank so he could learn the truth? Somehow, the image of Oku and Asger strolling side by side through one of the castle gardens with the sun beaming on their faces disturbed Casmir. It wasn't that he truly believed he had a shot with the princess—besides, he barely knew her—but imagining Asger as Oku's confidant was troubling. Surely, Casmir, as a fellow academic, would be a more logical match.

"I'm not so sure about that," Casmir said, giving his brain a boot to return it to present concerns.

"He was a war hero. That's what war heroes do to win wars."

"Hm." Casmir vowed to look up his progenitor as soon as he had time, to dig deeper than what the encyclopedias and online history texts said. If they'd gotten the face wrong, who knew what else was inaccurate?

He wished he could look in that book about great leaders of the Twelve Systems that Qin had in her quarters on the *Stellar Dragon*. It hadn't been published in the Kingdom, and she'd believed he looked "kind of like" Mikita, so maybe it had accurate information.

He also wished he was going off to help Qin and Bonita with their pirate situation, rather than helping find a powerful ancient relic that Casmir still questioned whether the Kingdom had the right to claim.

"Captain Ishii is going to want a destination as soon as we get on board," Asger said. "I hope for your sake that you've figured out where that gate went."

"Er, not yet."

Casmir squirmed under the disapproving look he got. He missed occasionally goofy Asger, who flexed his biceps and talked about having assets that women admired. Maybe he'd been lectured for helping Casmir the last time they had been in space together.

"I was going to suggest starting at Modi Moon to see if any clues were left behind." Casmir hoped that the entire stealthed cargo ship with the ancient gate inside had been left behind, and that the Fleet ship that had searched for it had simply missed finding it. But Royal Intelligence had confirmed that the wormhole gate out of the system had been activated by an invisible ship, so Casmir feared it was long gone.

Twin shuttle-bay doors came into view as Asger guided them closer, along the rotating hull of the warship. As their craft slowed, leaving them in zero-g, Casmir decided he looked forward to the *Osprey's* relatively stable partial gravity. Even if he looked forward to little else about his assigned task.

The doors yawned open, and Asger timed their entry perfectly. They settled to a magnetic deck, and with a lurch, the shuttle had gravity again. Casmir's stomach also lurched, and he took several slow breaths. He was the last one out of his pod.

The soldiers filed out quickly. Asger, wearing his silver liquid armor instead of a galaxy suit like Kim and Casmir, waited for them by the hatch. Kim unstrapped the luggage rack and started pulling off her several cases of belongings.

"I'm guessing that's not make-up," Asger remarked as Casmir joined him.

Kim, whom Casmir had rarely seen wear make-up, shot him a flat look. "I assume the captain will give me a laboratory where I can store my tools and specimens."

"I assume the captain will give me a brig cell," Casmir said.

Kim tossed Casmir's tool satchel and travel case to him, the latter full of a suitable amount of clean clothing, almost as much as his mother had insisted on.

"If you irk him, he will." Asger spread his hand, inviting Casmir to exit the shuttle next. "You might not want to bring up his nicknames from robotics camp."

"Right. Good advice."

Though he had an urge to make Asger go first, so he could hide behind his tall, broad-shouldered figure, Casmir shouldered his bags and hopped down to the deck. Captain Ishii waited in his Fleet galaxy suit with a stunner on his belt. Was that a typical precaution, or did he think Casmir would attack him?

Ishii eyed Zee, who walked behind Casmir, as they approached. That was the physical threat he was likely more worried about, but a stun bolt wouldn't affect Zee.

"Professor Dabrowski," Ishii said with a quick stiff bow. "You are here in the capacity of civilian advisor. You will interact as little as possible with the crew, report directly to me, take orders from any officer that gives them, and work on the solution to our mutual problem during all hours outside of meal and sleep time. Neither of those had better be leisurely."

"Civilian advisor?" Casmir did his best to offer a friendly smile—he would prefer to turn Ishii into an ally, or at least a colleague with a good working relationship, rather than to continue on as antagonists. "That sounds like the role of civilian lackey."

"The king, when he commed me directly to remind me of the importance of this mission, was imprecise on your actual designation and job duties. I gather I have some leeway."

Casmir glanced at Asger. "The brig scenario is looking more likely."

Ishii shifted his focus as Kim stepped out, porting two boxes that looked like they would have squished her in the full gravity of Odin. He bowed much more deeply to her.

"Welcome back to the *Osprey*, Scholar Sato. You also have the title of civilian advisor while you're here. You'll find that Dr. Sikou has cleared a dedicated laboratory for you. You have full access to the ship's fitness and recreation areas. My soldiers will carry your cases." Ishii waved for some of the men to hurry forward and take them from her. "If you need anything, you can ask any of my crew for assistance."

"Thank you," Kim said.

"Is it just me," Casmir said to her, "or are the parameters of our positions vastly different, given that we have the exact same job title?"

"I bet she's getting paid more too." Asger thumped him on the shoulder as Ishii headed for the exit, waving for them to follow.

Casmir stared at Kim. "You're getting *paid*?"

"You're not?" She sounded surprised.

"No, I'm proving myself to the king."

"Does that come with benefits and time off?" Kim asked, her delivery as deadpan as usual, even though he knew her well enough to recognize it as a joke.

"It doesn't even come with leisurely lunches."

"I won't be obnoxious and point out that you got yourself into this situation," she said as they trailed Ishii and his men into a wide corridor.

"That's very considerate of you."

Ishii took them first to sickbay, where he waved Kim into Dr. Sikou's waiting hands—she was the doctor that Kim had worked with on the research vessel *Machu Picchu* to find a cure for the pseudo radiation so many of them had been afflicted with while hunting for the ancient wormhole gate.

Casmir wondered if he would get to see Kim at all during this mission. He felt the urge to blurt an apology through the doorway after her, since he highly doubted she would be stuck up here if he hadn't hidden the gate from the government.

But the presence of Ishii and the soldiers kept his tongue still. The next stop was guest quarters, where Asger was given a cabin of decent size. Casmir hoped for one nearby, but Ishii took him another level up and toward the bridge. He stopped before reaching it and waved open a door to a room packed with servers and monitoring systems.

"Your quarters." Ishii extended a hand toward a display- and technical manual-filled desk with a chair locked to the deck.

"Uh, there's no bed."

"You'll be so busy researching that you won't need one. You have all the computer power you need to find the gate, and your robot can plug in over there if he needs to."

"While the crushers can plug into an outlet, Zee typically absorbs and breaks down simple inorganic material in his environment. He's kind of like a big autotroph, but instead of producing complex organic compounds, he creates pure energy."

Casmir expected Ishii to say "Whatever" and shove him into the little cabin, but he raised his eyebrows.

"Really? Will you send me the schematics? I've been curious about the crushers." Maybe Ishii hadn't completely given up on his childhood passions.

"Yes." Casmir saw little point in withholding the schematics since the government already had them. Oh, they were supposed to be top secret, and he'd signed paperwork agreeing to that, but Ishii worked for that government, and now that terrorists and who knew who else had the crushers, did it matter? Maybe it would help prompt Ishii to see him as less of an enemy.

Ishii's eyebrows rose even higher, as if he hadn't expected that answer. "Good."

Ishii sent a quick, admiring look toward Zee, but then his face closed off again. "Sit down and get to work, Dabrowski. No screwing around. Scour the networks and find out where the gate is. We've got Intelligence people looking now, but Jager presumably sent you along because he thinks you'll see something they won't." Ishii's lips twisted with skepticism. "Don't even think of having a seizure or getting sick. We're depending on you. I was reprimanded with demerits going into my record after you disappeared with the gate. This time, we're going to drop it on the castle doorstep and be blasted heroes."

Ishii spun on his heel and stalked away. The door closed automatically, sealing Casmir inside the computer cabin with Zee.

He feared his thoughts of befriending Ishii were in vain, and he regretted that his actions had resulted in the man getting in trouble.

"I guess I better get to work," Casmir murmured. So Ishii could be a hero. Or at least redeem himself in the eyes of his chain of command.

"Do you know where to look for this gate, Casmir Dabrowski?" Zee took up a guard position by the door, his six-and-a-half feet in height seeming even larger than usual in the tight quarters.

"I have some ideas."

"I have observed that when humans say that, the answer is truly no."

Casmir sighed. "You're more intuitive than you look, my friend."

CHAPTER 3

DR. YAS PESHLAKAI STEPPED ONTO THE BRIDGE OF the *Fedallah* and headed toward the briefing room at the back. He paused when he spotted Captain Rache speaking with Lieutenant Amergin, his security officer who specialized in hacking networks and gathering intelligence.

The four other men working on the bridge only glanced at Yas before their gazes returned to the forward display or their own stations. Their shoulders were hunched, tense. And Yas saw the reason on the display. The *Fedallah* was trailing four Kingdom warships through space. It was from a distance, but he wouldn't call it a *safe* distance. Rache's ship had a slydar hull coating that should keep those ships from detecting its heat signature or spotting it on a camera, but… this seemed a blatant flirtation with trouble.

"Briefing room, Doctor." Rache pointed a thumb toward the sliding doors, and he and Amergin headed that way, Amergin's face a smiling combination of biological and cybernetic parts under a broad-brimmed cowboy hat, and Rache's face, as always, hidden under his black mask.

"Yes, sir." Yas followed them.

He didn't yet know why he'd been invited to the briefing, as he wasn't usually a part of the mercenaries' missions, other than patching people up afterward. He hoped it had something to do with the research Amergin had been doing about Tiamat Station—Yas's home—and the murder of President Bakas. The murder Yas had been framed for…

A vain hope, most likely, since Rache was surely following those warships for another reason. Maybe he thought the Kingdom Fleet would lead him to the ancient wormhole gate that he'd almost had in his grasp the previous month. If it did, would he attack all four warships in an attempt to wrest it away? Yas would need to do more than a little *patching up*, if that was the case.

Two of Rache's senior officers were seated at the large briefing room table, along with the assassin Chaplain and Chief Jess Khonsari. She lounged sideways in her seat, one arm slung over the back, and one boot on the table.

Rache looked at her, looked at the leg, and looked back at her. When one couldn't see his face, it was hard to tell if he was glowering, but Jess grinned broadly, one of the few crew who never seemed intimidated by him, before lowering her leg to the deck.

Yas's stomach did a little flipflop when their eyes met, but then he winced, for her smile faded and she only gave him a wary nod. Because he kept trying to get her to agree to an exam and to look for alternatives to the addictive painkiller she didn't want to give up?

He resisted the urge to sit next to her, not wanting to make her uncomfortable, but a large part of him wished he weren't her doctor. If he were just her friend, maybe he wouldn't feel so compelled to look after her health, when she clearly didn't want to confront it herself.

No, he decided. He would still want to help her.

Rache waved at a display on the wall, and the same view of the four warships came up. "Amergin has ferreted out proof that those ships are being sent to find the gate that slipped through the Kingdom's fingers." His tone cooled. "And *my* fingers."

He didn't mention his genetic twin, Casmir Dabrowski, the one who'd been responsible for all that slippage.

"We're following them," Rache continued, "since, from what I gathered down on Odin, we have to head out of the system to find the gate anyway."

Yas was curious what Rache had been doing down on Odin for several days. Questioning Dabrowski? He'd returned to the ship with numerous injuries and combat armor that had looked like someone had dropped a mountain on it. As usual, he hadn't allowed Yas to treat those injuries, saying his enhanced immune system would handle them.

These mercenaries all fell into one of two camps: people who would take a bullet to the chest, deal with the pain, and wave it off as a mere scratch; or people who would get a scratch and act like they'd taken a bullet to the chest. There was absolutely nobody on the ship who treated health and injuries with an amount of gravitas appropriate to the situation.

"We're monitoring their communications and doing our best to decrypt encoded transmissions." Rache nodded to Amergin. "It's possible they'll report their destination to their headquarters, and we'll catch it, but I would prefer to figure out where the cargo ship carrying the gate went before the Fleet does. We know astroshamans were, before they died, piloting it and were likely the ones to steal the gate pieces from Skadi Moon. Amergin, you're the one who's been researching them. Where are the most likely places astroshamans would have taken the gate, assuming they didn't want anyone to find it?"

Yas sank back in his seat. This briefing definitely didn't have anything to do with his problem. He was disappointed, but he shouldn't have been. Rache had told him he would focus on finding the gate first and *then* help him. Assuming they survived this gate hunt. Yas couldn't help but eye the heavily armed and armored warships with concern.

"The astroshamans have bases and a presence in all the systems except this one," Amergin said from his seat. "The Kingdom doesn't forbid the blending of biological and machine components, such as almost all astroshamans embrace, but it's known to be unfriendly to all except pure humans."

"The astroshamans were the ones that seemed to be in charge of the bombings that took place on Odin," Rache offered. "There was a terrorist group down there led by a former Royal Intelligence chief superintendent who'd gotten a few noticeable cybernetic implants since he stepped down from his position."

Amergin hesitated, then nodded and adjusted his hat. "I read about those terrorists in my intelligence gathering, Captain. It was implied that you'd been to their base and had something to do with its destruction."

"It's not important." Rache flicked dismissive fingers. "Go on about potential locations."

"Yes, sir. Like I said, they've got bases all over, and a lot of the followers of their religion are normal citizens living in the various habitats and colonies around the systems. Usually, they don't make trouble or get involved in squabbles over resources or what they consider mundane things. At the core of their belief is the idea that ultimate enlightenment comes from leaving one's human body behind and embedding one's consciousness into a droid or computer. I don't know about that myself. Machine bits have their uses, but I'm fond of my human bits too."

Amergin smiled at Jess.

Yas frowned. Was that a flirtatious smile?

"Nobody wants to know about your human bits," she told him.

"That's disappointing." Amergin faced Rache again. "Despite them being pretty integrated into a lot of societies, there *are* rumors that the astroshamans have a secret headquarters that's part shrine and part laboratory where they test out human-machine interfaces and new cybernetic implants before sending out the schematics to the rest of their followers. The majority of the astroshamans exist as humans or hybrids until they near death, and then they seek that ultimate enlightenment of continuing on without their biological bodies. That secret testing headquarters seems a likely spot where they would take the gate to study."

Rache nodded. "Rumors of locations?"

"Oh, quite a few. I'm surprised I had trouble pinpointing it, given how many people must know. I'd figured the shrine was a place any of their followers could visit—but it seems that their high shamans are the only ones to know the location and go there, along with the devotees that work inside. I have been sorting through the rumors and trying to narrow things down. Something that keeps coming up is the idea that you can only get there with a submarine."

Yas sat up straighter, his interest rekindling. System Hydra, his home system, had two water worlds. Several of the other systems had planets with land and oceans, but a high number of astroshamans lived on and passed through Tiamat Station, which was centrally located in the system.

"That still leaves quite a few possibilities," Amergin went on, "but I'm assuming it's somewhere sparsely populated, since they're secretive with their comings and goings. They probably didn't hide their base on the continental shelf in front of the resort islands of Tlaloc. So I've got three likely possibilities. Planet Oceanus in System Stymphalia, an underwater facility on the stormy side of the water world of Nabia, or under the ice on Xolas Moon. There's a whole ocean under the moon's frozen surface, and it hasn't been visited much, except by science teams. At least that's what the public records say."

Rache looked at Yas. “Two of those possibilities are in your system. Have you heard any rumors of the existence of this shrine?”

Yas wished he had, so he could urge the *Fedallah* toward System Hydra. Maybe then, as long as they were in the neighborhood, Rache would send a team to Tiamat Station to help him investigate the president’s death.

“I haven’t heard of that shrine or laboratory before,” Yas said slowly, raking through his brain just in case he’d forgotten some useful tidbits. “There is a relatively high population of astroshamans in the system.”

Amergin nodded. “About two percent of the population in System Hydra, compared to .5 to one percent in other systems, barring System Lion here.” He waved toward the display and the stars outside.

“If two out of three likely possibilities are there,” Rache said, “it makes sense to start our search in Hydra.”

“What happens if the Kingdom warships are going to System Hydra?” Chaplain asked, speaking for the first time, his hands folded neatly on the table. He never did anything so assassinly as picking his teeth with his knife or sharpening the blade in public, but his eyes were intent as he gazed at Rache, and Yas had the feeling he wanted a fight. A bloody fight that resulted in a lot of dead bodies.

“We’ll attempt to get to and obtain the gate before they arrive,” Rache said.

“And if we don’t?” Amergin asked.

“We’ll find a way to get it anyway. As I said weeks ago, I’m not letting Jager squirrel away something so powerful.” Rache waved toward the exit. “Dismissed, everyone. Except you, Doctor.”

Yas paused, halfway out of his seat. Was he about to learn why he’d been called to this briefing?

“Does something ail you, Captain?” Yas hadn’t seen him limping or favoring any body parts, not the way he had been when he’d first returned from Odin, but for *normal* people, such injuries would take a while to heal.

“No.” After the door shut, Rache said, “Do you know of any poisons or bacteria that would have deleterious effects on humans with mechanical interfaces?”

Yas grimaced. He knew of a lot of poisons that would have deleterious—also known as *deadly*—effects on anybody. But he’d studied them so he could *save* people from them, not make recommendations to killers.

"If Amergin is right," Rache said, "and this base is underwater, we won't be able to bring the entire might of the *Fedallah* down to deal with the inhabitants. We'll likely be dealing with a lot of loaded droids and robot defenders. It would be advantageous to have a way to entice those with human parts to cooperate."

"I understand, Captain, but I'm not comfortable recommending poisons."

Rache gazed steadily at him. Yas waited for him to point out that he'd offered to help Yas with his problem, or maybe to suggest that he would only do so if Yas helped him *first*. But all he did was stare wordlessly. Somehow, that was worse.

"I'll look and see if there's anything in the toxicology dictionaries." Maybe Yas could find something that would inconvenience their enemies without killing them.

"Good. If there's time on the way or after, we'll stop by Tiamat Station. Did you see this?" Rache faced the display, sending some command with his chip, and the image changed from the warships to a news clip.

Yas recognized Vice President—no, he was *President* now—Chronis. And also… "Is that King Jager?"

They were standing together on a beach and shaking hands as they faced the camera, a clear blue sky behind them. That definitely wasn't Tiamat Station.

"Yes." Rache froze the image on the display. "The media is reporting that he visited Odin personally two weeks ago and is on his way back home to announce news of an alliance."

Yas grimaced. "At least half of Tiamat Station is going to be very unhappy about that."

"It's something that wouldn't have happened if President Bakas had been alive and in charge, I presume."

"No, she was vehemently opposed to the old-fashioned mindset of the Kingdom and any sniff of a tyrannical regime encroaching in our system. There could be some major upheaval over this. All of the citizens who have genetic modifications or who are in non-traditional marriages wouldn't be welcome in their own home if the Kingdom were to gain control of Tiamat Station. A lot of people will fight to prevent that. Tiamat Station is over three hundred years old, and many citizens trace their heritage back to the founders. They won't simply leave."

"If System Hydra is distracted by upheaval on one of its most populous habitats, that'll be a good time for us to slip in unnoticed and explore the moon and water world." Rache nodded and headed for the door. "Let me know what you find regarding poisons, Doctor."

As Yas stared at the image of his new president shaking hands with Jager, the only poison he could think about was the one that had killed President Bakas.

The door to Kim's lab slid open, and the *Osprey's* chief surgeon, Dr. Angelico, leaned in, knocking on the jamb.

"The glorious Kim Sato hath returned to our modest sickbay," he said with a cheery smile. "I'm delighted."

Kim turned in time to catch him checking out her ass. She sighed. The fact that galaxy suits were form fitting made them prized over the bulky spacesuits of earlier centuries, but she wouldn't have minded some bulk at that moment. She also wouldn't have minded if Angelico had been transferred to another ship in the weeks since she'd last seen him.

"I was never on the *Osprey*," Kim said. "We worked together on the *Machu Picchu*."

"Ah, but you're here now. Perhaps we can have a drink together? It's well into the night shift, you know. You should take off for the day. The R and R deck isn't as appealing as the café on that orbital station I was telling you about, but we do have coffee." He wrinkled his nose. "If you persist in being addicted to it. Did I, by chance, convince you that a green smoothie would be a far superior health choice?"

"No."

Not only that, but she'd brought bags of her own beans along this time, as well as a portable espresso machine and milk steamer. There was no way she would have gone into space unprepared a second time.

She pointed to a corner of the counter where she'd set them up, carefully securing the accoutrements so they wouldn't float off if there were hiccups in the ship's gravity.

Angelico wrinkled his nose again. "I'd have to check the regs, but I don't think that's allowed. If there's an inspection, Captain Ishii may insist that you put that in your cabin or in the mess hall."

"Captain Ishii can *try*."

Angelico snorted and smiled. "Why don't you let me show you around the ship later? Have you seen the hydroponics gardens? We're able to grow fresh vegetables and fruit."

"I'm busy." That wasn't really true. Kim had refined the bacteria that fed on the pseudo radiation before she'd left Odin. There had been little point in her being dragged along on this mission, as she'd informed Chief Superintendent Van Dijk, but the military was certain they needed her along in case there were any medical surprises related to the gate. "And also, I am not interested in spending recreational time with you or having intercourse."

She should have made that clear from the beginning.

Angelico blinked, his lips parting in surprise—or bafflement?—but he recovered quickly, and the smile returned. "You only *think* you don't want to have intercourse with me, but that's because you haven't seen me naked yet."

He winked and stepped out into the corridor before she could issue a retort.

Kim shook her head in disgust, missing her lab back home at Parvus Biologia Corporation headquarters where all of the men were old and married. Not that she was usually hit on left and right during her regular life. She wasn't sure how she'd managed to get two men asking her to dinners in the same month. Though who truly knew what Rache's intentions were? The idea of someone like him having intentions was still mind-boggling. Surely, some of his fellow space mercenaries or outlaw pirates would be more logical choices for his affections.

Though maybe not. If he was as book-loving as he seemed, he might have trouble finding kindred spirits in that crowd. If such things mattered. Men seemed to care less about common interests, at least *some* men. She couldn't imagine Casmir having a relationship with someone purely based on physical attraction. Though it was hard to believe Rache could *want* a relationship. How could that even work if he was constantly switching systems and always in hiding? Always putting his life in danger? Wouldn't casual sex be a lot safer for him? Or abstinence, for that matter. Rache had mentioned that someone had sent a female assassin to seduce and kill him. She was surprised he wasn't completely soured on relationships.

Kim pushed away the thoughts as she realized she'd been staring at her computer display for several minutes without seeing it. She was trying to think of what else besides bacteria might be used to protect people who came in contact with the gate and that pseudo radiation. But she kept coming back to what she'd suggested to Van Dijk as the most logical action, sending in Casmir, since he was immune, to see if the gate's defensive mechanisms could be deactivated.

Maybe she should suggest the idea to Captain Ishii. He seemed to be in charge of the mission. Perhaps he would be more logical.

She closed down her workstation and left the quiet lab—aside from a curly-haired female nurse on duty, the rest of the sickbay staff had departed for the night—and headed to the lift. She would see if Captain Ishii was on the bridge and make the suggestion to him. Maybe it was moot, since they hadn't found the gate yet, but she felt like she should be working on *something*, since she was, as Asger had pointed out, being paid by the military to be here.

Casmir's computer cabin—computer *closet* was a more accurate term—was on the way, so she stopped and knocked. She had little doubt that he would be there and doing research. It wasn't as if Ishii had given him the option of recreation, though Kim considered it inhumane to deny him exercise time. In the ship's low gravity, they all needed to spend time with the gym equipment on a daily basis.

The door slid open to reveal Zee filling the entryway.

Kim jumped. Even though she had grown accustomed to the crusher in the days he'd been her bodyguard, she hadn't seen him since arriving on the ship earlier in the week, and it was easy to forget how large, dark, and intimidating he was.

"Casmir, are you in there?" Kim asked. "I can't see around your butler."

Zee shifted aside and pressed his back to the wall. It still didn't leave a lot of room to maneuver past, but when she spotted Casmir rising from the cabin's only seat, Kim stepped inside.

The door closed automatically behind her, making the space feel claustrophobic. Heat radiated from the banks of computer equipment, and the air smelled faintly of ozone.

"Greetings, Kim." Delight blossomed on Casmir's face, and his arms twitched upward, as if he wanted to hug her. He turned it into a deep bow.

"I'm guessing you haven't seen many people these last few days." Kim felt bad that she hadn't come by to visit sooner. She hadn't been certain it would be permitted. She could envision Ishii storming in and dragging her out, saying that nobody was allowed to distract Casmir.

"Just Ishii." He smiled ruefully. "Hourly. And Zee of course."

"I don't think Zee counts as a *people*."

The stolid crusher did not react to the comment.

"How can you say such things? He's delightful company."

"I still think you need to get him a pink bow tie."

"I thought we agreed on periwinkle." Casmir stepped to the side and offered her the sole seat.

She declined and leaned against a rack of servers, careful not to bump anything. "I'm going to try to find the captain and suggest something to him, but I thought I should run it by you first."

"And here I thought you just came to visit. I brought my dice." Casmir waved to his tool satchel and personal bag—had he truly not been given any quarters?—hunkering under a console. "We could play a game."

"Are you allowed to do that?"

"No, but I would rebel for a chance at human interaction." He arched his eyebrows. "What do you want to run by me?"

"I think you're the best bet to figure out how to get those gate pieces to stop emitting the pseudo radiation. It doesn't make sense to keep trying to find treatments to help people who are exposed to it when it could presumably be turned off somehow. And since you're immune and an engineer, who better to do it?"

"Someone who's extensively studied the gate technology?" Casmir smiled self-deprecatingly, but he also rubbed the back of his neck and looked like he was considering it.

"Name someone who's done that and might be immune, and I'll suggest him or her to the captain. I doubt it's one of Rache's hobbies."

"Probably not. He's too busy reading about ancient whales. Does your mother have an engineering background at all?"

"No, archaeology and anthropology." Kim supposed she could mention her mother to Ishii—Casmir might do better if he had someone with knowledge of the gates at his side—but was reluctant to bring Kingdom attention to her. As she'd learned earlier, Jager was aware of her mother and aware that she had many friends outside of System Lion. It hadn't sounded like he trusted her. "You're good at figuring out mechanical things, whether you have a background in them or not. I think you could do it."

"I'd be willing to try. I'm still not sure…" Casmir glanced toward the ceiling—toward some hidden camera?—and adjusted what he'd intended to say. "It would be good to keep anyone else from dying, especially since everyone is determined to go cozy up with the gate pieces, so I'd take a shot."

Kim suspected he'd kept himself from saying he still didn't want the Kingdom to end up with the gate. She hoped he would give up on that idea and work wholeheartedly for Jager. Maybe it wasn't ideal for the entire Twelve Systems, but if he insisted on opposing the king, he would end up exiled—or worse.

"Good. I'll tell the captain."

Casmir leaned against the console, his expression glum, and Kim waved at the row of displays behind him. She was reluctant to leave so soon when he was starved for company.

"How's the search going? Have you found anything?"

"I've been researching the astroshamans themselves and have some possible places they might have taken the gate to hide it, but I find myself wondering if they would have taken it to a home base—I found information on secret laboratories and shrines in underwater locations few can get to—or if they're handing it off to someone else."

"You found evidence to suggest they're working for another party?"

"Not evidence, no. The astroshamans have their own private satellite network in most of the systems, so they leave a minuscule footprint on the public networks. I'm just debating why a religious order would *want* an ancient wormhole gate. Maybe they want to explore the rest of the galaxy or leave the Twelve Systems and find a new place to live, but why the terrorist stuff on Odin then? And why would they have cared about me helping Jager? Only people planning to stick around in the Twelve Systems would care about that."

"Weren't you hypothesizing that the terrorist activity was to distract the Kingdom so the astroshamans could slip in and get the gate in the first place?"

"That could be part of it, but I was also debating if the timeline matched up. The terrorist activity began months ago, before the gate was discovered and reported to our government. The crushers started coming after *me* about the same time it was unearthed, but it's not like that would have affected the government or military in a significant way. I feel like we're dealing with two separate events and two separate motivations. I wish we'd been able to question that ex-chief superintendent." Casmir grimaced, perhaps seeing the nightmare he'd shared—or the real event—over again. "I'm reluctant to tell Ishii to spend months hunting down all the astroshaman bases if ultimately, someone else is in charge. Though I don't know how that would work either. The astroshamans aren't mercenaries—not en masse, anyway. They're not known to have a lot of alliances or allegiances to humans outside of their religion. Who would think of them as the likely people to hire?"

"There were astroshamans in the cargo ship you boarded and astroshamans in the terrorist base, right? Whether they're responsible or not, they know *something*."

"True."

"So if you find someone high up in their organization—they have high shamans as spiritual leaders, don't they?—the captain could question him or her with a truth drug."

"I suppose. I'd just like to be able to point Ishii right to the spot where the gate is. Even though I have mixed feelings on whether we're the rightful holders of it, I… like being efficient." Casmir shrugged, almost appearing embarrassed. "You know, *good*."

"Well—" A faint hiss reached Kim's ears, and she broke off. "What is that? That's not a computer noise."

"It sounds like air blowing." Casmir glanced toward a small vent high on a wall. "Put your helmet up."

Kim held her breath and tapped the small control patch on the chest of her galaxy suit, and her Glasnax helmet unfolded from its pouch below the back of her neck, pausing only when it encountered her braid. She hurried to tuck it inside so the helmet could seal. The heads-up display came on, and she ordered it to check the atmosphere for unexpected elements.

The hiss was probably indicative of an innocuous leak or transfer of air somewhere—surely a Fleet warship had to be at the top of the list of safest places in space—but Casmir was doing the same thing.

"My suit is reading nitrous oxide in the air," he said quietly.

An instant later, her display flashed a similar warning. "That's a sedative, and it can be deadly if you inhale too much."

"Sounds like a good time to break for a non-leisurely lunch." Casmir headed for the door.

"Wait." Kim gripped his arm. "Someone may be trying to flush you out. If they assumed you would hear that and get your helmet on in time…"

"Who here would want me knocked out?" Casmir asked, but he didn't try to pull away from Kim. "Zee, check the corridor, please."

Zee took a step, coming right up to the door, but it didn't open.

"The door is not opening," Zee said needlessly. "Shall I force it aside?"

"Uhm. I don't know. This is weird. I'm going to comm the bridge." Casmir stepped back to the console, bumping Kim in the tiny space, and tapped the comm controls.

Kim eyed the door, expecting a couple of men in combat armor to stomp in at any second. She didn't have a weapon. She'd assumed she wouldn't *need* weapons here on a Kingdom ship.

"The comm isn't working." Casmir scowled at the control panel. "Give me a minute. I have access to all the systems from in here…"

"Do you have any weapons in your tool satchel? Or tools suitable to be turned into weapons?"

"That's Zee's job, but my power drill is vaguely intimidating if you want it." His back was to her, fingers flying across the interface.

A faint scuff sounded in the corridor outside.

Kim thought about lunging for his drill, but it wouldn't do anything against someone in combat armor.

Her helmet display flashed another warning, letting her know that she needed to hook up an oxygen tank if she wanted to continue enjoying air unaffected by the environment around them, an environment now filled with nitrous oxide.

Someone or something bumped against the door. A would-be attacker? Or someone coming to help them?

"Hah," Casmir said. "Figured out the override. That was some kludgy hacking. Bridge, I need to report—"

The door slid open, and two armored men lunged inside.

Zee blocked them, throwing his weight into it, and they bounced back into the corridor. Zee sprang after them, attacking them and denying entry to the cabin at the same time.

Casmir lunged to a side wall and pulled Kim back with him.

"Do you want your tool satchel?" She grabbed it as cracks, slams, and wrenching noises came from the corridor. Something clattered to the deck.

"No, I want to hide out of sight of the door."

"I'm not good at hiding." She poked into his satchel for the drill.

"I can give you pointers later."

A DEW-Tek weapon fired, and a crimson bolt sizzled into the cabin and slammed into a computer display. It exploded, tiny shards of metal pinging off the walls and Kim's and Casmir's galaxy suits.

Casmir cursed. "Are they trying to *kill* us?"

"You sure you don't want the drill?" Kim offered it to him.

"Pin them down, Zee!" Casmir yelled, even though they couldn't see the corridor from their spot against the wall. "Get them out of their suits! And get rid of their weapons, please!"

"Do you think he'll do better work if you add the please whenever you give an order?"

"Wouldn't you?"

Casmir grabbed his satchel and peered inside, but before he could find whatever he had in mind, thunderous footsteps rang above the cacophony in the corridor.

"Drop your weapons!" a female voice ordered.

Clatters sounded.

"Professor Dabrowski?" the woman called. "Are you all right in there?"

"Should I admit that my hands are shaking and I'm trying to remember if I took my seizure medication this morning?" Casmir whispered.

"No," Kim said.

"Right." He raised his voice. "I'm fine. We're all fine in here. Thank you."

"Could you, uhm, call off your robot?"

Casmir walked warily to the door. Kim was right behind him, though she hoped this intervention meant she wouldn't need to find out if his drill was powerful enough to break through the seam of some thug's combat armor.

Six armored and armed men and women stood in the corridor, pointing their weapons toward the deck at Zee's feet instead of directly at him or at the two armored men he held by the backs of their necks. One man hung limply and appeared unconscious. The other was squirming. Two DEW-Tek pistols lay on the deck under their feet.

Casmir retracted his helmet and pushed a hand through his hair. "Is anyone else confused by the fact that all of the people are wearing the same blue armor?"

"Don't worry, Professor," the woman said. "We'll get to the bottom of this."

The gas had dissipated when the door opened, but Kim left her helmet on.

"Zee," Casmir said, "thank you for apprehending those men. Hand them to the nice…" He looked at the woman's armor, but none of the suits had insignia. "Soldier."

"Sergeant Sekimoto," she supplied.

Zee lowered the men to the deck and thrust them toward the soldiers without letting go of their armored necks. It wasn't until the two attackers were surrounded and gripped by multiple people that he released them. He stepped back and loomed in the doorway, leaving Kim without much of a view.

"The captain has been informed of this incident," Sekimoto told Casmir. "I'm sure these men will be questioned under a truth drug, and we'll figure out what happened."

"Thank you," Casmir said.

"What happened," Kim murmured as the armored soldiers tramped off, "is that someone is still trying to kill you. The Black Star terrorists? Someone else?"

Casmir slumped against the wall. "Is it selfish of me to hope that there isn't more than one group?"

"No, that seems reasonable. Some people might hope there weren't *any* groups."

"I don't think I get to be that lucky." He closed his eyes.

Kim tried to determine if this was an occasion when the rules of friendship required a hug—would a hug make him feel better? He wasn't injured. After all he'd been through these last couple of months, he ought to be somewhat inured to danger. He looked more tired than overly distraught. She ended up patting him clumsily on the shoulder and wondering what it would be like to simply know what was appropriate and not need to go over a flow chart in her mind to determine the most human action.

Casmir smiled wanly and opened his eyes. "Thanks. I think I'll send a note off to Bonita."

"Are you hoping Viggo and his robot vacuums are in the area and will come to your rescue?"

Casmir snorted. "Is it strange to wish for that? I asked the king if I could ride on the *Stellar Dragon* instead of on a Fleet warship for this mission. Sadly, he said no. Granted, I don't know if Bonita would have agreed to come, but I knew even then that I would feel safer if I wasn't sleeping on the deck in Ishii's computer closet."

"You knew about the closet in advance?"

"I knew I wouldn't receive the luxury yacht experience. It's better than the brig, at least. Or it was until that attack." He shook his head. "I'm going to ask her if she can check for bounties. I wouldn't have thought I had to fear bounty hunters on a Fleet warship, but… otherwise, I really irked those two men. Whoever they were."

"That seems unlikely. You haven't been out of your closet."

"I don't know. I've been managing to annoy a lot of people lately. Jager is irked with me. Ishii is irked with me." His expression grew contemplative. "I *do* think I'm finally on better terms with Rache. We parted with a handshake."

"The underwear gift must have worked."

"Technically, those were from my mother. My point is that I've made progress with him. Maybe I shouldn't yet give up on my relationship with Ishii. If he starts to like me, maybe he'll try harder to keep his men from killing me."

"*That* shouldn't happen, regardless. Make sure to get the details of that interrogation."

"I will, but I think Bonita may be more forthcoming with me than Ishii or his sergeant. She finds me charming."

"Charming? I think *useful* may be the better adjective."

"Viggo and his robots find me charming."

"That sounds more plausible."

CHAPTER 4

CAPTAIN BONITA "LASER" LOPEZ SANK BACK INTO HER pod with relief as the blue-and-green swirls of Odin receded from the *Stellar Dragon's* rear camera. She hadn't been positive the government would allow her ship to use the launch loop, which was the only way her old freighter could escape the planet's gravity, nor had she been certain Kingdom fighters wouldn't swoop in and do their best to blow her out of the stars.

Yes, she had helped Casmir—and through him, the Kingdom government—bring down that terrorist base, but she'd also made a lot of threats to the law enforcers on Forseti Station a couple of months before. And then there had been that bioweapon… She hoped the Kingdom Guards were satisfied, after searching her ship on Odin, that she no longer had it in her possession, but they had never stated that she was free to go.

"Look at all that green," Qin said from the co-pilot's pod. "I'm going to miss it."

"The planet or the trees on the planet? I know you won't miss the people, since they kept trying to kill you."

"Yes, but that happens everywhere. I'm a professional warrior, so I'm used to it." Qin held out one of her long arms and flexed her lightly furred hands, her claws extending. She wore "metallic sparks" nail paint today. "I'll miss the trees most. And then the grass. And the smell of the ocean."

"Once we win your freedom, you can go back if you want. Though there are other places in the Twelve Systems with those things. Some of the space habitats even have all that. More lakes than oceans, I suppose, but they are there."

Qin made a noncommittal grunt.

Bonita wasn't as excited by trees and oceans. She'd grown up on habitats and ships, and she tended to feel uncomfortable on planets and moons with so much openness. They had a lot of gravity, too, and that made her joints creak and ache.

Although—she flexed one of her legs, bumping her boot against the console—maybe they would be less prone to that now. Usually, a bump like that would have made her knee twinge with pain, but the slight jolt was uneventful this time. Dare she hope the procedure she'd undergone would be a permanent fix? She'd forgotten what it was like to walk without pain. She liked it.

It made her want to pull out one of the treadmills in the lounge and run some sprints. It also made her want to solve Qin's problem so they could go back to bounty-hunting. She'd begun to feel she was too old for chasing after criminals, but with better knees—and Qin as the muscle—maybe she could finally earn enough money to pay off the *Dragon* and one day retire. Now that she had been paid by that medical company on Odin and had some Kingdom crowns in her account, the universe seemed less suffocating, the possibilities less limited.

"I did some research," Bonita said, "and confirmed that the Druckers were last seen in System Cerberus. I'm heading for the gate out of System Lion and plan to go there, but I'd like to have a solid plan in place first. You said you don't think they'll simply sell your contract for that fifteen thousand Union dollars?"

"That's just what they're offering for my *retrieval*." Qin bared her fangs. "I'm not sure how much it originally cost them to have us made and trained, but it must have been a lot more than that. And an investment of time as well as money."

"So, our options are either to convince them to accept the fifteen thousand as payment, by making them believe they were never going to get you back, and it's better for them to get paid something… or we need to take the person who issued the bounty out of the equation. One of the Drucker brothers, I assume? We can't sneak onto his ship and threaten him—these pirates with their big egos hunt you down and kill you later if you try moves like that. But maybe if there's a bounty out on *him*, we can capture him, turn him over to the law, and not have to worry about him until he gets out of prison in fifty years. Unfortunately, even if we could capture him, there's a whole family left to avenge him."

"Yes," Qin said bleakly. "They have a tradition of slaying anyone who messes with the family. Not all two-thousand-odd crew members are related, but the five brothers who run their five warships have a *lot* of relatives. Honestly, I think my best bet would be to stage my death somewhere so that they write me off as a loss."

"Let's put that down as an option, but it's not ideal. You'd have to spend the rest of your life worrying about being spotted. In addition to their two thousand people, they must have a lot of spies throughout the systems that report to them."

"If I was careful, maybe eventually, they would forget about me."

"If we're regularly collecting bounties among the demimonde, I'm afraid word will get back to the Druckers. You're very memorable."

Qin retracted her painted claws. "What do you think is best?"

"I think we need to talk to them, feel them out. Maybe we'll learn something. Like how badly do they want you back? Is it even one of the warship captains—one of the brothers—who put that bounty out? Or did some guy in accounting get reprimanded for the loss of an asset, so he's making a halfhearted attempt to clean up the books?"

Bonita hated that anyone might think of Qin like property or an asset reported on a balance sheet, but the systems were what they were. Even if she didn't like it, slavery was legal in some of them, and even the more egalitarian systems tended to identify genetically engineered creations that had been purchased from a lab as property rather than people.

"How likely is it that they know you work for me?" Bonita asked.

"Likely. Remember when we met? You helped me turn in two of the Druckers' men and collect the small bounties on them."

"Yes, true, but hopefully those men are still in prison and haven't had contact with their employers. Even if the Druckers *do* know you've been working for me, what if I, being a greedy bounty hunter, noticed there was money out for you and sent them a message saying I'd sell you back? But only if they doubled what they were offering. That might open the door for negotiations or at least get us in touch with whoever's in charge of your retrieval."

Qin grimaced. "Captain, I *do* want my freedom, and I appreciate that you want to help me get it, but I'm afraid you'll get in trouble on account of me."

"Let's at least talk to them. If it seems too dangerous, we'll try another approach. What are your thoughts on cosmetic surgery? Maybe if you had your ears snipped, your fangs and claws filed down, and glued some astroshaman machine bits to your face…"

Qin's eyes widened, and she touched one of the pointed ears sticking up through her hair. "My… ears snipped?"

"And some serious hair—fur—removal. That's our last option, I think. Try to disguise you. You could try a hood like Rache has, but those ears would try to poke out of it. They would definitely have to go."

Qin covered her ears protectively. "Comm them."

Bonita smiled. "I'll compose a message right now."

As she reached for the comm panel, a message landed on her personal chip. Casmir's words floated down her contact.

Greetings, Captain Laser!

I hope that you and your knees are doing well. I also hope Qin is doing well. I recently experienced a clumsy assassination attempt—technically, it may be less that it was clumsy and more that they did not anticipate Zee's sturdy presence—and I'm hoping you can tell me if my name has popped up again on that virtual bounty-hunter job board of yours. I assume Rache isn't after me this time, but it would be handy to know who is. And how many of them there are. Is it still the Black Star terrorists? Or is some other moneyed organization irked with me? I would be grateful if you could let me know.

Thank you, and good luck to you and Qin on your next adventure.

~Casmir

"Captain?" Qin asked. "Everything all right?"

Bonita realized her hand was hanging in the air over the comm panel, and she pulled it back. "Casmir sent me a message."

"How is he doing?" Viggo asked. "Has he decided to travel with us again? I'd like to get his opinion on a new brushless motor I'm thinking of ordering. And I've been debating ways to enhance the nozzles on the robot vacuums to more easily suck dirt from crevices. Perhaps he has an opinion on nozzles."

Bonita rolled her eyes. "I'm sure he does. Most men do." She looked at Qin. "Someone's trying to kill him."

"*Again*?"

"He's not sure if it's the same terrorist group or someone new. I'm going to search the bounty-hunter job board, as he called it, and see if there are any entries."

"Should we go help him?"

"He's on a Kingdom Fleet warship. If they can't keep him alive, nobody can."

"I'm going to arrogantly believe that I would be better at keeping him alive than a soldier who doesn't care about him." Qin extended her claws again. "Or even one who does."

Bonita smiled. "That's possibly true, but he has his mission, and we have ours. I'll send him whatever I can find, but *we* are going to confront the Druckers."

"I wonder if they have an opinion on vacuum nozzles," Viggo said, sounding mournful that Casmir wasn't on the way to visit them.

"Not unless they're gold-plated and worth a lot of money, I'll wager," Bonita said.

Qin, who knew the Druckers' tastes far better than Bonita, did not comment. She only gazed pensively at the stars on the display.

Less than an hour after the attack, a firm knock sounded on the door to the computer cabin. Casmir doubted an assassin would knock, but he was glad that Zee shifted to stand in front of it. Kim had gone off to speak with Ishii about her ideas, or maybe to lecture him on letting assassins prowl his ship, but only after Casmir had spent fifteen minutes convincing her that Zee would protect him and he was safe. And only after an armored marine had shown up to guard the computer cabin.

As the door slid open, Casmir sneezed. He needed to grab his antihistamines out of his bag. When he'd traveled on the *Stellar Dragon*, he hadn't needed them, but maybe the *Osprey's* air filters weren't as assiduously attended as Viggo's.

"Casmir?" came Asger's voice around Zee's head. "Are you all right?"

"Yes."

"I heard about the attack. May I come in?"

"There's only one seat."

"Knights have legs. We're capable of standing."

"An admirable skill. Let him in, please, Zee."

"He carries a weapon," Zee stated without moving. "Your life was threatened tonight. It is not wise to trust the humans on this ship."

"Yes, but we know Asger. He's a friend." Casmir tapped Zee on his hard, cool back. "He's not going to stab me."

Zee stepped aside, but he didn't go far. Asger had to turn sideways to ease past him and into the cabin.

Asger frowned, gripped Casmir's shoulder, and looked him up and down. "Do you need an escort to sickbay? Were you injured?"

"I'm fine."

"I'm sorry I wasn't here."

"I suspect that's the first time someone has ever said that in this cabin." Casmir waved to the rack of servers humming softly and emitting heat.

Asger didn't smile at the joke. He lowered his hand and shook his head. "I was in the gym, exercising and sparring with some of the marines. I need to be as fit as possible for this mission, and I know it, but… I should have been here. I've been tasked with keeping an eye on you. I just didn't expect you to be in any danger *here*."

"Do you know what happened? Nobody's told me anything."

"Not yet. Ishii said he'll give me a report after his security people are done questioning those two men. I did learn that they're kitchen staff, both on their first tour of duty."

"The *kitchen staff* tried to assassinate me? I haven't even complained about the food."

"I'm guessing someone suborned them, offered them a lot of money if they were successful. You'd think whoever it was would have picked someone with more combat training."

"I didn't mind them being inept."

Asger smiled for the first time. "No, I wouldn't have either. I should have been here. I will be from now on. I'll sleep on the deck while you work."

"If you sleep on the deck, how will I get out of the cabin to pee? You may have noticed the lack of floor space."

"When my cousins and I were little and went on long air-speeder trips with my grandfather, he would toss an empty jinga-juice jar in the back for us to use. He didn't like to make stops. He was focused on getting his desired number of miles in each day."

"Asger, I'm not using a jinga-juice jar for the sake of your beauty sleep. Zee doesn't need to lie down to sleep, so he takes up less space, and he can protect me just fine. He handled those two men by himself."

Asger's gaze drifted to the melted display that had been struck and a black scorch mark in the wall over the console.

"Those weren't even close to hitting me. I was hiding over there." Casmir pointed to the wall. "I'm good at hiding."

"I doubt that." His face screwed up into a conflicted expression.

"Look, I appreciate that you want to protect me. Really, I do. Especially since the number of people trying to kill me seems to be growing as fast as bacteria in one of Kim's petri dishes."

Asger's forehead furrowed.

"Bad analogy, sorry. They divide and increase their population. They don't grow." Casmir patted Asger on the arm. "You don't need to watch me. I'll be fine. Thanks."

Asger slumped against the wall. "I just want to do the right thing and earn my superiors' and colleagues' respect back."

"Back? What did you do to lose it?"

Asger opened his mouth, but he shut it again and looked at the wall above Casmir's head, instead of at him.

"Ah," Casmir said. "You helped me escape the *Osprey* last time, and I didn't put the gate into Fleet hands, as everyone in the Kingdom believes I should have. So you're getting blamed."

"Not fully. Nobody has any trouble blaming you for those things, but it didn't look good for me. They think you duped me."

"I'm sorry." Casmir studied the deck. "Did you tell them I'm not that clever?"

"No." Asger looked at him. "I just—you're not going to try anything shifty this time, are you? I understand that you weren't comfortable giving Jager the gate, but as you've seen, it's not wise to go against him."

"I know. This is my chance to prove myself to him, or so he said." Casmir tried not to think about Rache's conversation with the ex-chief superintendent of Royal Intelligence, about how *Rache* had once been asked to prove himself to Jager. Casmir wished he and Rache hadn't had to part ways in such a rush, that he could have asked for more details.

But would Rache have revealed them? Thus far, he'd been close-lipped about his past. "I'm sure if I go against Jager, I will be exiled. Or worse. He might send the *laundry* staff after me."

Asger snorted. "I'd find that more amusing if you'd actually answered my question."

"I promise to help the captain find the gate."

"Without being shifty?"

"I'm not sure. What if shiftiness is required to get it away from the astroshamans?"

"It won't be. You won't have to do anything. Just point us in the right direction, and we'll unleash the might of these warships on them."

Another knock rang out at the door. Zee moved into position.

"I don't think any more people are going to fit into this cabin," Casmir said.

"We could go to one of the rec areas."

"I'm not allowed out."

"Dabrowski," came Ishii's cranky voice as the door slid open. "Are you somewhere behind this mass of metal?"

"That's an impolite thing to call Zee, especially when I sent you his schematics."

"I haven't had a chance to look at them."

"You'll be much more impressed with him once you know him better."

"I'll bet. Is he going to move?" Ishii's boots, all that Casmir could see around Zee, shifted impatiently.

"This man is armed, and I do not believe he is a friend, Casmir Dabrowski." Zee remained solidly in position, blocking the doorway. "It would be unwise to allow him entrance."

"Oh, I'm certain of it, but let him in anyway, please."

Despite being a stoic and emotionless crusher, Zee managed to convey grudging acceptance as he stepped aside.

Ishii wasn't as tall or broad as Asger, being closer in size to Casmir, so he didn't have to turn sideways to enter, but the cabin grew even more claustrophobic with three men and Zee inside.

"What did the interrogation turn up?" Asger asked without preamble.

"They were in it for the money," Ishii said. "One of them was a dropout from the flight academy, and he knew enough that he thought he and his buddy could slip away in a shuttle after doing the job. They planned to ditch it somewhere, get paid, and live like kings in another system. They were genius enough to believe fifty thousand crowns would get them that. And that whoever put out the bounty would actually pay them. Idiots."

Before Casmir could chime in, a response to his message came in from Bonita.

El Mago, yes, there's another bounty on your head. This one wants you dead, not kidnapped and delivered somewhere. Who have you annoyed now? The man who put up the bounty is Prince Dubashi from the Miners' Union. He's offering fifty thousand Union dollars for your head, preferably detached from the rest of your body. Sorry to give you this news, but if you decide it's too dangerous to venture close to System Hydra—the prince makes his home there on a private asteroid in the middle of his fleet of robotic asteroid-mining ships and his claim on the entire Golden Belt—you can come with us to System Cerberus. Qin and I are going to figure out a way to get the Drucker pirates to leave her alone. A robot army would not be unappreciated.

Casmir sighed, both because someone else wanted him dead and because he couldn't go help Bonita and Qin. He didn't want either of them to be hurt, and facing a huge and deadly family of pirates alone sounded like an inevitable road to hurt.

"It's fifty thousand Union dollars," Casmir said. "Not Kingdom crowns."

"What?" Ishii asked.

"I got confirmation from Captain Lopez. A Prince Dubashi put out the bounty."

"Prince *Dubashi*?" Ishii asked. "Why would one of those Miners' Union money-grubbers want you dead? You've never been out of our system, have you?"

"No."

Asger scratched his bearded jaw. "Could it be for the same reason the Black Star terrorists wanted you dead? Did you figure out the reason for that, by the way? I assumed that someone who didn't want to see the Kingdom expand again worried about history repeating itself."

Casmir nodded. "That's what I inferred from my brief interaction with the leader."

Actually, that had been *Rache's* interaction. Casmir had been hiding in a crawlspace, other than that brief moment when Bernard had jumped up and tried to throw a grenade at him. Did that qualify as an *interaction*?

"History repeating itself?" Ishii looked from Asger to Casmir and back. "What does that mean?"

Asger extended a hand toward Casmir. "It's your secret to tell—or not—if you wish."

Casmir appreciated the gesture. He would have assumed that Asger and Ishii drank after-hours beer and sake together while sharing gossip. He figured all men in the nobility did that.

"How long have you known it?" Casmir asked curiously.

Ishii scowled and folded his arms over his chest.

"I had suspicions—I think I told you that weeks ago—based on some overheard comments the queen made, but it wasn't until I mentioned to the princess that you were interested in visiting the seed bank that she confirmed it for me. I hadn't realized she might be a resource."

"Thank you for that," Casmir said. "For letting her know about my interest. She was the one to give me an access card so I could get in."

"To a seed bank?" Ishii asked. "Are you planning to grow some rare heirloom tomatoes this summer?"

"No." Casmir thought about telling Ishii about his genes, but he already felt pressure due to the king's expectations. He wanted to change Ishii's opinion of him, but not by revealing that he'd been cloned from a three-centuries-past war hero. "I guess I'll avoid all asteroid miners and wealthy princes in the future. And System Hydra."

"And avoid bounty hunters," Asger said. "And ill-contented privates in the Fleet military who are looking for a way to get rich. Semi-rich. Can you even buy a good air speeder for fifty thousand? I suppose Union dollars are worth more than crowns."

Ishii scowled at this change of subject. He was squinting at Casmir, not Asger.

"Give us a minute, will you, Sir Knight?" Ishii asked.

Asger hesitated, looking at Casmir and lifting his brows. Asking for permission to leave? Or maybe wondering if Casmir thought he would be safe here alone with Ishii.

Casmir pointed at Zee and nodded, though he didn't believe Ishii would try to beat him up. He *did* expect Ishii to push harder on the "secret" he'd been made aware of but not brought in on.

As the door slid shut, leaving them alone, Casmir debated again if he should share it.

Was this why Rache never told anyone? He didn't want them to have expectations that he feared he couldn't live up to? Not that Rache probably experienced feelings of inadequacy. His desire to keep his progenitor a secret might have more to do with the very clear tie to the Kingdom that it would show. Since he always worked for people who were against the Kingdom, he might not want to give them a reason to be suspicious of him. Though it had also sounded like he hadn't wanted Jager to know who Tenebris Rache truly was.

"You find anything yet?" Ishii waved at the computer displays.

"A number of possible locations of astroshaman bases. We could try checking them one by one, but I'm still hoping a clue at Modi Moon will give us more to go on. And I'm also debating if the astroshamans are ultimately behind our troubles—the terrorists on Odin and also the theft of the gate—or if they were working with or for someone else." Casmir wondered if this Prince Dubashi was tied in somehow. It almost seemed like he had to be. Why would some random stranger put a bounty on Casmir's head?

His left eye blinked, and he rubbed it.

"Following the politics of who's involved in what always gives me a headache," Ishii said. "I prefer the logic of machines to the machinations of men."

"And yet you became a commander of hundreds of men."

"I wanted to be an engineer. But my father was a Fleet admiral, and so was my grandfather. It was assumed that I would follow in their footsteps and take the command track. The weight of family expectations."

At least Casmir hadn't had to deal with that. His parents had always told him he could be whatever he wished. Maybe if he'd grown up in the nobility with some generations-old tradition to follow, these new expectations would feel less onerous.

"We're three days from Modi Moon. I hope you find what you need there. All I'm worrying about is getting the gate, but…" Ishii frowned at the deck, took a breath, and looked into Casmir's eyes. "I apologize that two of my men attacked you on my ship. That's inexcusable. All of the men here are under my command, so I take full responsibility for this.

They will be detained until we return to Odin, at which point they will be handed over to the military police and held for a court-martial. I don't know what the outcome of that will be, but I'm positive they'll at least be dishonorably discharged from the service. It's likely that they'll also serve time in a military prison. Which, I'm told, is an unpleasant experience."

Casmir almost joked that it couldn't be much worse than being on the kitchen staff, or those men wouldn't have been so easily enticed, but Ishii was making a serious apology, so he kept himself from being flippant.

"Thank you. And it's fine. I mean, not *fine*, but we weren't hurt, so..." Casmir shrugged, not sure how to explain that he didn't particularly wish unpleasant experiences on the men, even if they *had* tried to kill him. If they had managed to hurt Kim, he might feel different, but he liked to think he wouldn't. "As long as they're not free to do it again, that's all that matters to me."

Ishii's eyebrows drew together, and Casmir thought maybe he hadn't given the right answer. Or at least not the expected answer.

"It will *not* happen again. Not on my ship." Ishii bowed stiffly and walked out.

Casmir hoped that Ishii wouldn't get in trouble with his superiors because they shared his belief that a commander was responsible for everything that happened on his ship. It sounded like Ishii was already in trouble because of actions Casmir had taken. He couldn't help but think about how Ishii's current assignment would be going a lot better for him if Casmir had never come into his life again.

He gazed at the door and resolved that he would help Ishii find the gate and, if at all possible, regain favor with his superiors. He made the same resolution in regard to Asger. Maybe hoarding the gate for the Kingdom wasn't the right thing to do, but neither was ruining the careers of those two men.

CHAPTER 5

REPORT TO THE BRIDGE, DABROWSKI," ISHII'S VOICE CAME over the speaker in the computer cabin.

It had been almost three days since the attack, but Casmir still had Zee enter the corridor first, and poked a wary head out before committing himself. A female corporal in combat armor stood on one side of the door. Asger was waiting on the other, his hand wrapped in a bandage.

"I warrant an escort?" Casmir asked him. "I'm honored."

"You should be. Not everybody receives personal attention from a knight." Asger pointed toward the lift at the end of the corridor, and they started walking.

"You're clearly a better than average knight. I'll have to ask my mother to buy more tubes of your underwear to support you. Maybe my father needs some."

The guard remained by the door, but she gawked after them—and glanced at Asger's butt.

"It's not *my* underwear. I was simply paid a fee so they could use pictures of me in their advertisements. And on the packaging, apparently. My agent failed to mention that part."

"Is something wrong with your hand?" Casmir pointed to the bandage.

"Just a bad punch in a sparring match at the gym. Dr. Sikou said she could fix it up later, but I wanted to make sure you weren't in trouble."

"Thoughtful, thank you."

They stepped into the lift for a brief ride to the upper deck and then walked onto the bridge, which was full of newer and fancier-looking pods than the ones on the *Stellar Dragon*. There were far fewer fluctuations in gravity on the *Osprey*, but Casmir knew from his experience on that cargo ship, which had also had artificial spin gravity, that things could get hairy during combat maneuvers.

A familiar moon marked by brown, tan, and gray striations dominated the forward display. Asger led Casmir onto the command platform that held the captain's pod.

"We've arrived at the moon," Ishii said without preamble, "and I've had the scanner team scouring its orbit for the last four hours."

"Find anything interesting?" Casmir assumed he hadn't been brought up here to admire the view.

"Have you got the mag-lock on it?" Ishii asked an officer manning a station to the side.

"Yes, sir."

"Put it on the display."

The distant view of the moon was replaced by what Casmir thought was a human body. He flinched at the sight of stiff legs and outstretched arms, clothes frozen solid, and a hand missing on one side. He didn't have a good view of the face, only a partial profile, but something about it seemed familiar.

"Is that a dead body?" Asger asked.

"A dead *android* body," Ishii said. "It's not giving off a heat signature or anything to indicate it's operational on any level. It's possible it's a piece of space trash that's been out there for who knows how long, but it was in a low enough orbit, and Modi's gravity is strong enough, that it would have ended up as a splat on the surface within a day."

"Can you rotate it so I can see the face?" Casmir pointed at the display.

"Adjusting the mag-lock," the officer said without checking with Ishii. He sounded young and eager to please.

The android shifted, and Casmir sucked in a startled breath. "That's Tork-57."

"Tork-what?" Ishii asked.

"It's the android that brought me to the cargo ship, hoping that I could *fix* the dead astroshamans on the bridge."

Asger tilted his head sideways. "You're right. It is. Someone dented in the side of its head, though, didn't they? Qin and I tossed it around a lot, but I don't remember it looking that bad. We didn't rip off its hand—or cut it off. That looks like a neat slice there."

"No, he wasn't that badly damaged when we left." Casmir closed his eyes, thinking of the last time he'd seen the android.

He'd deemed Tork-57 too dangerous to turn back on and add to his robot army, so he'd left him disabled on the bridge. Was it possible Rache's men had brutalized the android out of frustration? They'd been on the bridge trying to hack into the navigation computer. No, Casmir had seen Tork-57 again after he and Asger had dumped the mercenaries into escape pods. This was damage that had happened since then. Meaning…

"Someone was there after I hid the ship," Casmir said, then snorted, realizing it was a statement of the obvious. It wasn't as if the android would have powered himself up, mutilated his own limb, and jumped out an airlock.

"Whoever came to grab the ship?" Ishii asked.

"That's a fair assumption. But why would they have thrown away a good android?"

"It can't be *that* good," Asger said. "It's missing a hand."

"A simple repair, especially if the cut is as clean as it looks." Casmir gripped his chin as he gazed at the display. "It doesn't make sense."

"Androids record everything they witness," Ishii said, "until they need more space, and then they delete some of the old nonessential stuff. Since this couldn't have happened more than a couple of weeks ago, it should have a recording of who did that. And maybe it can tell us where the cargo ship went."

"Why would he be floating out there?" Casmir asked. "Especially if he has that information. Whoever took the ship wouldn't have wanted us to find it."

He winced, still wondering how someone had found the ship in the first place. He'd left the stealth generator on when he parked it in orbit, and he'd disabled the communications systems and tracking chip, so nobody should have been able to find it. Even *he* would have had to calculate its position based on the orbit he'd left it in and how often its thrusters had been programmed to fire to keep that orbit from deteriorating.

The bridge doors slid open, and Kim and Dr. Sikou walked in. Nobody batted an eye at their entrance. Kim's position of civilian advisor *definitely* allowed more wandering of the ship than Casmir's.

Dr. Sikou pointed at Asger's hand, waved her medical kit, and drew him off into a briefing room.

"You think it's a trap?" Ishii was looking at Casmir, not his newest visitors. "Or a diversion?"

"Maybe they—" Casmir waved nebulously to indicate he didn't know who *they* were, "—suspected the Fleet would be along and wanted to distract you. Or send you off in another direction. Maybe Tork does have footage, but it's been altered. Maybe the cargo ship went to a system with a water world, but the android will show someone programming in a course to System Cerberus, and when we follow, we'll spill out into the waiting hands of pirates."

"Pirates don't scare me. Wasting time does." Ishii rose from his pod and walked over to the scanner station. "I want as complete an analysis of that thing as you can give me," he told the officer working there. "If it's painted with an explosive substance or seems to be anything but an android, I want to know."

"Are you thinking of bringing it on board, sir?" The officer brought an interface arm to his embedded chip and tapped a few controls on the panel.

"Yes. And I'm thinking of having Grunburg and our civilian advisor take a close look at it."

"Is he talking about me or you?" Kim asked, stepping up to Casmir's side. It didn't sound like a joke, but it was often hard to tell with her.

"I assume me," Casmir said, "but why do you ask?"

"I thought he might want an analysis of the bacteria present inside it to possibly help determine its system of origin."

"You can do that?"

"It would be easier with a human, and if it hadn't been floating frozen in space for weeks, but I'm sure I can find some evidence of dead bacteria. Dormant endospores, if nothing else. Each of the Twelve Systems has its own signature ratio of common bacteria that humans brought with them from Earth mingled with native bacteria from the various planets and moons that had microbial life when the first colonists arrived. There's some commingling due to space travel, but it's usually still possible to identify a person's home system, if they haven't been away for too long. Odin was a bacterial paradise when humans arrived, in addition to having all manner of native flora and fauna. I could identify a Kingdom subject within seconds, simply by looking at a cheek swab under a microscope."

"Are you saying… if I'd thought to bring back a sample of the bacteria living on that cargo ship when I was there, you could have told me where it originated?"

"Very likely."

Casmir slapped a palm to his forehead. "Damn, Kim. If I'd known that, I would have licked the deck while my face was smashed against it, and then you could have cultured my tongue."

One of her eyebrows twitched. "A clean swab inserted into a properly labeled tube of sterile nutrient broth would have been preferable."

"I didn't have any of those in my tool satchel."

"A deficiency you should remedy."

"Absolutely." Casmir turned as Ishii walked back to his command pod. "Captain, your bacteriologist-on-loan wants to swab that android."

Ishii's eyebrows did an only slightly more expressive twitch. "Does that mean you think it's safe to bring on board?"

"Oh, not at all. I think it's a trap. But I bet its bacteria won't lie."

"Aren't its bacteria as frozen as it is?"

"Bacteria are regularly frozen for preservation," Kim said. "It would likely be possible to revive specimens collected in space. However, I don't need to revive them to identify them and make an educated guess where the android and the cargo ship originated."

"Which we would then hope is where they returned to and where we can now find them?" Ishii asked.

"I've narrowed down some likely spots," Casmir said. "If one happens to be in the system that matches Kim's bacterial analysis…"

"All right, good. We'll check all that, and I also want whatever footage that android recorded. Dabrowski, since you're sure it's not safe to bring it aboard, I'm going to send you to visit it."

"Uh." Casmir's one and only spacewalk had been when he'd leaped from the exploding refinery out to the *Stellar Dragon* with Qin and Zee. "Do I get an oxygen tank?"

"If you want. I was going to send you in a shuttle supplied with air."

"Oh. That sounds very reasonable. Thank you."

Ishii looked at Kim.

"Captain Rache took us onto an airless refinery without giving us tanks," she explained.

"That's criminal," Ishii said. "But that's not what I intended to ask. I was wondering if you want to go with him, but now that I think about it, you're too important to risk. I'll send my programmer, Grunburg, along with him, and they can bring you back a sample. Or the whole android if they deem it's not dangerous."

"That would be acceptable," Kim said.

Casmir thought about protesting the fact that he *wasn't* too important to risk, but he was so relieved he wasn't being forced out an airlock without an oxygen tank that he didn't mind. If Ishii was going to send one of his own men along—a programmer sounded like a promising colleague—he must not think it too dangerous a task.

"Shall I supply you with appropriate swabs and tubes?" Kim asked Casmir.

"Are you going to put some in my tool satchel whether I say yes or not?"

"Yes. You horrified me with the idea of trying to isolate exogenous bacteria from the endogenous microbiota of your tongue."

"Sorry. That was inconsiderate of me."

"Yes."

Casmir grinned. He wasn't sure, but he thought there might have been a glint of humor in Kim's eyes.

Yas sat at a table in the *Fedallah*'s mess hall, eating dinner, which consisted of bland vegetables, oddly textured vat chicken, and a lumpy brown sauce of indeterminate flavor. Supposedly, the concoctions served on board were optimized to be nutrient-dense with the ideal mix of fat, protein, and carbohydrates. Now and then, the meals neared the decent mark, but most of the time, Yas suspected the dubious flavors and textures were intentionally chosen to make the mercenaries grumpy and mean. And they were working, if the shouts and fist banging coming from the group two tables down were an indicator.

As always, he'd thought about dining in his cabin or sickbay, but that would have required an extra trip to return the dishes. As far as he'd seen, the ship lacked the service robots that had been typical on Tiamat Station. Or, if not typical, easily affordable on what he'd made as a surgeon there.

Jess Khonsari walked into the mess hall with her usual swagger, her high cheekbones and full lips as striking as always. More than a few of the men's gazes drifted in her direction. Yas hoped she would ignore them and join him, but he kept himself from making pleading puppy-dog eyes and pointing vigorously at the seat next to him.

He focused on the tablet he'd opted to do research on instead of his embedded chip and contact interface, mostly so he would look busy and nobody would bother him. A vacant expression seemed to be an invitation for a mercenary to stride up, thump him on the back, and shove up a sleeve or pull off a boot to get an opinion on some fungal growth or skin irritation around a cybernetic implant.

"How're you doing, Doc?" Jess slid into the seat across from him.

A few of the men looked over, either disappointed by her choice or hoping for something gossip-worthy to share in the gym.

Yas ignored them and focused on Jess, noting that her warm brown skin didn't quite hide the dark bags under her eyes. It was a wonder that she still managed to look beautiful, but the form-fitting galaxy suit tended to ensure men barely noticed her eyes. *Some* men. He wasn't that shallow.

"Doc?" she prompted.

"Yes," he blurted, realizing he'd been studying her… shallowly. "I am, at the captain's request, researching poisons that might have particular efficacy against astroshamans, though it's hard to find anything that wouldn't also affect all humans. I'm focusing on agents that attack the nerves, since those are usually altered during cybernetic surgery to network the new parts in with the human system."

"Half the people on this ship are altered in the same way as the astroshamans." Jess lifted her prosthetic hand and curled the fingers, then flexed them. "Well, maybe not in the same way. Those guys are usually interested in becoming one with their machine parts and achieving spiritual enlightenment, not kicking bad guys' asses. But you'd be finding a poison that would take out the crew as well as our enemies."

Corporal Xi, one of the men gathered at the other table, jumped on top of it. Trays rattled and a cup flew off as he pantomimed a sexual act.

"Are you sure *we're* not the bad guys?" Yas asked, looking glumly down at the chemical structure of a poison he was researching.

Jess waved a dismissive hand at the men. "We're just tools. Rache gets to decide if we're used for good or evil."

"Corporal Xi is most certainly a tool."

Jess snorted. "Good or bad, at least in regard to us, depends on whether you're pro-Kingdom or anti-Kingdom. Sometimes, we're fighting for pirates or Miners' Union barons, and it's just a matter of deciding who's the lesser evil."

"I think if you use poison to kill your enemies, you're evil even if you're rescuing school children."

"So find something that doesn't kill. Couldn't you *temporarily* paralyze people or otherwise mess up their nerve connections?"

Yas tapped his tablet, trying to think if he knew of such an agent.

"I doubt the captain requires that we be able to toss in some toxic gas that kills everyone before we go in," Jess said. "He probably just wants to stack the advantages in our favor, since it sounds like we're going to be doing the equivalent of storming some ancient Kingdom castle with giant walls and moats and dinosaurs in the moats."

"I believe you're thinking of alligators."

"What's the difference? They're green and scaly with giant teeth, right?"

"I gather you didn't have either in your habitat when you were growing up." Yas only knew of one moon that had been seeded with some geneticists' notion of what ancient Earth dinosaurs had been, based more on texts than any preserved genetic material. It was a tourist park. Alligators, however, filled an important ecological niche and existed in many places that had been terraformed with swamplands.

"Nah, our government decided that having giant predators around in an enclosed space station with a million humans wasn't the smartest idea."

Corporal Xi jumped down from the table and started trading punches with a private. Yas couldn't tell if it was a game or a genuine fight. One man flew backward, skidding on his ass across the deck.

"Yes, predators can be tedious." Yas flicked a casual finger toward Jess, not wanting to point out that she looked like she hadn't been sleeping, lest she think he was going to pressure her about an exam again. "How are you doing?"

"The usual." She shrugged and gazed toward a porthole. "I have mixed feelings about going after astroshamans. They don't seem quite so alien and strange to me these days." She flexed her prosthetic fingers again and lowered her voice. "I thought the captain's main goal was to keep the Kingdom from getting that gate. It seems like that's what's happening right now. Someone else has disappeared with it. Why can't we stand back and let that play out?"

This was the first time Yas had heard her question Rache, and he found himself also lowering his voice, feeling they shouldn't be overheard. "We saw four warships. Maybe he thinks it's likely that the Kingdom will find and recover the gate, if there's nobody else to oppose them."

"Maybe. I just…" Jess shrugged again. "I guess I've been a little curious about the astroshamans of late. It's said that some of them know how to rewire the gut and the brain so their people are more rational and less swayed by emotions. I was trying to find some studies on how that might affect dreams and the power of memories, but there wasn't much out there. I'm sure they do plenty of research, but they don't publish their findings on the public networks. They're reclusive, but if you want in, and you meet the qualifications…" This time, she waved to her eyes, though one had to look very closely to tell they weren't biological organs.

Yas tried not to find her admission alarming, that she'd found herself intrigued enough to look up astroshamans. Thoroughly.

It wasn't that there was anything inherently evil about their religion—they were a lot less likely to cause trouble than the Star Striders—other than their disturbing tendency to find humanity to be lesser, something to evolve away from, rather than something that could be accepted and improved as it was. Yas was mostly concerned that her desires stemmed from whatever nightmares and emotional pain she experienced as a survivor of the attack she'd described, the only one in her family *to* survive.

"It's true that many people have found solace by embracing the various religions out there," Yas said, not wanting to suggest that he could help her find a better solution if she would simply come to sickbay for an exam, "but the surgery you described wouldn't likely be reversible, so you might want to talk to some people who have had it done before making a decision."

"Yeah. Maybe I can chat with some of them while Rache is poisoning them and Xi is trying to blow them away."

"Perhaps you could find some members of the religion who weren't directly responsible for taking the gate," Yas said seriously, even though she'd been sarcastic. "If we end up at Tiamat Station, there are a few astroshaman communities. I even had a couple come in as patients. There are often complications to cybernetics surgeries."

"Tell me about it." Her mouth twisted, and Yas wondered how much tinkering had been required before she'd become a fully functioning human being again. And he wondered if she felt physical pain, not just emotional pain.

He stretched his hands across the table toward her, wishing he could take hers into his, but her hands were in her lap, and she was gazing toward the porthole again. He let his fingers press against the cool surface instead.

"If the captain is able to help me clear my name, and I can walk through the station without being shot, I would be happy to introduce you to some of the astroshamans there. I remember there was a woman I operated on who designed virtual-reality games, and was kind of like you."

"Plagued by demons of the past?"

"She'd been in an attack and had the surgery done to save her life. And she was snarky."

"I guess that's almost as good."

The men at the other table fell silent, the fight ended, and they all sat demurely. Yas spotted the reason. Captain Rache had walked in. He headed for the trays stacked in the dispensing station but noticed Yas and Jess and detoured toward their table.

Yas tapped his tablet so his research showed on the screen, wanting Rache to know he was working on the assigned problem, even if he'd shifted to thinking about non-deadly ways to achieve the objective.

"We'll pass through the gate later today," Rache told them without preamble, glancing at Yas before focusing on Jess. "Two of the warships diverted to Modi Moon, and two others appear to be delivering robots and supplies to rebuild those refineries, so we'll have a head start, assuming we guessed right and are going to the correct location."

"System Hydra?" Yas asked.

"System Hydra. We have to assume that Fleet will figure it out and be right on our tails. And that we may have to battle them as well as the astroshamans. Chief, I need you to spend the rest of the trip ensuring the ship is in top shape. If any parts were damaged during the refinery-station incident and weren't repaired to optimal, let me know, and we'll pick up replacements. We can stop at the Outpost Zeta on the way into Hydra."

"You really think their Fleet will figure it out soon enough to be a problem?" Jess wrinkled her nose, perhaps not having a high opinion of the Kingdom soldiers.

"Yes," Rache said. "I've learned that Professor Dabrowski and Scholar Sato are on one of those warships."

His matter-of-fact tone changed slightly for the announcement, but Yas couldn't quite read it. It didn't sound like wariness or dismay, which Yas might expect. It almost sounded like eagerness. Some desire to pit himself against his clone nemesis again? Or could Kim Sato's presence mean something to him? She had saved Yas's life, so he hoped Rache didn't harbor some resentment toward her.

"You think that'll make the Fleet ships more dangerous, sir?" Jess asked dubiously.

"Dabrowski is immune to the gate's pseudo radiation, and Kim knows how to cure people who encounter it and aren't immune. That could give them an advantage we don't have. And Dabrowski's like a neophyte fighter who ends up winning with a lucky punch, because he's so unpredictable that you can't use logic to defend against him." Rache shook his head. "Just make sure the *Fedallah* is in top condition."

"Yes, sir," Jess said. "I'll get you a list of parts."

Rache nodded, grabbed a tray, and walked out.

"Hm, he calls Dabrowski by last name and Kim by first," Jess mused. "Isn't that interesting?"

"I think he's spent more time with her."

"Makes you wonder what he was doing down on Odin, doesn't it?" Jess smirked.

Yas thought of the expressionless and aloof Kim Sato and couldn't imagine her flinging herself into Rache's embrace—into anyone's embrace—for a wanton sexual encounter. "I assumed he needed new socks and masks and prefers Kingdom wool to synthetic materials."

Jess laughed and clasped one of his hands. "You should make jokes more often, Yas. You're not bad at it."

Yas swallowed, abruptly aware of nothing else but her hand resting atop his, fingers warm where they touched his. That was her human hand, though he wouldn't have minded a touch from the prosthetic one. From any part of her.

"Thank you," he managed to get out.

She patted his hand, then took her tray to the disposal, the food barely touched, and walked out. Yas hoped she wouldn't decide to take up a new religion and leave the *Fedallah,* especially when he was stuck here for another four years and seven months… but he knew there was a lovely park on the way to that astroshaman community he'd mentioned taking her to, and he couldn't help but imagine walking through it with her while holding hands.

"I just need to survive four Kingdom warships and countless astroshamans first," he muttered.

CHAPTER 6

KIM WALKED WITH CASMIR TO THE SHUTTLE BAY, worried that he was being sent off to investigate a frozen, spaced android that he believed had been placed as a trap. Why did Captain Ishii think Kim wasn't expendable but Casmir *was*?

That irritated her. On this particular mission, wasn't he the *least* expendable person here? He had the gate immunity, was the one who'd been narrowing down likely locations where it had been taken, and had the engineering background to perhaps figure out the gate well enough to turn off its defenses. Though she hadn't gotten a chance to tell Ishii that yet. She'd been distracted by the assassination attempt and hadn't run into him since then.

She paused. Maybe she should tell him now. Before Casmir was sent off into danger.

"Kim?" Casmir paused a few steps ahead of her.

She caught up. "I was debating whether Ishii would send you off to do a dangerous thing if he believed you were the best bet to turn off the gate's defenses. I haven't yet suggested that to him. Maybe I should do so before you go."

"I'm not sure he'll believe that, especially since I doubt it's true, or that it would stop him from sending me. This *is* my job, after all. I'm probably more experienced with androids than anyone on his crew."

"You don't think there's another roboticist on a crew of five hundred?"

They stepped into the lift, and he ordered it to the shuttle bay without hesitating. Kim frowned.

"I'm sure they have an occupational specialty for repairing robots, but I've got almost thirty years of experience doing a lot more than repairs, and it's not like I had to split my time between academic studies and learning combat and how to be a good soldier."

"Thirty years ago, you were three."

"What's your point? That's when my father got me my first robot kit to assemble—a toy knight on a motor bike that you could program to zip around the kitchen and flee the fearsome predator living in the apartment."

She squinted at him.

"We had a cat when I was younger," he explained. "Anyway, weren't you cozying up to bacteria by the time you were three?"

"Not until I was five."

"And here I thought you were more advanced than I am." The lift doors opened, and Casmir bumped his shoulder as he stepped out, then apologized to the door.

"I'm *definitely* more advanced than you."

He grinned at her as they headed down the wide corridor, passing refrigerated holds and storage compartments.

"Even if he has robotics specialists," Kim said, "I think he's making a mistake by considering you more expendable than me."

"He may have been sarcastic about expendability. He's sending one of his men along."

"Maybe he doesn't like that man. If his kitchen staff is anything to go by, his crew isn't that appealing."

"Don't worry." Casmir waved at the sensor to a set of oversized doors, and they stepped into the shuttle bay. "I'll be careful. I have some pretty good guesses about how an android might be booby-trapped and what to look for."

Kim held her tongue, but when she spotted Captain Ishii and a young officer by a shuttle being prepped by a robot grounds crew, she vowed to use this opportunity to speak with him.

"Professor Dabrowski?" a chipper young voice asked. The officer walked—no, that was more like skipping—away from Ishii and toward Casmir. "It *is* you. I heard you were here. I thought about coming to see you, but the captain said you weren't to be disturbed."

The young man—a lieutenant, his insignia said—bounced to a stop in front of Casmir and started to salute. He seemed to realize that wasn't the correct address for a civilian and switched it to a bow and an offered hand. He had buzz-cut black hair and a strong jaw, but something about his goofy grin made Kim think he would fit in more at Casmir's robotics lab on campus than here on a military vessel.

"Davy Grunburg?" Casmir clasped the offered hand for a vigorous shake.

"You remember my name." The lieutenant straightened, and his goofy grin grew wider. "You were the best assistant professor ever. Your classes were so much more interesting than Professor Nowak's. Have you made full professor yet?"

"Yes. I even have tenure. Which may theoretically mean I still have a job when I return home, even though I've been MIA for months now."

Casmir looked down at his hand. Grunburg was still shaking it.

He realized it and let go. "Sorry, sir. Uhm, Professor. Professor, sir."

Ishii was scowling at what appeared to be an unexpected reunion, and he rolled his eyes at Grunburg's fumbling.

"I remember you saying you were going into the military," Casmir said. "Because of your father, right?"

"Yes, my father the admiral." Grunburg smiled and shrugged. "It's a family tradition. I promised him I'd serve at least six years before going out into the civilian sector, and he promised he wouldn't be terribly disappointed in me."

"Funny how much military service has more to do with parental expectations than a desire to protect the Kingdom and swear oaths to the king." Casmir looked over at Ishii.

Ishii's scowl deepened. "You two, load up. You can reminisce about Dabrowski's teaching style while you're flying over to pick up that android. I imagine it involved a lot of things blowing up in the lab."

"There's not much in a robotics lab that can blow up," Casmir said. "You're thinking of chemistry. Explosions come out of Professor Andric's lab all the time."

"Whatever." Ishii pointed toward the open hatch. The robot crew had finished fueling the shuttle and was retreating.

"You should come to one of my classes sometime when we're both on Odin, Sora," Casmir said. "You could see what we do in the lab. You might find it fun. At the end of the semester, we have competitions, which I know you're a fan of."

"The drone races were excellent," Grunburg said wistfully as he climbed into the shuttle.

"I'll bet," Ishii grumbled and shooed Casmir toward the hatch again. "There are oxygen tanks inside in case anything happens to the shuttle. Check your galaxy suits before you launch."

As Casmir was about to climb in, the doors opened, and Asger raced in with his pertundo in hand, as if he expected to face a legion of angry pirates. But his long legs took him toward Casmir, his scowl more than matching the one lingering on Ishii's face.

"You weren't going to tell me you're leaving the ship and going into danger? You are the *worst* body that's ever been bodyguarded." Asger frowned, as if he knew that only made dubious sense, but he was too flustered to correct himself.

"It's a good thing you're such a flexible and adaptable bodyguard then," Casmir said. "If a touch grumpy."

"You'd be grumpy, too, if you had to work with you."

"It's true that not everybody finds me as charming as Kim does. She's lived with me for seven years, bless her, and doesn't find my antics grump-inspiring."

"I close the door and lock myself in my room a lot," Kim said.

Asger gave her a look that may have been confused, disbelieving, or sympathetic. She wasn't as familiar with him and had a harder time reading his expressions than she did Casmir's.

"It's not that bad," she added, in case he expected clarification. "There's a private balcony."

Asger pushed his hand through his hair, tearing out a few strands. Maybe that wasn't the clarification he'd sought.

"You're staying here, Asger," Ishii said. "There won't be any assassins out there."

"What if that android has been programmed to be an assassin and kill whoever brings it in?" Asger pointed his pertundo, the telescoping shaft extended, toward the closed shuttle-bay doors and the frozen enemy that floated somewhere beyond them. "That is the android that we battled on the bridge of the cargo ship—the one you *tricked*, Casmir. Even if it *wasn't* programmed to kill you, it may make an exception because it's annoyed with you."

"The scanners showed that it's powered down," Ishii said. "As long as they don't activate it, it can't assassinate anyone. Probably."

"*Probably*." Asger thumped the shaft of his weapon on the deck. "Casmir..."

"You should stay here, Asger." Casmir stepped away from the shuttle and put a hand on his arm. "While I appreciate your willingness to protect me, it's better not to endanger more people than necessary, just in case there is a booby trap."

"Booby traps are the precise reason I *should* be there."

"You have experience with nullifying explosives and biohazard weapons?" Casmir asked.

"No, but I can stand in front of you if they go off, so you don't die."

Casmir's mouth opened and closed again. He didn't seem to know what to say to that.

Ishii squinted at Asger. "Do you actually have orders to do that?"

"The queen has always wanted him protected, and it's my understanding that the king does, at the moment, too. Until the gate is recovered."

Kim didn't miss that *at the moment* or the connotation that the king's preferences could change with the wind.

"Must be nice to get a knight for a personal bodyguard," Ishii said.

Grunburg poked his head out of the shuttle's open hatch. "Do you think he'd jump in front of *me*?"

"No, because he's not coming," Casmir said.

The doors opened once more, and Zee strode into the shuttle bay carrying several toolboxes.

"*He* is." Casmir smiled.

"I find it disconcerting that you prefer a robot's presence over mine," Asger said.

"Only because he bounces back better from explosives thrown at him and boulders landing on his back." Casmir waved for Zee to hop into the shuttle with the toolboxes.

"You're underestimating me, Dabrowski. Haven't you seen my calendars?"

Ishii rolled his eyes again. He did that a lot for the supreme commander of a warship.

"*Calendars*?" Casmir asked. "There's more than one?"

"One for each year. Ask Qin the next time you see her. She can attest to the sturdiness of my physique."

Casmir's lower lip drooped. "You gave her a calendar? Of your… sturdiness?"

"I signed it. I thought she would like it."

"You should probably run your future gift ideas past me. For refinement suggestions."

"I didn't think giving her underwear would be appropriate."

"Get in the shuttle!" Ishii roared, making both men jump.

Kim also jumped and stared at him. His face was red.

"It's like being in a frat house. Go do your damn mission so we can figure out where to find the gate." Ishii stepped toward Casmir, as if he meant to personally heft him into the shuttle.

But Casmir scrambled in on his own, joining Zee and Grunburg inside. Asger's fingers twitched as the hatch lowered, as if he meant to stop it and leap in, but maybe Zee's appearance had convinced him that Casmir didn't need another bodyguard. He grumbled something under his breath and stalked out of the shuttle bay.

"Scholar Sato." Ishii extended a hand toward the door in invitation.

Knowing they would have to leave for the bay to depressurize and the shuttle to launch, she walked out with him, but she lifted a hand as soon as they were in the corridor.

"There was something I meant to tell you earlier, Captain," she said.

"What?" He eyed her warily.

"When we actually find the gate, I believe Casmir is the best person to study it and figure out a way to turn off its defensive mechanisms, i.e. the emitting of the deadly pseudo radiation."

"Why him?"

"In addition to his immunity, he's good at solving engineering problems."

"Wait, his what? He's immune?"

Kim cocked her head. "You didn't know that?"

"Nobody told me. Why is he immune?"

Kim opened her mouth to give the full explanation but caught herself, realizing that would mean explaining that he had been cloned from a man who'd lived and died three hundred years earlier, before the Great Plague.

"He has unique mitochondria," she said.

"Lucky him."

"Only if we don't encounter the Great Plague virus in our travels." She worried about that now that they were heading out of System Lion. Even if the virus no longer ran rampant among human civilizations, she was sure pockets still existed out there, surviving in less desirable hosts, ever ready to pounce at an opportunity.

Ishii started to ask a question but shook his head and switched to another. "Is his immunity the reason the king and queen have given him a bodyguard?"

"That's tangentially the reason."

"What does that mean?"

"Tangentially? In a way that relates only slightly to a matter. Peripherally."

Ishii chopped the air with his hand. "I know what the *word* means. What I want to know is does this mean it's more important to keep him alive than I realized because of that?"

Kim wanted to state that it would be important to keep him alive under any circumstances, but all she said was, "Yes."

"It would have been nice if my orders had said that."

"Maybe your superiors believed you would do your best to keep civilian advisors alive, regardless, and did not feel the need to state that it was important." She couldn't keep her words from coming out cool and accusatory.

"I have a whole ship to worry about and a mission to complete." Ishii bowed stiffly. "Good day, Scholar Sato."

Kim frowned as he walked away, not sure her words would affect the way Ishii treated Casmir. She hoped he considered Grunburg invaluable and would do his best to keep both men alive.

There was no gravity on the shuttle. Casmir had known there wouldn't be, and he'd taken an anti-nausea pill before heading to the shuttle bay, but he'd forgotten about it until they launched and flew away from the *Osprey* and its spin gravity. He sat wrapped in a pod, cradled like an egg, but that didn't keep his stomach from feeling the effects of their acceleration, turns, and deceleration as the craft's autopilot took them around some space junk and toward the abandoned android.

"Do you get space-sick, sir?" Grunburg asked, his face not visible through the side of his pod.

"Yes."

"Me too. I got an injection of some gut bacteria when I first started space training, and that's helped lots."

Casmir snorted, remembering his conversation with Kim. "Is injection really the accurate word there?"

"Uh, perhaps not, but it worked pretty well."

"I wonder if Kim made the strain they used."

"I'm not sure. Dr. Sikou would know. There's the android. Let me have the shuttle's external mag-gripper snag it." Grunburg adjusted his pod forward and tapped a few controls.

Casmir was glad to let someone else handle the shuttle, since he didn't have any familiarity with the model—or shuttles in general. With his depth perception, he'd make a farce of grabbing something out of space.

"The captain said to run it through decon and bring it on board. Do you think that's wise?"

"No, but we're going to be limited with what we can do without direct access to it."

"Right. Bringing it in."

Casmir activated his helmet, and it sealed over his head. Just in case the android had been given some awful virus that the decontamination system didn't catch. And would that decon protocol destroy the bacteria Kim needed to look at? It hadn't sounded like she needed the bacteria alive to identify them.

A few clunks reverberated through the shuttle as tools extended, clamped onto Tork, and pulled him into the airlock. Casmir tried to wait patiently. Behind him, Zee gripped a handhold, his legs floating free in zero-g.

"We've got it on board," Grunburg announced. "Running decon." He leaned forward and eyed a display. "It's still not showing any heat signatures or anything to suggest it's powered up. The captain wants it to stay that way. Think we can find the footage without turning it on?"

"Maybe. We'll have to look under the hood to see if Tork is powered down because a switch was flicked or because of damage. Or if he's just playing dead."

Casmir patted his tool satchel, making sure the bulge in the side was still there. He'd swung by the ship's small robotics lab in engineering and been fortunate enough to find a spare hand for the android models the *Osprey* employed. It wouldn't be a precise match, but with a little tinkering, Casmir thought he could outfit Tork with it. If it made sense to do so. He had an idea, but he wasn't sure it would prove viable. Or that it was wise.

"That's an alarming thought," Grunburg said. "Do you really think the android is booby-trapped?"

"I am suspicious of Tork's presence here instead of inside his cargo ship."

"Right. I'm going to get it and strap it down in the back."

Grunburg left his seat and pushed himself toward the airlock. Casmir, telling himself that it would be wrong of him to advise from his pod while Grunburg did all the work, took a few breaths to steady his stomach, then hit the release tab.

The pod's embrace lessened, and he maneuvered himself toward a worktable in the rear where Grunburg was strapping down the inert Tork-57. The walls were full of wide, thin drawers of tools, in addition to the boxes Zee had brought on board and secured. This particular shuttle must have been used for repairs rather than sent out on combat missions. If nothing else, it would have everything they needed to tinker with the android.

"Its power switch is turned off." Grunburg had a panel in the back of Tork's neck open. "I'm going to see if I can get any data without switching it on, but that's probably not going to work."

"I doubt it. Let's search his physical body thoroughly first before we risk it."

Casmir grabbed a scanner and ran it over Tork as Grunburg finished strapping him to the table. The android's hand was missing, as they'd been aware, and his overalls were torn, the fabric frozen in rucked-up positions, and there were gouges and a dent in the side of his head. Some of the damage Casmir recognized from the battle, but the hand had definitely been there the last time he'd seen the android. He peered down and examined the severed arm. It had been a clean cut, as if by a bladed weapon, like Asger's fancy halberd. Had whoever collected the cargo ship been carrying a sword?

"No sign that he's online in even a backup capacity now." Casmir set an alert on the scanner, so it would inform them if that changed, and tried to set it on the table. It promptly floated away, and he grabbed it and found a place to wedge it into. It wasn't only his stomach that needed to get used to zero-g. "I'm pulling up his model schematics from the network so we can check all of the orifices for explosives or any other foreign material."

"If there's one thing I never expected to do with an old instructor, it's check orifices."

"Yeah, that's an activity the school board doesn't encourage professors to do with students." Casmir pulled out his drill and put in a tiny bit to open a hidden panel in Tork's side that he would have missed if he hadn't had the schematics.

"Weird. How's one supposed to prepare for a career in customs?"

"I can't believe that sense of humor fits into the military."

"It doesn't," Grunburg said.

Casmir carefully removed the panel, checking the scanner to make sure he didn't trip some virtual wire and cause the android to power up. And attack them. He glanced at Zee and was relieved to find him nearby, paying close attention.

He maneuvered himself lower so he could peer into the panel. There was a spare power pack inside, a few wires, and… a small rectangle of gray matter that looked a lot like a Mark-Pak amalgam explosive.

"We may have a problem," Casmir said.

"I am detecting electronic activity in the android," Zee said, just before the scanner beeped a warning.

Casmir couldn't tell if the activity was coming from Tork or from the explosive. He pulled out a flashlight and examined the gray rectangle, trying to tell if it had been wedged into the only available space or was hard-wired to Tork's insides.

"Uh, I didn't turn it on." Grunburg had hooked a tablet and data transfer cables to the ports near the ON/OFF switch. "Maybe some defensive security measure we triggered?"

"Maybe," Casmir said. "There's a chunk of Mark-Pak in here with a single wire going into the android. It was definitely jury-rigged. I don't see a detonator. I think Tork probably *is* the detonator."

Grunburg cursed. "Better get it out of there before the android fully powers up."

"Right." Casmir pulled out wire cutters, cursing when he tried to set his flashlight down and it floated away. Well, it couldn't go far.

Zee stepped forward. "Let me remove this explosive device while you humans take cover."

Casmir hesitated. He hated to foist something dangerous off on someone else, but Zee had a good chance of surviving an explosion and even reassembling himself back to his original state. Casmir's and Grunburg's odds of that were far less. "All right. Here."

Casmir tried to hand Zee the wire cutters before he fully remembered what his creation was capable of. Zee lifted his hand, and two of his fingers morphed into scissors.

"Right. Grunburg?" Casmir tilted his head toward the pods in front of the navigation console. Unfortunately, the small shuttle didn't have any separation between the front and back—no bulkheads to hide behind. Not unless he and Grunburg wanted to squeeze into the lav together.

"Hiding?" Grunburg glanced at Zee but didn't object. He removed his tablet, leaving the cables dangling from the back of Tork's neck, and followed Casmir up front.

"Go ahead, Zee," Casmir said as they crouched behind the pods. "Remove the Mark-Pak and throw it out the airlock."

"I suppose we can't get the footage the captain wants if we just throw the android out the airlock," Grunburg muttered.

"He already spent enough time out there." It was silly, especially since Tork belonged to their enemies, but Casmir felt sorry for the rejected android. "Wait," he blurted, an idea coming to him. "Hold on, Zee. If the guy who last tinkered with him wasn't wearing gloves…"

Casmir rummaged in his satchel again, snorting when he saw Kim's kit for swabbing bacteria samples. He would do that later. For now, he pulled out a brush with fine bristles.

He opened the bank of drawers near the worktable, items secured inside so they wouldn't float away, and found some clear tape and what looked like charcoal powder in a jar. It wasn't labeled. Hoping for the best, he grabbed it.

"Professor?" Grunburg asked. "Do you think we have the time to do… whatever it is you're doing?"

"What I'm doing is wondering why I don't carry lycopodium powder in my toolkit. That's what the detectives always use in the old murder-mystery comics."

Casmir took his borrowed goods back to the niche in the android's side, opened the jar of powder, and did his best to dust it over the interior with the brush before it floated away. Blowing while wearing a helmet did nothing useful, and he snorted as he caught himself doing it, glad the Glasnax faceplate had anti-fogging properties.

"Professor..."

"Almost done. I'm hoping to get lucky and snag a fingerprint. The oil left behind by fingers would have frozen in space, but it should still be here, right? In a crystalized form?" Casmir decided not to explain that he'd only read about lifting fingerprints, and it tended to involve identifiable powders, better brushes, and gravity-filled crime scenes.

"You're doing that *now*?" Grunburg asked instead of answering the question. He was still crouching behind the pilot's pod. "While there's a bomb ticking down?"

"Well, if it blows up, it'll be much harder to get fingerprints."

"You're a loon, Professor."

"You can call me Casmir."

Casmir worked quickly, sweat dribbling from his hairline even though the galaxy suit created a perfectly conditioned environment. In the nonexistent gravity, the bead of sweat floated away from his face and splashed against his faceplate.

He carefully brushed away the excess powder, stuck his clear tape inside, and hoped for the best. There were a few smudges on it. Fingerprints? Maybe. He smashed the tape to a white piece of cardboard and stuck it in his satchel.

"Done." Casmir dove behind the pod next to Grunburg. "Your turn, Zee."

As the seconds passed, Casmir kept his head down, afraid to watch Zee's progress in case the explosive blew.

Grunburg, crouching in a similar position, peered over at him. "When I became a military programmer, I didn't envision myself being flung into dangerous situations very often."

"When I became a robotics professor, I also didn't envision myself being flung into dangerous situations. I'm positive it wasn't mentioned in the job description anywhere."

"Well, you're working for the military now. When you sign the enlistment contract, there are a lot of lines about possibly dying and your family not being able to sue the government for a settlement."

"I didn't sign any contracts. I'm a civilian advisor."

"How's the pay?"

"There isn't any, not for me. I understand Kim is getting paid." Casmir almost joked that she should be the one over here trying to remove bombs, but he wouldn't wish this on anyone else. And it wasn't as if she was entirely safe back on the *Osprey*. This was only a pause in their journey to go fight astroshamans for possession of that gate.

He grimaced at the thought, reminded that he was once again responsible, however inadvertently, for her being dragged off into space and put in danger. He hoped she got a lot of story ideas from these adventures and that they resulted in her writing a bestseller in her spare time.

"I have removed the malleable explosive," Zee said.

"Excellent work, Zee." Casmir kept his head behind the pod and didn't look. They weren't in the clear yet.

A hiss sounded, the seal breaking on the airlock.

"Does he know how to cycle it?" Grunburg asked.

"He'll figure out the panel. It's not that hard."

A soft clank sounded.

"That's great," Grunburg said. "He's amazing."

"Yes, he is." Since Casmir didn't have children, he could only imagine what it was like to feel the pride of fatherhood, but he wouldn't be surprised if it was something like this.

"I am opening the outer hatch," Zee said from the airlock chamber, his voice now coming over a speaker. "The device is—"

The shuttle lurched hard, the deck tilting and hurling Casmir toward the side. He rammed into Grunburg, and they tumbled into the hull as the lights flickered.

"What happened?" Grunburg blurted.

"I assume our explosive went off right next to the shuttle." Casmir righted himself as the lights shut off completely. He looked at the airlock hatch, the night vision in his contacts compensating for the low illumination—only a few indicators glowed on the control panel. "There's not a gaping hole in the hull, so that's a plus."

Zee opened the inner hatch and pushed himself back inside, grabbing a handhold as he shut the hatch again. He gave Casmir a thumbs-up, his fingers having returned to their usual shape.

"Looks like we got rid of it just in time," Casmir said.

"A little sooner might have been better." Grunburg pulled himself to the control panel and thumbed on auxiliary lighting.

A thud sounded, and Casmir looked up as Tork, now fully online with his eyes open, arrowed into Zee with enough force to knock him from the handhold. Their momentum carried them toward the pods, and Casmir ducked for cover again.

"Get him, Zee!" he shouted, though it was unnecessary. Zee knew how to defend himself.

They slammed into his pod and bounced off, grappling. Grunburg's cables dangled from an open panel in Tork's head. The damaged android fought like a cornered cat in a back alley in Zamek.

Grunburg pulled out his stunner but only looked at it. The weapon wouldn't stop either of the combatants. Casmir trusted that Zee would come out on top, but perhaps not before android limbs littered the shuttle. An elbow slammed into the hull, leaving a dent.

When Casmir saw an opening, he pushed past them. His momentum took him to the worktable—they should have strapped the android down far more tightly and with stronger cables. He hunted around for his tool satchel and found it floating near the ceiling. He yanked it down and grabbed his screwdriver.

"Zee, can you bring him back here? Angle him so I can get to the panel in the back of his neck."

Zee launched himself off the ceiling, ramming into Tork's chest, and again, they flew through the shuttle, limbs tangled. Somehow, Zee forced the android around, then held him still so Casmir could access the panel. It was still open from Grunburg's tinkering, cables dangling from the ports. He did his best to get close enough to poke around but not so close that he risked an elbow like titanium striking him in the ribs.

The switch was clearly in the OFF position.

"Lies," he muttered, then jerked his head back as Tork reached his fingers over his shoulder, trying to grasp him.

Zee caught the hand before it got close to Casmir. He clamped down with force that would have crushed human fingers. And would crush android fingers, as well, if it continued.

"Try not to damage him further," Casmir said. "Please. Just hold him as still as you can. I appreciate it. Thank you, Zee."

Casmir pried open the entire panel, revealing a tangle of wires leading to the circuit boards inside.

"It is not always easy protecting you, Casmir Dabrowski."

"I know. You were probably better off with Kim."

"She *was* restful."

Casmir pulled wires from sockets so he could get deeper into the android's head, located his CPU, and levered the chip out of its socket. Tork stopped struggling.

"Did that finally knock him out?" Casmir asked, since the schematic showed both backup power supplies and an auxiliary CPU.

"I no longer read a power signature," Zee said.

"Let's hope he's not playing possum again." Casmir pointed to the table. "Strap him down, please. I'd ask you to also sit on his chest, but that probably wouldn't be effective in zero-g."

Casmir looked at the CPU, then zipped it into one of the pockets of his galaxy suit.

"We should have tried to grab the video footage while it was online." Grunburg returned to the table, holding one of the cables that had fallen free in the fight, along with his tablet. "We could have let your bodyguard tear off its limbs so it couldn't fight us."

"I suppose, but I would have felt bad beating up on him more."

Grunburg stared at him. "That thing tried to kill us."

"Technically, someone programmed him to try to kill us."

"That makes it all right then."

"Maybe *we* can program him to work for us. Ishii said that's your specialty, right?"

"Programming weapons software and making updates to the operating system for the *Osprey*, not androids, but yes."

Casmir waved for Grunburg to continue his attempts to download from the android's memory. "If you can't get anything, I can put the CPU back in, but here, let me reconnect the power lines without it, and see if that's enough. His memory cards and hard drives are still in place."

"Hopefully, that will work. Since your friend isn't able to sit on chests currently."

Zee had found a new spot he liked, his back to the ceiling as he looked down on the table from above.

While Grunburg worked, Casmir poked into his satchel again, grumbling in frustration as tools tried to float out. He needed to zero-g-proof his tools. But not now. Now, he had a project.

He pulled out the android hand he'd acquired.

Grunburg frowned. "You're not going to *fix* him, are you?"

"Sure. While you're handling the data, I'll handle the, uh, hand." Casmir waved it, fingers flopping.

"You're the boss, Professor."

"Am I? I think you're the only one here who believes that."

Grunburg looked up at Zee.

"The only one on the warship," Casmir amended and got to work.

"Only because they haven't taken your classes and don't know that you're a fun professor. And an easy grader."

"I'm not easy. All of my students deserve the grades they get." As Casmir worked on the hand, his foot hooked under the table to keep him in place, he felt a twinge of homesickness. He'd been too busy to think much about his colleagues and the students he'd been teaching, but the fact that he'd been chased off Odin in the middle of the semester had left him with a lack of closure. When he'd been back home for those brief days, he'd learned that his assistant and another colleague had taken over his classes, but he couldn't help but feel that he'd abandoned those students.

Would he ever get to return to his normal life again? Where he lectured and drew enthusiastically on holo-boards for students who almost always listened? Or, with more people gunning for him every month, would he end up as some renegade on the run? Maybe he'd end up working on Rache's ship, after all.

"What the hell is going on over there?" Captain Ishii's voice came over the comm so abruptly that Casmir dropped his pliers. Fortunately, the hand was already attached.

"Sir?" Grunburg looked toward the navigation console without leaving his data link.

"You transmitted a report, but when we opened it, it's a bunch of garbage. What is this? Computer code?"

"Uh." Grunburg met Casmir's eyes, fear flashing there. "I better look at our comm."

As he launched himself toward the console up front, Casmir checked the scanner again. Tork was the only thing he could imagine transmitting something, but it showed his power was still off. He registered as a dead lump of chips, synth-skin, metal, and wire.

"Zee?" Casmir looked up. "Do you read anything from the android?"

"Negative."

"Either he's fooling us, or Ishii is wrong."

"It looks like the comm opened itself," Grunburg said slowly, his hands checking and double-checking the controls. "But I don't show that we sent anything. Uhm, this looks like an update on our environmental statistics. Neither Casmir nor I did this, sir. It had to have been the android. Unless there's a stealthed ship out there that somehow piggybacked off our comm." Grunburg rapped his knuckles against the console. "Captain, are there any other ships in the area?"

"Not unless they're hiding behind a slydar hull," Ishii said. "The *Eagle* is in orbit on the far side of the moon, looking for any other clues that might have been left behind."

Casmir grimaced. What if there *was* a hidden ship? "Could Rache be around and still angling for the gate? Or is it possible the astroshamans left a hidden shuttle here to keep an eye on us?"

A garbled line of speech came back, Ishii's voice but now chopped and mangled.

"Can you repeat that, sir?" Grunburg checked the controls to make sure it wasn't something on their side, and shrugged helplessly back at Casmir. "I didn't read that."

"…a damn virus," came Ishii's words out of the garble. "Turn it off!"

"A virus?" Grunburg asked. "What's it doing?"

The channel cut off.

Grunburg cursed and hammered the controls. "I'm trying to get them back."

Casmir frowned down at the Tork-57 that was once again strapped to the table. "Are *you* the cause of this?"

Zee pushed himself down from the ceiling, rotated, and magnetized his feet to lock to the deck.

"Did something change?" Casmir asked him. "Did you detect him transmitting anything?"

"No, but if I dismantle him into his most constituent parts, whatever he's doing will cease."

Casmir imagined ten thousand bits of android floating around the cabin but shook his head. "It may be too late."

If Tork had done it, it must have been when he was powered up and fighting them.

"Is it not best to be certain?" Zee asked.

Casmir had seen numerous examples of very good stealth technology of late, both Rache's slydar hull and the astroshamans' stealth generators. He didn't think they could rule out the possibility of another ship being responsible, but maybe Zee was right. Maybe utterly destroying Tork was safest.

"Their power went out," Grunburg said.

"What?" Casmir gaped at the display. All of the running lights visible on the *Osprey* had gone dark. "The *warship's* power? What about auxiliary?"

"How should I know? I'm as in the dark as you are. No, as *they* are. I'm trying to comm them back, but nobody's answering. Readings definitely show that they're powered down. The heat signature from the engine compartment is dropping fast."

"So, they don't even have maneuvering thrusters? We're in a low orbit. That's going to deteriorate within days. If not hours."

"If they don't run out of air first," Grunburg said grimly.

CHAPTER 7

KIM DRUMMED HER FINGERS ON THE COUNTER IN her lab, waiting for the lights to come back on. Almost ten minutes had passed since they went out—since *all* power in her lab went out, including the power that opened the sliding door to the corridor—and she was starting to worry that something significant had happened. She'd tried the comm, but that was also out.

She was tempted to send a message to Casmir and get an update on his progress, but if he was doing delicate android surgery, she didn't want to interrupt him.

A knock sounded at the door.

"Finally." Kim raised her voice, wondering how much sound insulation there was in the lab. "I'm stuck in here. I don't have any power."

A wrenching noise made her jump. It sounded like the door being forced aside, but the light she expected to flood the lab did not come.

"Kim?" Asger asked, his voice muted, as if he wore his helmet.

"I'm here. What's going on?"

"Nothing good. Here, I brought you something." Footsteps clanged softly as he entered the lab, the darkness complete around them. "I'm glad you're in your galaxy suit. We're still spinning—an object in motion, and all that—but I'm not sure how much longer that'll continue. We might lose gravity, so you'll have to use the magnetic boots. Among other things."

Something hard bumped her hand, and she patted in the air. A cool metal cylinder.

"An oxygen tank?" The first tendril of fear wormed through her stomach as she realized this power outage wasn't local to her lab and that something bad must have happened. Something very bad.

"Yeah. Does your galaxy suit have night vision?"

"Yes." Kim tucked her braid out of the way and ordered the Glasnax helmet to unfold and snap into place. It had better night vision than her contacts. The feature came on automatically, and a green version of Asger came into view, complete with cloak and pertundo.

"I came from the bridge via the ladder wells—the lifts are, of course, out. The last I heard, someone—or something—transmitted a virus to us over the comm. There are *supposed* to be security protocols programmed in to prevent that, but the bridge crew was hypothesizing that it's something new that the computers haven't seen before. I just know that a virus got in, and we're screwed. It took down both the main and auxiliary power. The engines are off. We don't have thruster control, environmental control, or even power to the comms."

"No environmental control means no life support, I gather."

"That's right."

Kim thought of how many people were aboard—wasn't it a crew of five hundred and another hundred marines?—and wondered how long it would take for them to breathe all the air. Or, more accurately, expire toxic levels of carbon dioxide. If she'd known the cubic feet of space in the ship and the current air pressure, she could have set up the equation in her head, but she wasn't sure she wanted to run the numbers. Ignorance was bliss, and, as Casmir liked to add on, was therefore less likely to induce a panic attack.

"What about the other warships?" Kim asked. "When they realize they can't communicate with us, they'll send help, right?"

"Two of them veered off two days ago—I think they were dropping off robotic builders and supplies for reconstructing those refineries—with orders to meet us at the gate when we're done here. The other warship is also here, but it's in orbit on the other side of the moon, searching for clues over there. It *could* get to us in time to help if it figures out we're in trouble. Unfortunately, Ishii had no idea this was coming, and definitely not coming so quickly. He was in the middle of talking to Casmir and his officer in the shuttle when everything went out."

"We can just message them chip-to-chip to get the word out, can't we?" Kim tapped her helmet near her temple. Her chip ran off the energy her body created from oxidative phosphorylation and would continue to work for as long as the rest of her body did, even if she was fasting.

"I'm guessing Ishii has already spoken to his officer that way, but you can try Casmir. Ishii thought the transmission of the virus came from the shuttle—the android—so it's possible they're in trouble too."

Casmir, Kim sent a message. *What's going on over there?*

She grimaced, realizing his shuttle could have just as easily been deprived of power if someone was flinging viruses around.

Kim! Are you all right?

So far. We're without power.

I know. Is Asger over there?

In the lab with me.

Oh, good. I'm including him in my message. So far, we haven't been affected here on the shuttle. Grunburg sent a comm to the other warship, the Eagle. *I think they're coming to help. They're about six hours away, but they're concerned about being attacked with this virus, so they want us to make sure that can't happen before they get close. Which doesn't make us feel at* all *pressured. But we're working on it. We're trying to figure out if it was a virus, as Ishii said, and if it's possible to create an antivirus program. But we won't be able to upload it to the* Osprey*'s systems if there's no power whatsoever. I hope Ishii has a bunch of smart engineers working hard.*

I'm positive everyone even remotely skilled in that area is working on the problem, Asger said. *But I understand you did take Ishii's best programmer.*

I did? Ishii picked Grunburg without any influence on my part. I—hold on. Problem.

Kim waited, hoping the problem wasn't that their shuttle had also been affected. Or afflicted? Did computer viruses have the same vernacular as biological viruses?

Disturbed by the gap in her knowledge, she tried to access the network, but found she no longer had a strong enough signal from the nearest satellite. A transceiver aboard the *Osprey* must have been amplifying the signal. A transceiver that, along with everything else, was no longer working.

"What's taking him so long?" Asger shifted his weight, then sent, *Casmir?*

No answer.

Kim sank back against the counter, feeling helpless. She couldn't help Casmir and couldn't help the ship. The closest she could come was trying to breed some cyanobacteria to munch on carbon dioxide and produce oxygen, but there was no way she had the raw materials or time to grow enough bacteria to make a difference on a ship this size. She doubted she could even create enough to make a difference in her lab.

"The crew of the other ship wouldn't really let us die due to some possible risk from a computer virus, would they?" Kim asked.

"I'm hoping not, but I don't know. That was some virus. It took us out in less than a minute." Asger shifted to lean against the counter next to her. "I'm guessing they'll risk sending some shuttles. But it'll take time if they have to force their way aboard because there's no power to open the shuttle-bay doors or airlock hatches. And then there's going to be a limit to how many people they can take off the ship at once. I hope Ishii won't do something stupid like go down with his ship. Though I'd understand if he did."

Kim stirred in surprise. "Why?"

"He said he got chewed out for losing the gate. So did I, so I can imagine how it went for him. If he then lost his ship… It's not like a warship is inexpensive for the government to make. At a *minimum*, he'd lose his career. If not his family's nobility."

Kim would have laughed at the idea of the latter being anything to commit suicide over, but Asger sounded deadly serious. "I don't think that's happened for a long time."

"A couple hundred years, but there are precedents. If you screw up big time, you can screw up for your whole family."

Kim didn't know what to say. Beyond a hint of research for her thriller novel, she hadn't spent a lot of time studying the nobility and didn't know all the rules.

"If Casmir and the captain's best programmer are over on that shuttle," she said, "the odds seem to be in favor of them figuring out a solution, especially to a computer virus."

"Let's hope so." Asger dropped his hand to his pertundo, as if he might draw it and slay some enemy, but he released it. "I wish there was something I could do."

"Me too." Kim might not understand what it meant to be a part of the nobility, but she definitely understood the distress of feeling useless.

She wondered if Rache and his mercenaries were anywhere nearby. He hadn't told her where he was heading off to when he'd left Odin, but she assumed he still wanted the gate. Or more accurately, wanted to ensure that King Jager didn't get the gate.

A chill went through her as she wondered if it was possible that he'd sent the virus. Could the *Fedallah* be lurking out there under its slydar hull, positioned to make sure Ishii didn't get the clue that would lead him to the gate first?

She shook her head, not wanting to believe he would ruthlessly sacrifice Casmir for that. Or her. He seemed to like her. Who sacrificed someone they were trying to arrange a dinner date with?

Besides, if he had such a computer virus, wouldn't he have used it before? He could have sent it over to the cargo ship and knocked out all of its power instead of sending a team that Casmir's robots ultimately overcame.

Sorry, Casmir messaged. *Everything is fine here. I just had a hiccup in my surgery.*

Surgery? Kim asked.

Android surgery. I'm giving Tork a new hand and—hm, I have an idea.

He didn't add anything else. Kim and Asger exchanged looks.

"An idea?" Asger asked. "Should we be concerned?"

"Yes."

Casmir finished attaching Tork's hand while Grunburg alternated between hunting through the comm system, trying to isolate the virus they believed the android had sent, and poking around in his hard drives. Casmir was tempted to ask Grunburg to step aside so *he* could take a look, but he didn't know if he'd find anything the lieutenant couldn't. And he was contemplating an idea percolating through his mind.

"There's no sign of the file the shuttle transmitted in the comm system's memory bank," Grunburg said, returning to the worktable. "It's got to be in *him* somewhere."

"You haven't found anything on his drives?"

"Nothing obvious, but it's like sifting through a desert's worth of sand."

Casmir nodded. "I've been thinking about this. Logically, *he* would be the best one to find it." Casmir pointed at Tork, then stuck his hand in his pocket and pulled out the CPU he had removed earlier. "We believe this virus was created by an astroshaman, and he *is* an astroshaman android. Technically, he's an alpha model of a Tork-57, and the Torks are manufactured in several factories around the systems—I found his schematics on the network—but he has some enhancements that aren't standard. I've seen that while tinkering around to attach the new hand. I assume the astroshamans did some upgrades to him, just as they did to that cargo ship with the stealth generator. Putting all that aside, he's the vehicle for carrying the virus. He should know it well."

Grunburg blew out a slow breath. "We run the risk of him further sabotaging us if we turn the power back on. Or he'll attack us outright again." He glanced up to where Zee had once again positioned himself with his back to the ceiling, staring straight down at the worktable and its occupant. "Though I guess that's less likely to be a problem."

"Zee can immobilize him effectively, yes. But I'm hoping we can convince him to help us."

"How? It's not like you can torture an android into giving up information."

"No, but maybe we can rationally argue that it's in his best interest to do so."

Grunburg's forehead crinkled. "Is it? It's not like he's going to be harboring some resentment toward his owner, or whoever did that."

Casmir wasn't so sure about that, but he only said, "If he becomes our ally instead of our enemy, he may consider it ideal to help us."

"I think we'd have to wipe his memory and program him from scratch to convince him of that. But if we wipe his memory, we wipe the virus, and we'll never be able to figure out an antivirus program in time, not without the original to study."

"Let me try putting his CPU back in and having a chat with him." Casmir held up the chip between thumb and forefinger.

He expected more of an argument, but Grunburg sighed. "Let me double-check the straps first."

Casmir nodded. He didn't want Tork to escape and cause trouble any more than Grunburg did. He wouldn't have tried powering him up again if not for Zee's presence.

"Go ahead." Grunburg removed his cables and pushed himself back from the table.

Casmir slipped the CPU back into its socket. He also pushed himself back, not sure if Tork would immediately go on the offensive again—or try.

A soft beep came from the scanner monitoring the android. Tork was online. But he didn't open his eyes, didn't move at all.

Long seconds passed. Grunburg pushed himself closer to take a look.

Casmir lifted a hand, a warning on the tip of his tongue, but he was too late. The straps holding the android snapped, and Tork lurched upright.

Casmir tried to scramble backward and get out of Zee's way. He crashed into the built-in drawers behind him. Tork sprang not at him but at Grunburg, knocking him into the hull, his helmet cracking against it.

An instant later, Zee reached Tork and grabbed him. But the android did his best to ignore Zee, shoving himself toward the airlock hatch, as if he was trying to escape. Maybe he *was* trying to escape.

"The mission has been completed," Tork said in a robotic tone. "The unit must be destroyed."

Zee pinned his arms so he couldn't reach for the hatch, but Tork fought back. He bucked and twisted, even kicking Zee. But Zee was stronger and forced the android back to the worktable, pushing off the hull and deck wherever he could to gain leverage.

"Tork-57," Casmir called, pushing himself farther toward the rear to avoid their flailing limbs. "Tork-57, I need to talk to you. Do you remember me?"

He would have preferred to communicate with the android through a computer interface and was surprised when Tork paused struggling and twisted his neck to look back at him. Zee shoved him against the table, pinning him.

"You are Casmir Dabrowski, roboticist," Tork announced.

"Yes, that's right."

"I brought you to my handlers because I believed you could repair them, and you tricked me, powered me down, and took over the ship."

"Uhm, yes, that's also right."

Grunburg groaned, bringing a hand to the side of his helmet. He was floating in a crumpled ball near the hull.

"But I didn't want to trick you." Casmir met Tork's eyes, focusing on him and hoping Grunburg would be all right. "I'd been hoping to negotiate with your handlers when I came aboard. I didn't know they were dead. There was nothing I could do to bring dead humans back to life. There was nothing wrong with their interface pods. It was their human bodies that had been affected by the pseudo radiation from the gate pieces you gathered. It doesn't bother machines or androids in a significant way, but it's deadly to humans after a few days of exposure."

Tork stared at him. "*You* are not dead, and you were exposed."

Casmir didn't want to attempt to explain his immunity, so all he said was, "Because my friend on that warship over there, a bacteriologist, found a way to heal people of the cellular damage. But it only works if they're still alive when she gets to them. Even if she'd been with me on your cargo ship that day, there wouldn't have been anything she could do for your handlers. That any of us could have done." Casmir lowered his voice. "There was nothing you could do to save them either."

He knew Tork wouldn't have feelings like guilt, not in the traditional human sense, but he also knew that androids were usually programmed with a desire to complete their duties. He guessed that Tork might have a sense of having failed and that he might regret that in some way.

"I tried to save them," Tork stated. "It is my duty—was my duty—to protect my handlers and oversee the ship on the mission."

"I understand. I'm sorry we couldn't save them. I would have preferred to negotiate for the gate pieces, rather than simply take them." Casmir lowered his voice and, concerned that Grunburg wasn't moving, whispered, "Grunburg? Are you all right?"

The pained grunt that came back was not that reassuring.

"My handlers would not have given them to you. They need them. It was my duty to stop you from following the cargo ship home, and I have succeeded." Tork's head turned to look past Zee, who still had him pinned to the sturdy worktable, and toward the forward display where part of the *Osprey* was visible.

"What did you do?" Casmir asked quietly, silently ordering his chip to record the conversation.

This was their first proof that Tork had been responsible.

"I did nothing, but the subroutine ran. I am aware of this, even though I was…" Tork looked at him again. "You removed my CPU."

"Yes."

"Why did you put it back in?"

"I want to work with you." Casmir suspected honesty would go further than treachery, especially since he had already tricked Tork-57 once, or tried to. The android would be wary. "It looks like someone got cranky with you for losing that cargo ship, however temporarily, and decided to sacrifice you to make sure you took out any Kingdom people trying to follow him—or is it a her?—back." Casmir had a hard time imagining a woman lopping off an android's hand, but he supposed Qin wouldn't hesitate if it attacked her. He didn't believe she would do it out of spite though. Or to teach an android a lesson.

"I failed my original mission," Tork said. "This was an opportunity to correct that mistake."

"By sacrificing yourself? That's impractical. If the model information I looked up is correct, you're only two years old. In the Kingdom, quality androids are valued at forty to fifty thousand crowns."

"I am precisely two years old. And I *am* a quality android."

"An alpha edition is top of the line," Casmir said.

"It is. *I* am." Tork tilted his head. "Do you believe flattery will make me more inclined to do as you wish?"

"I'm simply stating facts. It seems pointless to sacrifice you. Didn't the astroshamans have a dishpan they could have thrown out the airlock with the explosive stuck to it instead of an expensive android?"

"You would not have stopped to pick up a dishpan."

"I would have if it was a particularly intriguing one. Or if there were comic book superheroes painted on it." Casmir didn't know if such things existed, but they definitely should.

"You seek to use humor on an android? All robots are ruled by logic, not laughter."

"Are you sure? Zee is only a couple of months old, and he makes jokes. I expect he'll be letting out guffaws after another couple of months of hanging around me."

"What is Zee?"

Zee tightened his grip on Tork. Casmir wasn't sure if it was because the android tried to move or if he was making a point.

"*That* is Zee. My bodyguard, golem, and friend." Casmir smiled.

"Humans and robots are not friends. Robots serve humans, as I served my handlers."

"Until they had no further need for you. I'm not going to let you destroy yourself, so why don't you come work for me?"

Tork looked toward the hatch he'd failed to fling himself out. "I am your prisoner, not your employee."

"Maybe now, but you can have the choice. Zee, let him go, please."

"That would be unwise, Casmir Dabrowski."

"I know, but you can capture him again if he tries to kill me."

"Or me," Grunburg grumbled, his helmet still leaning against the hull. "Professor, the *Osprey* has limited time."

"I know." Casmir waved at the arms locked around Tork. "Zee, please let him go."

"Unwise," Zee repeated, but he released the android and stepped back.

Casmir shifted to put the table between himself and Tork in case he attacked.

"You say please to robots," Tork said. "Even to robots that do not contain human consciousnesses?"

"Yes. Like I said, Zee is my bodyguard and friend."

Tork looked down at his new hand. For a few seconds, he simply stared at it, and Casmir imagined him checking his wiring and rerouting signals to complete the installation. Since Tork had been powered down, Casmir hadn't done that part yet.

"This is a new hand." Tork curled the fingers, then extended them one at a time and wiggled them, checking functionality. "My old hand was severed."

"So I saw. What severed it? A sword?"

Tork curled the fingers again but did not reply.

Casmir glanced at the display and thought the *Osprey* had dipped lower than it had been before. A sign of its orbit deteriorating already?

"I researched you briefly when you first contacted the cargo ship," Tork said. "I learned you were a roboticist."

"Yes." Casmir hoped this was going in a positive direction, but it was possible he was deluding himself.

"It was a superficial search. I did not have time to go into more depth. The cargo ship was engaged in battle."

"I remember."

"I am doing a more in-depth search now." Tork swiveled his head, more like an owl than the human he was designed to emulate. He looked at Zee, who still stood behind him, close enough to grab him if he tried anything.

"All right." Casmir tried not to sound wary.

What besides his profession could interest an android from another system?

"You have a reputation, Professor Dabrowski," Tork said.

"I suppose that's inevitable after thirty-three years." Casmir didn't know if he should ask what this reputation was. It would depend on what Tork was looking at. Commentary on his academic publications? Gossip about him on the university network? Or from the scientific community at large?

"What would you offer in exchange for my services?"

"What do you want? Not money, I assume." Though Casmir would try to get the android some if he wanted it.

"The freedom to work on my astronomy project—I had a telescope on my first duty station, and I was cataloging all the rogue planets that have strayed from their stars and attempting to locate more. Did you know that no significant astronomic finds have been discovered by androids?"

"I did not. Many have been found by computers."

"Computers are mindless automatons. Nothing compared to a Tork-57 alpha model that must balance his hobbies with his duties for his human handlers. I am more akin to a human than a computer."

"I won't argue that." Casmir would have scratched his head if he hadn't been wearing a helmet. "I'll be happy to get you a telescope and give you time off to pursue your hobby. All the hours when I'm sleeping or don't need you for a specific task. But the first task I need you to perform may be difficult for you, since it would go against your former handlers' wishes. I need you to search your drives for the virus you sent to that warship. We need to isolate it and create an antivirus program to knock it out."

"My handlers ordered me to sacrifice myself by blowing myself up along with the Kingdom soldiers attempting to hunt down the cargo ship. Should that fail, I was ordered to self-destruct. I failed at throwing myself out the airlock to slowly tumble down and crash on that moon. My programming ends at that point."

"Then it's time for you to start your new life as an amateur astronomer and valued assistant. You can program your own future. And if you want, I can find a way to compensate you for any work you do for me."

"Do you compensate the thuggish brute behind me for his work?" Tork gave Zee another look, more of a disdainful glance this time.

"No. I built him."

"So you consider him yours."

Casmir answered carefully, worried Tork was setting a trap for him. "Zee has been good enough to join me on my quest and protect me. He is too intelligent for me to own, like a thing. If he developed an interest in pursuing some other work, I would feel compelled to let him go."

"Yes. I believe this." Tork looked down at his hand. "You have returned me to a fully functional state. I will seek the virus program on my drives." Tork closed his eyes and lowered his chin to his chest.

Casmir had no idea how long that would take, so he moved around the table, pushing himself over to check on Grunburg. "Are you badly injured?"

"No. Well, maybe a little. I hit hard enough to crack my head against the side of my helmet, and my eyes are crossing. That was really stupid."

Casmir winced. "I know. Sorry. We both should have run and hid in the lav after putting that chip back in."

"I meant that *I* was stupid. I shouldn't have gone to check on him." Grunburg frowned through his faceplate at Tork. "Are you sure he's not doing something now to dupe us?"

"No."

"I wish you'd said yes in a wise and scholarly voice."

"Sorry."

"I have detected a virus stored on my third auxiliary hard drive," Tork announced.

"The schematic I downloaded for you shows only two auxiliary hard drives," Casmir said.

"I have been further modified and upgraded from my factory baseline."

"Handy. Can you encapsulate it so it won't activate when it's delivered to a new computer, and send a copy to Grunburg's tablet? We need to work on that antivirus program."

This would be the true test.

Long seconds passed. Casmir didn't know if Tork was figuring out a way to render the virus inactive or if he was having second thoughts about working for them.

"Yes," Tork said. "It has been deactivated. I will transmit it."

"Let's hope it's written in a programming language I'm familiar with," Grunburg muttered.

Casmir grimaced and nodded in agreement. But he wouldn't be surprised if the astroshamans favored something obscure or brand new. "At the least, we can contact the *Eagle* and let them know it's safe to come help the *Osprey*."

"Are we sure it is?" Grunburg murmured. "Is there some way to test if he's telling us the truth?"

"I think having the other warship fly over will *be* the test." Casmir patted Grunburg on the shoulder, hoping the gesture was reassuring.

Judging by Grunburg's bleak expression, he was envisioning two powerless warships spiraling out of control to crash on the moon's surface.

CHAPTER 8

"READY?" BONITA ASKED, HER POD NESTLING HER TIGHT as they approached the wormhole gate out of System Lion.

"Yes," Qin said from the other pod.

The navigation arm kissed Bonita's temple, interfacing with her chip, and she transmitted the destination code to the gate, the massive metal circle looking like little more than a huge dark gray donut hanging in space. That was how it appeared on the display, but Viggo's scanners lit up with the energy radiating from it, even before she sent the code and it appeared dormant. Panels all along its surface gathered power from the distant sun, storing it until a ship needed the gate to establish a travel link to one of the other eleven gates in the system.

Bonita wondered how the existing network would handle a thirteenth gate being added on after two thousand years. As far as she knew, humanity only had theories as to how the things worked now.

"We're heading in." Bonita relinquished control to the autopilot as they flew toward the gate.

The interior flared to life, glowing yellow, as if a tiny sun was contained inside its circular rim. Even though the display automatically dimmed, she closed her eyes against the intensity and against the strange sensation soon to come. She had traveled along the gate roads hundreds of times during her career, but it never ceased to feel surreal as she lost consciousness, and myriad strange colors and images writhed in her mind while the ship and her body seemed to enter a state of utter stillness. Sometimes, it reminded her of "trips" she'd taken with psychedelic drugs in her youth, and sometimes, it was an experience she couldn't describe.

Every time they passed out of the wormhole, she had the distinct feeling that the human body wasn't supposed to be exposed to such strangeness, but none of the countless research studies done on frequent animal and human passengers had ever found a correlation between wormhole travel and death or disease. If anything, experiments had shown that there was less cosmic radiation in whatever plane or dimension one entered while inside.

Her stomach lurched as they came out on the other side, entering System Cerberus, and full awareness returned. Beeps sounded, and alarms flashed on the control panel.

"We are being scanned by three ships in the vicinity," Viggo announced. "Four ships."

"Hopefully, they'll see that our cargo hold is empty and there's no reason to attack us." No *logical* reason. She'd had pirates come after her before just for the fun of it. A freighter made a large and appealing target.

She tapped the weapons panel to bring the rail gun online so anyone thinking along those lines would know they were armed.

Crimson beams streaked through space, followed by a missile launching.

Bonita tensed until she realized the *Stellar Dragon* wasn't the target. A small corvette wheeled away from the attack, which originated at a heavily armored private yacht. The corvette had enough time to adjust course to avoid the DEW-Tek bolts, but the heat-seeking missile shifted course to follow it. The projectile slammed into the armored hull and exploded near its rear thrusters. The corvette unleashed a barrage of missiles in response.

"Should we… help?" Qin asked uncertainly.

"Nope." Bonita steered them away from the gate and the conflict. Whatever was going on, it had nothing to do with them. "This is the kind of thing you hope for when you come to System Cerberus in anything smaller and less intimidating than a warship."

"People trying to kill each other?"

"People creating a big distraction while you slink past unnoticed. If nothing like that is going on, you're more likely to be targeted by the opportunistic bastards that loiter by the gate, waiting for easy marks. Back in the Kingdom days, their warships used to patrol all the gates to make sure nothing like this happened. It's one of the reasons some people actually wish they still governed the entire Twelve Systems. Or that *somebody* did. Now that the systems are so fragmented, nobody worries about what's happening outside of their own planets and moons." Bonita peered at Qin over the side of her pod. "But you must know all about this, right? If you were with the Druckers, you must have spent a lot of time in this system."

"I've been here frequently, yes, but nobody ever bothered the Druckers, and we—" Qin tapped a claw against her chest, "—were usually ordered to stay in our pen during space travel. We were usually only let out when it was time to board another ship or fight on a planet or moon."

"Your *pen*?" Bonita curled a lip, imagining Qin in something akin to a dog kennel.

"That's what we called it. It wasn't that bad. There were cabins that we shared, four girls to a room—the others like me in my cohort and the older cohort—and then there was an exercise and eating area. It was our own area of the ship."

"A private place where you could be away from the pirates?"

"Uh, no. They always made it clear that we were there to work for them, in all senses of the word, whenever they wanted."

"Assholes."

Qin didn't answer.

"That's why we're making sure you never have to go back to them."

"Did you ever get a response to your comm?" Qin's voice had a weird note, as if she wasn't sure to hope Bonita had or hope she hadn't.

"Yes. That's why we're here. I sent a message to their publicly listed address, saying I had you on board and was willing to sell you for the right price, and a Johnny Twelve Toes replied to my message with a very wordy text."

"Wordy?"

"It said: *Come to Cerberus so we can talk real time.*"

"I don't recognize that name. Are you sure it was the Druckers and that your message didn't get intercepted?"

"No. But there are two thousand people working for the Druckers, right? They must get new recruits from time to time. Maybe it's someone that came on after you left, or just someone on another ship that you didn't know well."

"Maybe." Qin sounded skeptical. "But someone with the authorization to make deals would be relatively high up in the organization, not a new recruit."

Bonita would be shocked if the Druckers intended to deal fairly with her, so she wasn't that worried that the pirates might already be scheming. She had schemes planned too.

Once they were clear of the skirmishing ships, Bonita set course for a space station in the middle of the system that she'd visited numerous times for work. There was a clan there out of Cabrakan Habitat, in the system where she had grown up, and they always welcomed her for meals and holiday celebrations, so long as she brought something good to eat.

"I'm taking us to Death Knell Station and will try to set up a rendezvous with the Druckers there." Bonita checked the scanner display to make sure none of the ships around the gate were following them. Most continued to ignore them, but a yacht that had come through the gate after they had was flying in the same direction as the *Dragon*. She would keep an eye on it. "I know the family that runs that place, and I doubt they're allies of the Druckers."

"The Amigos?"

"Yes, that's their pirate name. The family is the Delgados."

"You're right," Qin said. "They compete with the Druckers from time to time. The Druckers sneer at them because they mostly make money from the station now instead of going out to attack ships."

"Yeah, how terrible of them to legitimately earn money instead of preying on others. Viggo, run some deep scans and see if there's anything alarming going on in the system."

"Certainly. Do you wish me to search the bounties listed in this system to see if there are opportunities to make money on the side?"

"No. There's too much competition here and too many extremely dangerous people overall. I've never liked trying to do business here, unless it was just coming to hand someone in and get paid. But make sure there's not a mark on us, will you?"

She hadn't considered that there might be until Casmir had asked her to look him up, and they'd learned of the fresh bounty on his head.

It was possible someone looking for Casmir might have delayed intelligence and believe he was still on the *Dragon.* Bonita hoped not. She didn't need complications. This was already going to be a difficult mission.

"Do you have a will, Captain?" Qin asked.

"Uh, yes. A somewhat outdated one. The last time I updated it was after my divorce—my *first* divorce—because I wanted to make sure that dung-munching donkey didn't get anything from me if I died. In my foolish naïveté, I'd put him in the will. After that, I learned not to put anyone else in besides my cousins and nephews—real blood kin—because you can't trust husbands. Or men in general."

"Really, Bonita," Viggo said. "That's a dreadful prejudice. Some men are delightful."

"You're not going to talk about Casmir again, are you? Just because a guy lubes your robots doesn't make him trustworthy for life." Though Bonita admitted she would be inclined to trust the kid. Not enough to marry him, but fortunately, he hadn't asked. It was possible she was losing some of the beauty that had made her more of a target of the opposite sex in previous decades.

"Actually, I was talking about myself," Viggo said with impressive dryness.

"You don't have testosterone anymore. Or a body. I'm not that worried about you being driven to lie, brutalize, and murder based on imbalanced hormones."

One of Viggo's robot vacuums rolled into navigation and slurped up imaginary dirt around the base of the pods.

"Perhaps you'll meet someone nice one day," Qin said, "who will change your mind about men in general."

"Definitely not. Quickies are fine, but I'm not getting involved with anyone ever again. Why do you ask about the will?" Bonita wondered if she should add Qin to it, not that she truly had much to leave anyone. A bank back home owned half of the *Dragon*, and whoever inherited it would inherit the loan and tax payments too. And her savings, while not as bleak as they had been a few weeks ago, wouldn't change anyone's life.

"Just in case this doesn't go well, and I survive and you don't." Qin peered over her pod with worried eyes. "I'll do my best to protect you and make sure that doesn't happen, but I'm… I'm a little scared. I *want* my freedom and for them to leave me alone forever, and I appreciate you trying to help me win it, but I know what we'll be facing, and that has me concerned for you."

Bonita was debating how to answer that—she didn't want to wave away Qin's very valid fears, but she *did* want to comfort her—when the comm beeped.

The identification of the caller came up: Johnny Twelve Toes.

"He must have been watching the gate for us." Bonita wrinkled her nose, finding that degree of attentiveness discomforting. She'd wanted to reach the station before making real-time contact with the Druckers. And she'd hoped their fleet wouldn't be anywhere near the gate. She needed time to set things up.

"The comm is originating approximately ten hours away," Viggo said, "from a ship that is in orbit around Amber Moon. It appears to be a large warship, though it has no transmitter chip, so I can't give you an identification."

"It's them," Qin whispered. "Amber Moon is one of their favorite places. The clouds in the atmosphere make it easy for them to hide if they need to, not that they usually need to. Few risk pissing them off, and it's been more than a decade since any of the government fleets came through and tried to instill order in the system."

"Let's see what he has to say." Bonita accepted the comm, not sure whether to be pleased or not that there wouldn't be much of a time lag. "This is Captain Laser Lopez. Speak."

She braced herself for a snide comment about her name. Thirty years ago, few people had mocked it, but since her hair had gone gray, derisive snorts had become more typical. She hoped for a chance to prove to the Druckers that her marksmanship was as good as it had always been.

A request came through for video, and she grimaced. The pirate was offering it in return, but she would have preferred audio only. Maybe he wanted to see if Qin was sitting next to her in navigation instead of locked away down in a brig cell.

"Should I hide?" Qin whispered.

"Yes." Bonita waved for her to leave navigation. "They might be suspicious if I don't accept. Let's play by their rules for now, so they'll be caught off guard later when we don't."

Qin must have wanted to hear the conversation, because she opted for squeezing her broad frame and six-feet-two-inches of height under the main console.

"I guess that works," Bonita murmured and accepted the request for visual.

The face that popped up on the screen was about what she would have expected from a pirate—a tattoo of a barbed-wire dagger dripping blood on each cheek, cool steely eyes, a studded dog collar around his thickly muscled neck, spiky blond-gray hair, and a more determinedly gray beard, shortly trimmed except for two slender braids that dangled down past the camera's field of display. The only surprising part was that he looked to be around sixty, and Bonita wouldn't have guessed that many pirates lived that long. Just as few bounty hunters survived long enough to retire.

"Captain Laser." The man twitched an ironic eyebrow, but he didn't openly mock her name. "May I call you Laser? Or do you prefer Lopez? I wouldn't wish to presume inappropriate familiarity." *Very* ironic.

And he had a Kingdom accent. It was faint, and Bonita usually wouldn't have noticed it, but since she'd spent so much time with Kingdom denizens lately, her ear was tuned to it. He had the same stuffy way of speaking that Asger had, but there was no way he could be a noble from Odin. What stuffy Kingdom noble would turn pirate and maim his face with a tattoo gun?

"Laser works. What do you prefer? Twelve Toes? I'm going to need to see proof of those extra digits if you want me to use that. I hear they lop off mutations like that if you're born in the Kingdom. You sure you aren't Johnny Eight Toes?"

"The Kingdom is indifferent to extraneous digits, so long as they were legitimate mutations and not genetically engineered to confer some advantage. I find that my feet work like flippers in the water, so my swimming is excellent. Alas, I was not allowed to compete on the school teams as a boy."

Under the console, Qin's forehead creased. Yeah, it was a weird conversation, not at all what Bonita had expected.

"No doubt why you fled the Kingdom's embrace and took up residence on a pirate ship." Bonita couldn't imagine what route might have led this man to the Druckers. It sounded about as likely as Casmir joining pirates. She made a mental note to look him up later and see if he had a bounty on his head. Maybe he'd fled System Lion because of some crime he'd committed.

"Yes, a dearth of competitive swimming opportunities inculcates a desire for pirate life in a boy. I'm going to need to see evidence of Qin

Liangyu Three's capture if we're going to negotiate. If you are wasting my time, I will be extremely disappointed."

"Your disappointment would be like a lover's dagger to the heart." Bonita pointed a thumb over her shoulder. "I've got the freak in my brig cell." Bonita made an apologetic gesture toward Qin under the console with her other hand. She knew Qin hated that word. "There's not a camera in there. Let's figure out if we can deal. If so, I'll take a picture for you to stick on your refrigerator. If not, I'm going to offer her her job back. She's pretty handy."

"Yes, I have footage of her fighting to defend your ship." Johnny's eyebrow twitched.

Ugh, what footage had he found? Something from the terrorist attack on Odin? Maybe a camera at one of those air harbors had caught one of Qin's skirmishes.

Either way, he didn't believe she was truly willing to turn her over. She could tell. Should she abort this now, or was there a chance to convince him he was wrong?

"I had no intention of trying to turn her over to anyone," Bonita said, "until I saw that there was a reward for her safe return. Fifteen thousand is such a measly sum though. Hardly worth the trip to this system."

"And yet you came."

"I was hoping to see you and your extra toes swim."

He snorted, his eyes briefly glinting with humor, and Bonita decided he was attractive, despite his dubious fashion tastes. If she'd met him in a bar, she would have taken him for a ride. Though she wouldn't have asked to see his toes. He could keep his mutations under the blankets.

"If that was a request to see me naked," Johnny—that name definitely didn't suit him—said, "then I might be amenable to that. After business."

"I assumed you'd be wearing swim trunks."

"You go faster without them. Less drag. Send a picture of the girl, and we'll discuss a price. I've been authorized some leeway when it comes to bargaining, though not an unlimited amount. The Druckers have already ordered more furry females to be made for their use." His lip twitched in what appeared to be disapproval, though Bonita couldn't tell if it was for the idea of the pirates *using* the furry females or for their existence in general. If he'd come from the Kingdom, he probably shared their prejudices toward modded people. Twelve toes, notwithstanding.

"You've been authorized? What's your position?"

"I am the Druckers' accountant."

She waited, expecting it to be a joke. That couldn't truly be his job, could it? Though she supposed it made sense for whoever handled the books to be in charge of retrievals and payouts.

"You don't look like an accountant."

"No?" He looked to the side, then plucked a light pen off his desk and tucked it behind his ear. "Better?"

She almost laughed but caught herself. She wasn't going to show any interest in one of the animals who thought they *owned* Qin.

"Sure, I see it now."

"Send the picture," he said.

"Don't be so pushy, pirate accountant. I don't take well to being bossed around."

"*Please* send the picture, Laser, so that I may justify continuing to flirt with you." He didn't sound even vaguely imploring when he said that please. His eyebrows still had that ironic tilt to them.

"Is that what you're doing? Flirting?"

"You couldn't tell? I had no idea I was so rusty. It's rare that I meet a woman who doesn't rear back in disgust at the idea of my extra toes. Do I need to promise a picture of myself naked in exchange for one proving you have Qin Three as a prisoner?"

"Promise you *won't* send that, and I'll see what I can get for you."

His lips curved in a slight smile. "I shall eagerly await whatever you have for me."

A lurid thought popped into her head. Damn it. This wasn't going to turn out well.

She closed the comm and waved that it was safe for Qin to get up.

Bonita brought back a picture of his face. "You sure you've never seen him?"

"No, and I'd remember someone who talked like that. He doesn't sound like the others."

"Too many complete sentences?"

"With big words in them, yes."

"Viggo," Bonita said, "are you sure his comm came from that warship that we're fairly positive belongs to the Druckers?"

"It came straight from the warship, yes," Viggo said.

"Qin, let's take a picture of you in the brig looking surly, defiant, and completely trapped," Bonita said, "and we'll see what happens."

Qin made a face, but she tramped to the ladder to comply. She gave a long suspicious look over her shoulder at Johnny's picture before descending.

CHAPTER 9

CASMIR FLOATED BEHIND GRUNBURG'S POD, WATCHING OVER HIS shoulder as he worked and giving advice whenever he could. Tork was belted into the pod Casmir had occupied earlier, wired to Grunburg's tablet and helping come up with an antivirus program to eradicate the virus that had shut down the *Osprey*.

When it looked like they were getting close to a solution, Casmir sent a message to Kim.

Is everything all right over there?

Her reply was prompt. *I'm standing in a dark lab with Asger, reading periodicals on my chip, and wondering if there's something more useful I could be doing.*

Do you know what the Fleet techs are doing?

Praying and hoping, I believe.

I doubt their orders would allow them to do only that.

No, Kim replied. *Likely not. Footsteps sound in the corridor outside every now and then, but I'm staying in sickbay and out of the way. I don't know anything about engineering or programming.*

Grunburg, Tork, and I are working on an antivirus program right now.

Tork? Is that the android our enemies left us?

Yes, he appears to be an adept programmer.

Oh, I'm sure. How can you trust— Did you wipe his memory and reboot him?

Something like that. I'll explain later. We need a favor, and Ishii has never given me permission to contact him. This might not be the best time to reach out with overtures of friendship. Casmir had already tried contacting Ishii, but he'd either been too busy to notice or was already talking chip-to-chip with Grunburg.

What can we do?

We need to send you, or someone else over there, the antivirus program to install on the ship's mainframe in engineering. And we need someone there to figure out how to get the power running to the mainframe, even if it's just for a few minutes.

I think they've been trying to get the power back on for hours.

Hopefully, some clever engineer over there can figure out something. If nothing else, there ought to be battery-powered devices around the ship that aren't hooked up to the network and weren't affected by the virus. They could deliver power while you upload the antivirus program, enough to bring the system online briefly. It won't take long for it to run. Grunburg's program should give the computers what they need both to eradicate the virus and engage self-repair processes to fix all the damage that it did.

I'll see what I can do.

Thank you.

"This is quite the sophisticated virus," Grunburg murmured. "And I have quite the sophisticated headache."

"Did you take some painkillers?"

"Yes."

"Ah. What does a sophisticated headache feel like?"

"First, there's a stabbing pain in my skull, then the back of my eyes throb, and then a sympathetic throb comes from the back of my head and runs down my spine."

"Huh." Casmir was glad *he* hadn't struck his head. That sounded like the kind of thing that could cause a seizure. As it was, he was trying hard not to think about how much trouble everyone would be in if this didn't work. And if Tork was lying to him about coming over to his side.

Casmir checked the scanners to see the other warship flying closer, about an hour away now. How close did it need to be for the virus transmission? Casmir bit his lip and watched Tork work, his eyes closed as his android brain interfaced directly with Grunburg's tablet. Zee stood behind him, ever ready to snap his neck if he proved he was still an enemy instead of an ally.

"I think… Yes, it's working." Grunburg thumped his fist on the control panel. "Inside the quarantine I created on my tablet, the antivirus program isolated and eradicated the virus."

"I've got Kim and Asger going to engineering to help us deliver it."

"Does either of them know anything about programming?"

"No, but they're both willing to talk to me, unlike most of your crew members and officers."

Grunburg snorted. "I'll contact the captain again. Last I checked, he was on hands and knees in engineering, working alongside our men, trying to get an un-networked generator to power the environmental control systems." Grunburg looked over his shoulder. "How were you planning to deliver the program? Chip-to-chip?"

"I think that's the only option we've got, as long as the *Osprey's* comm is down."

Grunburg looked at Tork. He didn't have to say anything for Casmir to guess his doubts. If Tork was truly working against them, he could be wrapping another iteration of the virus or some new threat into this antivirus program. And it was possible he was good enough that they wouldn't detect it until it was too late.

"Right," was all Grunburg said. "Let's try this."

The corridors of the *Osprey* were dark and quiet as Kim and Asger headed to engineering, having to bypass the inactive lifts and use the ladder wells. The ship had hundreds of crew, but all other than essential personnel—those who might have some skill at fixing this problem—had been ordered to stay in their quarters or at their duty station. The clangs of Kim's and Asger's boots sounded particularly loud on the ladder rungs.

Kim had her helmet up to protect against the cold that had crept into the ship. The ambient temperature, according to her helmet display, had dropped below zero. And it would drop a lot lower if the antivirus program didn't work.

Asger paused when he reached the bottom of the ladder, not stepping into the corridor right away, and Kim stopped short of clunking him in his helmet with her boot.

"Problem?" she whispered.

Something about the cold silence of the ship made whispers seem appropriate.

"I saw a shadow out of the corner of my eye, someone moving out there, but I don't see anyone out there now."

"Probably just an engineer, right?" Kim asked. "People should be down here working on the problem."

"Yeah." Asger didn't sound that convinced, but he stepped into the corridor.

When she joined him, she noticed his pertundo in hand.

"Are you sure a shadow is all you saw?" she asked.

"I thought I heard a grinding, whirring noise too. When nothing is supposedly powered up now."

Kim looked up and down the long, wide corridor they had entered. There was nothing there except closed doors along either side. None of those doors would be working now, so if Asger had seen something, it had to have moved away quickly.

"Casmir mentioned that anything battery-operated and not hooked up to the ship's network should be able to operate without trouble. Maybe it was a cleaning robot."

"I guess." Asger headed down the corridor, not putting his pertundo away. "Engineering is this way."

Kim trailed after him, the corridors seeming longer than usual in the quiet dark. A clang came from somewhere up ahead. The engineers attempting repairs? Or kicking some housing in frustration?

Asger slowed as they neared open double doors to their left. Kim, not having been to engineering on this ship before, assumed it was their destination, but it was dark inside. The sign painted on the wall was hard to make out with the blurry imprecision of her night vision, and they were almost to the entrance before she could read *Shuttle Bay 02.*

A grinding noise came from the dark beyond the open doors, and Asger halted.

"Stop," a man inside whispered, the voice unfamiliar.

The noise halted.

"Get those damn doors shut so I can work," another man said. "If we vent the whole ship, they'll come after us."

"Not if they can't."

Kim was about to say they should run ahead to engineering and warn the officers that someone was up to mischief when Asger sprang into the shuttle bay.

"Stop what you're doing," he ordered.

She rolled her eyes. Casmir might read about superheroes in comic books, but Asger thought he *was* one.

The grinding noise started up again, four times as loud. Something roared toward the doorway.

Kim hurried forward so she could see what was going on, suddenly wishing she'd brought a weapon. Why did she keep running into trouble on a secure Fleet warship full of soldiers and marines?

A huge machine with wide treads rumbled straight toward Asger. Blue and white indicators flashed on the front, highlighting a massive tunnel-boring bit. Aimed at his chest.

Kim took a step inside, but she was too far away to help. Asger crouched as if he would spring to the side, but he jumped straight into the air as the machine roared toward him. His cloak flapped, the whirling six-foot-tall bit almost catching it as he sprang over it. But Asger cleared the machine, landed on top, then jumped off on the other side. His boots rang out as he ran toward something.

One of the men cursed.

From the doorway, all Kim could see were the parked shuttles and the boring machine as it stopped, turned ponderously, and rumbled after Asger again. There was Casmir's battery-powered machine that they could use… if it didn't run out of power while trying to kill Asger. Was someone driving it? She couldn't see a typical cab with windows. It looked automated.

Thuds rang out on the other side of it, followed by grunts of pain.

Kim was debating going for help, when a man raced out of the shadows toward her with a rifle gripped in both hands.

She leaped back into the corridor. The man rounded the doorway and charged out after her. He had the rifle, but he wasn't armored, and he didn't point it at her, so she lost some of her wariness.

"Where's your damn friend?" he growled.

Casmir?

Abruptly, she recognized him. It was one of the would-be kitchen assassins who'd attacked Casmir in the computer cabin.

She growled and sprang for him. He must not have expected her to attack, because his movements were startled and jerky as he lifted his rifle to defend himself. She feinted twice with a jab and a punch, and then, when his arms were raised to block the punches, rammed her knee into his groin and stomped on his instep.

He roared, bringing the rifle down like a club. She whipped up a block, knocking his forearm—and the rifle—aside, then slammed her helmet into his nose.

The rifle clattered to the deck. He cursed, moisture springing to his eyes, and tried to grab her shoulders. She brought both forearms up and out, knocking his arms aside, then rammed him in the face again.

The bastard deserved a broken nose twice over for trying to collect on some stupid bounty. She finished him off with another knee to the groin, then, as he curled protectively over himself, she shoved him to the deck.

Kim jumped back, fists up in case another threat appeared.

But only Asger stood in the doorway, grinning and giving her a salute with his pertundo. The grinding and whirring had stopped, so he must have taken care of whoever had thought to use the tunnel borer as a weapon.

Claps came from farther down the corridor. Ishii. Two armed men stood to either side of him, rifles pointed at the jerk on the deck, but they lowered them when it was clear he wouldn't be a further threat.

"I knew there was a reason we were paying you more than Casmir," Ishii said, though his smile was fleeting. "Sergeant, put that man back in the brig, and find out what happened to whoever was guarding him."

"Yes, sir."

The two men rushed forward to pick up Kim's foe.

Asger pointed a thumb over his shoulder. "The other one is in here. I think they were going to drill their way through the hull and try to take the shuttle and escape."

Ishii rubbed his face, the epitome of a man having a bad week. "I bet captains had it easier in the old days, when they could have men who disobeyed orders shot."

"What a shame that wanton murder is frowned upon these days," Asger said.

Ishii gave him a dark look. "What are you two doing down here?"

"Coming to help get the main computer online long enough for Casmir and Grunburg's antivirus program to be transmitted and installed," Kim said.

"We've been trying for hours to get the computers back online," Ishii said.

"He suggested a jumpstart from something with a battery."

"We already thought of the shuttles for that, but they're on the ship's network and got knocked out along with everything else."

"What about the tunnel-boring machine?" Asger waved behind him, though Ishii wouldn't be able to see it from his position in the corridor. "That thing has a battery. A *good* battery." He lifted his cloak, showing off a rip, though the SmartWeave fabric was already repairing itself.

"Mm, that might work. It'll only give us a few minutes though."

"Casmir said that's all we need," Kim said. "As soon as the antivirus program is installed, it'll clear out the virus and repair any damage it did."

"Casmir wrote the software program? Or Grunburg did?"

"It sounded like they were both working on it." Kim decided not to mention that Tork, who was apparently a good programmer, had also been working on it. She trusted that Casmir was smart enough not to be duped by an android. After all, he'd been the one to warn Ishii that Tork could be booby-trapped.

"All right. Good." As his men dragged the escaped prisoners away, Ishii peered through the door at the borer. "Let's find a cable."

CHAPTER 10

KIM DIDN'T NEED TO BE IN ENGINEERING, BUT she couldn't imagine going back to her lab and twiddling her thumbs while she waited for the lights to come on. She and Asger stood off to the side, and none of the officers had shooed them away. If she hadn't had her helmet on, she might have nibbled on a fingernail as the cable snaking through the doors from the shuttle bay down the corridor was plugged into a power converter.

A female engineer flicked a few manual switches, then opened a panel to adjust something. Kim wasn't the only one watching intently. If this didn't work, what was the alternative? When she'd walked into engineering to find wires and panels and tools strewn all over the deck, she'd gotten the distinct impression the twenty men and women working inside had already tried everything.

But they had been attempting to bring everything back online while finding ways to work around the virus. Now, they had an antivirus program. If they could bring up the main computer long enough to get it loaded…

"We've got power to the hub here, sir."

The engineer glanced at Ishii, who was also standing back and probably wishing he could bite his fingernails. He'd acquired a tablet and kept fiddling with it.

"Good work, Vestergaard. Here." Ishii strode forward and knelt next to the woman. "They sent me a copy of the antivirus program. I assume the wireless network is still down, so you'll have to load it manually."

Vestergaard fished a cable out of a pile on the deck and plugged it into Ishii's tablet. "How did they come up with an antivirus program they're sure will work?"

"They had the android carrying the virus to test it on." Ishii grimaced and tapped a few digital buttons.

Kim was glad she hadn't mentioned that Tork had been assisting with the testing. It would only make Ishii nervous. Right now, he probably thought his programmer had hacked into the android and taken control of it.

Ishii finished typing in commands and leaned back. He drummed his fingers. Vestergaard shifted her weight. Twenty people watched intently.

"Thank you for taking care of those men in the shuttle bay, Asger, Scholar Sato." Ishii glanced at them. "If you served under me, I would recommend you for promotions."

"You can recommend it to *my* superiors if you like." Asger sounded wistful. "Though I'm not sure punching a man in the face and taking his tunnel-boring machine counts as exemplary work above and beyond the call of duty for a knight."

"Is that what's required for a promotion?"

"More or less."

Ishii looked at Kim and raised his eyebrows. She wasn't sure what that meant. Was he wondering if she wanted him to put in a word with *her* superiors?

"Head butts and knees to the groin don't get you promotions in the medical research field," she said.

"No? But you did them with such finesse."

"I've had a lot of practice."

"Hopefully, that refers to regular martial-arts training, not a history of handsy roommates."

Kim frowned. She thought it was a joke, but she didn't like the implication that Casmir would be anything less than a gentleman. "The only things Casmir puts his hands on are his robots."

Belatedly, she wondered if she'd implied some kind of fetish for the mechanical. She was horrible at jokes revolving around sex.

"I would expect no less," was all Ishii said, though his eyes glinted with humor before he turned back to his engineer. "Anything happening?"

Vestergaard had taken out a monitoring device. "One of the auxiliary computers has managed to power up. It doesn't seem to be bringing any processes online though."

"Hm."

"It could be working on eradicating the virus."

A faint hum came from the wall of equipment. A couple of loud *ker-thunks* emanated from behind a bulkhead. The lights came on for the first time in hours, and Kim squinted against the abrupt brightness.

Relieved cheers went up from the engineers, and similar sounds echoed down the corridor from other departments in the ship. Ishii sagged forward, leaning his faceplate against the control panel.

I think you can come back to the ship now, Kim messaged Casmir. *The lights came on.*

Excellent. The Osprey's *current orbit is concerning.*

This whole day is concerning. And I must apologize because it's possible I've led Ishii to believe you like to have sex with robots.

Well, there are worse things. That's not even particularly uncommon. I did an internship at a sex-robot factory the summer before I started at the university. I got in some trouble with my supervisor though. Apparently, you're supposed to program the robots to be docile and acquiescing lovers.

And what did you program them to do?

Defend themselves and lecture people if they got rough.

How long did it take before you got fired?

Interns aren't fired; they're let go.

How long?

Less than a month. I decided to leave the experience off my résumé later in life.

Wise.

Yes. Grunburg is bringing us to the shuttle bay.

"The shuttle is coming back, Captain." Kim pointed at the power cable, realizing they would have to unplug it and move it out of the shuttle-bay doorway so it could close and the bay could depressurize. "Are you done with that?"

"I'll get it, sir," a young engineer blurted, waving for a couple of men to help him.

By the time the shuttle docked and Kim and Asger walked to the bay, the ship seemed to be back to normal. The thrums of power reverberating through the deck as the thrusters pushed the *Osprey* away from the moon's orbit were comforting. The silence earlier had been eerie. Silence in space was death.

As soon as Casmir climbed out of the shuttle, Kim trotted forward to pat him on the back, glad he and Grunburg had been able to come up with a solution—and glad they had returned without trouble.

"Are you all right?"

"Yes, fine. *Our* power never went out." Casmir squinted at her. "Are *you* all right?"

Did she appear disheveled after the assassins' attack? Hunting for a hairbrush hadn't been a priority since then. "Yes. Having the power go out was largely uneventful."

Asger stood a few feet away, talking to an officer, but he looked over. "What do you consider *eventful*?"

"A loss of limbs," she said. "Death."

"You should have been a knight."

Casmir lifted a finger, as if he wanted details, but he must have decided to wait for later. "I brought something back for you."

Casmir rummaged in his tool satchel as his programmer acquaintance stepped gingerly out of the shuttle, a hand to his head. A waiting nurse came forward to help him out of the bay. They passed Captain Ishii as he strode in.

"Here you go." Casmir held out a tube of the nutrient broth she'd prepared for his sample taking. There was tape stuck to it. And…

"Is that your hair?" Kim grimaced, squinting at the strand stuck to the tape—and the side of the vial. "Or the android's?"

The android in question hopped out of the shuttle with Zee, both stopping behind Casmir.

"I'm not sure." Casmir peered at it as he pulled out a card with black powder smudges taped to it. "I was trying to get fingerprints." He peeled the tape off her tube. "It could be *my* hair, but it looks kind of gray, doesn't it? I'll have someone run a DNA test. If it belongs to the person who booby-trapped the android, that would be more conclusive than fingerprints. Though I suppose it depends on if the astroshamans of the systems are in the various law-enforcement databases. And if Fleet has access to them. Let's see first if the Intelligence officers can pick up anything. On a ship this large, they ought to have a forensics lab, right?"

"Yes." Kim almost volunteered to run the tests herself—the medical laboratories had everything needed—but she didn't have access to any military or law-enforcement databases in the Kingdom, much less in the rest of the Twelve Systems. She merely accepted the tube, which was clearly for her.

"I also brought Tork back." Casmir gestured to the silent android behind him, its short brown hair mussed, its utilitarian overalls torn and disheveled.

Since androids didn't bruise, it wasn't clear that it had been in a fight, but Kim did get that impression.

"In case you want to swab him personally," Casmir added.

Kim eyed the android, wondering why he had activated it. He'd said Tork had helped with the antivirus program, but wasn't it also the reason the *Osprey* had been knocked offline?

"Or Zee will happily swab Tork for bacteria samples if you don't want to get close," Casmir offered.

"Perhaps not *happily*," Zee murmured, head turning briefly toward Tork. Briefly and dismissively.

Kim raised her eyebrows. "Casmir, is it just me, or is your crusher developing more… personality?"

"Zee has the ability to adapt and learn new things."

"Like personality?"

Casmir shrugged. "Sure. He *has* been my roommate of late. You got more personality after living with me for seven years. Remember how stoic and humorless you were when we first met?"

"I was neither of those things. I'll accept that I may have been more reserved."

"And I've cured you of that." He winked. "I rub off and stick."

"Yes, like honey from a leaky jar."

"Sweet and delicious?"

"Requiring intensive washing and chemical sanitation after handling."

Casmir's forehead furrowed, and he looked like he might object, but Ishii strode over.

"What is *that* doing here, Dabrowski?" He pointed at the android.

"Helping us."

Ishii sputtered. "*What?*"

"He located the virus he sent and ensured it wouldn't be transmitted again to other Kingdom ships." Casmir stepped back and patted Tork on the shoulder. "He's our new ally."

This time, when Ishii sputtered, no words came out. He did gesture in beseeching exasperation toward Asger.

Asger spread his arms. "You didn't let me go, remember?"

"I want it destroyed," Ishii said.

"He knows where the cargo ship went," Casmir said.

"And I'm sure he can be trusted to tell us." Ishii curled his fingers into a fist and glowered at him.

Kim frowned, feeling Ishii should be more grateful. She didn't know yet all that Casmir and the programmer had done out there, but she did know they'd been responsible for fixing the damage the virus had caused. And she hadn't heard any reports that the second warship had been attacked by the virus.

"I will share the destination of the cargo ship if Professor Dabrowski wishes me to do so," Tork said. "I work for him now. He has agreed to get me a telescope so I may pursue my astronomy hobby in my off time."

Casmir shrugged without any denial. Kim gripped her chin while she watched Ishii sputter some more. For someone with brown skin, his cheeks could get impressively pink.

"Where are you going to get a telescope?" Asger asked blandly.

Like Kim, he no longer seemed surprised by anything Casmir did, or caused to happen around him.

"If the ship doesn't have one we can borrow, I'll buy one at a space station," Casmir said.

Kim was tempted to ask him if he'd talked someone into paying him for coming along on this mission yet, but Ishii spoke again.

"It's not a stray dog. You can't keep it."

"As I told Tork," Casmir said, "it would be illogical to destroy or abandon such a valuable asset."

"Then wipe its memory. Wipe everything on it. Wasn't it carrying a *bomb* inside some panel?" Ishii must have gotten a preliminary report from his officer earlier, because Kim hadn't heard about that.

"Yes, because the astroshaman that found the cargo ship booby-trapped him. I did warn you that was a possibility, I believe, and that it would be dangerous to bring him aboard."

"It was dangerous *not* to bring him aboard too. I want it wiped." Ishii pointed a finger at Casmir's nose. "And *you're* not doing it. Take it to the programming lab. Grunburg can handle it."

"Sora," Casmir said gently. "If we wipe his memory, he can't tell us where the cargo ship went."

"So get that information and *then* wipe its memory. *Its*, Dabrowski. It's not a person, not a him."

"He may prove a useful ally when we reach the astroshamans and have to deal with them," Casmir said without commenting on the rest.

"I don't need any more *useful* and unwanted allies." Ishii stomped toward the exit.

Casmir patted Tork's shoulder before lowering his hand. "Don't worry. We'll make sure nobody wipes your memory."

"Do you have command of this ship, Professor Dabrowski?" Tork asked.

"No, but that hasn't stopped me yet from doing what I want."

Asger snorted. "No kidding."

"I believe you." Tork nodded. "I have been programmed to discern when humans are being deceitful, and you are not. I believe the research that I found in this system is true."

"Research?" Kim mouthed.

"Professor Dabrowski is a protector of robots," Tork said.

Casmir smiled, though he appeared puzzled. "You never did mention what you were reading for your research. Or is it who you were contacting?"

"Not who. What. Other androids in this system. You have a good reputation. Protector of robots."

"Just what you need," Kim said. "Another nickname."

Casmir still looked more puzzled than enlightened, but he patted Zee and Tork on the backs and nodded toward the exit. "Let's go get some food. And oil for those in need of lubrication."

"I am experiencing friction in my servo motors," Tork said.

"I am self-lubricating," Zee said.

"I'm sure that comes in handy with the lady crushers," Asger said as they passed.

Kim, Casmir sent her a message as he walked out with his odd entourage. *Tork already told me the cargo ship was heading to an underwater base on Xolas Moon in System Hydra. I'll tell Ishii, ideally in exchange for a promise not to wipe Tork's memory, but if you can verify that with your laboratory magic, that would be excellent. I think I won Tork over, but it is possible he's deceiving me and is still under the control of his handler.*

You mean he could be buttering your toast with that protector of robots *bit?*

It's possible. What's that old proverb? Trust but verify?

I shall attempt to do so. I hope this sample never came in contact with your tongue.

It didn't. I had my helmet on, so I couldn't have even breathed heavily on it.

Good. She decided not to complain about the hair. If it didn't belong to Grunburg or Casmir, it might give them a clue even greater than bacteria could.

Casmir settled on the deck on a blanket he'd acquired his first night on board, the servers humming near his ear, the displays dimmed for the night. Zee was a dark shadow standing guard near the door. All was back to normal.

With the crisis past, his mind whirred like an automaton, imagining different scenarios that they might face when they found Tork's original handlers. The android stood in the dark next to Zee, his eyes closed, his chin to his chest. Powered down, the stance said. Zee didn't have eyes in the traditional sense, but Casmir was sure all of his optical sensors were pointed at Tork.

A knock sounded at the door, and Zee shifted to block it as it slid open. Casmir squinted at the light that slashed in from the corridor, wrapping around Zee and leaving his broad shadow on the deck.

"Get your bag, Dabrowski," came Ishii's gruff voice.

"My tool satchel?"

"No, your *bag*. With your pajamas and underwear and beard gel in it. Come on. You're getting a bunk."

Casmir hadn't unpacked much—where would he have put anything?—so he was ready in a few seconds. "It's not in the brig, is it?"

"No. You save the ship, you get an upgrade to your accommodations. That's how it works."

"Oh, that's a nice perk."

Casmir squinted again as he entered the corridor, the light obnoxiously bright. His left eye blinked. He paused with his hand on the wall, feeling a flush of heat and the sensation that his mind wasn't fully connected to his body. Damn it, was he going to have a seizure *now*? After surviving all that crap earlier without collapsing?

"Dabrowski?"

Casmir shut his eyes against the light—why was the corridor so bright?—and fought off a wave of dizziness. He was aware of a hand gripping his shoulder, but it almost seemed like it was happening to someone else.

"I promise, Dabrowski—Casmir, I'm not taking you to the brig."

Casmir struggled to concentrate on the words, and his dizziness passed. He drew in a shaky breath and tried to force muscles that had gone painfully rigid to relax. He opened his eyes partway, wary of the light now. A blurry brown face was staring at him. Ishii.

"Sorry." Casmir blinked, and Ishii slowly came into focus. "I'm sorry."

His tongue felt thick, and he sighed, wishing Ishii had left him to sleep on the deck in his dark computer cabin.

"Did you just have a seizure?"

"No." Casmir tried to smile. Only half of his mouth wanted to work. "Maybe a partial one." He focused on enunciating. He didn't want Ishii to worry about him. Or drag him off to sickbay. "It's no big deal."

"Do you want to go to sickbay?"

"No."

"Do you want me to get Lieutenant Adjei? The night nurse?"

That was the nurse with the curly hair that Casmir had admired, shortly before he'd gone into anaphylactic shock and passed out from a full seizure. At her feet. He didn't want to see her again. In part because it would mean something was wrong with him, and in part because he now found himself thinking more of straight black hair and sandaled feet with pieces of grass stuck between the toes.

He smiled, wondering if Princess Oku had looked at any of his robot bee babble, or if she'd filed it away along with all the dead flowers and stale chocolates and whatever lame things would-be suitors had given her over the years. Asger, Casmir recalled, had offered her one of his calendars.

"Casmir?" Ishii squeezed his shoulder.

"Sorry, I don't need a nurse. Just that bunk you teased me with would be fabulous. Thank you."

Zee loomed behind them, perhaps not realizing there was anything wrong with Casmir. Because there wasn't. He would be fine. He nodded his head firmly. His eye blinked and watered. Sighing again, he rubbed it. He was just tired, the light of the corridor too much after the day's stresses.

Fortunately, Ishii set a slow pace as they walked, glancing back at Zee and Tork, who were trailing along behind them.

"You get the cargo ship's destination from that android yet?" Ishii asked.

"If I share it, will you agree not to wipe his memory?"

Ishii glared at him. "That's not how it works. As a civilian advisor, you joyfully give me all the information you learn without trying to make deals."

"Are you sure? The job title simply implies that I advise you. Joy isn't mentioned at all."

Ishii sighed and rolled his eyes.

"Xolas Moon in System Hydra," Casmir said, too tired to argue with him. He thought he could talk Grunburg out of wiping Tork's memory if it truly came to that. "In a base deep in the ocean under the mass of ice that covers the surface."

"That was one of your earlier guesses, wasn't it?"

"Yes."

"We're on the way to the gate. Hopefully, Scholar Sato's analysis of the android can confirm System Hydra before we have to choose a destination."

Casmir nodded, feeling the same way. Trust but verify.

"Did you have the seizures when we were kids?" Ishii glanced at him. "Or did you get hit on the head or something?"

"I'm sure I've been hit on the head plenty, but the seizures were actually worse when I was a kid. By the time I was ten—" Casmir waved at Ishii, since that was how old he'd been the summer they'd met and competed in robotics camp, "—we had them mostly under control with medication. They were *completely* under control until I started gallivanting around in space. I think all the extra stress on the body up here is making my medication not work as well."

"So, naturally you volunteered to return to space." Ishii waved Casmir and his robot mini entourage into the lift.

"I suppose I did volunteer, but I didn't have much choice. The king is giving me a chance to prove my loyalty, and I think bad things could happen if I fail."

Ishii frowned as they stepped out of the lift and stopped in front of the second door in the corridor. "Does he know you have a medical condition?"

"Oh, I'm sure Jager knows *all* about me."

"What do you mean? Why would he have been aware of your existence before you made off with his gate?"

"Because…" Yes, because why? Casmir had decided earlier not to mention to Ishii that he was a clone. Was he going to change his mind? He had a headache, and he wanted to go to bed, not get into a big discussion about his origins, origins he was still fuzzy on. "Because of the crusher project. And because he lives next door to Royal Intelligence. I'm sure he can learn all he wants to about anyone who catches his attention within minutes."

"Likely so." Ishii waved at a sensor, and the door opened, a soft red light coming on inside, nothing brighter.

Casmir stepped inside, welcoming the dimness and wanting to fling himself onto the bed. It was a delightfully *large* bed. If he'd had a wife or a girlfriend, there would have been room for both of them to spread out. Not that he would have wanted to take such a person along on a dangerous mission. He was better off with robots for roommates. Platonic roommates who would stand by the door, leaving him the luxuriously large bed to sprawl out on by himself.

"Casmir?" Ishii remained in the corridor.

"Yeah?"

"I'm sorry I gave you a hard time."

"It's all right."

Ishii's mouth flattened, as if he didn't agree.

"You can make up for it by giving me all the perks Kim gets," Casmir suggested.

"You want your own lab and an espresso maker?"

"You *gave* her an espresso maker?" Casmir had been horrified to learn that the new one in their kitchen back home, sitting next to the perfectly good old one she'd had for years, had been a gift from Rache. Was she going to return from space with another one? A gift from the military?

"She brought it with her," Ishii said. "I think your friend makes her own perks."

"That is quite possible."

Ishii offered a salute, even though Casmir was certain officers weren't supposed to salute civilians, and left him to his new cabin. Zee and Tork walked in, taking up positions on opposing walls where they could spend the night glaring suspiciously at each other.

Casmir dropped his bags and collapsed on the bed, delighted to have a pillow. The case crackled as if it had been starched, and it smelled faintly of bleach, but he didn't care. The deck had also smelled of bleach. It seemed to be the staple cleaning chemical on a military warship.

As he was about to nod off, a message came in, the alert flashing on his contact. He almost ordered it into do-not-disturb mode without reading it, but it was hard to miss seeing the name. Princess Oku.

He sat up, eyelids flying open. Princess Oku was sending him a message? Was it about bees? About how she thought he was charming and hoped they could get coffee when he returned?

"Yeah, I'm sure that's it." Casmir leaned back against the pillow as he accepted the request for authorization to contact him, then opened her message.

Dear Professor Dabrowski...

So formal! He wished he'd asked her to call him Casmir, but the last time they'd met, in the clinic where Bonita had been undergoing her knee procedure and Oku had been undergoing... whatever she'd been there for, she'd been surrounded by guards. He'd felt self-conscious. Also, his parents and Kim had been there. What man could interact smoothly with a woman when his parents and roommate were watching?

I wanted to thank you for the work you put into your robotic bee research. I had an associate look at it, and he thought it did seem promising. Please let me know if I can compensate you for your time. That must have taken you many long days to put together.

Compensate him? His mouth dropped. She thought he wanted payment? No, he'd just needed something to do while he'd been locked up in her father's dungeon...

Did she know about that? He was inclined to think it unlikely. Jager probably didn't tell his daughter about the miscreants, delinquents, spies, and innocent robotics professors he tossed into cells deep in the bowels of the castle.

At this time, I'm not prepared to give up on the idea that there may be a biological solution to helping bees handle a space habitat's lesser gravity and lack of a magnetic pole—we believe that's part of what's stressing them to such a state that they end up dying. At the suggestion of a colleague, I decided to look into bee bacteria, since I'm aware of the human-beneficial bacteria that has been used to improve the constitutions of our Fleet soldiers in space. I found a paper on a pathogen that caused deadly wing mutations among larval bees on the southern continents that a talented scientist isolated, studied briefly, and created a bacteriophage to kill. When the bees were inoculated with the bacteriophage, they ceased to have problems with the wing mutations, and within a few generations—bee generations—no traces of the pathogen remained. I thought I might contact this particular scientist and see if she has any interest in my project. It turns out that she volunteered for a mission for my father and is off on a warship at the moment. With you.

Casmir snorted, imagining Kim in her lab sipping coffee and vehemently stating that she had *not* volunteered.

I've never spoken with Scholar Sato before, the message continued, *and I understand that she now specializes in the human bacteria I mentioned. It looks like the bee research was something she did for an advisor during her postgraduate studies. You're probably both very busy right now, but would you consider asking her if she has any ideas and if I can send my data to her?*

Casmir felt a twinge of disappointment that Oku wanted to send data to *Kim* and not to him, but he didn't mind being the intermediary.

There wouldn't be any hurry. This is just a pet project of mine. There's no deadline. I can send her a message directly if you don't want to be involved, but I somewhat selfishly think she may be more likely to say yes to her roommate than to a stranger, even a royal stranger, especially if she was strong-armed into going on that mission rather than volunteering. I know my father fairly well.

Hm, maybe Oku wasn't as unaware of her father's machinations as Casmir had guessed.

He swung his legs over the side of the bed, thinking to find Kim that very minute, but the change of position intensified a twinge of lingering dizziness. He checked the ship's local time and realized it was almost midnight. He would wait until morning to bug her.

Zee had noted his movement and turned his head toward Casmir.

"I was thinking of going for a walk," Casmir said, though he doubted the crusher would have asked, "but I've decided against it."

He flopped back onto the bed.

"Humans are supposed to sleep during night cycles," Zee stated. "For your health, you should attempt to keep your circadian rhythms balanced while you are in space."

"Yes, thank you for the advice." Casmir was certain he hadn't included knowledge of circadian rhythms in the information set he'd programmed the crushers with. Zee was, indeed, adapting and learning on his own. It was possible his fearsome bodyguard had witnessed Casmir's health foibles enough times to decide to assign himself the additional duty of nurse. Or maybe nanny. "But I should definitely compose a response to Oku's message before I go to sleep. I wouldn't want her to think that I'm too busy to make time for her. Or aloof and unavailable."

It was probably his imagination that Zee's gaze was extra stern.

Casmir closed his eyes and laid his head on his pillow so Zee would believe he was pursuing circadian rhythm perfection, but his previously sleepy mind refused to doze off until he sent a response that said he would be delighted to assist Oku in any way possible. And that he definitely wasn't aloof or unavailable. Not that anyone had ever used those words to describe him, but she'd only met him twice briefly, so she didn't know him well yet.

Dear Princess Oku,

I will speak with Kim and see if your project would interest her. I don't remember her mentioning the bee study, but it's possible she did it before we became roommates. I do specifically remember her doing a project that involved enhancing a certain bacteria in a zindi tree's microbiome in order to encourage it to sequester more carbon dioxide from the atmosphere.

He grinned, remembering that project had involved Kim climbing the tree and being harassed by a campus security drone in the process. He'd been able to offer assistance with the drone, which, he believed to this day, was the only reason the fastidious Kim Sato had agreed to sign on as his roommate. At the time, his house on campus had been slightly less clean and tidy than it was now.

So, he continued, *even though she specializes in the human microbiome now, she likely has the expertise for insect work. I'm certain she would* love *to take on this project for you.*

He wasn't *that* certain of it, and suspected Kim was tired of doing things for the military and government, but he would be charming and promise her a favor. Or more chocolate-covered espresso beans.

He was tempted to ramble on to Oku and write a letter five pages long, but she might be horrified and never send a message to him again if she thought he had romantic intentions toward her. She probably got enough of that from men around the castle. If Asger was anything to go by, the knights that she encountered spent a lot of time on one knee around her, with their heads bowed.

"Maybe I could simply share a closing line about myself that she would find intriguing," he mused, ordering his chip to record his mutters in case anything brilliant fell out among the ramble. "Or would that be boorish? To talk about myself? I could ask her something about herself, something that requires an answer, thus ensuring that she messages me back. But no, I shouldn't be a pest. After all, if Kim agrees to work on the project, she'll probably get invited to the castle for a meeting sooner or later, and as her best friend and roommate, I would be allowed to go along, don't you think? Kim is an important scientist. She may need someone to hold her bag of lab specimens."

As he gazed at the ceiling, pondering the perfect closing line, Tork spoke.

"I am uncertain if an answer is required." He sounded puzzled.

Casmir realized he'd been rambling aloud.

"I do not believe so," Zee said. "The tone of Casmir Dabrowski's voice suggests he is engaging in a human practice called soliloquy."

"My definition of this word suggests it applies only to characters in stage dramas."

"There are broader definitions. I suggest you search the system-wide network database."

"I will do so."

"It is also possible he is experiencing a mental illness or psychological disorder, such as schizophrenia," Zee said, "but I deem this unlikely. Casmir Dabrowski is emotional but generally rational and coherent."

"I have located a definition that allows for soliloquies outside of dramatic performances," Tork said.

Casmir rubbed his face, wondering what he'd started by acquiring a second intelligent robot. Did this chatter mean they were getting over their animosity and suspicion of each other? Were his weird human idiosyncrasies bringing them together?

He turned off the recording, deciding nothing brilliant was going to come out of his mouth tonight.

On a whim, he attached Zee and Tork's exchange to the end of his message to Oku with the caption, *This is what happens when you ramble late at night and androids are around to hear it.*

With luck, she would think it whimsical and funny. And that *he* was whimsical and funny for sending it.

Only after the message sailed off into the network ether did he consider that she might believe there was a nugget of truth to Zee's alternative assessment.

He shook his head. "You are a multi-award-winning, sought-after-in-your-field professor with *two* advanced degrees. Have some confidence in yourself, Casmir."

Zee and Tork looked at him and then looked at each other.

"Soliloquy?" Tork asked.

"Soliloquy," Zee stated firmly.

Casmir went to sleep.

CHAPTER 11

MORE THAN A DAY PASSED BEFORE THE *DRAGON'S* comm panel lit up again. The freighter was flying toward Death Knell Station on Bonita's original course.

She had no intention of heading anywhere close to the moon where the Drucker warship housing Johnny Twelve Toes orbited, and she hadn't been delighted when Viggo had reported two other Drucker ships in the system. Fortunately, they were on the far side of the sun, orbiting the inhabited planets over there. She'd hoped the rest of the family would be off terrorizing innocent civilians in other systems, but if they were over a week's travel away, that should be fine. Though it wasn't like dealing with a single warship and four hundred pirates would be that much easier than facing the whole clan.

"It's just a file," Viggo said, his tone sounding disapproving.

"From Johnny and the warship?"

"Yes."

Bonita reached for the panel to accept it, but paused when Viggo added, "An *image* file."

"Er." She'd sent a picture of Qin supposedly trapped behind the barrier in a cell, as requested. She distinctly remembered requesting that Johnny *not* send a picture in return. "Are your vacuums mature enough to see whatever a dirty pirate decided to share an image of?"

Currently, two of them were sucking dirt out of crevices under the control console.

"I don't know," Viggo said. "I didn't open it. *I* may not be mature enough."

"You're over a hundred."

"I know."

Bonita let her finger drop and opened the attachment. If she was about to get an eyeful of penis, well, it wouldn't be the first time. People in her industry weren't known for being classy.

What came up was Johnny standing in front of a mirror with his shirt off, taking a picture of his smug reflection. She rolled her eyes. Cocky bastard.

He *was* nice to look at—the chest had fewer tattoos than the face, though the barbed-wire motif continued, making it look like he was wrapped with the stuff. He clearly spent time in the gym and tended to his diet.

"At least his pants are on," Viggo said.

"I confess to being flustered, Viggo. Guys don't flirt with me anymore. Is he messing with me? Trying to use sex to get what he wants?" Bonita didn't know why the Druckers' accountant would care that much one way or another if he got Qin back. Was there a nice bonus involved for him if he was successful? Maybe pirate accountants weren't on salary and had to save the outfit money in order to get paid.

"Sex usually *is* what men want."

"Tell me about it, but I haven't met many who didn't also like money."

Clangs floated up from the lounge. The last time Bonita had passed through, Qin had been down there working out on the gym equipment and lamenting that with Asger gone, she didn't have a sparring partner.

The comm flashed again. Johnny requesting visual communication.

"Qin," she said over the internal comm system, "stay quiet for a bit. The accountant is comming."

"Yes, Captain." The clangs stopped.

Before answering, an idea popped into Bonita's mind, and she ran to Qin's cabin.

"I'm borrowing something of yours," she called.

"That's fine."

She hopped into Qin's cabin, marveling that her knees now allowed her to hop. She ignored the unicorn duvet, cheerfully colored books, and mythological-creature candles mounted all along the walls and headed for the little desk. She pulled out a drawer and found the calendar that Asger had given her, the one where his bare chest—and other bare parts—were on display above every month.

Sad that Qin had stuck it in a drawer. Bonita would have put it to its proper use on the wall above the bed. For the ease of marking appointments, of course.

"Bonita, what *are* you doing?" Viggo asked as she returned to navigation.

"Planning to take our caller down a notch." She answered the incoming comm. "Captain Laser here."

Johnny's face appeared. "Such a delay before answering, Laser. Whatever were you doing? Admiring the picture I sent?"

"Nah. You'd have to do better than that to keep my interest. We recently had this fellow as a passenger, so I'm inured to sexy men right now." Bonita selected one of the pictures where Asger was dressed in nothing but an artfully placed bunch of leaves and turned it so her pirate would see it.

She lowered it in time to catch a startled look on his face. He quickly masked it, the cool sardonic expression returning.

"He appears young for you," Johnny said.

"I *like* younger men." She wriggled her eyebrows at him, guessing he was a good ten years her junior.

"I'm sure I have more experience than that puppy. But let us talk of work before pleasure, yes? I've been authorized to offer twenty thousand for the return of Qin Three."

Bonita leaned back in her pod, pretending to debate the offer. "Why do the Druckers want her so badly? Don't they have a bunch of others?"

"Each of those girls is worth ten trained soldiers in a fight. Just yesterday, I watched one of them stomp Jeb Drucker in the sparring ring, and he's modded up to android levels." Johnny smiled tightly, as if the sight hadn't displeased him. "Further, there's a matter of saving face. It's not the Druckers' way to look bad by losing things that belong to them."

"Who would even know?"

"*They* would know. Others close to them would know. It's enough."

"Will she be treated acceptably once she's returned? I'm not heartless. She's been a good worker for me. I need the money, I'll admit—who doesn't?—but I don't want to turn her over if she's to be tortured or punished for leaving."

"She'll be treated the same as before. The Druckers want loyal warriors, not super soldiers with a taste for vengeance."

Apparently, they didn't think taking those girls to bed could instill a thirst for the latter. Sometimes, Bonita wished Qin *was* the vengeful type. Instead, she seemed to accept her lot in life and only turned on her killer instincts when she was fully engaged in battle.

No, that wasn't completely true. She had fled the pirates once, after all. She didn't want to be with them.

"I'll sell her back for twenty-five thousand, and whoever you send to collect her will have to agree to a neutral meeting place of my choosing."

"Whoever we send? Why, I plan to come personally, dear Captain. Perhaps, after we've completed the transaction, you would be willing to join me for a drink."

"If everything goes without a hitch and you people don't try to betray me, then I would absolutely have a drink with you." Maybe this could go both ways. If he truly was interested in her and wasn't feigning that, maybe if she promised him a date, he would be less likely to set up a double-cross. It was a lot to hope for, but she found herself smiling and saying, "Maybe *more* than a drink."

"*More* than a drink? Whatever do you have in mind?"

"You seem a vaguely educated man. Perhaps we could talk about our favorite books together."

"*Vaguely*?" His eyebrows rose. "Dear Captain, I am a trained accountant. Not only am I well-read, but I can rub numbers together in the most enticing way."

"Number rubbing? What exactly does that look like?"

"Show up without that calendar, and I'll show you. What neutral meeting place do you propose?"

"Death Knell Station."

Johnny snorted. "How is that neutral? The Amigos are likely allies of yours, and they are enemies of the Druckers."

"I had to tilt the odds in my favor, since you have a warship and a crew of four hundred, and I have a freighter with little more than Viggo to assist me."

"Viggo? A man? Are you married, Laser? If so, my disappointment will be as intense as a tidal wave. Unless you and your husband have an open relationship, in which case, I'll gladly rub things for you."

"I thought you only rubbed numbers."

"I'm versed in many types of rubbing. Does that excite you?"

"I'll be excited by twenty-five thousand Union dollars in my account and nobody stabbing a dagger in my back."

"At Death Knell Station," he said, his tone flat.

"Yes. The alley behind the Fiery Comet restaurant across from Docks and Locks."

"Very well. I'll send the date and time that we can get a ship there." He smiled slightly. "I look forward to showing you how well I rub." He reached for the button to turn off his comm but paused to add, "I refer to numbers, of course."

"Of course."

The comm ended.

Bonita shook her head. "I do believe that man intends to double-cross me."

"Don't you intend to double-cross him?" Viggo asked.

"Yes. So, we'll end up with a quadruple cross, and that always gets complicated and messy."

"Perhaps it's fortunate you're meeting someone who's adept with numbers then."

Bonita sighed. "I doubt it."

She would have preferred to meet with someone who came across as a thug and an idiot. Despite Johnny's barbed-wire tattoos, she feared he was neither. And that made him far more dangerous.

It was well into the morning cycle—Casmir had slept longer than he'd planned—and the warship was less than two hours from the wormhole gate out of System Lion when he found Kim in a large multi-purpose recreational room next to the *Osprey's* gym. She was in a sparring area, wielding two wooden batons of similar length to the kendo bokken she practiced with back home. Her opponent, Asger, attacked and defended with a wooden staff the length of his extended pertundo.

They sprang into and out of each other's range, the clacks of the practice weapons ringing from the walls as they attempted to make contact. Each wore padded armor and light shoes instead of their galaxy suits. Judging by the other men and women in the gym, that was typical in here.

Casmir waved for Zee to stay by the door and walked to the side of their circular arena, lights in the deck defining the space and blinking and buzzing if anyone stepped over the boundary. He clasped his hands behind his back, trying to wait patiently and admire their speed and agility—they both had the grace of natural athletes who had practiced their craft for years, if not decades—but he mostly hoped they would notice him and take a break so he could ask Kim about bees.

"She's pretty good, huh?" said a young man coming to stand beside Casmir. His gray T-shirt only said Fleet in capital letters and didn't hint to his name or rank. "You'd expect a knight to have serious fighting skills, but not a biologist."

"Her family runs a kendo studio."

"I heard she beat up one of your would-be assassins that escaped during the power shutdown."

Casmir blinked. He hadn't talked to Kim much since his return—in addition to wanting to ask for this favor, he hoped to get an update on whether she'd found anything from his swab or that strand of hair—and was chagrined to hear that she might have been in danger. Especially if it was because someone had wanted to get at him. *Again.*

A heavy blow from Asger sent Kim flying, even though she'd blocked it. She twisted in the air and managed to land on her feet.

Casmir had the urge to run into the arena and play peacemaker. Did they need to whack at each other hard enough to leave bruises—or broken bones?

He snorted at himself. He was definitely his mother's son. Er, his *adoptive* mother's son. He was still puzzled by the revelation that he'd been cloned from a legendary military admiral. And not one who'd served during peacetime. Mikita had almost singlehandedly won the Twelve Systems for the Star Kingdom.

Casmir needed to read more about the man now that he'd figured out as much as he could about the likely destination of that cargo ship. Maybe he should be doing that instead of trying to arrange for bacteriologically superior bees for Princess Oku. Though he had been waiting to read about Mikita in the encyclopedias and books kept in other systems. He hoped he wouldn't regret that. What if what he read out there was unpalatable? What if Mikita had been far closer to the heartless killer Rache was than the caring professor that Casmir liked to think he was?

"That's stellar," the young man said, making encouraging gestures as Kim charged back in at Asger. "I'm Lieutenant Meister, Professor. We all appreciate you and Grunburg saving the ship from the bind it was in." He stuck out his hand.

Casmir shook it. "It seemed like a good idea, since I didn't want to stay in that shuttle indefinitely."

"They can be claustrophobic."

"It was more the lack of gravity that I objected to. My stomach doesn't seem to be made for space travel."

"No?" He looked curiously at Casmir. He had sandy blond hair and freckles that gave him a boyish look despite broad shoulders and a fit build. "I'm a historian. Both of my parents are scholars back in Zamek."

"I didn't know the Fleet had a military occupational specialty for historians." Casmir didn't recognize Meister's face or name but wondered if he should. The lieutenant was looking at him as if he was familiar to him. Had they gone to the same university?

"Oh, they don't. I'm in Intelligence. But I'm working on an advanced degree from Zamek University while I serve. I was stationed on Jotunheim Station for a year for a diplomatic mission, and I took a few classes at the university there. Zamek is being snooty and not letting me transfer the credits."

"Well, it is another nation's education system. As far as I've heard, there's not a lot of standardization across the systems as far as university requirements go."

Casmir shifted his weight and wriggled his fingers when Kim glanced at him. He didn't want to interrupt her training, but he did want to get an answer back to Oku as soon as possible. He wondered what she'd thought of the crusher-android conversation. Had sharing that been odd? Maybe she would think it had been an accidental upload. What had seemed whimsical the night before seemed a strange choice now, considering he had been messaging royalty.

"I think they just want me to pay more for their credits." Meister smirked wryly.

"Did you take any history classes while you were at Jotunheim Station? That's in System Hydra, right?" Casmir realized he might have someone right here who knew something about Admiral Mikita, the rest of the galaxy's version of him, not the edited-to-suit-the-Kingdom's-tastes version.

"I did, actually. Military history and early colonial politics." There was that curious look again.

Was *that* why he thought he recognized Casmir? Because he'd seen the same pictures in history books that Qin had seen?

"I've also studied the history of the pirate families and some of the newer independents." Meister raised his eyebrows. "That being as much for my work as for my education."

"Of course." Casmir smiled innocently, though he worried about what those elevated eyebrows might signal.

Maybe it wasn't that Meister recognized him as an Admiral Mikita lookalike but a Rache one. Did all of Royal Intelligence know who Rache truly was these days? Would they have shared that information with Military Intelligence?

Casmir remembered Jager's warning for him to stay away from Rache, that in order for him to be useful to the Kingdom, he had to be trustworthy. What if there were Intelligence officers on the ship—such as Meister—who were filled in on everything and had been ordered to keep an eye on Casmir?

"The pirate families sound particularly heinous," Casmir said, hoping to divert the man's attention from Rache, if that was indeed who Meister had in mind as a *newer independent.* "I have a friend who's trying to find a way to escape their interest right now."

"Qin Liangyu Three?"

"Yes." Casmir forced himself to keep a smile on his face, though he now had more evidence to support his hypothesis that this guy had been completely filled in on all things related to Casmir. "Have you met her? She's a sweet girl."

"That's not how she looks in the picture I've seen."

"Did the picture not show her holding one of her unicorn candles with freshly painted fingernails? Er, claws?"

"No, it was from security footage at the royal air harbor as she slung an intruder over her shoulder as if he weighed ten pounds."

"That was a bounty hunter trying to capitalize on her reward. I hope his hospital stay went well and that he didn't suffer too many ill effects from self-tranquilizing himself numerous times. Though maybe it's not technically *self*-tranquilizing if the drone you programmed does it."

"He was sent off to a penal colony for having worked with the Black Star terrorists."

"Ah. Better than being dead, I suppose."

"I'm going to assume you haven't been to a penal colony." Meister, who had seemed affable and innocuous early on, narrowed his eyes, as if to imply Casmir might end up in one if he didn't play his role satisfactorily.

"No. Is it worse than Ishii's computer closet here?"

"There's mental rehabilitation in addition to physical labor. Speaking of pirates, we've been trying to capture Captain Tenebris Rache and dump him into a penal colony for years." Meister waved his hand, as if the comment was meant to be casual and apropos of nothing, but Casmir had no doubt it was very, very intentional.

"Oh? I'd heard the goal was to assassinate him."

Meister's eyes sharpened. "Is that what he told you?"

"What? No. He's barely told me anything about anything when our paths have crossed."

"I understand they've crossed often of late."

"You go into space, and you run into pirates. I think that's just what happens." Casmir shrugged and spread his arms, also striving for casualness, even though he was positive Zee would point out his increased respiratory rate if he were close enough to do so. "The travel and tourism brochures fail to mention that aspect."

"Royal Intelligence believes he's after the gate and will try to get to it ahead of us."

"He did try to claim it for himself once." Casmir grimaced, imagining him and Rache ending up working at odds with each other again. He remembered their handshake, after they'd both climbed out of the rubble in that base, and wished… He wasn't sure what. That they could be friends and brothers? Some siblings found that challenging even when one wasn't a heinous criminal. He just wished they didn't have to be enemies.

"And is likely to do so again." Meister smiled, but his eyes were intent as he added, "Will you have any trouble fighting him if we end up battling his mercenaries to get to it first?"

"*Fighting* him? Do I look like someone who successfully picks fights with a lot of people?" Casmir waved at himself—he was certain he was the smallest male in the gym, in weight if not in height *and* weight—and then waved at Asger, offering him up for comparison.

Meister looked toward Zee. "You can sic your robot on him."

"I have done that before, but I truly hope Captain Ishii's plan doesn't hinge on sending me into a combat situation." Casmir's stomach twisted at the idea of even being on the *Osprey* if the Fleet went into battle with Rache's *Fedallah*, but surely, he couldn't be held responsible for anything that happened if the ships fought each other. Though he would feel strange if he was forced to watch his clone brother's demise from across the intervening space. Why couldn't Rache find a new hobby and leave the gate to Jager?

A hypocritical thought, since Casmir hadn't been willing to leave the gate to Jager. Not last time. This time, he would stay out of it, do what he had to do in order to return to his home a free man.

"I imagine Captain Ishii will do whatever is most likely to cause this mission to succeed."

Casmir decided he didn't need to break out in a cold sweat at the thought of being marched into battle against his brother's mercenaries. At the most, Ishii might order him to send Zee along with a boarding party. Even that made his stomach squirm again, the idea of commanding Zee to help against Rache. To help *kill* Rache. Because that was what their goal would be, not to simply keep him from getting the gate, but to eliminate him as a threat to the crown.

A couple of big men walked up, bare-chested and gleaming with sweat, and Casmir had an excuse not to reply. Though he wasn't sure their presence was an improvement.

The men stopped next to Casmir and Meister, looming over both of them. Casmir groped for something witty to say, his instincts and past experiences telling him that interest from beefy men was never a good thing. They didn't want to beat him up for some reason, did they? He didn't *think* he'd bumped into anyone or inadvertently knocked a towel off a hook on the way in.

Casmir readied a finger, prepared to wave for Zee to come loom over *them.*

One man wiped his palm on his damp trousers, looked at it, rubbed it on his friend's equally damp shirt—this earned him a punch that would have knocked Casmir on the deck, but which he didn't seem to feel—then stuck it out toward Casmir.

"Glad to have you aboard, Professor."

"Oh." Casmir was so startled by the pleasant words that it took him a moment to add, "Thank you," and clasp the hand, his own dwarfed by it, and accept the hearty shake. It was so far from the introduction he'd expected that he didn't worry about the fact that neither of the man's attempts to dry his palm had been successful.

"I'm Sergeant Kofler. That's Corporal Juric. You let us know if anyone gives you trouble while you're here."

"What if Captain Ishii gives me trouble?" Casmir didn't think that would happen, not now that Ishii had deigned to give him a bed to sleep in, but his was the first name that popped into mind.

The sergeant's forehead furrowed.

"You let us know if anyone lower in rank than us gives you trouble," he amended.

Casmir smiled. "Thank you. I will."

"We heard those idiots from the mess tried to kill you. For some stupid bounty they probably wouldn't have even gotten. If that happens again, you let us know." The corporal pounded a fist into his palm hard enough that Casmir jumped.

The sergeant nodded, duplicated the action, then slapped Casmir on the shoulder and headed for the towel dispenser.

"I see you're making friends," Kim said from behind him.

Only then did Casmir realize the clacks of wooden sticks battering each other had halted. He turned to face her, hoping Meister would trundle off now that he'd made his insinuations. Asger was grabbing a couple of towels.

"Yes," Casmir said. "The gym is my natural milieu and a place where I enjoy bonding with sweaty men."

"Using words like milieu in a gym is a good way to get beat up."

"And here I thought it was my scrawny build that made me an enticing target. Can I talk to you about bee bacteria?"

Kim blinked a couple of times.

Casmir willed Meister to go away. He turned his head and body toward another sparring match, but he was still close enough to hear their conversation.

"Here?" Kim asked.

"Ideally, somewhere with less grunting and clanking of weight machines." He thought about adding *somewhere private*, but would Meister find that odd? For the first time, he wondered if there were surveillance cameras around the ship keeping an eye on him. He knew there were security cameras in the common areas, but what about in his new cabin?

"I want to grab something to eat and clean up," Kim said. "I also have a report to share with you on that genetic material. Meet me in my cabin in a half hour. Or should I meet you in *your* cabin?" Her eyebrow twitched. "I understand you have one now."

"I do. Ishii promised to give me the same perks he gives you. Such as a bed. And if I'd brought an espresso maker, there would be room to set it up on the desk."

"Are you getting paid now?"

"Uh, I didn't think to ask about that."

"You have odd priorities, Casmir."

"Don't tell me you don't prioritize having room for your coffee accoutrements."

She flicked her fingers in agreement, said, "My cabin," and headed for the door.

Asger came over, and Casmir clapped him on the shoulder—never mind that he had to reach up to do that—and nodded toward the door. "Just the knight I wanted to see." He hoped Asger would take the cue and walk out with him.

"I'm the only knight on the ship." Asger headed for the door.

Meister watched them over his shoulder but didn't follow.

"Then it's convenient that you're the one I wanted to see."

"Were those men bothering you?" Asger pointed a thumb toward the sergeant and corporal—they were now grappling in one of the arenas.

"No, they offered to beat up people who bother me."

"Oh? So I should be careful about appearing to menace you?"

"They did mention that they could only beat up people of lesser rank, so unless a knight is outranked by a sergeant, I think you're safe."

"We have our own special ranking system, but our pay grades put us on par with officers."

"So you make the big money? Why do you need to model for underwear companies on the side?"

"I'm the lowest rank a knight can be," Asger said dryly as they stepped into the corridor, "until I prove myself worthy of a promotion by demonstrating leadership abilities, trustworthiness, and the ability to act independently while keeping the best interests of the crown in mind."

"Ah." Casmir decided not to ask if Asger's relationship with him had put his progress in jeopardy, because Asger had already hinted that it had.

"And even officers don't make piles of money. They've historically come out of the nobility, so they're expected to have family money. Which I do not have access to since my father is not—has not always been—pleased with me."

They stopped when they reached a lift, Asger perhaps wondering where Casmir wanted to take him. Nowhere, in truth. He'd just wanted to leave the gym without his spy.

"Why not? You seem like the kind of son every father would want."

"I'm not sure *most* fathers want their sons to be underwear models and pose nude for calendars. Would your father want you to do that?"

"My father would be flummoxed if I had the *ability* to do that."

"It's not that hard." Asger smiled faintly. "You just have to know the poses and how to pump yourself up to improve your vascularity."

"Vascularity? Like big visible veins? I'm pretty sure if that happened in my body, it would be due to excess stress causing an increased secretion of cortisol, which increases the glomerular filtration rate and renal plasma flow from the kidneys. Among other things, that increases sodium and water retention. That makes your veins stand out. And then, if you have my special brain, it increases neuronal excitability and gives you a seizure."

"That's impressive."

"The number and variety of things that can give me a seizure?"

"No, that you can spout things like that. I thought medical stuff was more Kim's venue."

"I did take a number of science classes on the way to getting my engineering degree. That's basic human biology." Which happened to be rather relevant to him, hence his knowledge on the matter. "But my point is that I'm surprised your father wouldn't be delighted with you. You're a good man. And you're—" Casmir waved vaguely up and down Asger's impressive height and build, "—manly."

"I wasn't the most responsible teenager, and I had a tendency to get into trouble. My mom suggested sports as a way to distract me from less noble pursuits, but it wasn't until she passed that I followed her advice. Bodybuilding wasn't what she had in mind, I'm sure, but I did get into it, especially when there was nobody else around to do things with." Asger grimaced and looked at the bulkhead instead of Casmir. "The last time my dad and I spoke, he yelled at me and told me to straighten up or he'd do more than cut me off temporarily. He'd name my cousin his heir and leave me with nothing. I didn't care about that—I don't even want his damn land or money—but it was just hard because when I was younger, I'd always wanted to be like him. But then he was never home, and it was easy to resent him for that, even if that was his job. Logically, I know that. As an adult. But I didn't get it that well as a thirteen-year-old kid, angry because Mom had died, and he was never there, and all I had were tutors to lecture me…" He shook his head and returned his focus to Casmir. "Sorry. I don't know why I'm telling you all that. In the middle of a corridor with people walking past."

Two officers strode out of the lift as he spoke, and Casmir stepped to the side with him.

"Did you say your father is a knight too?" Casmir asked.

"Yes, one of the ones who gets sent off to other systems for spy missions. It's been years since he was back home. The one time he was, I was graduating from my squireship and officially being knighted. I'd thought he'd come to see it, but he never showed up. He's never even given me a chance to show him that I'm not a screwup anymore. At least, I'm trying not to be one." The expression he turned on Casmir was on the sad side.

Once again, Casmir felt guilty for having caused him to get in trouble with his superiors. "Don't worry. We'll get the gate, and I'll be good, and the king will have no reason to doubt either of us again."

Casmir wasn't sure he fully believed that, or that he wanted to be the king's loyal servant, but Asger nodded, appearing heartened.

"Good." Asger clapped him on the shoulder. "Thank you."

CHAPTER 12

"DID YOU SAY *BEE* BACTERIA?" KIM ASKED AS Casmir entered her cabin. She'd been wondering if she heard him correctly in the gym.

There was only one seat, a swivel chair locked to the deck in front of the built-in desk, and she waved him to it, then sat cross-legged on the end of the bed.

"Yes." Casmir stood and rummaged in his tool satchel before taking a seat. "I got a message from Princess Oku, and she thanked me for my robot bee proposal, but she said she'd like to seek out ways to help real bees survive on space stations before resorting to the mechanical. I hardly see robots as a last resort, but I am always pleased to help people achieve their goals, even if they differ from mine."

Kim thought about asking if he had more interest in helping Oku with her goals than the average person but decided to be supportive instead of snarky. Besides, Casmir was usually willing to help *anyone*, from what she'd observed.

"She found a study you did—some bacteria you made—to help with a wing disease rampant among bees in the southern hemisphere."

"Oh. That was more than ten years ago. I had just finished my undergraduate degree and hadn't yet decided to specialize in human-bacteria relationships."

"Nonetheless, she was intrigued and wondered if you have any ideas of bacteria that could be produced to help her bees survive in the dubious environment of a space habitat." Casmir pulled out some kind of gauge or detector and stuck it to the control panel for the cabin's lights and comm.

Kim debated the proposal. She did like challenges, and she had been lamenting that she didn't have a lot to work on while they were en route for days and weeks.

"I would need all of her data, which I presume she collected from whoever was running the physical bee experiment. There are *so* many ways the rigors and alienness of space act on the human body. Humans and animals have been tested thoroughly over the last few centuries, and I'm certain there have been some entomological studies, but I doubt they're as extensive. I'm familiar enough with my previous work on bees that I could come up with some strains for an overall health improvement, but it's likely some key elements on the space habitat are having a deleterious effect, and while bacteria are myriad and versatile, they're not a cure-all. It might take genetic engineering to achieve what she wishes, assuming the problem can be isolated."

"It sounds like it could be a long project of months and years, especially if you're doing it on the side around your other work." Casmir nodded gravely.

"Give me some credit. Even for pet projects, I can usually at least get some bacteria to the testing phase in less than a month."

"But then there'd have to be lots of testing, right? You'd probably have to visit the castle often to confer with Oku. And since I was partially responsible for all this, I would volunteer to come along and assist you as needed."

"You were *entirely* responsible."

"Hence my offer of assistance. Maybe I can hold your petri dishes while you two converse." He smiled wistfully, his eyes growing unfocused, as if he was accessing the network. Or some daydream.

Kim shook her head, wondering if she would need to start looking for a new roommate. Though she supposed the likelihood of Casmir and Princess Oku wanting to shack up together was low. He'd only spoken to her twice, and as far as Kim knew, she hadn't given any indication that she fancied him as a romantic partner. She'd probably just given him that keycard as a thank-you for the bee research. Kim decided she would wait until Casmir convinced Oku to go on a date with him before worrying about roommate vacancies.

"Speaking of petri dishes, I found enough bacteria in your android sample to suggest he came from System Hydra. The water worlds there developed a lot of unique bacteriological life, long before humans arrived in the system, and humanity has since spread it to the various habitats and stations there. I let Ishii know too."

"Oh, good." Casmir beamed a smile at her. "Tork said his handlers had likely taken the cargo ship and the gate back to their base on Xolas Moon. The astroshamans have supposedly drilled a couple of access points in the ice and set up secret underwater facilities there. If you don't know where they are, you'd have a hell of a time finding them, since there's too much ice for satellites or ships in orbit to read the energy signatures under the surface. But he said he can direct us."

Kim still wasn't sure it was wise to trust Tork—what if he was leading them into another trap, and he planned to send a warning to his so-called *handlers* as soon as the warships entered the system?—but maybe it didn't matter. The astroshamans had to be reasonably certain the Kingdom was coming after the gate. They would be preparing their defenses no matter what.

She grimaced, uneasy at the idea of going up against a group of people—a very large group of people—that had so easily created a virus that had almost caused the destruction of the warship. Was she the only one who believed they might be in over their heads?

"Was that hair nothing?" Casmir asked. "Just one that I was carrying around on the outside of my suit?"

"Actually, it didn't belong to you, Grunburg, or anyone else on the ship—I checked the medical database here—so I sent it over to the Intelligence department. Maybe they can find a match in a systems-wide database out there."

"Interesting. I'd like to know who would lop off an android's hand and give him orders to self-destruct after his task."

"You sound more indignant when you talk about that than when you talk about people trying to kill you for some bounty."

"I'm not so much indignant about that as exasperated."

"Forty-five minutes to the gate," a voice announced over the speaker. "Station leaders, make preparations for the jump."

"I'll let the princess know she can send you her data now, before we leave the system and there are big delays in communication. And, uhm, there was something else I was wondering about." Casmir waved to the device he'd planted on the wall. It was beeping softly. He removed it and nodded. "That's nice. There don't seem to be any cameras or monitoring devices in your cabin."

"Are there in yours?"

"I haven't checked yet, but I figured we should have this next conversation in private." He put his device away and started pacing. "That Lieutenant Meister you saw talking to me was not-so-subtly letting me know he works in Intelligence and is filled in on the various encounters I've had with Rache."

"Including the details of the last one?" Kim wondered if Intelligence had figured out that she and Casmir—along with Qin, Bonita, and Asger—had invited Rache to dinner. Since the goal of that dinner had been to convince him to help them stop the terrorists, which they had successfully *done*, it was irritating that Intelligence would be suspicious of any of their motives.

She could understand them wanting to bring down Rache for all the crimes he'd committed against the crown over the years, but there was a part of her that felt indignant on his behalf. Oh, she wouldn't try to argue that he was a good man, or that he had acted against the terrorists because of a change of heart toward the Kingdom, but maybe King Jager and Royal Intelligence should consider that he *had* helped. Perhaps he could be convinced to help again, and he could become an ally to the crown instead of an enemy. Everyone kept talking about how the Kingdom, if not the entire Twelve Systems, was on the precipice of war. Wouldn't it be better to find a way to use Rache than to try to kill him?

Casmir poked her in the shoulder.

"What?" Kim asked.

"I answered your question and asked one of my own, but you kept staring darkly at that section of the deck there." Casmir pointed, then bent low to peer at it. "I don't see any dust or grime, so it can't be the reason for your ire."

"No, I was thinking about the situation. What was your question?"

"If you'd done any research on him yet and figured out where he grew up and why Oku was familiar with him."

"No. Why would I?" She didn't mean the words to come out defensively, but they sounded that way to her own ears.

Because Casmir had nearly fallen over when she'd mentioned that Rache had asked her to have dinner with him someday? And had made it clear the idea horrified him? Maybe that was it. She found herself reluctant to speak of him around Casmir now.

"Well, he asked you on a date. In this modern age, it's typical to look up a prospective romantic partner before going out with him. Did you check his network presence? How many people claim him as a friend? Whether his relationship history appears healthy and normal?"

Kim scowled at him. "Funny, Casmir. No, I haven't researched him further, though I'm sure it wouldn't be difficult with what we know now."

She didn't admit that she'd been *tempted* to research him, and had only decided against it when she realized she would likely never cross paths with him again. But did that still hold true? She'd assumed she would never leave Odin again, but here she was, heading to another system, in search of the same thing he sought.

Butterfly wings—or maybe bee wings—fluttered in her belly as she wondered if they would end up stuck in a shuttle together once more. No, only if he kidnapped her again. She hoped he was past that.

"Let's pool what we know about him," Casmir suggested, waving at his chip, "and figure out… I'm not even sure what I need to figure out, but I'm hoping not to have to go into battle against him."

"Did someone imply that would happen?"

"Lieutenant Meister thinks Rache is trying to beat us to the gate. And that there might be a showdown, not just with the astroshamans but with him. If we could figure out what his problem is—his *main* problem, I mean, since there are probably fifty million of them—maybe we could convince him to… go away."

Kim raised her eyebrows. "I had no idea you had such power over him."

"I think *you* might." Casmir grimaced. "Even if that disturbs me to acknowledge."

"I'm not a moral compass for him."

"But you've proven that he's willing to keep his word. He said he'd do a favor for you, and he did. Really impressively, I might add. He basically stormed that base himself while I crawled through a duct. I did most crucially deactivate the stealth generator, but I think I would have failed at that if he hadn't been keeping them busy. Not as the distraction, mind you, but as the main event."

Kim snorted. "He said that?"

She almost admitted that she would have liked to see Rache mowing down a bunch of terrorist bad guys—that was far preferable to when he attacked Kingdom soldiers—but she caught herself, feeling certain that an evolved scientist shouldn't find any manner of violence appealing.

"He did. He has a high opinion of himself, if you can imagine that." Casmir smirked.

Kim couldn't tell if it was because Casmir also had a high opinion of himself, and was admitting to some hypocrisy, or if it was something else. Probably something else. If anything, Casmir was too self-critical and underplayed his abilities.

"I thought if we—or you—could get him to somehow give his word that he wouldn't attack the Fleet and try to get the gate, we could avoid all manner of potential ugliness."

"And how am I supposed to do that?"

"You could ask him to knock it off and go away."

"Would that work on *you* if there was something you wanted? I seem to remember telling you to stop obsessing about that signed Remstar Robot first-run model that you were trying to convince other people not to bid on at the fundraiser auction so that you could get it. And now it's on top of your dresser."

"That's because you're my roommate and my friend, but not—" Casmir wiped his fingers, as if to remove something distasteful, "—whatever Rache would like you to be for him."

"I'm not sure he wants me to be anything, but I'm not using that against him, regardless."

"It wouldn't be manipulative. I mean, it *would* be, but it would be to save lives. His… *mine*…" Casmir splayed a hand over his chest.

"Why would your life specifically be in danger?"

The lives of everyone on the ship would be in danger if they flew into battle, but Casmir seemed to be alluding to something different.

"I jokingly said that Ishii wouldn't send me into battle against Rache and his mercenaries, and Lieutenant Meister less jokingly said that Ishii would do whatever it takes to complete his mission. He looked very significantly at Zee."

"Wouldn't that imply *Zee's* life would be in danger?"

"I'm just worried about all of our lives if we go up against him. And if Ishii orders me to send Zee after Rache. I'd hate to be responsible for his death. Why do we all have to fight each other, anyway? It seems like we should be able to get Rache and Ishii to work together, at least for this. They both want the gate. Someone else has the gate. Why shouldn't they jointly try to stomp the astroshamans instead of starting what already sounds like it's going to be a wire tangle from hell?"

"Because only one side can get the gate in the end."

"That's not really true. It's in five hundred pieces in the hold of that cargo ship. Rache could have a piece, Jager could have a piece, your mom could have a piece, and every government in the Twelve Systems with research teams could have a piece." Casmir had been pacing and flailing his arms about, but he stopped abruptly. "Kim, am I *mashugana*, or could that actually work?"

"If that word means crazy, then yes."

"No, I'm serious." He spun to face her. "I know what everybody *wants*—exclusive access to that gate to study, replicate, and use for their own gain—but I've thought from the beginning that no one person or government or organization should have that much power. This has the potential to end humanity's isolation in these Twelve Systems, to let us go to the rest of the stars, maybe even beyond our galaxy. It could also give us an opportunity to visit Earth again and find out what happened to our ancestors. But if *everybody* got a piece and a chance to study it, wouldn't that be a lot better? More *fair*? And, oh!" His eyes widened, and he grinned. "Maybe it would even mean that in order to get that gate working and use it, all of the systems would have to come together in a truce or even an alliance to plug the pieces together. We'd have to all work together."

"Do you know how Machiavellian you look right now?"

"Maybe that last part wouldn't happen, not if each piece had the basic building blocks of the entire gate within it and could be reverse-engineered to build a new gate, but isn't it a lovely thought? People coming together for scientific discovery?"

"More likely, some self-appointed warlord would go around the systems, conquering everyone and stealing their gate pieces."

"You're so pessimistic."

"You're so naive."

"I guess it's a good thing we balance each other out. Let's figure out what we can about Rache, just in case an opportunity to stop a war before it starts comes up." Casmir shrugged and clasped his hands behind his back, as if he'd given up on his crazy idea, but Kim knew him better than that. His eyes were practically gleaming as he calculated permutations in his mind.

Casmir sat on the deck, his back to the wall. "Let me tell you what I know, and you can tell me what you know and are willing to share. I'm going to run some searches based on my face too. Better get that done before we leave the system, as what we want would be on the Kingdom network if it's there. And it must be. There's a reason he doesn't show his face to people, presumably because it could be used to identify him and tie him back to the king and queen."

Yes, Kim remembered that Jager *and* Iku had been listed at the Zamek Royal Seed Bank on the day that Admiral Mikita's genetic material had been checked out. "You can sit in the chair. I left it for you."

"Thank you, but I thought you might want it. My back always starts to hurt if I sit like that for too long." He waved to her cross-legged-on-the-bed position.

"Perhaps you should do some exercises to strengthen it."

He stuck his tongue out at her. From Machiavellian to toddler-esque in twenty seconds.

"He signed one of his messages to me as David," Kim said. "Did he ever give you his name?"

"No, he's given me nothing. What little I know I got from listening to our nemesis at the base rant at him while his underlings were trying to strip him of his armor. Bernard seemed delighted to have some proof that he was who he'd long thought he was. Rache's hood was off then, you see. Bernard mentioned Rache used to get a hefty allowance, and that the king had sent a female assassin after him once."

"He mentioned that to me too, the assassin. I was his prisoner at the time and disinclined to ask for details. I believe I said something sarcastic in response."

"Imagine my shock."

"I'm not too old to throw a pillow at you."

"Did I mention how feeble my back is?"

She rolled her eyes.

"All right, I'm running an image search based on my face, throwing a bunch of negatives in here to try to weed out results with my name or anything to do with Zamek University or robotics in it… Hm, perhaps I should feel flattered at how many entries there are that mention me."

"Just don't look up any vid stars or sports celebrities for a comparison. Your ego might wilt."

"Yes, but have they been published in *Modern Robotics Analysis Quarterly*? Hm, here's something. Let me share my display with you." He pointed at his contact.

Kim nodded, and his search came up, along with the spot where he'd paused. An article shared the results of an air-bike race from twelve years earlier. The race had taken place six hundred miles down the coast from Zamek, near the city of Minato Doragon. Linked video clips showed hundreds of competitors zipping along cliffs and through a forested course, some being horribly maimed as they smashed into trees.

The winner that year had been a David Lichtenberg, who looked a lot like a younger version of Casmir. A little leaner in the face and more muscular in the fitted racing suit he wore in the picture, his helmet off and tucked under his arm, but not nearly as muscular as he was these days. He had graver eyes than Casmir, even though someone was in the middle of presenting a trophy to him, but there was a cocky twist to his lips. As if he'd expected nothing less than to win the race.

"That's him," Casmir, who had seen Rache with his mask off, said with certainty. "And Lichtenberg is not Jager's surname. Not any of the royal surnames. It sounds familiar though. One of the noble families?"

The image shifted aside, as Casmir ran a search on Lichtenberg. The first hit—one of many—that came up was of David Lichtenberg's death in a horrific air-bike crash. It had happened the year after the race, which was one of several he'd won over a span of seven years. He'd disappeared from the racing circuit for nine months before that final race, then come back for one of the most dangerous courses in existence, where he'd crashed into another competitor, spinning his bike into a tree before he tumbled over a cliff and disappeared into the ocean hundreds of meters below. The body was never found.

"Sounds like he staged his own death for some reason," Casmir said. "And here's more on the Lichtenberg family. They are nobles, longtime friends of the Dietrichs, Jager's line. The *orphan*, David Lichtenberg," Casmir read, "was raised as a ward of the family, where he had the best tutors and was trained to be a knight from an early age. He passed the knight training and was officially made a knight at age twenty-one, less than a year before the race where he supposedly died." Casmir's face scrunched up. "I cannot imagine Rache as a chivalrous knight."

"Maybe he was different then."

"I imagine most people *are* different before their deaths."

Casmir's search, which he'd display-shared with Kim, blurred down her contact until he paused again, on an obituary with word about the funeral and how the king and queen had come down from the capital to attend.

"There's nothing else?" Kim overrode his share to go back to the article of Rache—David—winning the race. "Something must have happened to prompt him to stage his death and go off to become a pirate."

"Maybe he didn't like his knight duties. Being chivalrous. Opening doors for women. Helping old ladies cross the street. Or maybe he didn't like the dress code. That purple cloak. It must have chafed at his villainous black-embracing senses. Just a riot of odious colors. I bet he cringed every time he put it on."

"Will you be serious?"

"Must I?"

"Unless you really do want me to throw something at you. You're an easy target down there on the deck."

"Damn, I shouldn't have ceded the high ground to you. A true military leader wouldn't have made that mistake." Casmir snapped his fingers. "Oh, I forgot. There was talk of a dead fiancée."

Kim stared at him. "He was engaged to be married, and the woman died? You didn't think to mention that right at the start?"

"May I remind you that I was overhearing this conversation from fifty feet away while I was wedged into a crawlspace and trying to pull myself forward without being heard?"

"No." Kim remembered the portrait of a beautiful young woman that she'd seen on the wall in Rache's quarters. "Tell me about the fiancée."

"They didn't mention her name or anything about her. He was definitely still bitter about the loss though."

Kim leaned back on her palms as she tried to imagine Rache being engaged to be married at twenty-one. That was so young, though she supposed not that atypical for the nobility. Those families still arranged marriages for their children, and many of them were finished with their private formal schooling by eighteen. Some went into the university systems to pursue advanced degrees, but a lot of them, especially the eldest, were simply apprenticed to their parents to learn to run the family estate and businesses. The younger children were often expected to train as knights or go into military service as officers.

But would any of that have applied to Rache? He had been a ward, not anybody's heir. Kim wondered why he'd been raised as a ward of the Lichtenbergs instead of by Jager himself. If Jager had wanted to ensure he had excellent training and became a model military leader, wouldn't he have wanted Rache at the castle where he could keep an eye on him from day to day?

No, Jager would have wanted his secret weapon kept a secret. If Rache had been raised at the castle as a ward of the king, everyone in the capital would have known about it. Someone might have figured out the secret early on—someone who'd seen authentic, unaltered pictures of Admiral Mikita. The Black Stars might not be the only ones who would have balked at the idea of Jager raising his own genius war leader to one day unleash on the Twelve Systems.

"Ah ha," Casmir said, having flipped to other articles while Kim mused. "Here's an announcement of the engagement. David Lichtenberg to marry Thea Sogard. It's just a one-line mention in their local news."

Kim looked up Thea Sogard, and a weird sensation crawled through her veins when her face came up. It was the same woman from the picture in Rache's cabin, a woman he clearly hadn't forgotten more than ten years later. She was—had been—from a rural noble family that ran vineyards and bred racehorses. Their estate was fifty miles farther down the coast from the Lichtenberg estate.

"I don't see an obituary," Casmir said, "but she went missing without warning, was searched for, and was never found."

"When did she disappear?"

"Hold on. I was trying to find any earlier mentions of her in regard to Rache. He sure competed in quite a lot of races from ages fifteen to twenty-one. And won often. It's hard to believe someone who shares my genes could be that good at racing air bikes. Between trees at a hundred miles an hour. Or maybe it's faster." He frowned at some article describing the races.

"Isn't your eye the main reason you're a klutz?"

"I'm not a klutz, schlemiel, *or* schlimazel if we're importing Yiddish terms that I was called in my youth. I simply have bad depth perception, not bad balance. Though I'm not sure I can blame my eye for a general lack of athleticism. It's mostly…" Casmir's expression shifted from indignant to thoughtful. "Come to think of it, most of the sports I was horrible at as a kid did involve throwing, catching, and hitting balls. Though even sports without balls seem to involve accurately judging the terrain around you. Bike racing, skiing, surfing, driftboarding. Maybe if I'd found some sport that you did blindfolded, I could have excelled. Is there such a thing?"

"We sometimes blindfold students in the dojo so they can learn to rely more on their other senses and hear when a bokken is whistling toward them or the rustle of a uniform as their opponent attacks." Kim hunted for other mentions of Thea.

"So I should have signed up for standing blindfolded in a room with people swinging sticks at my head? I'm not sure why my mother didn't think to suggest that." Casmir waved toward his contact. "You saw the time gap, right? When he was twenty-one, won that race, and then disappeared for months before entering another one. I don't see any articles or mentions of him during that time period."

"I did notice it. And I found the date Thea went missing. It was at the beginning of that time gap."

"I see it too. Rache was racing regularly that year. Almost every month. And then the gap. And then he comes back only long enough to die."

"I have his contact information," Kim said. "I suppose I could send him a message and ask what happened, though I'm not sure he'd tell me."

"You have his *contact* information?" Casmir stared at her.

"He gave it to me when you were setting up your kidnapped-by-Rache scheme."

"Well, that should make it easy to ask him if he would work with us instead of against us."

"Even if he agreed to that, which I doubt he would, do you truly believe Captain Ishii would go into battle with Rache's ship at his side?"

"Maybe we could simply not tell him…"

"Five minutes until we enter the gate," someone announced over the speaker.

Casmir pushed himself to his feet. "I better go strap myself to my bunk. I've heard gate travel is a weird experience. Which is probably a way of saying even more nausea-inducing than the rest of spaceflight."

Kim waved a hand as he left, but her focus was on the network search as she read more about Rache's race wins, more about Thea Sogard, and tried to find clues to hint at what had happened during that time gap in which Thea had officially been reported as missing.

Yas reported to the bridge with his medical kit, having been summoned about an injury. It had been three days since they'd flown out of the gate and into System Hydra, and there hadn't been so much as a hiccup to the gravity since then, so he didn't know what kind of injury anyone could have suffered. Had he been summoned to the recreation room or gym, where the mercenaries regularly pummeled each other, he wouldn't have been surprised. But the bridge, with Rache's briefing room and quarters nearby, was rarely a source of drama.

When he stepped out of the lift and saw the striated blue-and-white ice moon filling the forward display, his breath caught, both because Xolas Moon was beautiful and because it was in his system. He'd flown by it at a distance before, but he'd never seen it from this close up. It was striking. And looked very cold and intimidating.

As a boy, he'd even read a series of fanciful novels written about children stranded on the moon and learning to survive. Never mind that the moon's atmosphere wasn't breathable, and that the temperatures of -150C were sure to freeze unprotected visitors instantly. The children, as he recalled, had shared their adventures with a talking sled dog, who'd been stranded with them.

If the *Fedallah* flew straight to Tiamat Station, depending on where in its orbit the moon's gas giant was, they could reach it in two to three days. But the ship was orbiting Xolas, not flying past it on its way somewhere else. Looking for evidence of the astroshaman base, no doubt.

"Over here, Doctor," came Rache's cool voice from one of the monitoring stations.

He stood next to a seated lieutenant who was holding his nose, blood trickling through his fingers.

"What happened?" Yas dug into his kit for a roll of clotting bandage.

"I fell," the lieutenant said, glancing at one of the two navigation officers.

The man's back was to them, and he studied his console intently.

Rache stood behind the injured lieutenant, his arms over his chest, managing to ooze displeasure even through his mask.

"Into a fist?" Yas pulled the man's hand away and grimaced at the broken nose, cartilage crunched flat just below the bridge. "Here, press this against it."

He tore off a section of the bandage for him, then fished for painkillers, his medical scanner, and his programmable repair nanites.

"It's difficult to read anything in the ocean through the ice crust, Captain," an officer reported from the ship's small science station. "As we orbit, I'll try to find fissures where we might get a scan through. Sending a probe down wouldn't be a bad idea. Do we have probes?"

"It's not a science vessel, Neimanhaus," Rache said. "Do your best. We'll buy probes if we determine this was that cargo ship's destination. Amergin, what have you got on those satellites?"

"I've confirmed that two were set in orbit by the two planetary governments in the system to help provide whole-system network coverage, and two other satellites appear to be privately owned civilian models. I hacked into one, and it was only transmitting data related to weather and climate conditions below. I'm guessing it belongs to some corporation with interest in the moon. The second one…" Amergin swiveled in his chair and grinned. "It was too well protected for me to hack into it, but I intercepted a few transmissions that weren't encoded. Mostly boring stuff—lots of downloading of media entertainment and shopping from stores in the system—but some pedestrian messages heading to and from locations in the system with known astroshaman colonies and communities. It's not proof, mind you, and the messages themselves are nothing useful, but there's far less chatter heading off to habitats and terrestrial colonies *without* astroshaman communities."

"How many astroshaman communities are there in this system?" Rache asked. "And how many don't have a significant astroshaman presence?"

"There are four known astroshaman communities of notable size and twenty-seven human habitations without a major astroshaman presence. Enough that we can consider the results statistically significant, I should say." Amergin lifted his wide-brimmed hat and inclined his head.

Rache nodded. "Can you pinpoint what locations on the moon the transmissions are targeting?"

"Yes. They're all going to one spot. There are several bulk transmissions during periods of the moon's rotation when that spot has line-of-sight with the satellite."

"All to one spot? Can we send a shuttle down to visit it? Is it a known city or outpost?"

"Er, not exactly, sir."

Yas's patient winced as his jet injector delivered the nanites. Yas knew those always had a bite, but it seemed insignificant next to the pain of a broken nose.

"It's not an outpost," Amergin continued, "and the relay node—as I'm guessing it is—appears to be in the water under a gap in the ice."

"How *deep* in the water?" Rache asked. "It can't be too far down, or the satellite's signal would have trouble reaching it."

"Oh, not that deep, sir. About three hundred meters, maybe. But unless you've got some submarines I don't know about stored away on the ship, we won't be able to go check it out personally."

"We don't even have probes," the officer at the science station muttered, sounding truly indignant.

He wore a spiked metal collar, as well as spiked accessories to his galaxy suit, and his muscles were large enough to border on the ridiculous. Yas was certain he'd seen him go on combat missions. There was something odd about such a man complaining about a lack of proper scientific equipment.

"We can get those things if we need them," Rache said coolly, a warning note in his voice.

"Yes, sir," the man said with a few vigorous head bobs. He had to be a foot taller than Rache and weigh twice as much, but he glanced nervously at him and seemed to genuinely regret his sarcastic muttering.

"What's the moon's gravity?" Rache asked. "If we fly down to take a closer look at this fissure, will we be able to fly out again?"

"Oh, easily, sir," the navigation officer replied. "Only twenty percent of Odin's. The gravity won't be what we need to worry about when we want to leave."

"What does that mean?"

"Four Kingdom warships just flew into the system."

Rache lifted his chin. "I'm not worried about them. It'll be interesting to see where they go. If they head to this moon, it'll mean we guessed right. And more quickly than they did." He sounded a little smug.

"Yes, sir."

"Is there any point in getting closer, Amergin?" Rache asked. "I'm curious about this fissure and whether it looks like it's an entrance to the ocean the astroshamans are using."

"I think so, sir." Amergin put his hat back on and turned to his station, tapping a few controls. "From closer, we might be able to tell where that relay station is sending its transmissions to, and it's possible we'll be able to get some readings from under the ice if we're near a substantial-enough opening in it."

"Can you tell if that fissure is natural or manmade?"

"Not from up here in orbit. That's something else we might be better able to determine if we go down."

"ETA to get in and out?" Rache asked.

"About six hours to that spot on the moon, and if we go straight back up to orbit, that's a matter of minutes," Amergin said. "I'm sure I don't have to remind you that our slydar hull won't be as effective at hiding us in atmosphere. It would be worse on a planet like Odin, but the disturbance of our passing would be detectable to someone looking in the right spot, and we'll make a shadow if we go down on the sunny side."

"Understood," Rache said. "Lieutenant Woo, take us to Amergin's fissure."

"Oh, we're naming it after me?" Amergin asked. "I'm honored. I'd prefer to have a mountain or canyon or something more substantial named after me, but I guess you have to start wrestling smaller pigs."

Yas crinkled his brow at the metaphor but focused on Rache instead. "*Is* it likely that the Kingdom ships will be looking for you? Us?"

He reluctantly admitted that as long as he was on the *Fedallah*, he was essentially one of the mercenaries. He would be fired on, the same as they would, if the ship flew into battle.

"They know I tried to get the gate before. I'd be surprised if they don't believe I'm still determined to keep them from getting it. They may not suspect we're ahead of them, but if I were them, I wouldn't underestimate our team."

"My nose itches, Doctor," Yas's patient complained.

"Nanites are fixing your smashed cartilage."

"Do they have to do it itchily?" The officer's fingers twitched upward, as if he couldn't control them.

"Yes. It's how you know they're working."

Yas was amazed that the mercenaries had no trouble walking into battle and getting their limbs blown off, but then complained about tiny discomforts.

"Maybe it would make sense to skip investigating with the ship," Yas told Rache, "and go straight to Tiamat Station to buy some submarines."

"They make them?" Rache sounded surprised.

"Yes. There are a number of tourist outfits based out of the station that take people to the water worlds, and you can rent equipment. The manufacturing is cheaper in space, and there's a zero-g industrial annex anchored near Tiamat."

"Cheaper?" Rache tilted his head slightly. "I'm looking at the network site for WaterZoom, the manufacturing facility based out of your station, and it looks like a model large enough to fit six people is two hundred thousand crowns. No, Union dollars. That's even worse."

"It's something you buy as an investment if you're starting a tourism business."

"Are the margins better on that than on the mercenary business?" Rache asked dryly.

"I think that's a question for your accountant. I'm your doctor, remember."

"Ah."

"They rent them out," Yas said. "Maybe you can rent one."

"What kind of damage deposit would be required for a notorious mercenary?"

"Probably a high one. I assume you have fake names."

"I'll look into it more closely," Rache said, "but take us down to the fissure, Woo. I'm not making a trip to pick up submarines unless I know the astroshamans and the gate are down there."

Yas told himself not to be disappointed that Rache hadn't jumped at the opportunity to head to the station. Even if he had, it wouldn't have been an opportunity for Yas to meander through the streets and parks with Jess—or anybody else. Until his name was cleared, he couldn't go anywhere near those parks. He forced aside a twinge of homesickness, reminding himself that Rache had promised to work on his problem next.

His gaze drifted toward a small display someone had brought up that showed the four blips representing the Kingdom warships as they moved away from the gate and into the system.

Yas tried not to think about Amergin's statement that they wouldn't be as camouflaged down on the moon, and he also tried not to guess how the *Fedallah* would do in a battle against that many warships. He had a feeling he didn't want to know.

CHAPTER 13

ON THE *OSPREY'S* FOURTH DAY IN SYSTEM HYDRA, Casmir was called to the captain's briefing room. He put his tools away—he'd been doing a few repairs to Tork, damage left from his handlers and also from the times he'd grappled with Zee on the shuttle—and headed to the lift.

Knowing Ishii didn't trust Tork, Casmir had been leaving him in his cabin, and he only took Zee along. It would take time before any of them truly knew if they could trust Tork, so Casmir couldn't object to leaving him out of important planning meetings. Assuming that was what this was.

When he crossed the bridge to the briefing room, he found Kim, Grunburg, and Asger already seated at the large oval table inside, along with several of Ishii's department heads and two high-ranking marines. Unfortunately, Lieutenant Meister from Intelligence was also there. He smiled easily at Casmir, and Casmir made himself nod back, but he hadn't forgotten the probing conversation in the gym.

Casmir slid into an empty seat next to Kim. Zee stood against the wall behind them. Kim quirked an eyebrow at his silent presence.

"Do you really have a reputation among the robots of the system?" she asked.

A few other conversations were going on at the table while the officers waited for the captain.

"I'm not sure." Casmir had also wondered about that comment, and about what robots Tork had been in contact with.

As far as he knew, there was no dedicated network for androids and quasi-intelligent computers in the Kingdom. That didn't mean there couldn't be an underground one though. Ever since artificial intelligences had left their home worlds and habitats in droves to claim Verloren Moon for themselves, most governments had been careful to put a ceiling on how intelligent computers and robots could legally be made. He didn't know if he found it natural or alarming that the robots of the system might have a way to communicate with each other without using the public network.

"I guess it's better to have a good reputation than a bad one," Kim said.

"Yes, maybe I'll be spared if there's ever a robot uprising."

"That's not very funny."

"Don't worry. I'll stand in front of you so you're protected."

"That would be more comforting if you were taller than I am. And knew how to do a decent roundhouse kick."

"You have such stringent demands for a bodyguard. I don't think Zee knows roundhouse kicks, and look how effective he is."

Ishii came in, and the conversations around the table ended.

"We're a day from Xolas Moon and three days from Tiamat Station," he said without preamble as he settled into the deck-locked chair at the head of the table. "The latter is relevant because it's the closest location for submarines."

"Submarines, sir?" one of the sturdy marine officers asked, his buzz-cut hair speckled with gray.

"We've been told the gate was likely taken to an underwater base on Xolas. Submarines would be the only way to reach it. And if we intend to attack the base in order to take the gate, we'll need plenty of them. Fortunately, the Kingdom has a good relationship with the new president of Tiamat Station. Perhaps we could borrow the necessary craft instead of being forced to purchase them. They're not inexpensive."

"Sir," the marine said, glancing at his fellow officer, "while my men and I are ready for an infantry incursion in any setting, land, air, or… underwater, it seems unwise to attack them on their own ground. Especially if they're expecting an attack. Is there no way we could flush them out?"

"For that matter," Grunburg said, "how would they have gotten the gate down to an underwater base in the first place? From what we saw when we battled them, their cargo ship was a spaceship, no different from ours."

"Not *no* different," Ishii said. "They had that irritating stealth generator and who knows what other technology our Intelligence people are unaware of?"

Meister frowned at this slight to *Intelligence people.*

"Dabrowski," Ishii said. "You were on that ship. Did you see anything that would suggest it had some sort of amphibious capabilities?"

"No, but I wasn't looking for anything like that. I'm not the expert on spaceships, but isn't it possible they landed or lowered the gate pieces down to the ice, and they were transferred to this base by submarines?"

"It is possible. I wish we had more proof that this base exists and that this is the right spot." Ishii looked at Kim for the first time.

She turned her palm toward the ceiling. "I could only determine that it's likely that Tork originated in or spent significant time in this system recently."

"Yes, it's Tork who told us about this base specifically." Ishii grimaced and looked at Meister.

"There are a *lot* of rumors on the network, especially the network here in System Hydra, of an underwater base and shrine for the astroshamans. I'm actually inclined to believe it exists and is on the ice moon. I think if they were flying in and out of the two water worlds—the two fairly heavily populated water worlds—they would have been spotted numerous times and their base would be reality rather than a rumor."

"They may know we're coming," the older marine officer said. "Rented submarines designed for scientists and tourists to use would not be ideal troop carriers."

"We've got some manufacturing capabilities in the lower decks," Ishii said. "We could beef them up. But I do concede your point, Colonel. I'd prefer to use some trickery to flush them out before attempting a forward assault."

The colonel's bunched shoulders relaxed slightly. "Yes, Captain. Good."

"That may be more possible now that we have a face and a name of one of the astroshamans involved," Ishii said.

Casmir sat straighter in his chair. Did that mean Intelligence had identified the owner of that strand of hair?

Ishii extended a hand toward Meister, who tapped at controls built into the table, and a holographic photograph of someone's head appeared in the middle. The woman had bronze skin, milky whitish blue eyes, and short white hair swept back as if she'd exited a wind tunnel. Casmir couldn't tell if the eyes signified blindness or that she had some high-powered contacts that hid her irises. Other than that, she appeared fully human, at least on the outside. Not all of the astroshamans got cybernetics that identified them as blatant hybrids, but it did seem to be a hallmark of the religion, perhaps a way they easily identified each other when they traveled.

"This is Kyla Moonrazor, one of the high shamans of the religion," Meister said, "and the owner of the strand of hair that Professor Dabrowski picked up."

"I *thought* it looked too light to be mine. And I was pretty sure it wasn't Zee's." Casmir smiled and waved at his silent bodyguard.

Nobody else smiled. Most of their faces had grown serious at the appearance of the holo picture.

Casmir ran a quick search on the name. So far, he'd found that his access to the System Hydra public network was limited, and he wondered if the various servers and routers had a list of chip numbers of Kingdom subjects and restricted what databases they could poke into.

Moonrazor appeared, first as a teenager more than fifty years earlier, apprehended for a number of juvenile crimes on the cloud city of Nuevo Caracas on Nabia. In her twenties, she had received three degrees from two different universities, all in systems engineering and programming. She also had numerous certificates of mastery for various programming languages. In her fifties, she'd left her lucrative job at a software company and disappeared for years. Family members had proclaimed her dead. Ten years ago, she'd reappeared, named as a leader of the astroshamans but with no known residence listed. She had consulted—that was the term used, but it had quotation marks around it—with several mercenary outfits that attacked government installations throughout the systems, including a couple of hits back in System Lion. Unlike Rache, she didn't seem to target the Kingdom specifically, but she was one of the few astroshamans listed with a criminal record and the only one with a warrant out for her arrest in multiple systems.

"I think we can assume she made the virus," Meister said, "and is smart enough to have found the cargo ship that Dabrowski *thought* he hid." His eyebrow twitched.

"I didn't know I was hiding it from someone with more degrees than I have," Casmir said.

"Just us idiots in the Fleet?" Ishii asked.

Casmir hesitated, then opened his mouth.

Kim elbowed him. "There's no way you can answer that without irking him," she muttered.

"Right." Casmir folded his hands on the table and did his best to appear politely attentive.

Ishii still looked disgusted, but he returned his focus to Meister. "Can you dig around and see if we can confirm that she's in the system?"

"I've looked for recent mentions of her, but nothing came up in the news feeds. Since that cargo ship has stealth technology, it's unlikely anyone recorded it coming into the system. Though maybe I can find out if there was a gate activation where a ship *didn't* come through, much as the one we recorded of a ship not leaving the system."

Ishii snorted. "Let's just hope that stealth technology isn't widespread."

"I don't think so, sir. I haven't found any mentions of it on the public network. But there are numerous rumors of the astroshamans having some more advanced devices than the rest of the systems."

"No kidding."

"Maybe we could try talking to her," Casmir suggested. "Do the astroshamans have a network portal with information on joining their organization?"

Ishii gave him a dark look.

"Casmir enjoys chatting with his enemies and trying to learn things directly from them," Asger said.

"I doubt the contact form on their generic network portals goes to her inbox," Meister murmured. "You'd probably get to chat with some lowly janitor that scrubs the floors in their shrine."

"Such a person might know quite a bit and be easier to get information out of," Casmir said. "Even better, maybe there's a robot that would answer our communication."

Ishii snorted and started to make a chopping motion with his hand, but he paused, eyed Zee, and then eyed Casmir again. "I suppose if anyone could suborn an enemy robot and inveigle information from it, it would be you. I…" Ishii trailed off, his eyes growing distant as he read some message on his contacts. "Shit. Wait here."

He stalked out of the briefing room and into what looked like a private office.

Murmurs started up around the table, a few people glancing at Casmir. He couldn't tell if they were hostile or puzzled glances. Or hostilely puzzled glances.

"I'm wondering why I was invited to this meeting," Kim murmured when he looked her way. "Ishii didn't ask for anything from me."

"Did you help with the hair analysis?"

"His forensics people did have me check for bacteria on it. It read similarly to Tork, meaning they both probably came from the same system."

"And meaning we may get to face a nemesis who can out-program and out-clever me? That should be fun."

"My corporation, Parvus Biologia, has a small lab on Tiamat Station. Maybe I'll reach out to my colleagues there and see if they know anything beyond what Military Intelligence knows."

Casmir nodded, but Ishii returned before he could say anything. The room fell silent again.

"There's been an incident at Tiamat Station, and we've been ordered to assist, so we'll be heading straight there." Ishii looked at the marine colonel. "Run some station infiltration drills and prep your men for combat."

"Yes, sir."

"Dismissed." Ishii stalked out to the bridge without further explanation.

The rest of his officers filed out, leaving Casmir alone with Kim and Asger and Zee.

"Only in the military would orders to *assist* involve prepping marines for combat," Casmir said ruefully.

Asger frowned. "It sounds like there may have been an invasion. I'll check the news." He turned his frown onto Casmir. "You don't think Rache would bother a civilian station, do you?"

"I suppose it would depend if someone was paying him to." Casmir shrugged. "I thought he was focused on getting the gate, though, so you wouldn't think he would take side jobs."

"I guess we'll find out soon enough." Asger pushed himself to his feet and walked out.

"Is that true? Will *we* find out anything?" Casmir met Kim's gaze. "Or will we be shuffled off to the side and kept in the dark until the incident is handled?"

"I don't know, but I now have even more of a reason to contact Parvus Biologia's Tiamat Station branch," Kim said. "I've met one of the researchers there a few times. I'm going to be distressed if he's in danger because some mercenaries or other hostile invasion fleet have decided to claim the station."

"Is that likely?" Casmir rubbed his head. "I know we've been hearing that the systems are on the brink of war, and the Kingdom is somehow wrapped up in it, but this is our first time encountering anything first-hand."

"It's also our first time going to a new system. I would normally have heard if something major was going on in any of the other systems where my corporation has labs, but it's been months now since I've been in to work back home. I've been receiving the generic company announcements, but I haven't been contacted specifically by anyone since I let them know I've been pressed into government work." She shrugged. "I'll reach out to my contact and see if he can update me."

"Good. I'll see what I can dig up in the system news."

"I," Zee said, "will stand by assiduously and protect Kim Sato and Casmir Dabrowski while they work."

Kim glanced at him. "He's definitely gotten more personality."

"Chattier too," Casmir said. "I like it."

"You could definitely suborn and inveigle an enemy robot."

"I'm hoping I already did that." Casmir waved vaguely, indicating Tork in his cabin several levels below.

"Me too," Kim said.

Casmir smiled, hoping it didn't come across as bleak. If he *hadn't,* they might have a lot of trouble on their hands when they faced this Moonrazor and all her astroshaman buddies. In a submarine under kilometers of ice and water.

Kim was standing in her lab in sickbay, doing some research into Princess Oku's bee problem, when the response she'd been waiting for came in. Scholar Tom Chi sent a request for a live video call rather than a simple text message, and she put aside her work to answer it.

"Scholar Sato?" The man she remembered as being round-faced and quick to smile had new crow's feet edging his eyes and a tense, worried expression as he spoke loudly to make himself heard.

Clatters and shouts in the background made it difficult to understand him, and she focused on his face.

"Yes. What's going on, Scholar Chi? I can't hear you well."

The ship was still a day from the station, and there was a pause of a few seconds before his response came back.

"That's because there's chaos everywhere here. I'm locked in my lab, but—" A bang sounded, and he shifted out of focus as he leaned forward to look at something.

Kim tried to figure out where in his lab he might be, since there was a gray background, and he appeared to be hunching under a low ceiling. Was he under a *desk*?

"Door's still locked." He leaned back into view. "I'm all right for now. They *shouldn't* target me, but you never know. Innocent people are being shot."

"*Who* shouldn't target you?" Kim had looked on the news for talk of some invasion fleet or attack on the station, but she hadn't found anything, not on the limited public network she could access.

She clenched her fist, annoyed at the lag. Chi looked like he was in danger at that very second.

"The station inhabitants," Chi said. "It's civil war in here right now. Did you see the news? About our new president visiting King Jager on Odin personally? Were you there for that? Wait, where are you *now*? I'm sorry, I've been distracted. I only just realized that you have to be in System Hydra for us to be having this communication. Scholar Sato? Did the corporation send you or…?"

"It's a long story. I essentially got drafted by the government, and I'm on one of four warships that have been ordered to assist with the trouble at Tiamat, but I'm just a civilian advisor. Nobody's told me what the trouble is."

Chi's face vacillated between horror and greater horror as her words played for him. There might have been more emotions in there, but Kim wasn't adept enough to read them on his face. All she could tell was that her news distressed him, and she thought it was more that the warships were coming. Her corporation was apolitical, with headquarters in three systems, so he shouldn't professionally fear the Kingdom, but if he was among the inhabitants that opposed a Kingdom presence in the station, he might personally object to their arrival.

"Warships are coming?" Chi gaped at her. "*Kingdom* warships? I may be… Damn, damn."

The view blurred again as he leaned too close to the camera to look at something else.

"There's already been talk of taking hostages," he continued, "and bartering them to the Kingdom representative here to talk them into leaving Tiamat alone. I'm afraid that since Parvus Biologia has a headquarters on Odin, they might think *I'd* make a good hostage. Maybe they don't know about me. Hardly anyone pays attention to my work on this station. Most of our clients visit from elsewhere, like Shango Habitat. Their princess is here right now. She got stuck when the riots broke out." Chi groaned, letting his head thunk back against the desk behind him.

Kim didn't know what to say. This wasn't anywhere close to the mission she'd been drafted for, and she suddenly felt uneasy, since she'd answered his comm on an open channel. If officers on the bridge—or in the Intelligence office—were bored, they might be monitoring her contact with the station. Or maybe all outgoing messages would be automatically recorded for security purposes. She was sympathetic to her colleague, but she had to be careful not to say something that might incriminate her.

"Perhaps the appearance of the Kingdom warships will end the conflict," Kim said.

Chi shook his head. "You're not here. You don't know the hatred that's fueling people. And the fear—a lot of the citizens here are genetically modded and are terrified they'll be exiled, or worse, if the Kingdom takes over. I'm afraid those warships will only make everything escalate. Scholar Sato, is there anything you can do? I need help, if only to get out of here with my research. There have been explosions, and I'm afraid our lab is in danger, and oh dear, the princess. She came because she's a customer, picking up bacteria to help with biodiversity and improve the health of the birds on her station, and now she's trapped. I feel responsible. We're the only reason she's here."

"I empathize, but I don't know what I can do. I'm just a science advisor."

"I don't suppose you can tell them there's an outbreak of a virulent new strand of *Mycobacterium leprae*? And that people's limbs are falling off left and right all over the station, so they dare not come close?"

"I'm sure Captain Ishii's doctors would be able to recognize and treat leprosy even if I wasn't here," Kim said.

"Something more exotic then. I could make something up. Or I could *make* something." A dangerous, manic light entered his eyes.

Kim swallowed, afraid he wasn't joking. That he was desperate enough to try something like that. What if he thought he could make some horrible virus that would only affect those from the Kingdom? She could think of a few ways it might be possible, and she had no doubt her colleague could too.

Kim lifted her hands in the air in what she hoped was a calming gesture. "Don't do anything drastic, please, Scholar Chi. I'll talk to a friend of mine. He specializes in crazy ideas. Maybe we can figure out a way to help get you out."

"Could you? And my freezers? We've been working on all manner of flora and fauna bacterial enhancements to help plants and animals thrive on the ever-expanding number of space habitats around the systems."

"I don't suppose you've done any work with insects lately? And, uh, how *many* freezers? Can you pack everything up to be portable?" Kim tugged on her braid, wondering how she was going to convince Captain Ishii to take aboard a Kingdom-hating scientist with a daisy-chain of freezers strung out behind him.

Maybe Chi just needed help getting to a shuttle bay in the station, and he could find civilian transport from there. Though she feared it wouldn't be that easy. The station was probably on a lockdown.

"We do have several insect experiments ongoing," Chi said. "I'm currently attempting to genetically rewire spiders so that they can spin their webs in low-gravity environments. Have you read my papers?"

"Not the recent ones. I do remember some tinkering you were doing last year to help birds lay eggs on space stations."

"Indeed, yes. The chicken egg is a staple on Mawu Habitat. They paid the corporation quite handsomely for a solution to their eggless coops. When will you be here? Is there any chance you can get me off *before* your warships arrive?"

How was she supposed to do that when she was *on* one of the warships? Toss on a pair of wings and fly ahead of it?

"Let me talk to my friend. He's clever." And excellent at scheming ways to get into trouble. What were the odds that Casmir could scheme up a way to get Chi *out* of trouble?

He probably could, especially if they brought in Asger and his private shuttle, but at what cost? Casmir was already in Jager's sights. This might make matters worse for him. Maybe she shouldn't bring this to him. Maybe she should try to come up with something on her own. But what? Asger was more Casmir's friend—and was supposed to be keeping an eye on him—than Kim's. If anyone was going to talk him into taking his shuttle out against Ishii's wishes, it would be Casmir. And Casmir also had Zee. And apparently Tork now too. They were as good as a couple of armored marines. Maybe better since they would be loyal to him rather than some Fleet chain of command.

Kim forced herself to smile, since Chi still wore a worried expression. "I'll get back to you soon. I promise."

A bang and what sounded like gunfire came over the comm, and Chi jerked, cracking his head on the desk above him. "Good. Thank you. Hurry, please. My work is very important. I'm sure the corporation will talk to your king on my behalf if you incur someone's wrath to help me."

The channel went dead.

Parvus Biologia *was* powerful and did have deep pockets. Maybe it was possible that their chief operations officer could sway the king if need be.

Though ideally, Kim could help Chi with his problem with*out* getting herself or Casmir into trouble.

Casmir? She sent a message to his chip. *Will you come by when you get time? I have a new problem, and I need someone schemy to brainstorm with.*

Schemy? Is that a legitimate adjective?

It seems to describe you effectively.

Asger is forcing me to lift heavy weights and bounce on a trampoline with cables pulling me down, all to keep my muscles from atrophying in half-gravity. I think this is why people transfer their consciousnesses into android bodies. To avoid the evils of exercise. What's your mother's opinion on trampolines?

We haven't discussed them. Kim grimaced. She hadn't received so much as a brief update from her mother since leaving her on the *Machu Picchu* and had no idea if she was still on the research vessel or even in System Lion. But then, she hadn't sent her mother any updates either. She wished she knew how to have a relationship with her.

No? Odd. I thought mothers and daughters discussed all manner of important things.

Such as trampolines?

They are on my mind since—ow, this crazy knight is torturing me. How much would I have to pay you to come up and beat him with your wooden sticks?

More than you're getting paid.

I'm still not getting paid anything.

Exactly. Casmir—

No, I got it. As soon as I can escape him, I'll come see you. Schemily. Also not a word.

And yet, also appropriate for you.

Thank you. You're fabulous too.

Kim checked to make sure she had a recording of Chi's message, so she could show it to Casmir. He would need all the details, or as many details as she had.

She wished she'd gotten further on her research of bee bacteria, so she would have something to trade him when asking for a favor. Not that he would want anything in exchange. He would help her simply because he was her friend. And he would get himself in trouble for the same reason.

She grimaced and hoped it wouldn't come to that.

CHAPTER 14

"WHAT DO YOU THINK, DOC?"

Yas considered the ragged edges of the blueish-brown mole he had been called up to the bridge to inspect—a medical emergency, Neimanhaus had proclaimed over the comm. "It might be cancerous. I can biopsy it and take a look."

"Cancer!" Neimanhaus twisted his arm around so he could look at the suspicious growth near his elbow.

"Told you," one of the navigation officers said. "We all get it out here. Doesn't matter how modded you are. Radiation gets ya eventually."

"But *I've* never gotten it."

Perhaps not, but Neimanhaus had visited sickbay no fewer than six times in the scant months Yas had been on board, complaining of everything from itchy skin, to abdominal pains, to foot cramps, to a weird tickle in the back of his throat that wouldn't go away. He certainly seemed a magnet for afflictions. This was the first time he'd called Yas to the bridge. Yas gathered that heckling about the mole from nearby mercenaries had worked Neimanhaus into a panicked state.

This wasn't the best time for that since Neimanhaus was supposed to be keeping an eye on the scanners to make sure the captain and his team didn't get any surprises. The *Fedallah* was flying lazy circles around a deep fissure in the ice below while Rache investigated closer. He'd taken a shuttle that was small enough to fly into the narrow gap and land on a ledge.

As far as Yas had heard, this was one of only a handful of spots on the moon where the water was exposed to the surface. Periodically, hot geysers shot up, spattering the surrounding terrain before the water froze into lumpy mounds around the area.

Now, Rache's team was tramping around on the ledge, taking readings and examining the ice. The officers on the bridge were split between watching the men via the forward display and snickering at Neimanhaus's problem.

"It might be nothing." Yas dug into the large medical kit he'd chosen to bring up, expecting a more grievous injury to deal with. He selected a fine needle for aspiration. "Let me take a sample."

"You can take the whole thing. It's ugly."

"Yeah, take the whole thing," the navigation officer said. "He'll never get a woman to sleep with him with that thing leering at her from his arm."

"My mole is still better looking than your face, you ass." Neimanhaus gave his comrade a screw-you finger gesture that would have been more effective if he weren't still twisting his arm at an awkward angle for the exam. He turned to face Yas with urgent eyes. "Doc, I can't die from cancer. I want to go out in a big battle where I save everyone's lives."

"Noble." Yas drew a tiny sample and stuck it in his portable examiner, the computer humming to life to analyze the tissue.

"We've located the node," Rache's voice came over the comm. It was easy to pick him out on the ice, even though everyone wore the same black combat armor. He was shorter than the other men and also pointing into the water. "The ice is thinner in this polar area than on most of the moon, but the node is still hundreds of meters below the surface here. We're reading cables running from it in two directions. They look like power cables, so there's probably a fusion generator down there, unless the astroshamans are using the geothermal vents for energy. It's possible we could follow those cables to their base."

Rache walked along the edge of the water, adjusting his scanner.

"I'm still trying to find proof that there *is* a base," he added dryly. "The ice blocks our readings, which I'm sure is why they might have chosen this spot."

"Sounds like the submarines are our best bet, sir," someone else on the channel said.

As Rache walked farther, the gap in the ice widened. It still wasn't large enough that a substantial ship could fly into it, but Yas didn't think there were any spaceships with amphibious capabilities, anyway.

Rache knelt close to the edge, running a black-gloved hand along the ice. He shifted back a few feet away and crouched to study something else on the frozen shelf.

"It looks like a ship landed here, or maybe some big machinery was brought up," Rache mused aloud. "A crane? There are fresh scrape marks along the edge there, like something large was lowered down." He shifted to examine different locations along the edge of the shelf. Rare excitement crept into his voice as he added, "A *lot* of somethings."

"The gate pieces?" Corporal Chaplain asked, his flat voice easy to recognize. "Are they waterproof?"

Rache snorted. "I hope so. Or I hope the astroshamans had time to wrap them with something protective."

Yas hadn't yet seen the gate pieces himself, which seemed unfair since he'd been exposed to the pseudo radiation and almost died from it, but he knew from seeing the live gates in the network that the pieces had to be huge. He imagined them wrapped in the insulating and protective molds that some of his medications were shipped in. Or maybe bubble wrap.

"Captain," Yas said, a new thought popping into his mind, "I want to point out that we don't know exactly how far that pseudo radiation can go or how close people need to be to the gates to activate its defenses. If that base isn't that far from you… I still have some of Scholar Sato's bacteria, but we would have to return to a more advanced medical facility to treat anyone if they were exposed."

"I think we'd get energy readings from the astroshamans' base if we were anywhere close to it," Rache said, "but I concede your point. Neimanhaus, how far away are those Kingdom ships now?"

"Er." Neimanhaus had been squinting at Yas's examiner, waiting for the results, but he spun back to his station. "Less than a day, but it doesn't look like they're angling for this moon."

"No?" Rache's head came up, like a dog sniffing the wind. "Did their clues lead them to some other destination?"

Maybe it was Yas's imagination, but Rache seemed to sound disappointed. Did he *want* a battle with four Kingdom warships? Did he think he could best them and leave their wreckage scattered across the ice? Thus far, he'd been fairly prudent about avoiding battles if the odds were against him or there was nothing to be gained, but who knew what went through the man's head?

“They’re on course for Tiamat Station,” Neimanhaus said.

“They may already know they need submarines. Unless there’s something going on at Tiamat this week. Someone check the news feeds.” Rache turned back toward the shuttle, waving for his men to return as well.

Neimanhaus’s fingers darted across his console, though he glanced several times at his elbow and at Yas’s examiner as he worked. News feeds scrolled down a display in front of him. Wanting to put him out of his misery, Yas focused on his tissue analysis instead of the news. Until Neimanhaus whistled and spoke again.

“Looks like there’s a big kerfuffle at Tiamat Station, sir. Civil war, some reporters are calling it. Rumored to be dozens killed so far and hundreds injured.”

“*What?*” Yas fumbled the medical device, almost dropping it.

Civil *war*? In his home? And people dead?

His parents were there. His old colleagues. Fear clashed with regret in his gut. He should have contacted his parents and let them know what was going on. He hadn’t wanted them to be implicated in his crime, or accused of aiding him. And, he cowardly admitted, he had been afraid they would believe the reports that he’d killed the president—the *former* president. This new president who was buddy-buddy with the Kingdom was the reason for all this. Former Vice President Chronis. Yas wanted to strangle him.

“Looks true,” Neimanhaus said. “Lots of different reports from around the system, and look at this sexy blonde. She’s reporting from under a table in a cafeteria. Wish I was there to help her. You know, protect her so she’d feel grateful and want to jump in my bunk.”

“Nobody’s going to jump in your bunk as long as that thing is on your elbow, Neimanhaus,” the navigation officer said.

“Shut up, Marks.”

Yas poked Neimanhaus on the shoulder, wanting his full attention on the search. “See if you can find a list of the dead.”

Yas couldn’t imagine that his sixty-something-year-old parents would have been out running around someplace they might get shot, but what if this internal conflict involved more than simple fighting over sides? What if people started taking hostages or shooting influential people? His parents had wealth and influence—at least they had under the old regime. Who knew what they had now? They might seem like easy targets.

"Blondie looks too busy to publish lists like that," Neimanhaus said, "and she's the only one reporting from inside the station."

"News anchorwoman Zoe Demopoulos," Yas supplied numbly, "and it's usually brown hair, though it was green and blue briefly last year when she lost a bet on the air."

Neimanhaus looked over his shoulder. "Oh, is this where you're from, Doc?"

"Yes." Yas stared at the video of Zoe reporting—she ducked as some projectile flew by. In the background, someone drove a duct-cleaning vehicle over a table, crunching it flat.

"Sir," Marks said. "I'm reading something new under the water. Looks too small to be a ship—or a submarine—but something is heading your way. Actually, it looks like four somethings."

Yas barely heard the words, and it wasn't until someone cursed and shouted a warning over the team's comm channel that he tore his gaze from the small news report to look at the bridge's large forward display.

He almost dropped his examiner again at what he saw.

Four drones shot out of the water and streamed bursts of rapid-fire energy bolts. The team was still out in the open on the ice, fifty yards from the shuttle.

Two of the drones fired at the men, tracking them with deadly accuracy—and power. One man took a hit to the shoulder, and even though his armor protected him, the force behind the blast hurled him ten feet. He skidded across the ice, and only a wild roll kept him from being hit again.

The other two drones flew toward the shuttle, but Rache and Chaplain fired relentlessly at them until they turned away.

A couple of the men sprinted for the shuttle, zigzagging their paths. Rache and Chaplain stayed back, blasting at the drones even as they jumped and dove to evade sizzling pale blue bolts of energy that blew craters in the ice when they hit. Shards flew everywhere, and cracks appeared on the shelf.

"Shit," someone said, "they better get out of there before the ice breaks and the shuttle falls through."

"Can you fly us down there to help them?" Neimanhaus asked.

"Negative. The fissure is too narrow for the *Fedallah*. We could fly above it and shoot some nukes, but that would be overkill and likely to hurt our own team."

"Hurry, hurry," Yas whispered, his eyes locked on Rache and Chaplain, frustrated that they were staying behind, as if they *wanted* to be hit, while the other two men escaped into the shuttle. Yas was even more surprised to realize that he cared what happened to them. Maybe not to Chaplain, whom he'd never spoken more than five sentences to, but Rache was… he didn't know what. His only way to clear his name, at the least.

"They're drawing the fire on purpose," Neimanhaus said. "So the others can get the shuttle in the air."

Rache and Chaplain hit the drones several times, but they were armored, and the DEW-Tek bolts ricocheted off. One drone zipped down low, flying straight at Rache, strafing the ice and blowing holes as it came in.

Yas expected Rache to dive to the side, but he waited until the bolts were slamming into ice scant inches from his feet. Then, instead of jumping aside, he sprang straight up, fifteen feet into the air, and swung his rifle like a club—and with the power of a wrecking ball.

It slammed into the drone, knocking it from its path. The channel was still open, and the sound of the crunch filled the bridge like thunder erupting.

Chaplain kept sustained fire on the second drone as it focused on Rache, firing mercilessly, as if furious that he had destroyed its mechanical comrade. How much armor did the thing have? The bolts started burning through instead of ricocheting off. Abruptly, it veered toward the water, trying to escape Chaplain. Just before it dove in, it exploded.

The shuttle lifted up, thrusters melting ice. Yas gripped the back of Neimanhaus's chair, afraid the rest of the team intended to leave Rache and Chaplain.

The remaining two drones kept firing at the shuttle, but it zipped straight toward the armored men. It tilted on its side, the hatch open, but not slowing down. Rache and Chaplain had to time it perfectly. Yas held his breath as they sprang ten feet to throw themselves through the hatch.

The drones pelted the shuttle with energy bolts, but it shot away, the hatch slamming shut. It picked up speed as it flew toward the *Fedallah*, and the drones fell behind.

"We've got our shuttle-bay doors open, right?" someone asked.

"Yes, sir."

The forward display lost track of the shuttle as it whipped around the ship toward the bay, but an officer soon reported, "Shuttle safe on board."

"Good. Get us back up to a safe orbit."

Yas sagged with relief as they left the ice far behind and flew back up toward the stars. But he didn't know how long that relief would last. His parents were in danger, and Rache now had the proof he'd sought that the astroshamans' secret base, or at least something worth defending, was under the ice.

Casmir rubbed his chin as the video of Kim's colleague's half of the conversation played on the tablet propped on her desk. They were in her cabin, her in the chair this time and him sitting cross-legged on the end of the bed.

"Is that someone *shooting* in the background?" he asked as the conversation neared its end. "Like with guns with chemically-propelled bullets? Is that even allowed on a space station?"

"I don't think rioters care that much about obeying the law."

"It sounds really bad there. If Ishii knows exactly what's going on, he hasn't told me."

"Are you surprised?" Kim asked.

"No, I'm not his confidant."

"Do you think Asger is?"

"Not really. Asger has given me the impression that he got in trouble for losing the gate—for helping me—and that he's fairly low in the pecking order of knights, as it is. I don't think he's known Ishii much longer than I have. Technically, I'm sure he hasn't, though there was a gap of twenty-two years when Ishii and I never ran into each other."

"No reunions for summer robotics camp, huh?"

"Oddly not. Maybe I should put something together when I get home. Do you want me to call Asger down here to see this?" Casmir pointed at the video.

Kim hesitated. "It did occur to me that he has a shuttle. But I'd hate to get him—or you—into hot water over this. I've been thinking… maybe Ishii would help if I asked him. Even if this isn't my corporation's Kingdom branch, and Chi is far from a loyal subject, maybe Ishii would see the value of getting a scientist and freezers full of valuable specimens and interesting research projects out of a danger zone."

"Are the interesting projects genetically engineered?"

"Possibly. We don't do much of that kind of work on Odin, but the headquarters and laboratories in the other systems aren't so constrained."

"Don't mention that to Ishii if you ask him."

"Do you think I *should* ask him?"

Casmir bit back his natural response to flippantly point out that Ishii was paying her so he must like her a lot more than him. Kim's colleague was in danger, and she seriously wanted his advice.

"If we don't go through him, we'll get in trouble, and if we ask Asger to use his shuttle to take us over there, we'll get him in trouble too. I was hoping to avoid doing that again." Casmir smiled sadly. "But I think Ishii's primary, and perhaps only, concern is going to be… whatever his orders are exactly. And if he believes we'll be in the way, he'll never let us go."

Casmir let his gaze drift to the video. It had ended, but Scholar Chi's worried face was frozen on the screen.

"I'm guessing he has orders to stop the riots and trouble," Casmir said, "by whatever means are necessary. Unfortunately, the means he seems prepared to use could make matters worse. Even if he's able to force the citizens to calm down, is it likely a company of marines can do that without injuring a bunch of people and jailing others? Make that *four* companies of marines. The other warships are heading to Tiamat Station too. If our people end up killing some of the Tiamat citizens, however inadvertently, it's only going to give them more fuel for their hatred of the Kingdom."

As Casmir spoke, he realized the problem wasn't just finding a way to get Kim's friend out but finding a solution that wouldn't turn the Kingdom into heinous warmongering conquerors in the eyes of Tiamat Station.

"You don't think we should talk to Ishii, then?" Kim looked dubious, even though she'd claimed she needed a schemer when she'd called him down.

Casmir knew she preferred to be straightforward and wasn't one to skirt the law. Usually.

"I don't think he'll let us go, but I also don't think we should—or even could—blindside him by trying to sneak away with a shuttle," Casmir said. "There's not even any point in that until we're at the station, because the warship can accelerate a lot faster than those little combat shuttles."

"Scholar Chi seemed worried about what would happen when the warships showed up on their doorstep."

"Yeah, I got that." Casmir waved at the video. "But they're going to show up. I don't think we can stop that. But maybe we can alter what Ishii plans to do once we get there. Do you mind sharing that video with him?"

"No." Kim grabbed the tablet. "I would rather have his permission than not."

"That's because you're his favorite civilian advisor, and you don't want him to take your bed away."

"I also don't want him to think we're betraying the Kingdom and shoot at us if we try to sneak away in a shuttle."

"But it's mostly about the bed, right?" Casmir smiled and waved for her to accompany him to Ishii's office, Zee silently trailing behind them. He sent a note to Asger, asking if he would join them, and giving him a quick warning about what it would entail. "Do you want to do the talking or should I?"

Kim debated that for a while, and they were in the lift before she responded. "I'm not sure. I'm not good at finagling people, but you're not good at keeping from annoying Ishii."

"Maybe we could ask Zee to do the talking."

"That doesn't sound like a good idea. The new personality he's developing is too akin to yours."

"Maybe he needs to be someone else's bodyguard for a while."

"Nobody else gets in as much trouble and *needs* a bodyguard."

"That's possibly true," Casmir said.

They rounded the corner and found that Asger had beaten them to Ishii's office. He was waiting outside, leaning against the bulkhead by the door, his arms folded over his chest.

"He's fast," Kim said.

"He probably used the trampoline to bounce here."

"He's not going to say yes," Asger said without preamble as they walked up.

Kim glanced at Casmir. "You already told him my problem?"

"Briefly. He hasn't seen the video yet. I thought we would show both of them at once."

"Unless I can talk you out of this." Asger lifted a hand, stopping Casmir from pressing the door chime. "The captain isn't going to send his civilian advisors to the station ahead of his ship if there's a civil war going on. You'd be in danger of becoming hostages yourselves."

"Nobody there knows who we are," Casmir said.

"They'll know that you came from the Kingdom warships. Other than a dubious pirate fleet a day away, there aren't any other ships loitering around that station. The news is that their airlocks and shuttle bays are all locked down, and nobody's been allowed to come or go for days."

"You have news?" Casmir perked up. "More than what's on the public feeds?"

"I have some. I got my own orders independent of Ishii's."

"What are they?"

"Not to escort the two civilian advisors into danger."

"Does that mean you're supposed to go over there?" Casmir asked.

Asger hesitated. "Why do I feel that nothing good is going to come of me sharing my orders with you?"

"You shouldn't have teased us with them if you didn't want to share. That's rude. Kim, isn't that rude?"

Her eyes were tight with worry, and she didn't play along with him. Casmir, reminded that her colleague was in danger, affixed a more serious expression on his face.

"My orders are to go ahead of the main incursion team, if at all possible, and get President Chronis to safety," Asger said.

Casmir pounced like a cat. "A mission that would surely be easier to accomplish if you had allies."

"Doubtful."

"How can you say that? You're very fit and athletic, and you have a scary weapon and a voluminous cloak, but you're just one man. Wouldn't you like to have Zee along to help? And we could even take Tork. There shouldn't be any conflict of interest for him on this mission. And while you all are fighting the bad guys—or, in this case, the indignant, angry freedom fighters—Kim and I can skulk in the shadows, hack into the computer system, and find out where the president is. And also where any important civilian scientists are." Casmir almost added that maybe he and Kim could creatively find a way to make it unnecessary for Ishii's marines to storm the station and drive fear and hatred into the residents. But Asger might not go for that. Better to focus on how they could achieve what they wanted while helping Asger achieve what *he* wanted. A win for all.

"I knew I shouldn't have told you," Asger said. "You're already scheming."

"Schemily," Kim murmured.

"I'm simply being logical," Casmir said. "You need to do something in the station. We need to do something in the station. Clearly, we should carpool, work together, and help each other."

"Carpool. Right." Asger shook his head. "I ought to—"

The door opened, and a gray-haired man in a gray civilian galaxy suit and fur-trimmed robe walked out of Ishii's office.

Asger bowed. "Ambassador Romano."

"Sir Knight." The man—Romano—frowned at Casmir and Kim.

Casmir imitated Asger's bow, in case the lack of appropriate deference was a problem. Kim frowned, but she also managed a curt bow.

As the ambassador strode toward the lift, Ishii leaned out of the office and pointed at the empty bulkhead. "Do you see a sign that says briefing room?"

"No, Captain," Asger said.

Casmir considered commenting, but Kim elbowed him and gave him a warning look. Casmir shut his mouth and wondered how someone who claimed to be bad at reading people had a telepathic gauge on his brain. He also wondered if Ishii and the ambassador—where had he been lurking the whole trip?—had heard them talking in the corridor.

"Get in here," Ishii growled and stalked into his office.

Casmir gestured for Asger to go first. Asger shot him a dirty look, as if he was being invited to walk first across a mine field. Casmir followed him, and when Kim and Zee entered, the space in front of Ishii's desk grew quite crowded.

"You're not going anywhere," Ishii said preemptively, then frowned at Asger when he opened his mouth. "*Any* of you."

"I have orders to protect President Chronis." Asger pointed at the chip in his temple. "I'll transmit them to you."

"You can transmit them into a toilet. My marines are going in to deal with the uprising, as they're trained to do, and they'll find and protect the president. He's a Kingdom ally now and has appealed to us for help. We'll ensure he's not harmed."

"Your marines lack the subtlety of a knight."

"I've seen your calendar. You're as subtle as a sledgehammer to the face."

"That's not quite how women describe me," Asger murmured.

Ishii rolled his eyes, then looked at Kim and Casmir. "I don't know why you two are even up here, but you're definitely not leaving the ship. This has nothing to do with you. You're here for the gate, which we will retrieve as soon as we finish up here. Ideally, we'll acquire some submarines here to further assist us with that." Ishii looked at a tablet on his desk, a map of the station visible on the display. "Maybe the president will be so grateful that we've saved him that he'll arrange for a hefty discount."

Casmir looked at Kim. They hadn't had a chance to decide which of them was going to do the talking.

She took a deep breath. "Captain, I received a message from a colleague, a scientist and researcher who works for my corporation, and he's stuck in the chaos. He requested that I help him get himself and his freezers full of samples and research material off the station and to somewhere safe."

"Why would *you* be able to help him with that?" Ishii asked.

"I'm not sure why he thought that. He was desperate and likely felt he didn't have any other options. He implied they're taking hostages there or that they might. Further, he mentioned a princess there from Shango Habitat, and that she might also need sanctuary."

Casmir had forgotten about that. He had no idea who the princess was, but the name of the habitat was familiar for some reason. Simply because he'd learned the name back when he'd been a kid in school, encouraged to memorize the geography of the various systems? No, it had come up more recently. Oh, now he remembered. Princess Oku had mentioned it.

"That's the habitat that Princess Oku just got some dead bees back from." Casmir blinked, realizing this might be used to sway Ishii. "Captain, if that princess is from Shango Habitat, it's likely that Princess Oku has a relationship with her. At the least, the princess—er, our princess—has been doing humanitarian work there. I assume that's what you would call it. She might consider it a personal favor if you were to rescue her friend."

Casmir smiled, knowing he was making a lot of assumptions. It was entirely possible that Oku was working with some random gardener on Shango Habitat and didn't know the royal family there at all. That seemed unlikely though. She ought to have at least passing familiarity with them if she was sending bees to their station.

"*Bees?*" Ishii gave Asger an is-he-pulling-my-leg look.

"Oh." Asger scratched his head. "I do remember Oku mentioning that habitat. But it's not even in this system." His forehead furrowed as he looked at Casmir.

Casmir shrugged. "I imagine people travel great distances to acquire biological materials from Parvus Biologia."

"That is true," Kim put in quietly. "We fill a unique medical niche and can sometimes provide solutions to people who aren't interested in genetic modifications, or problems that can't be solved with them."

"This conversation doesn't make any sense to me," Ishii said. "The princess is a flower-picking dilettante who cavorts around the system on the Kingdom's tax money."

Casmir exchanged frowns with Asger, tempted to correct Ishii, since he now knew better. And he knew Asger also knew better. But Asger kept his mouth shut. He was in danger of not being able to obey his orders if Ishii didn't let him leave.

"Whether her interests are flowers or bees or both," Casmir said, "the very fact that she's well-traveled implies that she has relationships with the various royal and leading families around the Twelve Systems. For all we simple peons know, Shango Habitat may be cultivating an alliance with Tiamat Station, which we *know* is trying to cultivate an alliance with the Kingdom. Rescuing this princess could win you a medal, Sora." Casmir smiled cheerfully at Ishii.

Ishii looked like he was about to start sputtering again. Kim shook her head.

"Why does talking with you always give me a headache, Dabrowski?" Ishii asked. "Is it because my blood pressure skyrockets whenever you're in the room?" He looked at Kim.

"A mild blood pressure increase rarely causes symptoms," Kim said. "It's possible you're having a hypertensive crisis, in which case you should see your doctor as soon as possible."

"I think it'll go away as soon as Dabrowski leaves my office." Ishii focused solely on Casmir. "Why are you even *here*? Asger has some orders he's going to show me, and Scholar Sato has a colleague in trouble, but you don't have an air bike in the race, as far as I can tell. Did you just come along to vex me?"

"I don't want to vex you, Sora. I'm quite tickled with you these days, ever since you gave me a bed." Casmir offered his most winning smile, though he felt like he was scrambling to stay above the surface in a quagmire of quicksand. "I'm just here to help my friends, if I can." He spread his hands toward Asger and Kim.

Ishii looked toward the ceiling, as if seeking guidance from some god lurking among the stars. "Yes, I see your file, Asger. All this says is that you are to make sure President Chronis is still alive after our warships have taken over the station."

"It specifically orders me to find him early and guard him while you're taking over the station, so that nobody tries to make a hostage out of him as soon as your marines deploy."

"Are you going to go whether I forbid it or not?" Ishii was still looking at the ceiling.

Asger sighed. "I can't screw up again, Ishii. I can't fail at a mission I've been assigned."

"Aren't you already on a mission to protect Dabrowski and help us find the gate?"

"Yes, but I have been, the same as you, diverted to deal with this new crisis because I'm the only knight in the area. Just as you command the only Kingdom warships in this system."

"Are you going to take them with you when you stealthily sneak off my ship against my wishes?" Ishii waved at Casmir and Kim.

This was a strange way of giving permission, but Casmir held his breath, hoping Ishii was getting around to it.

"I was planning to go without them, as I'm sure they'll be significantly safer here—" Asger looked sternly at Casmir and Kim, "—but Casmir does have some points worth considering. If this scientist is anywhere near as talented as Kim, we should make sure to get him out. Maybe he'd feel grateful to the Kingdom and want to expatriate."

Kim's eyebrow twitched ever so slightly, but she didn't reject the idea aloud.

"And if the princess is a friend of Princess Oku's, then she may look favorably upon us rescuing her as well." Asger's eyes grew wistful, and Casmir hid a grimace, reminded that Asger had a crush on Oku. If he ever found out that Casmir was trying to… help her with her bees, he might not be pleased.

"*Oku's* favor isn't going to advance your career or anything that isn't in your pants," Ishii growled, apparently interpreting Asger's wistful look correctly. "She has nothing to do with politics or the military or with ruling the Kingdom at all."

Asger's face reddened, and he leaned forward, either to protest or to spring across the desk to throttle Ishii.

But Ishii lifted a hand and headed him off. "Nonetheless, I agree that royalty, even royalty from different nations, should be protected, and that there might be unforeseen consequences if she were to die in some accidental violence during an incursion."

What the hell was *accidental* violence? If Ishii sent his marines in, Casmir was certain any violence perpetrated would be very purposeful.

"Are you giving me permission to go?" Asger asked stiffly.

"No."

Asger's fingers curled into fists.

"But I'm not forbidding you to go. As far as my record is going to show, we never had this meeting."

Asger hesitated, then nodded curtly. "I understand."

Casmir wasn't sure he did, but when Asger turned for the door and Ishii flicked his fingers for Casmir and Kim to follow, he walked out after Asger.

When they were all in the corridor again, the door shutting behind Zee, Asger said, "I can't outpace the *Osprey* in my shuttle, but as soon as we reach the station, I'm going to fly over and attempt to get permission to dock."

"And are you taking us? Your steadfast and useful allies." Casmir pointed at Zee rather than himself, gesturing to indicate his height and brawn.

Asger snorted. "So long as you understand what Ishii just implied."

"That he's not responsible for what you or we do?"

"More than that. I think he was implying that he'll claim he had no knowledge of what we're planning to do, should we get ourselves and the Kingdom in trouble. I don't know what he and Ambassador Romano were talking about—I thought Romano was just along to smooth ruffled feathers as we flew through other nations' territories on our quest for the gate—but he reports directly to the king, so Ishii essentially has Jager's eyes watching him out here."

"We won't get in trouble," Casmir said firmly. "We'll help you, we'll help Kim's friend, and we'll help the princess's possible acquaintance."

"I hope you're right." Asger looked more worried than reassured as he walked away.

CHAPTER 15

DOES ANYONE WANT TO HEAR MY IDEAS?" CASMIR asked as Asger piloted his sleek purple shuttle through the open bay doors and toward the stars outside.

Kim smiled at his enthusiastic tone, but she was worried because she hadn't been able to reestablish contact with Scholar Chi. The night before, and again that morning, she'd tried to comm him to let him know they were coming. She'd also commed the general office contact code for the lab, but nobody had responded to that either. Over the last day and night, there had been a dearth of news updates from the reporter who'd earlier been transmitting coverage of the skirmishes from inside the station.

"*Ideas?*" Asger asked when Kim didn't say anything. "How many are there?"

"Specific to our rescue mission? Uhm." Casmir's eyes shifted upward as he counted. "Thirteen."

"Is that all?" Asger murmured.

"I didn't want to assume we would do things my way, so I brainstormed a few options for us to consider as a group."

"A few as in thirteen?"

"Yes. I had twenty, but I narrowed it down. It looks like it'll only take us a half hour to reach the station, so I thought brevity would be important. Especially since you didn't answer your comm when I messaged you a few hours ago."

"Because I was sleeping. It was the middle of the night."

"I was too excited to sleep. Also, my roommates were feeling chatty."

"Your… roommates?" Asger twisted in his pod to peer at Tork and Zee, both of whom Casmir had brought along. They were floating and gripping handholds rather than sitting. "They chat?"

"They're gradually getting over their natural distrust and aversion toward each other. Last night, they were competing at network games. I believe most of their communication was silent, but occasionally they asked me for input when emotional human reactions played into the games."

"You're the strangest ally I've ever had, Casmir."

"*They* were the ones playing the games, but I don't mind being considered strange." His expression grew more sober, and he bowed in his seat. He was looking surprisingly perky, given the lack of gravity in the shuttle and his known nausea issues. Had he taken some medley of space-sickness medications to achieve the effect? "I'm honored you consider me an ally now."

"Let's hear your ideas."

Casmir beamed a smile at Kim, then responded seriously. "Some of this will depend on how they react to *us*. Who has the upper hand over there right now? I wasn't able to find out via the public feeds, and Kim said her colleague has gone comm silent. So we don't know. If the Kingdom-friendly president and his people are in charge, they should welcome a knight and be pleased to invite you to dock, and they should be heartened to see all of these warships stopping at their front door."

Casmir leaned forward to gesture at two of the four warships that were visible on their forward display, having anchored in space on the far side of the station. The *Osprey* and the last warship were behind the shuttle now, also anchored in space. Kim thought it looked very much like they were an invasion fleet here to attack. There was no question that they had the station surrounded.

"And if Kingdom-friendly people *aren't* in charge?" Kim wondered what kind of defenses Asger's shuttle had.

"Then we won't be welcome," Casmir said. "Asger, can you find out if Ishii has been chatting with the president and can give a status report?"

"He hasn't and can't." Asger glanced at them. "I checked before we left. The station hasn't responded to his attempts to hail them. He tried the president's office, security, and a couple of other comms. Nothing."

"It's possible someone sabotaged the station's comm system," Casmir said. "It's also possible that the Kingdom-friendly people have lost power, and those who are in charge now don't want to talk to us."

"That seems likely."

"Even if the station's central comm system is down," Kim said, "there's nothing wrong with the closest satellite—otherwise I wouldn't be able to get news feeds from around the system—so I should be able to use chip-to-chip contact to speak with my colleague."

"But you can't, right?" Casmir asked.

"He hasn't answered since we talked that first time."

"If there are roving bands of rioters, everybody may be too afraid to draw attention to themselves by sending transmissions. Someone may have also forbidden them from talking to anyone on these warships."

"Or they could all be dead," Asger said grimly.

"That seems unlikely," Casmir said.

Kim shifted uneasily in her pod, remembering that Chi had been contemplating making some virus to unleash on the rioters. She hoped his sanity hadn't stretched so far that he'd truly considered that a good idea.

"I do think, given the silence, that we should assume anti-Kingdom people are in charge." Casmir pointed at the station. "Then, if we're wrong and Kingdom people welcome us with open arms, it'll be a plus. And if not…"

"If not, they could be targeting us to fire upon right now." Asger tapped a button on the control panel, and a shield status display flashed at 100 percent. "We're not defenseless, but we're a more vulnerable target than the warships. It's possible the station will use us to make a statement."

"Which is why Ishii should fire at us first."

"Uh—what?"

"If the *Osprey* fires at us and orders us to return at once, then the station will think we're fleeing and we may be on their side." Casmir leaned over and patted Asger's armored arm. "Suggest that to him chip-to-chip, please, and then use the comm, which we'll assume is being monitored, to call him a hairy turd not fit to command. And then prepare to impressively evade his attacks—though maybe if we took a little damage, it would lend verisimilitude to our ploy, eh?—and go skidding into the station by the seat of our pants."

Asger gaped at him throughout this speech. "I thought we were only brainstorming and that you weren't presuming to make decisions for us."

"Things were taking too long. This is simpler. Chip-to-chip to Ishii, please. Or I'll contact him. I'm *positive* he won't mind shooting at me."

"Oh, I'm positive too." Asger faced the control panel, his hands flat on it, not moving. Because he was debating or because he was sending a message?

"I see it may not be advantageous to be caught standing next to Professor Dabrowski," Tork observed from behind the pods.

"It is because of his impulsive nature that Casmir Dabrowski needs a bodyguard," Zee said. "That is why we are here."

"It is why *you* are here."

"Why are you here?"

"To offer advice. I have extensive knowledge of this system." After a pause, Tork added, "Also, Professor Dabrowski said we might be able to acquire a telescope if there's a gift shop here."

Kim rubbed her face. Maybe they *did* chat all night while Casmir was trying to sleep.

"Tighten your pods." Asger's fingers burst into movement. "The *Osprey* is going to fire at us, and then the *Eagle* is going to take a few pot shots too." Asger looked over at Casmir. "It's not a bad idea. Which one was it?"

"Number three," Casmir said. "We probably shouldn't judge it until we see if it gets us a free pass into the station."

"Right."

The comm panel flashed with an incoming message.

"Dabrowski," Ishii snarled on the open channel, "get your scrawny ass back here. That shuttle belongs to one of the king's personal knights. As if your betrayal isn't getting you into enough trouble as it is. You're dead if you ever return to System Lion, do you hear me?"

Casmir blinked. Maybe he hadn't planned to be the one exchanging vitriol with Ishii.

He recovered quickly and tapped the reply button. "Did you really think I was going to help you and the king after he threatened me and my family? I've already arranged for their secret escape from System Lion, and I hope I never see that backward hell again!"

"You won't because we'll blow you out of the stars." The comm ended, and the firing began.

Asger accelerated in a burst that had Kim's stomach knocking out her vertebrae. A massive railgun blast sailed past, scant feet from the rear of the shuttle. Her pod hugged her tight, and she closed her eyes as the craft accelerated and decelerated, then lurched sideways. A groan came from Casmir's seat, suggesting that their manic flight might be overcoming even a double dose of his space-sickness medication.

An alert flashed on her contact, not affected by her closed lids.

Scholar Sato? Chi's words came in. *Are you, by chance, in the shuttle being fired on outside of our station?*

Yes. She almost told him it was a ruse, but reminded herself that Chi wasn't himself friendly to the Kingdom, and withheld that information. *We're coming to help you.*

There was a long pause, even though there shouldn't have been any lag time now.

Are you sure?

We're trying, she amended as Asger jerked the shuttle into some wrenching, twisting move that seemed to defy the laws of physics. *Why didn't you respond to me earlier?*

I was unconscious.

Sleeping?

No. They gassed four levels of the station. To ensure compliance. They kept it going for more than twenty hours.

Kim's mouth dropped open. She'd used the chemicals in the sickbay labs to craft a few homemade knockout grenades—technically, knockout vials—but at small dosages that would probably only make people groggy unless they took a big sniff. Even then, they would only lose consciousness briefly.

That's insane, she replied. *People could have died.*

People did die. It was a blanket dose, not designed to accommodate variance among individuals. I've already heard of six who never woke up. Two were children.

Kim felt sick for reasons that had nothing to do with Asger's mad maneuvering. *Was the president responsible?*

Station Civil Security. They're loyal to him, yes. Nobody has seen the president in two days. We're not even sure if he's alive. Right now, a group of loyalists calling themselves the Bakas Vengers have the admin and control levels. I'm not sure if they control communications.

There was an attack, and someone tried to knock out the comm array. I've heard. This is all being reported to me secondhand by Princess Tambora, who refuses to stay in the lab and hide with me. She is driving her bodyguard insane.

What's she trying to do? How old is she? She sounds young. Kim would look her up later, when Asger was done trying to turn their stomachs inside out. Right now, even sending messages and reading Chi's replies threatened to make her sick.

She is twenty-one, and she has a jet-powered float chair that she rides through the corridors like a flaming chariot. She's refusing to accede to my wisdom.

What's she trying to accomplish? Kim wondered if she should mention that Casmir wanted to rescue her. This probably wasn't the time. Once they made it onto the station, she and Chi could, she hoped, have a long discussion.

She wants to escape and to help me escape with my freezers and the samples she ordered and came personally to pick up. It's a noble thought, but she only has an advisor and a bodyguard. Neither is able to control her.

This was sounding more like someone who would be a friend of Casmir's—or maybe be one of his students—rather than Princess Oku's. The one time Kim had met Oku, she had seemed quiet and refined.

They have a ship in a shuttle bay, but there are security robots guarding it. They've been stunning anyone who attempts to leave the station—I think both sides are afraid the other side will get reinforcements that will turn the tide of the battle if they let anyone go.

Tell her to stay in the lab with you. We're trying to get to the station. Once we dock, assuming they'll let us, we'll come for you. Send a map of how to get to your lab, if you can. I—

A massive jolt wrenched the shuttle, and Kim would have been thrown headfirst into the forward display if her pod hadn't held her tight. The hull groaned, and the force pressing against her changed from forward to back, up to down. It felt like the shuttle was tumbling head over heels through space. Was that even possible?

"We don't need quite so much verisimilitude, Ishii," Asger muttered.

Casmir groaned, and the sound of him throwing up followed. Kim's stomach wanted to join in, and she took quick deep breaths, trying to steady it as Asger steadied the craft.

"We're flying around the station's rings," Asger said. "The warships should stop firing now, since they'll risk hitting the station if they don't. And since I think they've made their point. Shit, Casmir. Did you puke on the back of my pod?"

Casmir groaned.

"And the *ceiling*?"

"To be fair," Kim said, "the ceiling was where the deck used to be a minute ago."

A giant strut passed in front of the display, and Kim had the sense of them circling it.

"It's on the deck too. Damn, Casmir. Does anybody fly with you twice?"

"Just Laser," Casmir said weakly. "She's a hero."

"She should get a medal. Maybe a statue."

"All I had to give her was a patent."

"All right, everyone be quiet. I'm going to try to comm the station. Let's hope they'll answer me after that display." Asger tapped the comm panel. "Tiamat Station? This is the recently liberated shuttle, *Thor's Hammer*. I'm carrying refugees Professor Casmir Dabrowski, a roboticist of some renown back in the Kingdom, and Scholar Kim Sato, a bacteriologist who works for Parvus Biologia. They have a lab in your station, and the senior researcher there should be able to vouch for her." Asger glanced at Kim.

"Scholar Tom Chi," she put in.

"We're requesting asylum. Do you copy?"

Asger continued to fly close to the station as they waited, not yet presuming to head to the docks and locks area. Kim got another look at a strut. It was covered with a lumpy gray material that reminded her of mycelium packing material she'd seen used for shipping medicines. Maybe it was something to insulate the station against radiation. All of the Kingdom stations were buried in asteroids and used the rock as natural insulation. This one was exposed to space, its rings spinning to give gravity to its wide cylindrical core.

"*Thor's Hammer*?" came a woman's voice over the comm. "That's a cocky name for a little shuttle, isn't it?"

Kim was inclined to agree—she hadn't even known Asger's shuttle had a name—but she kept her mouth shut.

"It belonged to a knight." Asger's voice came out stiff.

He had been careful, Kim noted, not to identify himself when he sent his message.

"That explains it then, doesn't it? I'm afraid we're not able to provide asylum to you or anyone else at this time. As you might guess from those brutish warships, we have problems of our own. We—our faction—also don't have control of the shuttle bays today." Her voice turned bitter. "You should have come five days ago. We were in a better position then. We thought… It doesn't matter. That was before the Kingdom entered the system. Completely *unopposed*." The bitterness was dripping from her teeth now. "What are the water worlds doing? Waiting to see if they blow us up before they send ships?"

"Tell her we'll take control of the shuttle bay we land in and hand it over to her," Casmir whispered.

"What was that?" the woman asked.

Casmir raised his voice to be heard from the back seat. "This is Professor Dabrowski, ma'am. Fugitive of the Kingdom. We're willing to help you in exchange for our asylum. I assume you're among the independent forces who oppose Kingdom rule?"

"You can bet your ore I am."

And originally from one of the mining colonies, Kim thought.

"And the president who's been sidling up to the Kingdom controls the shuttle bays?" Casmir asked.

"We don't know where he is right now, but his people control it, yes. And his damn robot army."

"Did you say *robots*, ma'am?"

Only Casmir would get excited at the idea of the enemy having a robot army.

"We can *definitely* help you take over that shuttle bay," Casmir said.

"If you can get in, you're welcome in the station, but I don't think you'll find this is the sanctuary you're hoping for."

"Anything is better than a Kingdom warship, ma'am."

"Tell me about it." The channel closed.

Asger twisted to look back at Casmir. "It's a little alarming how easily you spout anti-Kingdom propaganda."

"If Ishii wanted me to say glowing things about his warship, he should have put me on the payroll." Casmir patted the back of Asger's pod. "Find us a nice airlock or shuttle bay guarded by robots, please."

"I will do that if you find a towel and sanitizer and clean my ceiling."

"Can it wait until we have gravity again?" Casmir rested a hand on his stomach.

"No. Things fall and spatter on innocent people when there's gravity."

"Ah, yes. Unfortunate."

Casmir released himself from his pod and pushed himself toward the lav, patting Zee and Tork on the way past. The shuttle was traveling slowly enough now that there wasn't much danger of being creamed against the back bulkhead.

Kim was bemused, as always, that Casmir didn't have the robots clean up his mess. It had never bothered him to use the mindless cleaning robot back home for that purpose, but he seemed to elevate androids—and crushers—to something akin to human status.

"Did the king really threaten you and your family, Casmir?" Asger asked quietly as he guided the shuttle around the curve in the great cylinder, and numerous shuttle-bay doors and airlocks came into view.

"No. I think he's more subtle than that. He's giving me a chance to prove myself. I'm hoping the only thing at stake if I fail is my own livelihood and right to live on Odin, not that my parents or cousins or anyone I care about will be in danger."

"And do you think taking a shuttle bay back from Kingdom-loyal troops will accomplish that?"

Casmir had returned with sani-wipes, and he pushed himself toward the ceiling. "It sounds like they are robots loyal to the president's security forces. As far as we know, the president isn't officially a Kingdom subject, so I don't believe we're taking action against Jager or the Fleet personally."

"Do you know yet how you'll suborn those robots?" Kim asked.

"No, I haven't the foggiest idea what make and model they are, and we're not close enough yet to attempt to hack our way onto their local wireless networks."

"Would anybody else have been more comforted if he'd said yes?" Asger asked.

"Yes," Kim said.

"Yes," Tork and Zee said as one.

"I don't know his new android very well yet," Asger said, "but I've already got the gist that it's an alarming thing if they agree with each other."

"What's alarming," Casmir said, pushing off the ceiling and toward Zee, "is how far vomitus can travel in zero-g."

As Kim watched him clean his robot, she realized she'd broken off in the middle of her conversation with Chi. She tried to establish the connection, but once again, he did not answer. She hoped the princess on the float chair hadn't led an angry mob to his lab.

Yas came up to the bridge personally to let Neimanhaus know his mole was benign, at which point the bridge crew ribbed the lieutenant about how something so ugly was most certainly *not* benign, and found the view on the display even more alarming than the one from his last visit. The *Fedallah* had flown away from Xolas Moon's blue-and-white ice and was in a stationary position near Tiamat Station.

Normally, Yas would have boiled with excitement and hope at being so close to his home, but there were four Kingdom warships surrounding the great spinning cylinder. Yes, *surrounding*. He shuddered at the precise way they had located themselves at four points around the station.

"Join me, Doctor," Rache said and headed for the briefing room.

When Yas trailed him inside, he expected to find more crew there, waiting for a briefing to start, but the room was empty, save for another display showing the view of the station and the warships.

"Is this an alarming and unexpected development for you too?" Yas pointed to the Kingdom fleet. "Or what you expected?"

"I've been more focused on learning the moon's secrets, but as soon as Neimanhaus let me know the warships had passed Xolas by, I realized they might have been ordered to deal with the unrest here. You remember that image of your president shaking Jager's hand on Odin."

"I've been trying to block it from my mind." Chronis was still the vice president in Yas's mind—and a schemer who'd probably had something to do with Bakas's death.

"Do you think he's responsible for your former president's assassination?" Rache asked, as if he could read Yas's thoughts.

"I'd make him a suspect if I were doing an investigation."

"You *are* doing an investigation, Doctor. You and Amergin. He's picked out a handful of parties that would have gained from an alliance with the Kingdom, or even rule by the Kingdom, but only Chronis directly gained leadership and power after Bakas's death."

Yas nodded.

"My first thought when I saw all these warships was that this is a perfect time to sneak in and get some submarines, but if it's possible to dethrone the new president and clear your name while we're here…" Rache spread his gloved hand.

"You know that's what I want, sir. Just let me know what I can do to help. Also, I think you can only dethrone royalty. Throne-owning royalty."

"Not true. The word has evolved over the millennia and means simply to remove someone from a position of authority or dominance. No thrones are required."

"I stand corrected."

"An Old Earth author once said, 'If you are afraid of being lonely, don't try to be right.'"

Rache didn't sound annoyed or like he truly meant to censor him, but Yas bit his lip, realizing that was perhaps too apropos for his life. He'd been proud of how often he'd had the answers as a doctor on Tiamat Station, of how often he'd been correct. It had taken being rousted from his life and having his world turned upside down to realize how lonely a life it had been.

And had anything changed for him here on the *Fedallah*? He'd deemed the majority of the mercenaries to be thugs and had avoided anything but superficial interactions with them. Except with Jess, but he was always so sure he could heal her of her addiction—and that she must deep down want that—that he feared he'd driven her away. Even when he hadn't brought it up, she'd probably sensed it. Sensed that his desire to help her stemmed out of the certainty that she was wrong and hurting herself. And that he was right.

"Yes, sir," he said, doubting Rache had truly meant to instill that jumble of thoughts in him. Surely, he had the station on his mind, not Yas's social life. "*Is* there something I can do to help?"

Rache clasped his hands behind his back and turned his mask toward the display. "Right now, we're staying far enough from the warships that we shouldn't be detected. From what Neimanhaus and Amergin have gleaned, the shuttle bays in the station are locked down, and if you try to latch onto one of their airlock docks, you'll find the hatches secured. We couldn't bring the *Fedallah* in, regardless. The slydar hull works out in space, but if we sidle up to a dock, the station will notice, and it's possible the warships out there will too. My hope is that they'll *do* something, and we can take a shuttle over, dock, and force our way in, while everyone is distracted. But the Kingdom ships are just floating there, staring at each other."

"Wouldn't your shuttle also be recognized once it docked?"

"I've got Chief Khonsari painting the outside of a new incognito one. It was aggravating to lose the other one on Odin, especially since I didn't earn any pay for my mission down there."

Yas was tempted again to ask what that mission had been, but Rache was staring intently at the station, and Yas was far more interested in the current mission.

"I'm still willing to pay for your help in this, sir. I don't know that I could come up with enough to purchase a new shuttle, but maybe it would at least help."

"That's not necessary." Rache zoomed in on one of the Kingdom ships. The *Osprey*. "That's the ship that came to the *Machu Picchu* at Skadi Moon. It's also the ship that, according to Amergin, Scholar Sato and Professor Dabrowski are aboard."

Yas couldn't tell from Rache's tone what his feelings were toward them. "Does that change the situation at all? I assume they were sent because of their experience with the gate."

"It might," Rache murmured. "But it shouldn't affect our submarine retrieval and assassin-finding mission. I'm going to take a small team to the station, and I want you on it. You know the place better than I do. You can take us to find the president, where we'll have a frank chat with him."

"Yes, sir. I'll bring some eslevoamytal along."

Rache gave him a long look over his shoulder—maybe he'd been envisioning more physical ways to extract the truth—but he didn't object. "If we can, we'll convince him to make an announcement to the station that a mistake was made and that you're innocent. And we'll make sure he lets your civil security institution know."

"If he was the one responsible, he won't want to admit he was wrong and let the case be opened up again." Yas snorted. They'd condemned him so quickly that he doubted there had been a case to start with.

"A dagger to the throat tends to make a man amenable."

"Right," Yas murmured, closing his eyes.

The idea of threatening Chronis—would Rache go so far as to kill him?—didn't sit well with Yas, but what had he expected when he asked a mercenary to take on this mission? That Rache would hire a high-priced lawyer to argue Yas's case in court? Yas had asked for Rache's help, and it sounded like he was going to get exactly what he'd asked for. He couldn't object now.

"That's unexpected," Rache said.

Yas opened his eyes. The display was still focused on the *Osprey*, but a second spacecraft had appeared, a much smaller shuttle. It was flying away from the warship.

"Are they sending someone over to negotiate?"

The warship started firing on the shuttle, and Yas jumped.

"I think not," Rache said dryly.

"What are they—"

"It doesn't matter. That's our distraction." Rache strode for the bridge. "Gather your gear and meet us in the shuttle bay, Doctor. Hurry."

CHAPTER 16

THOR'S HAMMER CONNECTED TO AN EXTERNAL DOCK IN the middle of a bank of dozens of them on the long side of Tiamat Station's great cylinder. They had flown past several sets of shuttle-bay doors, but none had opened for them. As promised.

Casmir sat in his pod while Asger finalized the hookup. He was running three software programs on his chip, one scraping data off the public network in search of the accounts of personnel with access to the locked security network, one trying to crack passwords for those accounts, and one trying to find a back door from the unlocked public network into the locked security network that wouldn't require any accounts or passwords.

"Their hatch is locked, so we'll have to force our way in," Asger said, rising from his pod as soon as they were docked and piggybacking off the station's spin gravity. "That's not a problem, but we'll need to be ready for a fight as soon as we board. There are extra rifles in that cabinet for anyone who wants a weapon."

"I'll take one," Kim said. "Especially if we'll be fighting robots."

"I'm aggrieved, Kim," Casmir said. "Robots shouldn't be needlessly destroyed. If you give me a chance, I may be able to find a way to get into their control interfaces and turn them off—or even turn them to our side."

"You can do that while Asger and I are shooting them." Kim strode straight to the cabinet.

"I like the way you think." Asger handed her a rifle.

"I like the way Professor Dabrowski thinks," Tork said.

"Thank you." Casmir went to peer into the cabinet, hoping for a stunner. He'd hoped, by arriving before the marines did, that they could *avoid* using deadly force, on people *and* robots.

Without being asked, Asger opened a drawer and pulled out two stunners. He took one for himself and handed one to Casmir.

"Oh, thank you," Casmir said, inordinately delighted. He patted his tool satchel. "A stunner, a power drill, and a ratchet set. I'm ready to infiltrate a station full of enemies."

"Did I mention that you're the strangest ally I've ever had?" Asger asked.

"About forty-five minutes ago, yes."

"Just making sure." Asger held out his cloak and turned his back toward them. "Did you get all your puke off me?"

Casmir silently thought Asger might be one of the strangest allies he'd had too. Kim reached out and scraped at a suspicious glop on the purple cloak.

"Sorry, Asger," Casmir said, trying not to feel like a failure at space adventuring. Admiral Mikita couldn't *possibly* have had this problem. "People need to stop taking me on zero-g shuttles."

"If you keep throwing up on the pilots, I think that will happen." Asger smacked him on the shoulder, then stepped into the shuttle's small airlock chamber. "I wish you two had combat armor."

"This will have to do." Casmir tapped his galaxy suit. "I'm planning to hide behind you. And, as soon as I can acquire them, an army of robots."

"I don't think you're going to be able to wave a wrench and talk them over to your side." Asger glanced at Tork. "Or stick a missing hand back on one to win its loyalty. Unless you want me to go lop off their hands so you can try."

"I was planning to sneak onto their network and take control of them the old-fashioned way. By pretending I have the authority to give them orders."

"How long will *that* take?" Asger stood with his hand on the hatch, ready to go.

"Uhm." Casmir checked his programs. "Actually, I'm in now. I'm logged in as Brandon Oswald, who is listed as the assistant chief of Station Civil Security. The chief had a password that my cracking program is still working on, but this fellow should do. Let me try to find the models and network IDs of the robots guarding this area." He waved toward the station on the other side of the hatch.

"You're in?" Asger stared at him. "We've only been docked for seven minutes."

"True, but the wireless network extends beyond the station hull. I've had access for longer."

"How much longer?"

"Three minutes."

Asger looked at Kim. "Is he serious?"

"Rarely," she said with her usual deadpan delivery.

"Should we just stand here and wait while you take them over?" Asger asked. "Does it work like that?"

A clang sounded on the hatch, and they all jumped.

Asger spun toward the control panel and hit a button. A display flared to life, a camera showing the view outside of their airlock hatch. Surprisingly, the hatch on the station side of the short connector tube had swung open, as if to invite them in.

Unsurprisingly, eight six-foot-tall barrel-shaped robots on treads were staggered in the bay in front of the hatch, each with cannon-arms pointed at the shuttle. A few other robots rolled around the large bay behind them, doing patrol circuits.

"I don't see any humans in there that we could reason with," Kim said.

"Waiting inside for—what does Bonita call you, Casmir?—sounds like a good idea," Asger said.

"She refined the robot whisperer to El Mago." Casmir rose on his tiptoes for a better view of the display—Asger's broad shoulder partially blocked it. "At least I can more easily get the model numbers this way. It should make it easier to match up their network IDs."

"Just let us know—"

Another clang interrupted Asger. One of the robots had rolled closer to bang on their hatch. It backed up to its original position among its cohorts, and an android with a blow torch strode into view.

"Hell." Asger pulled out his pertundo and flipped his helmet into place. "I can't let them melt holes in my shuttle, or we won't be able to leave again. I'm going in."

“Zee and Tork will go with you.” Casmir waved his mechanical allies forward as he gestured for Kim to stay back, hoping she would listen to reason. She was in a galaxy suit, the same as he, and they couldn’t stand up to the same kind of damage as the armored Asger or the sturdy robots, especially Zee.

Asger eyed Zee and Tork, not looking like he wanted to storm the shuttle bay with them. Casmir didn’t know why. They were the most logical options. As good as Kim was with her practice swords, she couldn’t flatten enemies as efficiently as Zee could.

All Asger said was, “I’m going to try to charge across and lead them off into the station. Assuming that hatch on the other side of the bay is unlocked. If it’s not, I might need you and your tools along.”

“I’m positive either Zee or Tork can open the hatch for you.” Casmir patted them on their backs as they stepped into the airlock chamber behind Asger.

“My strength is greater than a Tork-57 android,” Zee stated.

“I have been upgraded,” Tork said a little stiffly.

“It was a simple matter for me to subdue you.”

“I had been damaged and was not able to defend myself optimally.”

“Uh, they’re not going to fight, are they?” Asger had his back pressed against the hatch and looked like he wanted to back up even farther.

“I think that *is* how they fight,” Kim murmured.

“They’re simply warming themselves up for the battle ahead,” Casmir said.

An alarm flashed on the control panel.

“Let’s do this then,” Asger growled, facing the hatch and hitting the button to open it.

Casmir scooted out of the line of fire, relieved when Kim joined him.

But no energy bolts streaked into the shuttle. Asger sprang out, leaping over all eight robots and the android and landing on the other side. Zee and Tork charged out, hurling themselves straight into the mass of mechanical enemies. As the first shots fired, punctuated by destructive clangs from Asger’s pertundo, Casmir pressed himself against the wall and concentrated on finding the robots outside on the network. It didn’t help that there were numerous ship bays full of robot sentries, and Casmir didn’t know the number or network designation of the one where they had docked.

Kim stood between him and the hatchway, her rifle poised to fire if any of the robots tried to enter.

"I've identified the type of robots we're dealing with," Casmir whispered, feeling the need to keep her up-to-date. Or maybe to let her know he was doing something, not simply cowering and hiding while Asger risked his life. "And those are Aegis Defenders, models 14A… located on, this has to be level 1…"

Logically, everything on the outside rim of the cylindrical station would be the first level. But what sector? There were more than twenty of them. Ah, there was a ship bay in Sector C with a breach recorded and Aegis Defenders and a security android on the move.

"That's us," Casmir murmured, then commanded the robots to cease, desist, and wait for new orders. Ah, damn, the assistant chief didn't have a high enough level of security access for the job. Back to his programs. He had to find the chief's passcode.

Asger shouted something inarticulate from across the bay. Casmir couldn't tell if it was a battle cry or a cry of pain. Or both.

Kim shifted, as if she might run out to help, but she glanced back at Casmir and hesitated.

"You can go help, if you want," he whispered. "I need a few more minutes. *Seconds*. This shouldn't take long."

"I'll stay here. They—" Kim heard something and leaned around the corner to peek into the bay. She jerked her head back.

A crimson energy bolt zipped through the hatchway and ricocheted off the opposite bulkhead. Casmir flattened himself to his stomach, but the bolt streaked the other direction, slamming into the back of a pod. Stuffing flew out, and the top half of the frame blew into pieces.

"I'll definitely stay here," Kim growled.

She hadn't hit the deck, but she'd dropped into a low crouch. She leaned around the corner and fired several bursts before pulling back again.

"Stay down," she ordered, as two more energy bolts streaked into the shuttle. They ricocheted into the lavatory, and the sink blew up.

"Oh, I was planning on it." Casmir pressed his cheek against the cool textured deck. If his program didn't find that passcode, he was going to have to think of something else. Other robots on the network were being ordered to come to the bay to assist with the intruder problem.

A soft bing sounded in his mind, and the second passcode appeared on his contact.

"Finally," he breathed, copying it into the wireless interface.

Then he was in. He zipped around the security interface, ordering robots all over the station to stand down until they received new orders from him even as he isolated the ones fighting Asger, Zee, and Tork. He ordered them to halt and was tempted to power them down, so there wouldn't be any delays or mistakes, but he might need those robots online to help his team if human security officers showed up. And Casmir was sure they would once they realized their network had been infiltrated. He hoped it would take them time to figure out it had been at the highest level.

By the time he changed the passcode for the chief, it had fallen silent out in the bay.

Kim poked her head quickly around the corner and back. Then she leaned out for a longer look.

"I think you can stop kissing the deck now," she told Casmir.

"You don't need a bacteria sample while I'm down here?"

"Please, no more offers of swabbing samples with your tongue."

Kim walked into the bay, and Casmir pushed himself to his feet. He jogged out to make sure Asger hadn't been injured. Or Tork. The android didn't have the self-repairing abilities of a crusher.

Tork and Zee stood still, facing a clump of the Aegis robots. Neither appeared damaged. Asger was in a crouch, his pertundo out and extended to its eight-foot halberd form, as he faced two robots he must have been battling when they had stopped moving. Their cannon-arms were now down at their sides, and none of the sensor discs that resembled eyes and a mouth on their heads moved.

"They're not going to bother us now," Casmir said, "and I think I've effectively ordered the rest of the robots on the station to stand down."

"How many is that?" Asger tapped whatever invisible button drew in the telescoping handle and hung his pertundo on his belt.

"A couple thousand, it looks like."

Asger stared at him. "Can you mobilize them to fight for us?"

"Maybe, but a lot of them are just cleaning robots and the like. And if I do more than power them down, someone will get suspicious right away and log on to investigate and try to override my work." Casmir waved at the still robots. "This might be interpreted as some network error. And if any security robots out there were fighting the inhabitants, the humans will be able to get away." Casmir nodded, pleased at the idea, even though he was acting against the side of the station forces that had Kingdom leanings. He couldn't help it that they had been the ones denying entrance to the shuttle bay. Hopefully, Jager would never find out.

"Get away? If robots had been chasing me down the corridors where I lived and suddenly stopped, I'd grab the nearest club or other weapon—" Asger patted his pertundo, "—and hack them into pieces."

Casmir rocked back, aggrieved. "Robots are just following programs written by humans. They can't be blamed for their actions." He looked at Kim, who'd walked out of the shuttle with him. "You wouldn't do that, would you?"

"No."

He let out a relieved breath, certain Asger's reaction was extreme. Maybe he had been joking.

"If I felt particularly abused, I might graffiti them," Kim said.

Casmir squinted at her, hoping *she* was joking, though it was always hard to tell with her. "That one over there shot at you, and you haven't graffitied it yet."

"I didn't think to bring spray paint." She poked his tool satchel. "Do you have any?"

He shifted it away from her. "No."

"Disappointing."

"You have a map of this place, Casmir?" Asger asked. "I've never been here. We need to find Kim's friend and President Chronis. And this wayward princess. Hopefully, before anyone realizes we're here."

"If the princess is in a float chair, she ought to be easy to identify," Kim said.

"I can probably find them through the network, though it would be handy if they could all meet us in the same place. Like here, for example." Casmir pointed toward the shuttle.

"Let me see if I can contact Chi," Kim said.

Beeps came from farther down the bay, followed by a few clunks and clangs.

Asger and Kim whipped their weapons in that direction. It sounded like another shuttle was docking, but there weren't any portholes, so Casmir couldn't see it. A few indicators blinked to the side of a hatch.

"Did another of the warships send someone?" Casmir asked. "Do we need to get out of here?"

Almost unconsciously, he ordered the robots to form a phalanx and face the airlock hatch with the blinking indicators beside it. Casmir stood behind them, and Kim let him pull her behind cover with him.

"Ishii says he doesn't know whose shuttle that is," Asger said. "A fleet of pirate ships that was heading for the gate has turned in this direction, and that's got all the Kingdom captains distracted."

"*Pirates?*" Casmir thought of Qin and Bonita and the Druckers. They couldn't possibly be in this system, could they? No, Bonita had been heading to System Cerberus to deal with the Druckers.

"They're probably not coming to the station to pick a fight with the Kingdom," Asger said, "but there are enough of them that everyone is watching them."

A few more beeps sounded.

"Maybe we should get out of here before whoever that is comes out." Asger took a couple of steps toward the exit, but the airlock hatch swung open before he reached it.

He sprang behind one of the Aegis robots for cover and leaned out, pointing his rifle toward the newcomers.

At first, nobody came out. Maybe the shuttle passengers had also expected to have to fight robots and were waiting to see what came to greet them.

After a moment, someone in black combat armor leaned into view, quickly spotting their group and pointing a rifle in their direction. Asger pointed his rifle right back at the man—or maybe it was a woman. Casmir was too far away to see through the faceplate.

"Shit, Dabrowski," a familiar voice said. "Don't you go *anywhere* without a robot army?"

Casmir gaped. "Rache?"

The armored man—Rache—lowered his rifle and walked fully into view. Several men in identical black combat armor walked out after him, similar rifles in hand but also pointed toward the deck instead of across the bay.

"To answer your question," Casmir said, recovering from his surprise, "I acquired these robots here. Recently."

"Not that one, you didn't." Rache pointed at Zee. "It's an army all by itself."

Zee lifted his chin. "Yes."

Kim lowered her rifle. Asger did not.

"Is there any chance we have a common goal instead of an opposing one?" Casmir asked.

He didn't want to work against Rache again, not after they'd defeated the terrorists and shaken hands. He couldn't imagine trying to shoot him. But did Rache feel the same way? Had he read Casmir's gift of comic books? Maybe Casmir should have brought more gifts. He'd already promised Tork to find a gift shop with telescopes. Maybe he could find something appropriate for a clone brother.

"It's doubtful," Rache said. "What are you here for?"

"We're rescuing a princess."

"What?" Rache sounded startled—it was probably the first time Casmir had caught him by surprise. "What princess? There's no reason Oku would be here."

"No, no, it's another princess. And a bacteriologist. I think." Casmir looked at Kim.

"Technically, he's a veterinary virologist," Kim said, "but his knowledge base is great, and he works on plant and insect projects too."

"Is that Scholar Tom Chi?" a voice Casmir didn't recognize asked. It came from inside the airlock. A man in a galaxy suit holding a medical kit leaned out.

"Yes," Kim said. "It's good to see you again, Dr. Peshlakai. Alive and upright."

Casmir guessed this was one of the people who Kim had worked with when she'd been kidnapped.

"Scholar Sato, I'm aggrieved that you're delighted to see my doctor but don't even acknowledge me." Rache's tone was dry, and Casmir couldn't tell if the following bow was mocking or self-deprecating or what, but he did direct it at Kim.

"Let's get out of here, Casmir," Asger murmured. "Someone is bound to check on this bay sooner or later."

Casmir itched to know what Rache was up to—he couldn't be tied in with the political mess on the station, could he? What if he'd brought his mercenaries to help the half of the locals that were *against* having Kingdom-influence brought to the station? But if that was his reason for coming, why hadn't he brought his warship over and more men to fight?

And what about the gate? He'd been determined to keep Jager from getting it, ideally by getting it himself first.

Was it possible he'd also gotten clues leading him to this system and even Xolas Moon? Maybe he'd already visited it and learned the gate was being stored under the ice. But like Ishii, he'd deduced that they needed submarines or some other type of aquatic vessel to retrieve it. Which had led him here…

Casmir squinted at Rache, debating if he should ask and see what kind of answer he got.

"Wait," Dr. Peshlakai said, waving both at Kim and Rache. "Are you in contact with Chi now? He's a friend of my father's. I haven't been able to contact my parents, and if he knows where they are, I definitely want to talk to him."

"Our contact has been off and on," Kim said. "He seems to be in the center of a combat zone."

"His lab is in a combat zone?" Peshlakai gripped the hatch, his voice almost squeaky with what sounded like genuine concern. "My parents don't live that far from his lab."

"You can come with us if you wish," Kim said.

"What?" Asger blurted. "No, we're not inviting *pirates* along with us."

"This system considers us mercenaries," Rache said blandly. "Only Jager spouts reductive hyperbole about me being a pirate."

I think he's here to get submarines, Casmir sent to Kim and Asger at the same time, *and to go get the gate out from under the ice of Xolas Moon while the Kingdom warships are occupied here.*

Shit, Asger replied.

Kim didn't send back anything.

"But I accept your offer, Scholar Sato," Rache said. "Dr. Peshlakai and I will come with you to find this virologist and to ensure his parents are safe."

"My offer was only to him." This time, it was Kim's turn to be dry.

No, wait, Casmir messaged his allies. *This is perfect. You can keep an eye on him, Kim. You and Zee.* Casmir balked at the idea of splitting Kim off to go on her own mission, *especially* with Rache, and he wouldn't consider it at all if Zee couldn't go along to protect her. *Asger and Tork and I can go find the president, and try to put an end to the fighting here without the need for an invasion force of marines.*

Asger shot him an exasperated look. *You didn't mention having* that *as one of your plans.*

I assumed it was implied.

"I am distressed that you don't wish to go places with me, Scholar Sato," Rache said, "but I assure you my intentions are honorable. Dr. Peshlakai may have told you the story of how he was framed for the former president's death. I've promised to help him clear his name, and it would be useful to know that his parents are safe and cannot be used against him. In case we end up bargaining at gunpoint with the local authorities."

"Is that true, Yas?" Kim asked.

Rache lifted his head higher, as if he couldn't believe Kim would doubt him. It sounded like an unlikely story to Casmir, but maybe it was true in the way that he and Asger were here for the princess. Technically true, but Asger's main orders were to protect the president.

"Yes," Yas said without hesitating or looking to Rache.

"Very well." As always, Kim's voice was flat and hard to read.

"Your heartfelt acceptance warms my soul," Rache said. "Allow me to confer briefly with my men."

"You can't tell me that man has a soul," Asger grumbled as Rache turned to the five armored men and his doctor.

He's going to send them to get the submarines, I bet, Casmir messaged. *Kim, if you can keep him and the doctor busy while we try to solve Asger's problem, then he won't be able to slink off and get the gate while the warships are anchored here.*

How am I supposed to keep him busy? Kim replied. *What if it takes you longer to find the president than it takes us to find Scholar Chi?*

Be creative. Didn't you want to discuss penis symbolism with him?

Asger sputtered. When Rache glanced over, Asger turned it into a cough and thumped his armored chest.

I believe I once said I would be capable of discussing the symbolism of Moby Dick *with him to buy you time to come up with a plan.*

Yes, but we failed to do that last time. Now's your chance. But hopefully, you won't need to bring up old boring books. Asger and I will be fast. Tork knows the system, and he's probably been to the station before. With luck, we'll finish before you.

Asger held up a finger, looking like he meant to protest further, but Rache and Peshlakai strolled over as the rest of his men headed for an exit into the station.

“Where are they going?” Asger asked.

“A brief shore leave,” Rache said. “Mercenaries get so little time off, you understand.”

“Shore leave in a violence-filled station in the middle of a civil war.”

“Do you not think the brothels will be open?”

Kim snorted.

Casmir frowned at her. She wasn’t supposed to find Rache amusing. Even if he’d helped with the terrorists, he was still an odious criminal.

“Come on, Casmir.” Asger headed for the door. “Bring your robots.”

“Right.” Casmir commanded the Aegis models to trail after him, then gave Kim a quick encouraging pat on the shoulder, hoping to convey that she could do this and he appreciated her willingness to keep Rache distracted. “Tork, this way, please.”

“You’re not coming with us?” Rache asked, suspicion leaking into his dry tone.

“No, Asger and I are excited to explore those brothels you mentioned.”

“With your robots? That’s asking a lot of the ladies there, isn’t it?”

“Robots like to be serviced too.” Casmir waved and hurried into the corridor, not caring if Rache was suspicious.

For now, he was worried more about the station than the gate. If the Kingdom wanted Tiamat Station as an ally, the Fleet couldn’t come in wielding force and alienating half of the population. Did the warship captains truly not see that? Or was it Jager who’d given this order?

Asger, Casmir, and their small robot army had to figure out an alternative, or this station might tear itself to pieces over fear of the Kingdom and what rule under Jager would represent.

Casmir didn’t know *what* alternative he could come up with yet, but he hoped for a lot of inspiration along the way.

CHAPTER 17

BONITA SET THE CHARGES IN THE BOTTOM OF the hover-capable freezer case in the cargo hold and threw a blanket artfully over them.

"They're very stable," Bonita promised Qin, who was gripping her chin as she watched the set up.

In a change from the norm, Bonita wore combat armor and Qin wore only her galaxy suit.

"You can't set them off by bumping them," Bonita added. "You'll have to roll over and set the timer to activate them. It only goes up to ten minutes, but that's too much time anyway. You'll want to set it for a minute, two at the most. And then leap out under the cover of smoke, which I will provide." Bonita tapped the belt purse she'd strapped on. She'd intentionally picked something feminine that looked like it would be full of make-up and perfume, not smoke grenades. "Take a circuitous route back to the ship, keep your helmet up, and hope nobody notices you. At least no Druckers."

Qin hadn't said much about the plan, and Bonita couldn't tell how she felt about it. Her expression was definitely dubious as she regarded the freezer box.

"Are you all right with this?" Bonita hoped so. They were docked at Death Knell Station, and she'd already deposited two thousand Union dollars into the account of an acquaintance who'd promised to arrange the distraction she needed. Afterward, she had promised to pay him another three thousand.

It was a lot of money for a half hour's work, but if she pulled this off, they wouldn't have to come up with money to buy Qin's contract from the Druckers. They wouldn't have to give those bastards a damn thing.

"I don't know," Qin said.

"I know it requires you to trust me, but I hope you know that no flirty pirate accountant is going to win me over. We're going to make sure they believe you're dead, and that's going to work best if you appear to blow up right in front of their eyes."

"I understand the plan—I always thought that would be a good way to get them to forget about me. I'm just not sure I can fit my Brockinger in that freezer." Qin patted the huge anti-tank gun slung over her shoulder and the bandolier of explosive shells draped across her torso.

"The whole top of it is clear." Bonita patted the glass door of the coffin-like freezer case. "You can't have that in there, or they'll know you're not a prisoner."

"I thought I could lie on it so they wouldn't see it."

"You're going to be busy lying on explosives."

"I can do both. I'm a big girl."

"Just let me carry the Brockinger. I'll hand it off to you once you've escaped and we're out of their sight. If this works, you shouldn't need it."

"You're already carrying your Starhawk." Qin waved at Bonita's DEW-Tek rifle. "Don't you think they'll find it suspicious if you show up with two weapons?"

"No. I used to hunt criminals with two pistols, a rifle, a dagger, and a grenade-pack on my belt. A girl needs to have the proper accoutrements for her profession."

"It's likely," Viggo chimed in, "that Johnny Twelve Toes will find a woman with a portable armory sexy. He seemed to find the name Laser appealing."

"Yes, thank you, Viggo. That's my main concern today. Making the pirates horny."

"It may not work on all the pirates. Johnny seems to be a unique individual."

"No kidding. I hope that's not going to be a problem."

Ideally, Johnny would send a team of mindless and easy-to-fool thugs instead of coming in person. Wasn't the fleet accountant too important a person to go out on field work? She couldn't imagine there were *that* many accountants on board those warships. How many well-educated number-loving people would agree to work for a pirate family?

Qin sighed deeply and shook her head, slowly removing her beloved weapon. "I do trust you, Captain—Bonita. You know I do. I always did, but especially since you let me help Kim and Casmir escape from the dastardly Captain Rache."

"The dastardly Captain Rache whom we later had dinner with." Bonita accepted the heavy Brockinger and the bandolier, arranging both over her shoulders. They were large weapons for her, but she didn't care. It wasn't as if she had to go far. The *Dragon* was snuggled up to a dock only two hundred yards from the restaurant she'd named as the meeting place.

"That was kind of weird," Qin said. "Life is weird."

"Tell me about it. See if you can fit in that freezer box." Bonita plucked a rock-hard steak that she'd missed earlier out of the corner and tossed it into the open hatch that led below the deck to the ship's frozen-food storage area.

Qin wrinkled her nose dubiously but complied. She had to scrunch her knees up and turn partway onto her side.

Bonita lowered the glass door to make sure it would close. "Good. You fit." Barely. She opened the door again to make sure Qin heard her. "See? This will work. Now close your eyes and do your best to appear unconscious. And hide your claws."

Qin had started to close her eyes, but she opened them again. "My claws?"

"Yes, your claws. Are those sequins? When did you bedazzle them?"

Qin grinned. "While you were flirting with the enemy."

"Well, hide them. The pirates aren't going to believe I gave my prisoner who's been locked in a cell for weeks bedazzling tools."

"All right, but they look good, don't they?" Qin wiggled her fingers.

"They look fabulous."

Bonita closed the case and took a deep breath. Her nerves tied themselves in knots in her stomach. She tried not to think about how much faith she was putting in people she hadn't seen in over a year and who ran a space station that advertised itself as an amicable place to trade slaves, illegal animals, and illegal drugs, while also satisfying all of one's carnal pleasures for a reasonable hourly fee. She wouldn't have taken the risk if the Amigos weren't known competitors of the Druckers.

"Shall I open the cargo-bay hatch, Captain?" Viggo asked. "The hour approaches."

"I know. I'm ready. I just wish I had Casmir's robot army at my back. It's too bad they were largely obliterated at that terrorist base."

Bonita pushed the button to activate the freezer box's hover capability, and it roared to life as it hefted its unorthodox cargo into the air. She'd turned off the freezer component, not wanting Qin to be in danger of turning into a cryonics patient if this took longer than expected. She pushed the case toward the hatch.

"I believe you would need El Mago here to operate them," Viggo said. "I watched him program them and add them to a network, and it did not seem intuitive."

"That's my nickname for him. You're going to have to make up your own."

"We can't share?"

"No, you don't speak my native tongue."

"You don't speak *my* native tongue, but I still let you use the sauna."

The sauna with instructions in a language she couldn't decipher. She was never sure if she was relaxing in it or irradiating herself.

"All right, you can share my nickname."

The hatch opened, and Bonita took another deep breath and strode onto the station. Countless people, androids, and robots of all types walked, rode, and flew past. She'd intentionally parked at the freight end of Docks and Locks, so nobody should think twice about someone pushing a big box around, but she did boost it a couple more feet off the deck so the average person wouldn't be able to see inside and wonder at her odd cargo. Not that anyone here would likely bat an eye at a corpse or unconscious woman stuffed in a box.

She kept her eyes and ears open as she strode toward the restaurant facing the dozens and dozens of portholes and airlocks, most with ships docked at them. According to the *Dragon's* scanners, the Drucker warship that Viggo had been watching was still at that moon, so Johnny must have sent some smaller craft. That was a relief. If it was a combat shuttle, it shouldn't bring more than twenty people along. That was still an intimidating number, but not nearly as intimidating as four hundred.

As she walked, Bonita looked out the portholes, hoping to spot their ship coming in. Not that it would wave a Druckers pirate flag and be easily identifiable. It was possible, if not likely, that it was already there, one of the innocuous shuttles or yachts that Viggo had scanned on the way in.

Bonita turned into the alley at the corner of the restaurant and carefully pushed the freezer box around massive trash and composting bins attached to the walls on either side. When she reached the alley running parallel to the main concourse, she spotted a partially open door in the back of the restaurant.

A dish girl with her dark hair swept into a ponytail met Bonita's eyes and whispered, *"¿Nuevo Popocatépetl va a erupciónar?"*

"Sí, señorita."

The girl ducked back inside. Bonita's shoulder blades itched. She wanted to put the helmet up on her armor, turn her back to a wall, move Qin's box out of the way, and hold her rifle—or maybe the big Brockinger—in both hands. But she had to look like she was here to make a deal, not start a war.

She leaned casually against a trash bin and yawned a few times. The alley was largely empty, other than a robotic garbage vehicle trundling toward her from a few blocks away. It paused frequently to collect refuse.

Six big men in forest-green combat armor strode around the corner, their steps in sync, rifles in their arms. Bonita did her best to look bored, and she didn't reach for her weapons as they approached. Two of the men's helmets were back, their faces easy to see. They walked ahead of the others. Neither was her graying accountant.

As the men came closer, she could make out the faces behind the faceplates of the others. None of them belonged to Johnny.

Her shoulders relaxed an iota. These six pirates could make plenty of trouble for her, but she had a hunch she'd have a harder time tricking Johnny. These pups all looked to be in their twenties.

"Where's your backup, Grandma?" one of the leaders asked, eyeing her and the freezer case.

"I never had kids, and it's *Laser*."

"Laser, right. So scary. That our Qin?"

Bonita unclenched her jaw—she hadn't realized it was clenched—and patted the side of the case. "Should be. You got my twenty-five? I assume you brought physical currency since I haven't had any money pop into my account."

"We got it." One of them tapped what looked to be a toolbox full of screwdrivers. "Let's see it, or you don't get the key to unlock the case."

"Let's see the money," Bonita said.

"Sarge?" the man with the box asked.

"Show her, Xun."

"What if she really *doesn't* have backup? We could just take everything. Leave her dead here. No one would even have to know. The bosses wouldn't care."

"Johnny said to deal fair with her," the sergeant said. "Do *you* want to cross him?"

The case holder—Xun—seemed to shrink inside his armor. "No. But he's not a boss. The bosses wouldn't care."

"They also wouldn't care if Johnny killed you. Show her the money."

Xun walked forward, opened the box, and displayed crisp white and red Union dollars. They had either come straight out of a bank machine, or they were counterfeits. Bonita would have preferred digital currency but reminded herself she hadn't come here to take their money.

"Let's see inside the case," the sergeant said. "Is that a freezer?"

"Hard to find a suitcase large enough to stuff her body in," Bonita said.

The men snorted.

"They are big girls."

Bonita adjusted the hover control, and the freezer case lowered to within a couple of inches of the faux pavement. Qin remained inside in the same position, her eyes shut.

"Yup, that's one of the Qins," the sergeant said. "She drugged or stunned or what?"

"Tranqed." Bonita waved indifferently. "You've probably got thirty minutes until she wakes up."

Or thirty seconds. Assuming her people came through. Bonita had been reassured by the dish girl giving the pass phrase, but Jaco's men should have attacked by now.

The garbage truck rumbled a block closer and paused to unload another trash bin. She picked out people inside the cab of what had appeared to be an automated vehicle. Maybe *they* were the distraction she had paid for. If so, she needed to buy a little more time for the vehicle to make its way to this section of the alley.

Two of the men stepped forward to grab the freezer case.

Bonita held a hand up. "I want to count the money."

The men exchanged exasperated looks.

"It's not that I don't trust you, but—no, I definitely don't trust you." Bonita snapped her fingers and pointed at the money box.

"You *sure* we can't just kill her, boss?"

"Not here." The sergeant looked toward the restaurant and up and down the alley, his gaze lingering on the approaching garbage vehicle.

Bonita stepped forward. The man holding the money sighed and let her count it.

A message came through on her contact. Viggo.

Bonita, my external cameras show that two men in armor have taken up a position in front of my airlock tube. They have rifles with grenade-launcher attachments.

Is their armor green? she replied.

Yes.

Is either of them Johnny?

I can't tell. Even if they weren't wearing helmets, I wouldn't know how to recognize him with clothes on.

Ha ha.

A couple of men in the local gray of the station militia have paused to look at them. So far, the authorities are not approaching or making aggressive gestures, and the green-armored men are only standing and watching, but if you intend to return to the ship with Qin in tow...

I understand. I won't, not right away. We rented that slot for two days, so if we need to, we'll disappear into the station for a while. Worst case scenario, if they keep watching, I'll leave on my own and come back in a few days to pick up Qin.

"Satisfied?" the sergeant asked.

"Yes." Bonita returned the money to the box and waved to the freezer case. "She's all yours."

No, she thought. The worst case scenario would be if her putative allies didn't show up, and these pirates walked back onto their ship unopposed, and Qin believed Bonita had abandoned her.

As the pirates backed away, Bonita feared that scenario would come to pass. Maybe the garbage vehicle was just a garbage vehicle.

"You taking this money or what, lady?" the man holding the box asked. "Because if you're not, me and my buddies will enjoy spending it ourselves."

Bonita reached for it, but she didn't want to take it and then disappear with Qin. That would make the Druckers more suspicious than if Qin seemed to die in the explosion and Bonita ran away without taking the money. If she vanished with both, the Druckers might put their next bounty out for *her*.

"Yeah, I—"

Something lofted out of the front of the garbage vehicle, and Bonita jumped back. A clank sounded as a grenade landed between several of the armored men.

"No Druckers on our station!" someone cried from around a corner.

"Death to Druckers!" came from another corner.

Bonita scurried for the nearest trash bin as the armored men whirled toward the threats. She commanded her helmet into place and resisted the urge to pull the freezer case back with her. She couldn't let the Druckers see her showing too much attachment to Qin.

The restaurant door opened, and someone leaned out, firing several times with a rifle. The bolts splashed harmlessly off the pirates' armor, but then the grenade blew. It hurled two of the Druckers into walls. Bonita grimaced as Qin's case rocked violently under the force of the shockwave.

The glass door on top opened slightly.

Not yet, Bonita messaged with her chip as she yanked out one of her smoke grenades.

The Druckers opened fire at the garbage vehicle and the restaurant entrance as another grenade lofted toward them. One of their bolts hit the projectile midair, and the thunderous boom echoed from the walls. Sirens started up in the distance. It wouldn't be long until the station militia showed up.

Bonita made herself wait until none of the pirates were looking her way before rolling her smoke grenade out into the alley. It came to a stop right under the freezer case and spewed a gray-blue cloud. Weapons fire streaked down the alley from both ends now. Bonita carefully rolled out two more smoke grenades. Billowing clouds from the first filled the air, and the case grew difficult to make out.

Now, she messaged Qin. *Set the explosives and slip out. I'm back by this trash bin.*

Coming, came the quick reply.

A crimson bolt tore off the partially open restaurant door, and the man who'd been firing jerked back inside. Thuds and clanks sounded, the smoke swirling around as the pirates found someone to fight. Bonita wanted to shoot at them, to help her allies, but she had to play the role of startled bystander, surprised by this unexpected development.

"Hurry, Qin," she whispered.

Since she couldn't see the case through the smoke anymore, Bonita didn't know if Qin had slipped out yet. Was she having trouble setting the charges? Bonita was on the verge of asking when a familiar figure leaped out of the smoke and joined her behind the trash bin.

Before Qin had fully crouched down, the charges went off. A squad of security robots rolled around the corner in time to witness it, and they rocked back as the shockwave hit them. Broken glass and the warped shards of the freezer case clanged off the walls, the robots, and the armored men.

As the security robots rumbled into the alley on massive treads, unperturbed by the explosion, Bonita rolled out her last smoke grenade. As fresh gray clouds filled the alley, she tapped Qin on the shoulder, and they ran off in the opposite direction she'd last seen the Druckers. Only the firing of weapons and thuds of armor striking armor proved they were still there.

Something slammed into her shoulder as they ran, and she would have pitched to her knees, but Qin caught her by the arm. Bonita had a feeling that had been a DEW-Tek bolt and was glad she'd opted for armor.

They ran down the alley, staying behind the shops instead of returning to the main concourse. The smoke faded, and Bonita felt vulnerable.

She blew out a relieved breath when they reached a grate for the large central ventilation system that connected the levels of the station. It leaned next to the duct entrance, four screws resting neatly on the pavement beside it. Bonita ushered Qin into the duct, relieved when she fit. Bonita hadn't been certain she would.

She couldn't put the screws back in from the other side, but after she climbed in, she twisted and pulled the grate into place. She hoped her allies would come and replace the screws so there would be no sign of their passing. She also hoped the Druckers would be driven back to their ship and wouldn't have time to investigate the remains of that freezer case in too great of detail. If they could scour it at their leisure, they were sure to notice the lack of Qin bits in the wreckage.

"Are we going to try to come out farther down and make our way back to the ship?" Qin whispered.

"We're not going to try to come out at all, not for a while. Viggo says there are two Druckers watching our airlock."

"Do you have a plan?"

"Yes, hide until they get bored and go away."

"Oh."

Bonita thought that *oh* sounded worried. She hoped it was a needless worry. They'd gotten this far. They just had to wait until opportunity favored them again.

CHAPTER 18

THE LONG CORRIDOR LEADING AWAY FROM THE SHUTTLE bays and airlocks was quieter than Kim expected. The patrolling robots must have kept the area free of rioters. Now and then, they passed a deactivated Aegis Defender sitting silently on its treads in the middle of the corridor or in front of a door.

Kim thought Casmir might truly have been able to take over the station if he'd ordered all the robots to detain the inhabitants at once, but she couldn't blame him for shying away from the idea. Countless things could go wrong, and if the robots ended up killing people, how would they be better than Kingdom marines?

"Are you deep in thought?" Rache asked quietly. "Or trading text jokes with Casmir?"

He was walking at her side while Yas led the way, Zee walking at *his* side in case anyone jumped out at them from the front.

"Should I be alarmed that you've learned enough about me to know that both are equally viable possibilities?" Kim asked.

It was safer to make a joke than share her thoughts. She didn't doubt Casmir's assessment of why Rache was here, so she would have to be guarded around him. She would prefer to be able to trust him, but if they had opposite goals, it did not seem safe.

For some reason, that gave her a twinge of sadness. Hearing his voice and seeing him come walking out of the shuttle had startled her, even though she should have realized their paths might cross once more on this quest for the gate. Would he ask for that dinner date again? Not here, surely. She ought to be safe from having to come up with an answer.

"Not alarmed, I should think," he said, his voice even softer. And faintly amused. "Might I suggest being pleased by my attentive perceptiveness?"

Yas glanced back. Kim couldn't see his face well through his helmet, but she thought she caught a flash of alarm from *him*. Maybe he wasn't used to Rache flirting with a woman. If that was what he was doing.

Rache must have caught the glance, too, for he didn't try another joke. Kim told herself she wasn't disappointed and that she wouldn't like to walk somewhere private with him so she could ask him about the mysteries of his past. The months of his absence from the race circuit, the fiancée that had been reported as missing but who Rache and the ex-chief superintendent had known was long dead.

Yas stopped in front of a lift.

"I think it'll be hairier on the upper levels," he said grimly.

"If there's a circuitous route to the lab that's less likely to be occupied, that would be ideal," Rache said, "but if we need to fight our way there, so be it. The locals are probably using broken chair legs and rotten vegetables for weapons."

"It's unlikely they'll be in combat armor, aside from Station Civil Security—" Yas stepped into the lift with Zee, "—but it's legal to own personal firearms and DEW-Tek weapons here, so there may be more resistance than you expect."

"Understood." Rache gestured for Kim to enter first, bowing his head slightly, as if he were inviting her into a restaurant.

She walked in, wondering what it would be like to simply have dinner somewhere with him. She imagined he'd be an intriguing person to debate literature with.

The lift hummed and rattled as it went upward, then jolted and came to an abrupt halt. They were between levels.

"And here we have the real reason nobody was on Level 1," Rache muttered.

"Maybe we should have kept Casmir and his tools with us," Kim said.

Yas hit a few buttons, but nothing happened. Rache slung his rifle onto his back and planted his gauntleted hands on the two sliding doors. He pushed hard, something snapped, and the doors jerked open in fits. Kim found herself on eye level with the floor of Level 5 and the ceiling of Level 4, with two feet of space for them to squirm out through.

"I don't object to tools," Rache said, "but sometimes, brute force is simpler."

"Force need not be brutish," Zee said, then morphed himself into something liquid and indistinct to ooze out onto Level 5 through the gap.

"Is it me, or is that robot chattier than it used to be?" Rache said.

"Casmir's been encouraging it to develop a personality," Kim said.

"How does he do that?"

"He talks to it."

"Huh."

Rache lowered his hands to offer Kim a boost. She didn't need the help and was debating whether to accept it or to simply pull herself up when a shout came from the corridor.

At first, she thought Zee had run down it and attacked someone, but his legs were visible, shaped back into their usual form, in front of the lift.

"It's one of those monsters from Stribog Station," someone yelled.

"It's the *Kingdom's* monster!"

Shots rang out, clanging off the elevator shaft above their car. Next came the *ssh-boom* of something more powerful firing. The lift rattled, slipping two inches.

"Wonderful," Rache muttered, pulling himself out as Zee raced down the corridor.

Rache ran out of sight after him.

"I suggest we wait while they handle the violence," Yas said.

"I'm not good at waiting." Kim didn't want to needlessly throw herself into danger, but she had her vials along, and it might be better to knock out the inhabitants rather than shooting them.

The shots had stopped by the time she climbed out, one of her vials in hand. She sucked in a startled breath at the carnage in the corridor ahead. More than a few bodies lay tangled among garbage, doors torn off hinges, broken furnishings, and spent bullet casings. Zee and Rache hadn't done all that—or *any* of that.

Facades of residential apartments and commercial shops lined the corridor—it was designed more like a street, with cross passages creating intersections—and corner lampposts burned with cheery fake firelight that was at odds with the rundown surroundings.

Zee stood in the middle of the first intersection with two young men in his grip, their feet dangling six inches above the faux pavement. Rache was picking up a couple of fallen weapons.

Not seeing any further danger, Kim helped Yas out of the lift. A woman screamed in the distance, and shots rang out.

Kim grimaced, fearing her vials would be of little use in quelling the chaos here. She tucked the one she'd pulled out back into a pocket.

"What was that?" Rache asked, glancing at the pocket.

"I made some knockout vials."

"Nice." He almost purred the word, and his approving tone made her smile before she could catch herself. "Is it the same stuff Casmir used in the Black Stars compound?"

"No. Just a sedative. I didn't have the urge to make confused station inhabitants vomit and drip snot onto their chests." She waved at the men—almost boys—that Zee still had in the air. They were flailing and trying to kick him, but Zee might as well have been a steel wall.

"I managed not to vomit." Rache's tone turned dry. "However, I was unable to still my nostrils' snot-secretion reflex."

"No? Perhaps your prowess isn't as great as I assumed."

"Really." He gripped the rifle and homemade grenade launcher that he'd retrieved from the boys, bent them in half with a wrenching that rang from the walls, and tossed them through a broken window.

"Shit," one of the dangling boys said.

The other one, less intimidated, snarled, "Screw that Kingdom ass-licker. He's probably a girl when he's not in armor."

Kim resisted the urge to point out that girls were not ineffective, with or without armor.

Rache strode back to Zee, patted down his captives, and removed pistols tucked into their boots. He bent them as easily as he had the larger weapons and tossed them aside.

"Perhaps you should have asked before firing," Rache said. "I loathe the Kingdom. And their asses."

"Screw you," the brave one said.

The other one looked like he wanted to disappear.

"Let them go," Rache told Zee.

Zee looked toward Kim instead of complying.

"How do you call him off the hunt?" Rache asked Kim.

"Casmir says please."

"Of course he does."

"I am only programmed to obey Kim Sato and Casmir Dabrowski," Zee stated.

Ah, that was the problem.

"Let them go, please, Zee." Kim would have preferred the boys be tied up somewhere, but that might make them targets for opportunist opponents that chanced past.

Zee released the boys, and they sprinted away.

"That was Tenebris Rache," one whispered, the words just reaching Kim's ears.

"Was not."

"Was too."

The boys raced around the corner, and their conversation grew inaudible. Rache gazed after them. Was he pleased to have been recognized? Proud of the reputation he'd established?

"What were your captain's orders?" Rache asked Kim without commenting on his infamy.

"The guy in charge of the ship I got stuck on?" she asked.

He faced her, though she had the sense that he was paying close attention to their surroundings, as well. "That person usually has the rank of captain, yes."

"I have no idea what his orders are."

"Truly?" Rache asked softly.

Did he think she would spill everything she knew, even when it might be considered treason? No, there was no might about it. To give intelligence to this enemy of the Kingdom would absolutely be considered treason.

"We're not on the same side, Rache," Kim said, resisting an urge to use the name he'd given her. His real one. David.

"Ah."

Rache gestured for Yas to lead again, and Kim waved for Zee to walk at his side. She would have volunteered to lead herself if she'd known where she was going, but the map she'd been able to pull off the system's public network was basic. She should have asked Casmir for the passcode to get onto the station's security network.

"Would you tell me what *Casmir's* orders are?" Rache asked, his tone more amused than dry this time.

"He doesn't have any orders. He's a civilian advisor, the same as I am. We're not in the loop."

Maybe he would believe that and drop the subject. Kim hoped they were close to Chi's lab.

"He doesn't have orders to… rescue the princess, was it?"

"No."

"Or your colleague?"

"No."

"Are you sure he's not an independent contractor rather than a civilian advisor?"

"He is independent."

"I only ask because if Jager takes this station by force, it will be seen as an act of war by the rest of the system, perhaps by governments in other systems. He's not trying to hide his presence here. There's no room for debate, as there was at Stribog, where the crushers mysteriously showed up and the Kingdom was blamed, but somewhat uncertainly blamed. Here, there would be no uncertainty."

"Do you care?" Kim hadn't wanted to continue the conversation, but she couldn't help but wonder.

He hated the Kingdom, didn't he? Or was it just Jager that he hated? After all, he'd been born and raised on Odin. He'd fallen in love with a woman from there…

"That Jager is starting something he may not have the capability to finish? No. But it's likely that someone, perhaps a band of wealthy families such as Dr. Peshlakai is a part of, will hire mercenaries to evict whatever forces the Kingdom leaves behind. And I *am* in the area."

She squinted at him, though he wore his usual mask under his helmet, so there was nothing to see on his face. Had he *already* been hired? Maybe Casmir was wrong, or only partially right, about the submarines. What if Casmir and the Kingdom and Rache and his men were on opposite sides because of more than the gate quest?

Yas took them up a narrower side street. The ceiling ended, giving the illusion of a sky high above them, commercial and tenement buildings rising, as if they'd been built outdoors instead of in a station.

Trees arose from circular openings in the sidewalk, growing tall in the half gravity, and expensive-looking cabs and air bikes were parked at the curb. Most had been damaged, windows and frames smashed, doors ripped open and interior compartments rifled through.

"This is my parents' building." Yas stopped in front of double Glasnax doors. "There's usually a security guard stationed here."

Gunfire in the street a block away made him wince.

"We're not far from the lab. It's just around the corner." Yas pointed, fortunately in the direction away from the gunfire. "Mind if I go up and see if they're home?" Yas hesitated. "You can go on without me."

"We'll stay together." Rache waved at the door. "Check."

Yas hurried inside, and Rache strode after him. Kim thought about waiting outside, but Zee might draw unwanted attention again. Better not to give the people here any more reason to fight, especially such a dangerous opponent. Fortunately, Zee hadn't been programmed to kill, just to defend, and Rache… she had no idea how programmed he was at this point in his life, but at least he wasn't inclined to get rough with surly teenagers.

They rode a lift that worked better than the last one and came out on the top floor, with large windows allowing faux sunlight to stream inside. The residence should have felt opulent, with its marble floors and elegant architectural details, but displays had been torn off walls, doors forced open, and furniture destroyed and left in pieces in the hallway.

Yas muttered worriedly to himself, and Kim wished she could think of something to say that wouldn't sound inane. She thought of her family back home and what would happen if war came to System Lion and Odin. Was it possible the capital city could end up looking like this? Or worse?

Yas groaned when he spotted what Kim assumed was his parents' apartment, and the door had been forced open. He rushed inside. Rache peeked in long enough to check for danger, then decided to wait in the hallway.

Kim waited warily with him, afraid he would ask more questions that she would have to dodge. He faced her, and she had the sense that he wished to speak. Maybe he was trying to come up with something to say that wouldn't put her on edge. As if that was possible here.

Even though she was sympathetic to Yas's plight, Kim wanted to hurry up and find Chi. She'd tried to contact him again when they'd arrived at the station, but once more, he'd gone silent. Not gassed into unconsciousness again, she hoped.

"I've just finished Ajda Basheer's *The Sun Never Sets in Space*," Rache offered. "Have you read it?"

She stared at him. He wanted to talk about literature? *Here?*

Was this an attempt to bring up something they could safely discuss without worry of treason or betrayal?

"I'm familiar with the author," she said, "but I haven't read anything of hers, save for a few poems in a literature class. I remember them as nods to the collective existential crisis that mankind seems to feel in wondering if we have the right to remake space and entire worlds to better suit us."

Rache chuckled. "That sounds about right. The book has a narrative structure, but she does lean toward poetic prose. There are chapters from the point of view of bacteria that existed on Yemaya when humans arrived and terraformed the planet, and now the bacteria are almost extinct, and they're struggling to adapt and survive on a world with a vastly different climate than they evolved in."

"The bacteria are sentient?" Kim suspected it was a literary device, but she'd read a few papers hypothesizing the existence of a collective intelligence among some species of bacteria.

"A bit of anthropomorphism. I assume. Perhaps you could read it and let me know your opinion as a bacteriologist. Or simply as a reader of literature. I would be interested in your opinions, either way." He bowed. Formally.

She couldn't tell if this was his way of flirting or if he simply longed for someone with whom he could discuss the things he read. If most of his men weren't educated, or if he felt he had to keep a distance from them, she supposed he couldn't wander down to the mess hall and chat about books with them.

He had picked a lonely existence for himself, surrounded by people but with nobody to talk to. Though if she was honest with herself, her life wasn't much different. Before she'd met Casmir—before he'd befriended her, winning her over almost against her wishes—she'd never had a best friend. Especially when she'd been younger, she'd been that weird kid who skipped grades in school and went to the university early, who hadn't known how to connect with *normal* people. She'd found colleagues she could speak with easily enough at Parvus Biologia, but many of them were as stiff and socially awkward as she was, and she'd never felt the urge to invite them for social activities outside of work. And they'd never invited her. Most of them were much older, but she wasn't sure that was the only reason she never truly felt she fit in.

Yas burst back into the corridor, and Kim jerked her thoughts back to the present. She was here on a mission; this wasn't the time for daydreaming—or wallowing in her own existential crises.

"They're not there, and everything is broken or stolen." Yas had retracted his helmet, and he gripped his hair with both hands, as if he might tear it out in clumps. "The household robots were smashed. There's moldy food on the floor in the kitchen and a dead bird on the balcony. I don't think anyone has been here for days. Or longer."

"We'll find this Scholar Chi and ask him where they went." Rache gestured back toward the lift.

"You think they went somewhere? Or—" Yas glanced back toward the open door, the apartment in disarray, "—I thought they might have been kidnapped. Because of their wealth and power in the system. The *old* system." He grimaced.

"We'll find out."

As Kim trailed them out, she tried not to think about the fact that the Kingdom sympathizers might be the ones who'd taken Yas's parents. And that she and Casmir—or at least Asger—were here to find the Kingdom-sympathizing president and help him stay safe and maintain his position. She also tried not to think about Rache's comment that his mercenaries might be hired to fight that president and his people, to evict him from power.

"I'll read that book," Kim said quietly as they walked back out into the street.

She didn't know what else to say. It wasn't an olive branch, not exactly, but maybe an acknowledgment that there could never be anything between them but she still wanted him to have someone to talk to about literature.

Rache gave her a long look. "Good. Thank you."

She swallowed. It seemed a strange thing to thank a person for, but it filled her with an unfamiliar emotion she couldn't quite identify, and she said, "You're welcome."

CHAPTER 19

I F THIS PRESIDENT CHRONIS HAS A CHIP, IT'S not on the network," Casmir said as he and Tork rode with Asger in an open tram car that zipped them toward the government end of the cylinder-shaped station. Lights streaked past, and their passage created a breeze that ruffled his hair. He'd had to leave his small army of Aegis robots behind when they hadn't fit through the car entrance.

Casmir tried to focus on finding the president, not on the fact that he was leaving Kim—and Zee and Rache—far behind when his main reason for coming to the station had been to help her. He also tried not to dwell on the rotting bodies they had passed on their way to board. His stomach was churning for reasons that had nothing to do with gravity.

"He must be in hiding," Casmir added. "I'm sure lots of people are trying to hunt him down. They may believe that the Kingdom threat will go away if he goes away. Or is killed."

"In hiding, yes, but somewhere protected, I'm sure." Asger watched the route ahead, platforms and signs for stops blurring past. "He has control of all the security forces and *had* control of the security robots until recently."

As their car slowed for the final stop, Casmir got a better look at walls covered in graffiti, including an image of two men holding hands crossed out by a huge crown—the Star Kingdom symbol. The idea of his government being boiled down into some monolith that stood for stamping out freedoms made him sick. The Kingdom wasn't perfect, and he'd often lamented its restrictive genetic engineering policies, but it wasn't the most tyrannical government in the Twelve Systems.

One had only to look to System Cerberus and the asteroid-states of the Miners' Union to find slavery, laws that only served the wealthy, and systems that allowed the poor to die in the streets.

Admittedly, those governments hadn't taken over the Twelve Systems in the past and forced their rules on huge swaths of people. Casmir could see why those who enjoyed freedoms that weren't allowed in the Kingdom would fear a second coming.

So, why was he here, helping Asger find the man who wanted the Kingdom to be in charge of this station? Casmir rubbed his face, wishing he had a better answer. Because if they didn't restore order, the marines would? And with more violence?

As the car stopped at the last platform, Casmir almost missed spotting sudden movement in the shadows.

"Down!" Asger barked.

Casmir ducked as gunshots rang out. He scooted away from the door opening, using the low sides of the car for cover.

Asger sprang out to the platform, and Tork followed him.

"A knight!" someone screamed.

"They're here, they're here!"

More gunshots fired. They clanged off metal at least twenty feet away. Whoever was out there wasn't targeting the car—not when they had Asger to shoot at.

Casmir pulled out his stunner and peered over the top of the car wall. Asger had switched his pertundo for a stunner of his own. He dodged a huge barrel thrown at him, then fired at two men with DEW-Tek pistols, backed up by a woman with a hunting rifle shooting bullets.

His armor protected him, but Asger dodged and leaped so rapidly that none of their attacks even glanced off. He fired three times, and the stun beams caught each target precisely in the chest.

A few meters to his side, Tork grappled with an android that had been given a shotgun. It must have been someone's independent servant, not one on the security network that Casmir now controlled. Tork tore the weapon from its grip and hurled it onto the tracks.

A whisper of fabric sounded behind Casmir, his only warning. He spun as someone thudded down in the car behind him. He tried to bring the stunner to bear, but big strong arms wrapped around him from behind and hefted him off his feet.

"Kingdom scum," his attacker snarled.

Casmir threw his head back as the arms squeezed with rib-crunching pressure. His attacker must have seen it coming, because Casmir didn't connect with the nose-splattering satisfaction he'd hoped for.

He tried again, apologizing to his neck as he whipped his head back. This time, he struck a glancing blow to his captor's chin.

It hurt the man enough to loosen his grip. That gave Casmir a split second to twist around enough to point the stunner at the man's torso.

He fired, but the nimbus caught him, too, and even though his opponent released him, Casmir's legs were numb when he landed, and he crumpled to the deck.

Idiot, he swore to himself, realizing that anyone with more than twenty minutes of experience with weapons would have foreseen that. At least his attacker pitched to the floor of the car, head clanging on the metal wall.

As Casmir dragged himself backward, his legs barely working, another thud came from behind him, someone landing in the front of the car. Damn it.

He twisted and pointed his stunner.

Asger gripped it and turned it away before he could fire. "Easy, killer."

"Sorry." Casmir jerked the weapon down. "I'm sorry."

"You don't need to be sorry. You need to yell when you're in trouble. That's the way you signal to your friends that you could use some assistance."

"I thought you might be busy."

"Not for long. Not with these people."

The platform had fallen silent, the attackers all unconscious. Casmir was thankful that was all that they were, that Asger hadn't used deadly force on any of them. Not that he'd expected a knight to be unchivalrous in battle, but these people clearly hated the Kingdom, and Asger was a symbol of all that the Kingdom was. It would have been easy for him to lash out against hatred directed at him.

Asger hauled Casmir to his feet and leaned him against the side of the car, keeping a hand on his shoulder to help him stay upright. Casmir couldn't feel his toes, and his legs only halfway supported him. Thankfully, Asger didn't tease him about the rookie move. It took

Casmir a long minute to pound feeling back into his thighs. Asger waited, constantly scanning their surroundings for more threats.

"I feel like the bully here," Casmir admitted, though as soon as the words came out, he thought they sounded silly. Maybe like he was on the bullying *side*. If ever there was an ineffective bully—he pounded on his numb thighs again—it was he.

"I know," Asger said, apparently understanding perfectly.

"Are we sure we want to help this president take control?"

Asger smiled sadly. "I have my orders."

"Is that enough to make it all right? I don't mean to condemn you—I'm just as Kingdom as you are, but…" Casmir licked his lips, not sure what he wanted to say. "This feels wrong."

"I think if we can bring stability back to the station, we'll be doing the right thing. It's the lack of either system being fully in control right now that's allowing this. Anarchy." Asger pointed at Casmir's legs. "Can you walk?"

Casmir shook them out and stepped away from the side of the car. "I think so."

Tork was already waiting on the platform. As Casmir exited on still-shaky legs, he questioned whether Asger was right, but he didn't want to argue with his friend.

They'd reached the stop where the government buildings were located. If the president wasn't in his office there—Casmir doubted he would be—maybe they would at least find a clue to lead them to him.

They passed more bodies, two men in civil security uniforms, and Asger checked them for signs of life before shaking his head and moving on. They turned a corner and walked toward wide steps of a large government building, the corridor ceiling disappearing and a gray-blue sky opening up, some technology creating the illusion that they were on a real planet with a real atmosphere.

A few mutters came from side buildings, and up ahead, a woman with a torn dress ran away from them. Casmir only glimpsed her bruised face for a second before she disappeared, but she looked like she'd been running away from a lot of people over many days.

One of the almost ubiquitous Aegis security robots lay tipped on its side.

"Tork," Casmir said, trotting over to it. "Let's tip this guy up."

Asger sighed. "Casmir, there's not time to fix things."

"Just this one thing. I'm realizing that I could do more with the robots. I powered them down so they wouldn't fight us, but they exist to protect people, presumably. Maybe I can program them to do that again."

"There's not time."

"I'll do it while we're walking." Casmir helped Tork lift the security robot—mostly, he pointed at the robot while leaving the far stronger android to handle the lifting—then hurried to catch up with Asger.

"I thought you were worried that someone would realize you were on the network and had disabled the shuttle-bay robots if you did too much tinkering."

"I was, and it's a valid concern, but maybe I can install some new defenses and keep other people from getting on the network to make changes, at least until we get everything straightened out."

"I think there may be a law about taking over an entire station's network." Asger climbed the wide stairs to the building.

"There probably is, but laws don't seem in much danger of being enforced right now."

Casmir concentrated on his new project, letting Asger pick the route through the building. It was empty, some of the lower-level offices looted, though a security door barred entrance to the second level. Casmir hoped they would find undisturbed offices with more clues in them up there.

Before he could volunteer to try to mechanically get past the locking mechanism, Asger used his armor-enhanced strength to rip the door open.

A woman's alarmed curse came from somewhere up ahead. Asger jogged in that direction while Casmir followed more slowly, peering into open doors to either side of the wide carpeted hallway. Couches and plush chairs dotted seating areas. On the back wall of one large office, he spotted a great seal featuring a two-dimensional rendering of the station overlaid with justice scales. A bookcase had been pulled away from the wall, revealing a hidden doorway leading into a dark corridor.

"Asger," Casmir called. "This looks promising."

Asger returned, marching a short, sturdy woman with a pointed jaw and short gray and black hair in front of him. She carried several folders and a couple of books that Asger hadn't taken from her. His grip on her arm was light but firm, and her jaw was clenched.

"I think this may be the woman we talked to on the comm," Asger said. "I thought I recognized her voice when she cursed, but she doesn't want to speak with me now."

At first, the woman glowered at Casmir, but then a startled expression crossed her face. Almost like recognition.

She wouldn't be familiar with Rache, surely, not the way Princess Oku had been. Had this woman looked up Casmir after Asger had introduced him on the shuttle? Casmir had publications in scholarly journals in other systems, so there ought to be records of him around.

He bowed as the woman stopped in front of him. "Professor Casmir Dabrowski, ma'am." He didn't think the woman on the comm had ever identified herself. "When I asked for asylum, I didn't realize your people were just as in need of protection as we are."

She snorted. "And you didn't mention you had a knight for a bodyguard. I am disinclined to believe your request was authentic."

"Does that mean you won't take me to see your president?"

"President Chronis can stuff his head up his own ass, if he's still alive."

"That sounds uncomfortable. Will you tell me your name, ma'am?"

She hesitated, squinting at him. Casmir tried to look friendly and harmless.

"Linh Nguyen, Secretary of Education on Tiamat Station."

"Oh, you're a teacher." He grinned. "My father is a professor of mathematics, and I teach—or *was* teaching robotics before all of this started. I run the lab at Zamek University."

"On Odin in the Kingdom," she said coolly.

"Yes, I gather you were one of President Bakas's supporters rather than one of President Chronis's."

"You gather correctly. The cabinet has been split this past couple of years, trying to figure out how to deal with increasing threats from pirate and mercenary activity in the system, but only Chronis had any interest in appealing to the Kingdom for protection—why, I don't know, since you people don't have a presence in any of the other systems anymore—and he's been acting alone behind a lot of people's backs. Nobody wants you here." She glared over her shoulder at Asger—well, Asger's *chest*, since he was a lot taller than she. "Go back to your ship and tell your military to leave this station and this system. You're not welcome."

"I'm afraid they wouldn't listen to us," Casmir said. "Certainly not to me. I'm a civilian advisor. That's all. What did you teach when you taught? I assume your government duties preclude you working with students now."

She squinted at him again, oozing suspicion.

"Uhm, anyway," Casmir said, "I think your president asked for the Kingdom ships to come. I'm not sure on the details, but Asger and I would love to help you solve your problem in such a way that the marines don't need to come stomping over here and make a mess."

Casmir wondered how much time they had before that became a reality. Was Ishii waiting to hear from President Chronis before sending his troops over?

"What are you talking about?" Nguyen asked.

"Asger and I—and my friend, Tork, here—" Casmir reached over and patted the silent android, "—went against Captain Ishii's wishes to come visit, in part to locate a friend, and also because we, being less surly and militant than those Fleet fellows, would prefer a non-violent solution to your problem."

"It's too late for *non*-violence. And don't tell me your armored knight is a pacifist."

"No, but he's a goodhearted man who doesn't want to see innocent people mowed down by large-scale military maneuvers. Or for people to be pressured into making decisions out of desperation. Speaking of that, is there a place where we can go to make an announcement to the entire station? I've been working on something to help provide protection." He tapped his temple.

Nguyen was scrutinizing him like he was a puzzling specimen in a science experiment. Or maybe a recalcitrant toddler in need of a spanking.

"Is there a comm station that way, perhaps?" Casmir pointed toward the open bookcase.

Nguyen flinched and looked away. Maybe she'd been the one to leave it open when she came to search for those books and folders.

Casmir headed for the secret entrance, and Nguyen sighed and muttered something in a language he didn't recognize.

Asger kept his grip on her, waving for her to follow Casmir. He would have preferred not to take anyone prisoner or hostage, as she would no doubt see it, but she was an ideal person to have run into—someone from the president's cabinet. He just had to figure out how to woo her with his charms and win her to his side.

No lights came on as they passed into the corridor, and Casmir ordered on the night-vision program in his contacts. They traveled far enough through the long passage that he assumed they'd left the building and gone under a few others. Their route sloped downward and then back upward before ending at a metal door full of rivets. Two blue indicators blinked on the side, though Casmir didn't see a spot for a fingerprint or retina scan.

Asger pushed Nguyen up to it, perhaps hoping it would identify her and open for them. She lifted her chin defiantly and smirked when nothing happened.

"I'll see if I can force it." Asger started to hand Nguyen off to Casmir but must have decided Tork would be better at keeping someone from escaping.

Casmir didn't disagree. He stepped back as Asger attempted to force open the door, and he continued to work on his refinements to his robot plan.

The door looked like it should swing away from them, so Asger pushed against it, first with his hands and then with a shoulder.

"I think this may be thick enough and strong enough to even keep out people in combat armor," he admitted after several tries.

"That's correct," Nguyen said.

"How did *you* get through it?" Asger asked.

"Someone on the other side controls access." Nguyen glanced up to a tiny lens on the wall. A camera.

"And they're not opening it since we're with you?"

"Correct."

"Either that or they took a bathroom break." Casmir paused his work with the robots to see if he could find a map for this part of the station and maybe a code for the door. He was already in the highest-level secured network, so if the door was connected to it, he ought to be able to open it.

"Would an ally of Secretary Nguyen who is watching this not open the door out of concern for her welfare?" Tork asked.

Unease flashed across Nguyen's face before she masked the expression.

"If you're suggesting we threaten her to get her buddies to open the door," Casmir said, "that's not how noble knights and roboticists operate."

"Right," Asger said. "How *do* we operate?"

"Like this." Casmir had found the door on the network. He stepped forward, raised his arms, and said, "Open, Sesame!"

The door swung open with impressive dramatic flair—and revealed two armored men with rifles. Casmir sprang to the side as Asger charged past, pushing him to the floor.

Casmir spotted Nguyen and Tork still standing and barked, "Get her down," afraid she would be caught if the men fired at Asger.

And they did. Several energy bolts ricocheted off his armor and into the walls before he smashed into them, throwing elbows and punches, then grabbing their helmets and smashing them together.

But they were also in armor and could withstand the brutal tactics. He was too close for them to use their weapons, but they threw kicks and punches of their own.

Asger drew his pertundo. Casmir, having seen the charged, bladed weapon cut into armor like an axe cleaving through the thinnest of aluminum, yelled, "No killing, Asger. Tork, go help him, please!"

Tork released Nguyen and charged past to join Asger.

Only when Nguyen jumped up and sprinted down the corridor back the way they had come did Casmir realize his mistake. For a second, he was tempted to run after her. The secretary of education would be a valuable person to work with, to win over if he could, but what were the odds that he could do that if he was holding her captive? She would resent them and work against them. Maybe he could prove from afar that he wanted to help.

A crack sounded, followed by the buzz of a stunner.

Casmir pushed himself into a crouch and turned in time to see Asger shoot the second defender. The first man hung limply from Tork's grip, already knocked out. Asger had used his pertundo to cleave open the men's armor, but it didn't look like he had used deadly blows. He'd managed to peel back the protection enough that a stun nimbus would catch his opponents and knock them out.

"Nguyen got away," Casmir admitted when Asger looked back. "Maybe we'll see her again later."

"Yes, escaped prisoners often come back to check on their captors."

Casmir waved for him to lead the way down the corridor. If there were people hiding at the other end, they'd likely been warned that intruders were on the way.

Asger removed the unconscious men's weapons and took off at a jog with Tork running at his side. Casmir followed at a slower pace, finishing up his work on the robots.

They didn't have far to go. They came to a cluster of metal doors that weren't as sturdy as the one they'd passed through. They were locked, but Asger used his shoulder to force two open, revealing windowless bunkers with crates of food, tanks of water, and racks of beds. The third one was a control station. It was empty, but cups and food waste sat on the consoles, suggesting recent occupation.

There were numerous tall cabinets large enough to hide people, as well as doors that likely led to offices, so maybe those occupants lurked nearby. A huge display like that on the bridge of the *Osprey* caught Casmir's attention, and thoughts of ferreting out scared people disappeared from his mind. He and Asger were looking at two of the Kingdom warships and… four more warships. They were painted the same shade of green, and they were definitely *not* from the Kingdom.

"Uhm, what are *those*?" Casmir asked.

"A problem," Asger said grimly.

"Because they want to dock and visit the shops, but the station isn't open for business?"

"Because they're pirates. The Rogue Asteroids, unless I miss my guess."

"Any chance they're just here to visit the brothels?"

"I doubt it." Asger pointed at a control panel under the huge display. "If it helps, there's a comm system there. You can say what you wanted to say to the station. Though it had better be orders to man the defenses, because the scanner display over there shows two more pirate warships on the other side of the station."

"Is it concerning that they outnumber the Kingdom warships?"

"Yes."

"That's what I was afraid of."

CHAPTER 20

AS SOON AS THEY WALKED INTO THE FOUR Nebulae Laboratory and Clinic Center, a black building full of gleaming blue-tinted windows overlooking a park across the street, Kim knew something had happened. Something more than the looting and wanton destruction in the other areas they had passed through. The air in the lobby had an acrid burned-chemicals smell, and she put her helmet on, in case it was toxic. The helmet display registered poor air quality but no hint of the nitrous oxide gas that Chi had described.

"Wait here." Rache held up a hand and trotted around the lobby, peering into all the open doorways, his rifle at the ready.

Kim, deciding on a loose definition of the word *wait*, headed for a directory.

"If memory serves," Yas said, walking at her side, "your corporation's labs are on the third floor. There's a toxicology lab on the second floor that I was occasionally invited to in an advisory capacity, and I remember running into Scholar Chi a few times in the lift."

Yas pointed at a short lift hallway behind a tall reception desk, the only piece of furniture remaining in the lobby, likely because it was bolted to the floor.

"I'm more inclined to use the stairs." Kim nodded toward steps at the end of a corridor full of vision and dental clinics.

"Understandable."

She headed that way with Zee trailing comfortingly behind. She wasn't sure when she'd started to find Zee's presence comforting, but he was like a reliable guard dog.

Footsteps sounded as Rache caught up. "This is very mobile waiting you're engaged in."

Yas was the one who got the hard look—Kim assumed it was hard under the mask—probably because he was in Rache's chain of command. Kim refused to be chained to him in any way.

"I assumed you meant wait in the building," Kim said.

"No, I meant wait on that floor tile back there without stepping over the crack."

"That's a tyrannical definition of the word." She crinkled her nose as they climbed the stairs, for the smell grew stronger, with a hint of smoke hazing the air.

"I prefer to walk into danger first so the bullets are less likely to hit the doctors and scholars in my party."

"That's very noble of you. It must be why you consider yourself the main event."

Rache caught his toe on one of the steps. He only flailed slightly and for a split second, but it was the first ungraceful thing Kim had seen from him, and she grinned.

This time, Rache gave *her* the hard look. "Is there anything Casmir *doesn't* tell you?"

"Very little. He's chatty."

"No kidding."

Rache trotted ahead at the landing, making *sure* he placed himself into danger first. Kim didn't object to that—he was the one in armor. She just bristled at people telling her what to do, even if it was a logical thing to do.

The smoke was thicker on the second floor, but on the third floor, it was so dense that Kim couldn't see more than twenty feet down the hallway. She could make out that doors had been blown inward, some hanging warped and twisted from a single hinge. The floor tiles were scorched or missing entirely.

Her gut knotted with fresh worry, and she quickened her pace. They found wreckage in the first two laboratories, equipment blown asunder and holes ripped in walls. A portable freezer unit half blocked the doorway of the third, the white material warped and blackened.

Kim remembered Chi talking about the freezers he wanted to leave with, and she knew it was his lab before Yas pointed to a soot-darkened plaque on the wall with her corporation's name and logo. Rache led the way in, boots crunching on shards of glass, broken equipment, and shattered panels that had fallen from the ceiling. A wall in the back had been targeted with an explosive, cabinets and counters and huge cases toppling, and half the lab from the level above had tumbled down through the floor. Countless people could be buried under that rubble.

"Why would anyone attack a medical research lab?" Kim asked, as angry and frustrated as she was worried. She remembered Chi talking about the potential of one side taking hostages to force the hand of the other.

She paused at a pile of ceiling panels half burying a float chair tipped on its side, its hover engine off. Hadn't Chi said something about the princess racing around in her float chair?

Were they too late? Would they find Chi and the princess dead under the rubble?

"There's someone alive back here." Rache tossed a broken support beam aside.

A feminine groan escaped from under the rubble. Kim started forward to help, but Rache pushed the heavy pieces aside far more easily than she could, so she paused, not wanting to get in the way.

"Zee," Kim said, realizing that might be the princess under there, "will you help me unbury this chair?"

"Yes, Kim Sato."

She had no idea if it would still work—maybe Casmir could fix it if it didn't—but if the princess couldn't walk, she would need it. Kim doubted anyone would volunteer to be carried by Zee, though she was sure any robot that Casmir had designed would be amenable to giving piggyback rides.

Another groan came from the pile, and Yas squeezed past Kim and Zee to wait at Rache's side, his medical kit in hand. Rache tossed aside the last of the rubble covering the crumpled girl, and stepped back so Yas could attend her.

"Huh," Rache said, glancing from the girl to the chair. She was dark skinned with tight rows of black hair that probably hung to her waist when she was sitting upright. Now they were tangled all about her, covered with pale dust. "There really is a princess."

"You recognize her?" Kim asked.

"Princess Tambora of Shango Habitat in System Boar. She's the second born. The women lead there, so she's theoretically second in line for the throne after her sister, but it's a matriarchal society full of warrior women, so I don't know if she's considered a possible heir. I think I remember something about her being groomed as a diplomat. There's another younger sister too."

"I've heard of the habitat but don't know much about it," Kim admitted.

At first, she was surprised that Rache did, but she reminded herself that Odin and System Lion hadn't been his home for a long time. He'd probably been to the rest of the systems often in his travels for work.

"We've stopped a few times for supplies and so the men could take leave." His tone turned dry. "Some of the men get excited by warrior women."

"You don't?" Kim got the float chair positioned upright and tried to turn it on.

"No," Rache said shortly. More tersely than she expected.

She thought of the pictures of Thea and thought she'd appeared athletic—and beautiful—if not a warrior woman. The Kingdom allowed women to serve in the Fleet and the Kingdom Guard, but there was an unsubtle implication that it was more desirable and traditional to be a mother and caregiver than a soldier or law enforcer.

"Shit," Rache said.

"What?" Kim glanced at Yas and the princess.

He was giving her a shot of something, but that wasn't what Rache was looking at. He was simply staring at a wall. Getting an update from his team?

"A bunch of pirate warships showed up. The Rogue Asteroids."

"Is that the name of the pirates or a hint as to what their ships look like?"

Rache looked at her. "It's one of the biggest pirate families. They brought six ships that are visible, and I wouldn't be surprised if there were more out there with slydar hulls. It looks like they brought their whole fleet. I'll check with my intelligence officer, but at last count, they've got twelve ships total. They do a lot of mercenary work as well as simple marauding and mayhem. It's rumored the Miners' Union uses them and considers them more privateers than pirates, at least around their space."

"What are they doing here?" Kim thought of the new bounty on Casmir's head, courtesy of that Miners' Union prince, and her stomach sank. This couldn't have something to do with him, could it? Who would send an entire fleet of ships to collect a bounty on one man?

"No idea, but they have the station surrounded."

"What are the Kingdom ships doing?"

"Nothing yet."

"*Nothing?* Isn't that a little odd?"

If the Kingdom ships were outnumbered and didn't want a fight, Kim would expect them to back away. If they intended to fight to keep the pirates from attacking the station, they would start maneuvering and posturing, wouldn't they? Maybe the two fleets were negotiating—or threatening each other—right now.

"If this was happening to a Kingdom station in System Lion, they would be attacking already, but Tiamat Station is very much in dispute right now, and backup for the Kingdom ships is days away."

"Are the pirate ships equal to the Kingdom warships?"

"In firepower and crew size, they're similar."

Kim grimaced. The *Osprey* was her ride back home, so she'd been hoping he would say the Kingdom ships had four times the firepower. Especially if there were potentially three times the number of pirate ships out there.

"Easy," Yas murmured. "Easy. We're here to help. I'm a doctor."

He helped Tambora to sit up, and she peered blearily around at them with dark brown eyes tight with pain. Her gaze skimmed over Kim and Yas and lingered on Rache in his black combat armor before settling on Zee, her mouth dropping as her eyes opened wide in alarm.

Kim wished Casmir had gotten him that pink bow tie she'd suggested.

"You're from the Kingdom," Tambora whispered, her tone not implying it was a good thing.

"Only I am," Kim said, "but we're not soldiers."

Tambora glanced at Rache.

"*I'm* not." Kim held up her open hands, hoping the rifle slung across her back wouldn't belie the words. "I'm a civilian, and I work for Parvus Biologia. We came looking for Scholar Chi. He's a colleague of mine. He mentioned that you were here picking up specimens and got trapped when the chaos broke out."

Tambora groaned and slumped back against the rubble. "They took him. I tried to stop them, but I'm not a warrior." She dropped her gaze to her slender legs. Kim wondered what injury or affliction she had that modern medicine hadn't been able to cure. "I did throw a book at one of them. After I tried to run over him with my float chair. They were dragging off Scholar Chi! But my efforts were ineffective." Her shoulders slumped low. "And then they blew up the lab. I didn't think—I thought I would die." She glanced toward the ceiling—the collapsed ceiling—above.

"Who took Chi?" Rache asked.

"Do you know if they took anyone else?" Yas added. "My parents—the Peshlakais—are missing too."

"I don't know them. I've only been here a week." Tambora frowned at Rache. "You are not from Parvus Biologia."

"You don't think so? Maybe I'm Scholar Sato's bodyguard."

"I am a Z-6000," Zee proclaimed, sounding indignant, "programmed to protect Kim Sato and Casmir Dabrowski."

"Is that robot arguing that I can't be your bodyguard because he's already got the gig?" Rache asked Kim.

"I think so."

Tambora started to say something, but a couple of clicks and a beep sounded from the wall near the door.

Rache spun toward the noise with his rifle ready to fire. He lowered it when he saw a speaker dangling from the wall by a tangle of wires.

"Greetings, Tiamat Station," a familiar voice said. Casmir. What was he *doing*? "My name is Professor Casmir Dabrowski, and I'm here as a civilian advisor to try to help with some of the problems. For starters, I've reprogrammed your security robots—the big Aegis Defenders with cannons and grippers. They were working for Civil Security and helping round up prisoners, I understand, but they are now programmed to protect anyone who is in trouble. I'm placing them in key places around the station, so if anyone is bothering you, just run up to one. They will do their best to stop any conflict in their presence. Thank you for listening. I'll update you when we've made more progress on—uhm, other fronts."

"Does he know the meaning of the word *stealth*?" Rache asked. "You're not supposed to take over an enemy's network and then tell the enemy all about it over an open comm."

"I'm sure they'd already noticed," Kim murmured.

She didn't know what Casmir was up to—maybe he genuinely only wanted to help the locals—but wouldn't be surprised if he had a plan. She *hoped* he had a plan. Someone here needed one, or the entire station might be stardust soon. She doubted all of those pirates had shown up to check out the brothels.

"That name is familiar." Tambora's face scrunched with concentration. "Dabrowski. Does he know Princess Oku?"

Rache snorted.

"Yes," Kim said. "He—we're—working on a bee project for her."

"Yes." Tambora pointed at her as if to award her a prize for the right answer, and she smiled for the first time. "The bees are for my habitat. Shango. We've been working together for a year to—"

Rache held up a hand. "Let's save bee chat for after we've found the missing people. Tell us anything you know about where they may have been taken. And tell us *who* took them."

Kim frowned at him, but Yas was nodding vigorously, and she admitted Rache was right. It was possible the people taking hostages might think to sacrifice some of them soon to make a point. She didn't even know which side had them right now.

"I don't like him," Tambora whispered to Kim.

"He takes some getting used to. Will you help us find Chi?" Kim tapped the power button on the float chair and was relieved when it rumbled to life, air kicking at her legs as the hover jets activated and it rose a couple of inches off the floor.

"Yes. It's the group who calls themselves the Bakas Vengers—like avengers, I think. They took the hostages. They've been collecting people for days, but they got extra worried when Kingdom warships showed up. They're saying they'll do whatever it takes to keep the Kingdom off their station."

"Mild-mannered, one-hundred-and-fifty-year-old President Bakas inspired a group calling themselves avengers?" Yas gathered Tambora into his arms and carried her toward the chair.

"*Vengers*." Tambora sighed, looking indignant at being carried, but she probably would have struggled to get past the rubble and over to the chair on her own, especially since she was holding her wrist gingerly, had a gash in the side of her face, and a swollen knot on one temple.

"These people are working *against* the Kingdom?" Rache's tone had a weird note in it.

Kim realized it was probably because he thought he should join them, not oppose them.

"If they have my parents and think using them as hostages is a good idea," Yas said wearily, "I don't care who they're working for or against."

"Hm," was all Rache said.

"Do you know where the hostages were taken?" Kim asked Tambora, hoping Rache wouldn't balk at helping get them out. If he did, she still had Zee. And it sounded like she might have Yas, too, though he wouldn't be effective in a fight.

"The Vengers have Levels 6 and 7, and I heard the men say something about taking Scholar Chi to the *Astrikos Gymnasium*. The president's Civil Security troops have Levels 1 and 2, which means all of the shipyards, industrial facilities, and shuttle bays." Tambora grimaced. "Including the shuttle bay where *my* ship is parked. When the Kingdom fleet showed up, my bodyguard and advisor left me here with Scholar Chi so they could try to find a way to the bay, clear it, and then come back and get me. They were worried I might be taken as a hostage and that the fighting would escalate even further. Which it did." She frowned around at the mangled lab.

Booms, shouts, and gunfire continued to sound in the distance, though not as frequently as before. Maybe Casmir's robots were helping calm down the situation.

"We'll help you find a way off," Kim said, following Rache as he led the way out.

"Onto one of the Kingdom warships?" Tambora asked dubiously, steering her float chair out the door.

Yas came right after her, lifting a steadying hand whenever the chair wobbled.

"If you're a friend of Princess Oku's, you'll be safe with the Fleet," Kim said.

"Are you sure? From our conversations, I've gathered she's not… well, she says she's found it safest to stay out of politics and let her people think she's decorative. Which is a sentiment I can understand completely, but if you're not crucial to the workings of a society, sometimes people see you as expendable."

"You'll be safe," Kim said firmly. "Also, if you tell Casmir that you know Oku, I'm sure he'll move galaxies to help you."

Rache glanced back at that comment, but he didn't say anything, simply leading the party down the stairs, Zee now walking at his side.

"Are roboticists powerful in the Kingdom?" Tambora asked skeptically.

"Anyone who can arrive at an unfamiliar space station and take over all the wireless networks and robots within ten minutes is powerful. Casmir just has a knack for making people not realize it." Because *he* didn't realize it, Kim added silently.

Rache stopped when they reached the empty lobby and drew Kim aside. "What are the odds that you would wait here with the princess and Dr. Peshlakai while I go and free the hostages?"

"I don't know. How many tiles would I get?" Kim waved at the floor.

"I'd be willing to grant you the whole lobby. Or maybe that short hallway over there behind the reception desk. There aren't any windows. You and Casmir's hulking bodyguard could more easily defend the space."

Kim wanted to object to the idea of hiding while he risked himself searching for *her* colleague, but it wasn't logical to drag an injured princess and doctor around a station with threats around every corner. Still, *she* wasn't useless. She could help in a fight, or maybe provide a distraction for him while he went in to fight.

"You don't think you'll need help?" Kim didn't know how many people these Vengers had, but a gym full of hostages would be well guarded. Rache wouldn't be the only one with combat armor.

"I can call up some of my men if it looks too challenging."

"But if it's only mildly challenging, you'll fling yourself into danger alone?"

"I *am* the main event."

She snorted, wishing he weren't wearing the mask, because she would have liked to see his eyes crinkle with humor as he said that. He might have been serious when he'd told it to Casmir, but she was positive he was smirking now.

"I'm willing to be the distraction." Kim pulled a couple of vials out of her pouch, held them on her palm, and raised her eyebrows. "And I'm sure Zee is too. You could get one of your men to come here and keep an eye on Yas and the princess, couldn't you?"

He hesitated, face tilted down toward the vials.

"If there's a point where negotiating might be better than outright violence, I may be a better person to do it, since I have a connection to the station through Chi and my corporation." Kim could envision Rache mowing down people left and right, as he'd done with those terrorists, but they weren't dealing with terrorists this time. There might be some opportunists out there, but those in charge were doing what they believed they had to do to defend their home and their freedoms.

"All right," Rache said. "Dr. Peshlakai, I'll send Chaplain to protect you two while I find your parents. Stay out of sight until he gets here."

Now Yas hesitated—maybe he also wanted to go along—but he glanced at the injured princess and nodded. "Yes, sir. Thank you."

Kim headed toward the front door with Rache. "I will also thank you for helping, especially since it means you're helping the Kingdom."

"The Kingdom can hang itself. I'm helping my doctor. And *you*."

Again, she wished he weren't wearing the mask, because a weird tingle went through her, and she had the urge to see his face. Or maybe touch his face. But she didn't like touching, so that couldn't be it. She was glad that, for whatever reason, he was willing to risk himself to help them. To help her.

"Thank you," she said quietly.

When they walked out of the building, a robot identical to the ones Casmir had suborned in the shuttle bay said, "Good afternoon, sir and ma'am. If you are in need of protection, you may hide behind me."

Rache laughed shortly and gave Kim a long look as they passed it. Even with the mask, she could tell he was oozing sarcastic thoughts.

Kim was glad Casmir had altered the robots and hoped it made a difference. After all the people here had endured, they needed someone to stand up for them. Even if that someone was robots.

Casmir was about to join Asger in searching the rooms adjacent to the control room when a beep came from the comm panel. He looked around. Since the secretary of education had fled, and they'd stunned the door guards, only he, Asger, and Tork were in the area.

"Do we answer that?" Casmir asked.

"It's the pirates." Asger eyed the flashing indicator as if it were attached to a venomous, armor-piercing snake.

"Who do you think they're expecting?"

"Not a knight." Asger looked at him.

Casmir lifted his hands. "I'm positive they don't want to talk to a Kingdom roboticist either."

Asger pointed at Tork. "That's our only alternative, unless you want to poke through all the rooms and see if we can find someone who actually lives on the station."

The comm flashed again. What if this was the main control room for the entire station? And what if the pirates opened up fire if they didn't get an answer?

If that happened, Casmir hoped Ishii would command the Fleet to swoop in and stop the pirates, especially since Jager had interests here, but since the Kingdom ships were outnumbered, he doubted they could count on that. Casmir reached for the comm, praying he wasn't about to instigate an attack.

"Good afternoon," he said in as polite a tone as he could manage. "This is Professor Casmir Dabrowski. How may I assist you?"

"This is Admiral Chaos Cutty, head of the deadly Rogue Asteroids," a bass voice said. "I will speak to your president."

"The president isn't available."

"If he's seen my fleet, he should know he must *make* himself available."

"We're experiencing a tiny bit of civil unrest at the moment, and it's making it difficult for people to come to work. Why don't you give me whatever message you have for him, and I'll make sure he gets it. I hope you're having a nice day, by the way. Are you here to enjoy the station amenities? I understand there are nice brothels."

Asger dropped his face in his hand. That couldn't be a good sign.

Did Casmir sound nervous? Was he babbling? It seemed understandable, given the situation.

"Are you in charge, *Professor*?"

"Of the brothels, no. I'm in charge of a small but cutting-edge lab doing important research into bipedal self-aware robots." No need to mention that it was back on Odin and he didn't even live in this system… "Do you wish to leave a message, Admiral? I'm not sure where the president is, but we're trying to locate him." He turned around to Tork and whispered, "Can you start recording this in case we need to play it back to someone?"

"Yes, Professor Dabrowski," Tork said.

"I command whoever is in charge to surrender the station to us immediately. We are taking it over as our new base of operations. You can make it easy on us and open all your airlocks and shuttle bays, but if you resist, we will take it by force."

"That is an interesting method of acquiring real estate," Casmir said. "Is it legal in System Hydra? I may need to consult with the station lawyers before I pass along the message. Lawyers bill by the hour and like to draw things out, as you may know. I'm going to need three or four months to get back to you."

"Give the message to the president, roboticist. You have fifteen minutes to get him on the comm to give his answer."

The channel went dead.

Casmir flattened his palms against the control console, vaguely aware of how damp they were. And how fast he was breathing. "Is this typical? I had no idea the other systems were so—what's the word I'm looking for?—*insane*."

"Your voice is getting squeaky, Casmir," Asger said.

"That's what it does when I'm on the verge of a panic attack. Where are the leaders of this place and why aren't they here to answer the completely unreasonable demands of self-aggrandizing pirate *admirals*?" Casmir spun toward Asger. "Do you think they'll open *fire*? Why would pirates want this station? What are they even doing in this system? I thought Hydra was reasonably stable. Aren't there local governments with militias that help keep this station safe? And what about our warships? Why aren't they telling the pirates to go get screwed?"

Because they were outnumbered. Casmir knew that, but shouldn't Ishii and the other captains be doing *something*? They weren't just sitting in their chairs and watching this unfold while they munched popcorn, were they?

Asger rested his hands on Casmir's shoulders. "Calm down. You and Tork check those rooms and see if there's anyone helpful hiding back there. I'm going to go find that secretary of education. She's more qualified than we are to answer demands about the station."

"The brutes that attacked us on the *tram* are more qualified than we are to answer demands about the station."

"No time to debate that now. Don't fall apart." Asger patted him on the shoulder and ran out of the room. "And don't have a seizure," he called back.

"I'm having a panic attack, not a seizure. Anyone with basic first-aid training should recognize that." Casmir tried to slow his breathing, well aware that stress could *lead* to a seizure. "I need to be calm and rational. Tork, will you check those rooms and cabinets, please, and see if anyone is hiding?"

"Yes, Professor Dabrowski."

In the meantime, Casmir would find some contact information for the leaders on the station. He had all of the network addresses of people. Surely, someone would accept contact from him. And even if they didn't, if their chips were connected to the local network, he could probably use his new access to force contact.

The comm flashed before he'd done more than bring up a list of the president's cabinet.

"What now?" he groaned, not wanting to accept another comm, but knowing he dared not ignore it.

"Good afternoon, Tiamat Station," a cultured voice with a Kingdom accent said. "This is Ambassador Romano, authorized to negotiate on behalf of King Jager of the Star Kingdom. We've noticed that you have what we believe to be an unwelcome pirate *infestation* loitering near your station."

Casmir stared at the comm panel. Was this the snooty guy he'd seen walking out of Ishii's office?

"We had originally come to Tiamat Station hoping to acquire a few goods for a research mission," Romano continued, "but since we are in the area, we are prepared to come to your defense and drive these pirates away. They did bring a large number of warships, however, so it would be dangerous for us to engage them, likely resulting in the damage of our vessels and loss of men. We would wish something in return. With whom am I speaking?"

As Casmir looked around at the empty control room, he felt a manic—or maybe maniacal—laugh bubbling up in his throat. He swallowed hard, trying to force it down.

"Uhm, this is Professor Dabrowski. Sir Asger and I have... I guess you could say taken over the control room. But we haven't found the president or any of his cabinet or anyone even vaguely in charge yet. Other than the secretary of education, but she ran away from us. Oddly."

"*Dabrowski!*" The ambassador said it like a curse, his smooth cultured voice turning into something close to one of Ishii's sputters. "What are you *doing* over there?"

Casmir wondered if Romano was comming from the bridge of the *Osprey* and if Ishii was standing next to him. He dared not get Ishii in trouble for looking the other way when Casmir, Kim, and Asger had left the ship.

"Taking initiative, sir."

"Where's President Chronis?" Romano snapped.

"We're looking for him, among other people. It's kind of a war zone over here. Oh, and about those pirates... An Admiral Chaos just commed and said he was going to take over the station in fifteen minutes if we don't surrender."

"We're aware of what he plans to do."

At first, Casmir assumed that meant the Kingdom had been listening in on the conversation, but he realized they wouldn't have been surprised when he answered the comm if that were true. Romano must have already spoken to the pirates—it did seem likely that the warships would have chatted each other up when they all realized they were going to be sharing the same space—or...

Casmir rocked back on his heels. Was it possible Romano—or even Jager—had arranged for the pirates to show up? So they could threaten the station and the Kingdom could *rescue* the station?

"If you want the people here to be beholden to you," Casmir said, "maybe you could drive off the pirates preemptively. Without that being contingent on deals. To show good faith."

"Dabrowski," Ishii said, sounding like he was standing right next to Romano, "that's a big request. You may have noticed we're outnumbered here. Can you find out if the station has any defenses?" He didn't sound as surprised to be negotiating with Casmir instead of the station president.

"I'll check." Casmir looked around the panel, then started checking the networks for something that looked like external defense systems. "Can you—"

An alarm beeped.

"Incoming attack!" a computer announced.

"What?" Casmir blurted. "That was *not* fifteen minutes."

He queried the network database for information on weapons and found the control panel on the far side of the room. This place was meant to be manned by multiple people. People who lived and *worked* here and were familiar with the controls.

As he raced over to turn on the station's defenses, the first attack hit. Whatever it was struck close enough and hard enough to make the floor shake. Casmir slipped, tumbling shoulder first into the defenses station. The alarms shifted from beeping to wailing.

He lunged to his feet and quickly learned two things. The station had defenses—that contoured gray stuff that coated the exterior could energize and harden to repel simple attacks. And the defenses weren't adequate to keep six pirate warships from blowing them to pieces.

CHAPTER 21

KIM LET ZEE AND RACHE LEAD THE WAY through the station, avoiding groups of people, though she had to pause and gawk when someone with two extra arms and head growth that looked more like tentacles than hair ran past. She had no idea if that represented genetic engineering or some post-birth modification.

Before leaving Odin, she'd never encountered anyone genetically modded in person. Meeting Qin had been a surprise, but it made sense to her that people would slice and dice DNA to create superior warriors. To create tentacle hair… Her rational mind struggled to find the purpose.

"The streets are a lot quieter now," Rache murmured, pointing at one of the Aegis robots stationed in an intersection with two young women and a group of children sitting beside it. Safe, at least for now.

Even though Kim worried that Casmir would one day get himself into more trouble than he could handle by snubbing authority to help others, she was glad he cared enough to do so. Few people did, not to that extent. She liked helping people through her work, but she wouldn't sacrifice her own life or career in order to aid some stranger. She just wished Casmir wasn't quite so cavalier with his own future, that he would weigh his own self-interest against the risks of aiding others.

But if he did that, would he be here, helping her?

"We're almost to the gym." Rache pointed to a group of signs at the next intersection.

They were moving through corridors again, the sky replaced with the high ceilings of Level 6. Catwalks ran along those ceilings, and now and then, a set of curious eyes peered down at them from above.

The station shuddered, the faux pavement quaking underneath them, and Kim dropped into a low crouch, arms spread for balance.

"What was that?" She eyed the nearby structures and the catwalks as the shaking stilled.

"An attack," Rache said, never stopping. If anything, he picked up his pace. "My people say one of the pirate ships has started lobbing shots at the station. I don't know what its defenses are, but let's hope someone is manning the control room and can get them up."

"The Kingdom warships should stop it."

Rache gave her a long look over his shoulder. "We'll see."

"Will your ship do anything? The *Fedallah*?"

"Against no fewer than six pirate ships? And with the Kingdom warships that loathe me like no other lurking in the background? No."

"Not even to save you?"

"I won't need saving," he said firmly.

They turned onto a new street, and she glimpsed two men in gray combat armor standing outside glass double doors under a large sign that read *Astrikos Health Spa and Gymnasium.* Rache, Kim, and Zee veered into an alley. The gym was two blocks away, and Kim didn't know if the men had spotted them. Zee stood out, but there was a large Aegis robot sitting in the middle of the street that would have impeded the view.

"We need a plan." Rache stopped now that they were out of sight. "I can go charging in with Large and Hulking there—" he waved at Zee, "—but since those two men are armored, I'm sure more men inside are armored. I'm not opposed to facing numerous men at once—if you're fast enough, you can usually get them caught in each other's crossfire—but if there are unarmored civilians in an open space, it could turn into a bloodbath."

"Casmir Dabrowski would use subterfuge rather than a forward assault," Zee announced.

"That's because he'd get his ass kicked in a forward assault," Rache said.

"He would not. I would protect him. I am a Z-6000."

"And you're quite impressive." Kim patted his arm, since she knew that was what Casmir would do, and also because she didn't want her two allies to waste time arguing.

"Yes," Zee agreed.

She was positive Rache rolled his eyes behind his mask.

"Let's figure out a way I can help and we can avoid blood baths," Kim said. "You brought me along to be a distraction, right?"

"I brought you along because I was afraid your mobile waiting would get you in trouble," Rache said.

She gave him a cool look.

"And because I'm certain you can help," he said, losing his sarcasm. "What do you suggest? Those two were wearing helmets, so your vials wouldn't do anything, but it's possible, even likely, that not all of the guards inside will be."

"Would it help if I could get in, get the layout and how many guards there are, and send that information back out to you? Then you could decide whether to come in with guns blazing or try something else."

Another jolt shook the station, and an alarm wailed in the distance. Maybe their plans wouldn't matter. Maybe the people holding the hostages would flee the gym any second and try to get to the shuttle bay to escape the station. Except that the other side held the shuttle bay—or had. Who knew what the president's Civil Security was doing now?

"Yes, but if you're suggesting letting yourself be taken prisoner, they would search you and remove your vials. If they wanted you for a prisoner at all. They've been selective about who they've taken."

"I have an idea," Kim said.

"Will I like it?"

"I think Casmir would approve."

"Does that mean it's harebrained and too creative for its own good?"

"I see you've worked with Casmir before." Kim waved Zee closer. "I've seen you morph into other shapes. What all can you turn yourself into?"

"Anything of equal mass without sophisticated moving parts."

"Have you ever seen a Trojan horse?"

Rache snorted.

Zee said, "I am not familiar with that reference."

"How about a dog?" Kim considered his mass. "A *large* dog."

"I am familiar with numerous breeds of dog, but I cannot change my color. Or grow fur."

"No, I wasn't expecting that. You'll still look like a robot, and that's fine. I just want them to think you're more of a pet than an intelligent, thinking creation."

"I understand."

Zee morphed before their eyes, melting like a candle and then re-forming into a dog-shaped creature with four legs and a stout stubby tail. His head was level with Kim's, and he had the stocky build of an ox, but he also had pointed canine ears and a semblance of a tongue that lolled out slightly. As promised, he was all the same shade of tarry black.

Kim smiled slightly, thinking he still needed a pink bow tie.

"What do you want me to turn into?" Rache asked dryly.

He was eyeing one of the catwalks that ran near the gym, so she suspected he already had ideas of his own.

"Just do what you do. I'll send you video footage of the interior, and then I'll get out of the way. Or at least duck down and hide behind Zee."

Kim pulled out her vials and considered them. Assuming this worked, and the guards were willing to let her in, Rache was right that she would be searched. They would take her stunner. They might take everything. If she were a guard, she would find the vials suspicious.

"Zee, can you hold these?" She held them toward him.

"What's he supposed to do?" Rache asked. "Put them in a pocket?"

A black tendril extended from Zee's shoulder, wrapped around the vials, then drew them into his body, liquefying his surface enough to bury them out of sight.

"Even better than pockets," Kim said.

"I am a little envious."

Another attack jolted the station. The alarm klaxon continued to sound, but thus far, there hadn't been any orders to evacuate or warnings of sections being damaged and cut off.

"Can your people tell how serious the attacks are?" Kim asked.

"So far, it's just one ship. Scare tactics, I suspect, but if the pirates don't get what they want, it'll escalate."

"I hope Casmir and Asger found the president so he can tell them to knock it off—or bribe them. Whatever it takes."

"I don't know what it'll take. It's odd that they're here. It's possible they heard about the civil war and came to take advantage, but it's also possible someone paid them to take advantage." Rache pointed at the street. "If you're going to go, go now. We need to get the hostages before things get worse."

"Going. I'll do my best to get you useful intel."

"Good." Rache trotted off down the alley and scaled the side of a building that didn't appear to have any handholds. He headed across the roof toward the catwalk, disappearing from her sight.

Kim strode around the corner with Zee clacking along behind her. That was a new sound from him—he'd grown dog-style claws to go with his costume.

They rounded the robot and headed for the gym doors. Kim worried that the guards would have seen Zee when he'd been in human form and be suspicious of this new look, but they were busy arguing with each other and pointing at the ceiling. She stopped five feet from them before they noticed her.

"We can't protect you, woman," one man said. "Go hide behind one of the robots."

Kim tilted her head, as if she were puzzled. "I do not need protection. I brought my hound."

Zee startled her by growling. She hadn't expected that, but since he could speak, she supposed she shouldn't be surprised.

"That's one damn big hound."

"Yes. My name is Scholar Kim Sato. I work for Parvus Biologia Corporation, and I came to help a colleague escape the chaos of your station."

"We don't care. We've got other problems right now." The man who'd been pointing toward the ceiling before flung his hand in that direction again. "There are pirates out there."

"Which is why I need to find Scholar Chi and remove him from the station. He's a renowned expert on veterinary virology."

"If he's in here—" the guard jerked a thumb over his shoulder, "—he's not going anywhere. These are valuable hostages, er, respected citizens, and we might need them."

"I'm authorized by my CEO to pay for Scholar Chi."

"Nobody's paying for anything. Money doesn't matter right now. We—"

His colleague put a hand on his chest and stepped forward. "How much are you paying?"

"Tate. Knock it off."

"What? The station's gone to shit, and we're all going to be lucky to get off it with our lives. Some money could go a long way. How much you paying, lady?"

“At least check her ID to make sure she’s with that corporate thing.”

Kim held up the finger with her embedded banking and identification chip. “I don’t have an ident reader. Do you?”

“No.”

Kim sighed. Maybe Rache should have run up and mowed these two down. She had a feeling that their armor couldn’t protect them from losing to someone with more than three brain cells.

“I’m prepared to pay ten thousand Kingdom crowns if you let me take Scholar Chi. Assuming he’s inside.” She raised her eyebrows. “Is he?”

“We’re not the ones with the list.”

“I’ll take her in and show her around.”

“Tate, we’re not supposed to leave our station.”

“Don’t worry. I’m not going to lunch. I’m just going inside. And I’ll cut you in. But we want Union dollars, lady. Nobody in System Hydra deals in Kingdom crowns.”

“Not yet,” the other guard muttered.

“I’m sure a currency exchange can be arranged,” Kim said.

“This way.” The greedy guard—Tate—reached for her arm.

Zee growled and stepped forward.

Tate shifted his reach into a wave. “Come on.”

Kim wondered what Casmir would think if she told him she liked the dog version of Zee best.

The corridor inside was dimly lit, save for a desk with a guard sitting at it, light spilling onto a display. He was tensely watching a view of the outside of the station as an ugly green ship lazily flew past, occasionally slinging weapons.

“Got a new one, Tongen,” Kim’s escort said. “Another scientist.”

Kim had a feeling her escort was actually her captor, and that he was thinking of making money by selling her, not by selling *to* her. She should have guessed as soon as he hadn’t asked to see proof of funds. Well, it wouldn’t matter. Her goal was only to get inside.

She trusted Rache would either break her out or that she could escape while he was breaking in. Briefly, she wondered when he’d become someone she knew she could trust rather than someone she feared would betray her.

“Good, but we’re going to need to bribe pirates it looks like, not the Kingdom, and I’m not sure if scientists are going to interest them.

We should be finding sexy women to tempt them with." Tongen stood up—he wasn't in armor, and Kim thought about asking Zee for a vial—and looked her up and down. "She's not hideous, but I don't think she's gonna be any pirate's fantasy. Some of those strippers from Boink Boink would be a lot better."

Tate snorted. "They always are."

Kim couldn't decide if the proper response was to feel affronted by their dismissal of her beauty or annoyed at the time this discussion was wasting. She chose the latter.

"She's got a stunner."

"Right." Tate removed the weapon and patted Kim down, fishing out a ration bar she'd brought along. Fortunately, the search didn't involve any extra groping. Both men kept glancing at the pirate ship on the display.

If one hadn't been wearing combat armor, she might have tried to knock them out, so she could let herself inside unaccompanied.

"And she's got, uh, that." Tongen pointed at Zee.

"I'm not sure how to remove it. Or even what it is. Some kind of robot dog. I don't see a power button or access panel." Tate poked Kim in the shoulder. "How do you turn it off?"

"He's voice-activated but only programmed to respond to my voice."

"Tell it to stay here. No dogs allowed in the gym."

Kim gazed at Tate. "I am not your prisoner. I'm here to barter for Scholar Chi."

"Uh huh. Just get going. We don't have time for drama. Sergeant Nails better be negotiating with those pirates already, Tongen."

"Let's hope. The Kingdom ships aren't moving. They're just watching the show."

"Fantastic."

Tate shoved Kim farther down the corridor, eliciting another growl from Zee. She caught him looking toward her face. Waiting for the command to attack? She was tempted. He ought to be able to handle a single man in combat armor.

But when she spotted the gym doors, they were far more solid than she would have expected, gleaming silver steel with a lock panel at eye level on one side. A sophisticated lock panel. Casmir could have waved a wrench at it, and the doors would have opened, but Kim didn't know anything about getting around locks. She was glad she hadn't made her move yet.

Her captor, who didn't seem that worried about Zee, lifted his faceplate and leaned in for a retina scan. The doors swung open, and they entered a short corridor with entrances to locker rooms on either side. Farther down, there was a foyer with an empty smoothie and espresso cart, as well as the clear walls of racquetball and thudmoon courts.

Tate walked her past open doors that might have been offices once but were now packed with bunkbeds with people sitting in them or gathered on the floors. Some were playing holo-games, others gazing at nothing as they read or tinkered on chip applications, and others were clumped together and sharing concerned whispers about the attack. At first, Kim thought these people were the hostages, but most of them had rifles within reach. She realized this gym must be the base for the entire group of vigilantes. The Bakas Vengers. How many of them were there?

Her unease grew as they walked past converted office after office, each with at least ten people passing time inside. Would it be worth tossing vials in and trying to knock some of them out? She was sending the feed to Rache so he wouldn't be caught unaware, but if he had to fight hundreds of people… being aware of it would only help so much.

In front of one of the doorways, she stopped and slumped against Zee.

"Vials," she whispered, pressing her hand to his side.

But she was touching the wrong side. He'd sucked the vials into his other shoulder. She was about to move her hand when Zee's hard surface softened, and a bulge pressed up against her palm. The vials.

"What are you doing?" Tate demanded.

"Sorry, I got dizzy."

"Dizzy?" He squinted. "What are you trying to pull?"

"Nothing."

Kim shook her head as she pulled out several of the vials, hiding them with her hand. She slumped further to cover the motion of unstoppering one, resting it on the floor, and sliding it into the room. The men inside weren't paying attention to her, but Tate was.

"I have vasovagal syncope," she said, "and I faint sometimes if I'm not careful."

That attempt at an excuse might have worked better on someone who knew what that was. She straightened and made a pained face as she walked to catch up with him, hoping he would truly think her in the middle of medical difficulties. But Tate snarled and snatched at her arm.

Zee lunged and butted him back. Tate shifted his rifle toward Zee. Kim took a few more steps to the next doorway and unstoppered a second vial, holding her breath. She didn't try to bend low and skid it across the floor again—Tate was sure to notice that, even if he was focused on Zee—and instead tossed it onto the closest bunk.

Someone was looking at the doorway this time, and she feared he would notice the vial, but he only said, "Holy crap, is that a *dog*?"

Tate fired at Zee. The DEW-Tek bolt bounced off and burned through the door to a sauna.

Tate gaped at Zee. "What *is* it?"

"He's made from a proprietary metal alloy." Kim's knowledge ended there.

"So it's immune to energy bolts?"

"Most metal is, isn't it?" Kim waved for Tate to continue forward so she could toss another vial. She didn't know if this would do any good. She only had a few more. Maybe she should save them.

To her surprise, Tate backed up and didn't fire again. He spun, muttering something about how someone called Spencer could take care of the weird freaks, and Kim had the opportunity to toss two more opened vials spewing her sedative gas.

Someone back at the first room snarled, "What *is* that?"

Tate either didn't hear or just wanted to get Kim—and Zee—off his hands. He pushed her through a door to the left and into a gym full of people sitting on blankets or pacing in agitation, throwing glances toward the high ceiling.

Kim grimaced because none of them were armored, but the guards standing around the entrance area were. If Rache rushed in and started a firefight, the hostages would have nowhere to hide. A lot of them were older men and women, people chosen because they would be deemed valuable in a negotiation with the Kingdom.

A man shambled past with a fresh gash at his temple, blood dried on the side of his face. Were the guards letting people fight? With weapons? Only a blade could have caused a wound like that.

She looked all around, trying to take note of all the details in case Rache would find something useful, and made sure to send the video to him while she could. She spotted Scholar Chi in a far corner, sitting against a wall with his knees drawn up and his face against them. Before she could take more than a step toward him, she spotted something else on that wall.

A man hung from a hoopball frame, a rope around his throat, his face purpled and eyes bulged out. There was no mistaking it. He was dead.

"Who's that?" Kim whispered.

"President Chronis." Tate grunted. "The rest of the hostages decided they blamed him for this."

Kim stared bleakly at the man, fearing it was the truth. If the president was dead, who was left with the power to clear Yas's name? And who was commanding the Kingdom-aligned side of this war? Did the Civil Security troops know their president and leader was dead?

"Over here, woman," a man at a table said.

The twang of a switchblade sounded, and Kim spun, her fists coming up defensively.

"Nobody keeps their chip."

What? Was *that* why that man had been bleeding?

Kim stepped back. She wouldn't let them take her only way of communicating with the rest of the universe—and sending footage to Rache. But several guards were within a few feet. Before, they had been watching the prisoners, but now they focused on her, shifting their weapons to point at her.

The man at the table pointed a blade at her temple. "Grab her, Tate."

CHAPTER 22

THE SECOND AND THIRD ATTACKS DIDN'T SEND CASMIR to the floor, but even with the station's defenses activated, he felt the jolts. Indicators flashed all over the control room, the alarms battered his ears, and the comm panel lit up with internal messages. He couldn't take the time to answer them. He was trying to figure out the weapons.

"There they are. And ugh—what is this schlock?"

Simple DEW-Tek spitters mounted at various points along the exterior were all he saw. Casmir doubted they would give the pirate ships so much as a nosebleed. Was it better to fight back, knowing it would be futile, or to pretend utter helplessness?

"The *warships* need to fight back," Casmir grumbled, running across the room again. He hit the comm, not to answer anyone, but to establish an outgoing call to the *Osprey*. "Ishii, are you there?" he blurted as soon as someone answered.

There was a pause. Ishii probably *hadn't* been the one to answer it.

Another blast slammed into the station. A green pirate ship flew past, showing off with a lazy barrel roll. So far, that was the only enemy ship that had fired. Maybe the pirates were seeing if the Kingdom would do anything to stop them before fully committing.

They had better.

"I'm here, Dabrowski," Ishii said warily.

Why was *he* wary? Casmir was the one being fired at.

"I'm sure King Jager would give you medals for saving civilians from a pirate fleet," Casmir said. "How about making that happen?"

"Are the station inhabitants willing to concede to Kingdom rule and accept us as their saviors?" That was Ambassador Romano. He sounded bored. Was the show not entertaining enough?

"I have no idea," Casmir said. "They're not here. I am. I'll *happily* accept Kingdom rule over myself."

"You should be in a brig somewhere. Find someone in charge of that station. Surely, now that they're in danger they'll be amenable to negotiating."

"Why is this a negotiation?" Casmir wished the ambassador were standing in front of him so he could punch the man in the nose. "Let's be heroes and do the right thing. Ishii, I know you didn't bring all those marines along to just scratch their armpits and throw heavy things around in the gym."

The channel closed.

"Assholes."

Tork strode in from one of the side rooms. "I have not located anyone, Professor Dabrowski."

Casmir pushed a hand through his hair. He was sure someone would *eventually* rush back to this control room now that the station was being attacked, but he had to do something in the meantime.

"Tork, do you still have that virus stored on one of your drives?"

"I do."

"How did you deliver it to the *Osprey* and get them to open it?"

"The comm was open because your shuttle was in contact with the warship. It was a simple matter to sneak the file into one of the automatic updates transmitted. The virus itself has self-executing capabilities."

"Once it's accepted onto the destination computer."

"Yes."

Casmir hadn't known there were automatic updates from the shuttle to the warship. Unfortunately, a pirate comm officer wouldn't accept automatic updates from an enemy station. Casmir could have Tork send the virus, but someone would have to manually download the file before it could execute.

"Maybe we could trick one ship into accepting it. Hm, Tork, you've got some good programming skills, right? Can you tinker with it and add a wrapper that gets it to automatically open comm channels to all of its ally ships and pass it along?"

Casmir fantasized about all of the pirate ships going dark and powerless as the *Osprey* had. Too bad there were no gravity wells nearby that they could be sucked down into.

"My handler did all of the programming related to the virus. I have only modest skills in that area."

"Send it to me then." Casmir waved at his temple, trying not to wet himself at the idea of Tork transmitting a horrible virus to the chip linked to his brain. He reminded himself that he and Grunburg had created an antivirus program, and Tork probably still had a copy. "I'll see what I can cobble together."

"Very well."

Another attack slammed into the station. An alarm in the control room battered at Casmir's eardrums like a dozen sledgehammers.

"Tork, can you try to turn that off, please? At least in here?"

"Yes, Professor."

Casmir closed his eyes and concentrated on writing code. What he wanted to do was simple enough. The virus itself was brilliant, and he couldn't imagine creating something like it, but all he had to do was add on a basic attachment. The hard part was concentrating.

Footsteps rang out in the corridor. Finally, someone coming to see what was going on? Casmir hoped for the president or someone with the authority to negotiate with those pirates.

Asger ran in with the secretary of education slung over his shoulder.

"What are you doing, Casmir?" Asger asked when he spotted him standing in the middle of the room, eyes glazed with concentration. "Doesn't this spinning block have any weapons?"

"Inadequate ones. I'm writing code." Casmir waved at the weapons panel in case Asger wanted to try firing back.

"Set me down, you hairy orangutan," Nguyen growled, slamming a fist into Asger's armored back.

"I'm a handsome knight, not a hairy anything. If you'd seen my calendar you would know." Asger set her on her feet. "Don't try to escape again. Your station needs you."

"I wasn't trying to escape." Nguyen ran for the comm panel, reached for it, but hesitated. She looked daunted by all the flashing indicators. "I was trying to find a weapon so I could shoot you two invaders and get back here." She glanced at Casmir. "Have the pirates commed?"

"Oh, yes. They want you to surrender the station. They were supposed to give us fifteen minutes to think about it, but they apparently come from a system with very fast minutes."

"Surrender the station! What are the Kingdom ships doing?"

"Nothing. They're willing to help if you agree to Kingdom rule."

Nguyen swore and kicked the console.

Casmir shrugged helplessly, trying to braid together if-then-go-to lines in a logical way as he glared at Asger, as if he were an appropriate conduit for his irritation with the Kingdom in general.

"I spoke to Ishii," Asger said quietly, waving at his chip. "This isn't his idea. Ambassador Romano was supposed to be along to negotiate with the local governments so they would let us pass unimpeded on our gate hunt. But when this all started, he stepped up and took command of the Fleet. Ishii and the other captains want to fight the pirates, but Romano is one of the king's handpicked diplomats and has the power to take control of the military."

"Diplomat!" Casmir threw his hands up. "I've only spoken to him once, and I know he's an asshole."

"He probably doesn't think he needs to be diplomatic with you."

"Or the entire station?"

"Shut up!" Nguyen glared at them and pointed at the comm panel, to an open channel. "This is Secretary of Education Nguyen. I need to speak with your leader."

"This is Admiral Chaos Cutty," the bass drawl of the pirate purred. "I'm still waiting to hear from your president."

"The citizens objected to his presidency, so we impeached him. The secretary of the treasury and I are the only two members of the president's cabinet currently holding office until such time that new elections can be held. What is your purpose in being here?"

"Did your robotics minion not make my purpose clear? We intend to take over your station and claim it for ourselves. If you surrender immediately, we will allow the current inhabitants to continue residing on it under our rule. You may serve us."

Casmir expected Nguyen to sputter as much as Ishii usually did, but she lifted her chin and glared at the display as she calmly answered. "We objected to Kingdom rule, and I am positive that pirate rule would not be a superior option. I am, however, open to listening, if you wish to argue your position." Her gaze rolled toward the ceiling, and Casmir knew she was only buying time.

He approved. He wanted to tell her his plan, but the channel was still open. He hunted around the room, found paper and a pen in a drawer, and wrote a quick note.

"I don't intend to *argue* why we would be superior leaders," Cutty said dryly. "We are here to take over your station, not compete at a debate bowl. Your options are to comply without a struggle and let us have it, or to put up a fight. In which case, my men do enjoy a good challenge and are always in need of training. That will, however, mean we have to force your people to work for us and do repairs when we arrive."

"It sounds like we have to work for you either way."

Casmir hurried over with his note: *I have a virus to send to them, but we need to trick them into accepting a file.*

Nguyen looked at him—squinted at him—as if she were seeing him for the first time and trying to figure out whether he could be trusted. He spread his hands and tried to look inoffensive. She had to see that, no matter whose side he was on, he would want to survive the pirate attack.

"Not necessarily," Cutty said. "If you cooperate fully, we will let those residents who wish to relocate leave."

"Residents who've lived here for generations and consider this their ancestral home?"

"It would be their choice."

"Some choice," Nguyen breathed, staring down at Casmir's note. "But I see we have few alternatives. I assume that if you take over the station, you will wish to protect it, even from Kingdom warships. We have no desire to side with the Kingdom."

Casmir tried not to wince. Asger *did* wince.

"Is our presence not proof enough that they fear to deal with us? They will not attack the station if the Rogue Asteroids protect it."

Casmir wondered if Ishii and the other ships were listening in on this conversation. He also wondered if Jager or Romano truly had set this all up. It distressed him to imagine the Kingdom dealing under the table with brutal pirates. Surely, Admiral Mikita had never resorted to that.

"You do seem to have them cowed into inactivity." Nguyen didn't bother to hide her disgust. "We officially surrender, Admiral. What do you want next?"

"We will send some of our ships to dock at your station. Allow them to attach to your locks without impeding them. I will come personally to speak with you and find an appropriate leader to be my second-in-command there and a liaison between your people and mine."

Nguyen's dark eyes flared with indignation—at the suggestion that *she* was not an appropriate leader?

"I understand. The president's chief of security programmed the airlocks and shuttle-bay doors to go into a lockdown mode so nobody could come or go. I'm not sure where he is currently, but I do have a transmission code here that I can send." Nguyen rested a hand on Casmir's note. "You'll need to transmit it from the outside to the sensors on the docking side. It was intended to be shared with the Kingdom ships, but since it's clear they are uninterested in helping us…"

"Quite. Send it. And prepare to receive me, Secretary." There was a lewd innuendo in the man's tone.

Nguyen sneered but made herself say. "We'll be ready."

She nodded to Casmir. Since he was already linked to the station's network, it was a simple matter to transmit his newly wrapped file to the comm computer and then over to the admiral's ship.

Once it was whisked away, he waved for Nguyen to close the comm.

"Please tell me that's something that will seriously screw them up," she said as soon as the channel was closed.

"It knocked out all the power and auxiliary systems on our ship," Casmir said.

Her brow crinkled. "You made it?"

"No, I only added an element to hopefully spread it among all their ships. It was the work of an astroshaman leader named Kyla Moonrazor."

"I've heard of her. She's infamous in this system."

"The Kingdom is learning about her now too." Casmir doubted Ishii would want him to share any more details than that, so he looked at the scanner display, hoping to see sign of the pirate ships losing power.

"How soon will we know if it worked?" Asger asked from behind them.

"Soon," Casmir said. "I hope."

As Tate reached for Kim's arms and his buddy strode toward her with his switchblade, Zee attacked. He morphed back into his human form so that he had hands and grabbed Tate, throwing him against a wall hard enough that his armor crunched. The wall buckled.

The man with the switchblade lunged at Kim. She dodged as she whipped up a block, batting aside his knife arm. His hand hit the wall, and he dropped the weapon. She shifted her weight and slammed a side kick into his groin. He partially blocked it, but the force was enough to knock his butt backward while his head pitched forward and down. Without dropping her foot, she rocketed a second kick into his jaw. This time, he flew backward and hit the floor in a jumble.

More guards rushed toward Kim, but Zee moved at light speed, blocking attacks and hurling people halfway across the gym before they knew what struck them.

"Look out!" more than one hostage cried.

Rache, Kim sent a message to go with the footage she'd been streaming to him. *Now would be a good time for—*

An alarm shrieked throughout the gym and spa. "Station breach on Level 6. All personnel must evacuate to a lower level. The atmosphere is venting. I repeat, station breach on Level 6. Evacuate immediately."

Everyone sprang to their feet, shouting and screaming in alarm. The guards were closest to the gym exit, and they rushed out the doorway first. Some of the hostages started forward, but a figure in black armor landed in front of them, and they jumped back.

Get the hostages up the rope, across the roof, and away on the catwalk, Rache messaged Kim as he raced past her and after the guards, slamming the doors shut behind him. *I'll make sure the guards don't follow.*

Weapons fire opened up outside of the closed doors, and the hostages that had been determined to run that way and obey the computer voice faltered.

Is there really a station breach? Kim replied.

No. Not yet. The pirates have stopped firing. I'm using subterfuge, as your hound suggested.

It's delightful.

I'm glad you approve.

Kim looked for the rope he'd mentioned and spotted a long chain dangling down from a tidy circular hole freshly cut in the ceiling.

A man ran past her, not caring that thumps, screams, and the buzz of rifles firing came from the corridor outside. He grabbed the door and tried to yank it open. It didn't budge. Rache had either locked it or blocked it somehow.

"That's the way out!" Kim ran into the middle of the gym, with Zee sticking close to her side, and pointed at the chain. The thirty-foot climb would be easy enough for her, but she could tell from the average age of the hostages that many people would need help. Still, it was better than remaining captive.

This is a chain, not a rope, Rache, Kim messaged before thinking better of distracting him.

Forgive my hasty word choice. I shall endeavor to use more precise vocabulary when we discuss literature.

I expect that. Thank you.

"Up to the roof." Kim waved and pointed, now standing right under the chain. "Scholar Chi. Over here."

"Scholar Sato! It's so good to see you." Her chubby colleague ran up, his mussed black hair sticking out in all directions, a bloody gouge in his temple where his chip had been removed. "Unless you wish me to go up that first. Then I'm less delighted."

A lean athletic man lunged for the chain and climbed up it.

"No, I expect you to go second," Kim said.

"I may need a boost." Chi looked up the chain. "Of thirty feet. Why is that ceiling so far away?"

Others who had the strength to make the climb hurried to follow the first man. Kim almost told them that the warning had been a fake, but they were moving so quickly and efficiently that she decided to let them believe they needed to get off the level. If Rache couldn't handle all the guards, it would be better to get the hostages out quickly.

She *hoped* he could handle them all. If he couldn't, she would have to figure out a way to rescue *him*.

"I can't climb that," a woman in her sixties said.

A bronze-skinned man in a rumpled but expensive hand-tailored suit stood beside her, gripping her hand. "And I won't leave without my wife."

"This situation is intolerable," the woman said, rubbing her face with a shaky hand.

"Zee?" Kim asked.

The crusher loomed closer, and the couple skittered back with wide eyes.

Kim lifted a hand, trying to let them know Zee was on their side. "Can you carry people up that chain on your back?"

"Certainly." Zee morphed, and his legs seemed to shrink a little as he reallocated his mass into an extra set of spidery arms.

Kim gaped, though she shouldn't have been surprised by now at what he could turn into.

"If you can grab onto his back…" she started, but Zee swooped up the couple, locking the husband under one arm, the wife under the other, and using the remaining two to climb. "That also works," Kim finished.

She ushered more people up the chain. As soon as Zee dropped off the couple, he jumped down, landing with a heavy thud that left dents in the wood floor. Without pausing, he snatched up two more people—older ladies who shrieked louder than the alarm Rache had sounded—and headed up again.

Scholar Sato, Rache messaged her. *Some of my opponents are sleeping. Do you know anything about this?*

I thought you might prefer them that way.

It does help end the combat more quickly, but for a man who enjoys a challenge, walking into a room littered with snoring enemies is a disappointing experience.

I'm sorry. Next time, I'll leave them awake, let them know you're coming, and tell them about all your secret weaknesses.

After Zee carried the last hostages up the chain, Kim shimmied up herself, afraid that he would come back down for her if she dawdled.

All *of my secret weaknesses? Surely, you can't imagine that I have more than one or two.*

Kim pulled herself up the chain easily, noticing how much of a difference the lesser gravity made. As she scrambled onto the rooftop—Zee was already leading people to the catwalk and giving them boosts up to it—a soft thud sounded behind her. She spun and found herself face to face with Rache. Had he climbed? Or jumped from the street outside the gym? She wasn't sure.

Smoke wafted from a couple of melt marks in his black armor, but he did not appear injured. He held out his gauntleted hand.

Not sure what he meant to give her, she lifted her palm. He laid five empty vials on it.

"In case you wish to reuse them," he said.

"Thoughtful of you."

"I try to be a conscientious ally. Let's see if we can find the control room and talk those pirates into leaving, shall we?"

"Don't you need to rejoin your men and escape the station?"

"Not yet. They're still loading the shuttle and the special cargo hauler they brought over."

"Looting?"

"Borrowing. I had Lieutenant Neimanhaus fill out a rental form, and we even left a deposit."

"Considerate." She hoped his people weren't taking all of the submarines on the station. Not that she cared much about the gate at this point. Mostly, she wanted the chaos to end here and to make sure Chi and the others wouldn't be threatened again.

"Yes. Did you happen to see an older couple that look vaguely like Dr. Peshlakai?"

Kim wasn't good at picking out resemblances among people, but she did think of the married couple that Zee had helped, and thought they might be the right age to be Yas's parents. "Yes. They went that way."

"Good. Follow me."

CHAPTER 23

THERE WAS NO DAY OR NIGHT CYCLE IN the ventilation system of Death Knell Station, and if not for the clock integrated into Bonita's helmet display, she wouldn't have had any idea how many hours passed before Viggo contacted her. It seemed like she and Qin had been hunkered in the large duct for days, recycled air flowing past them in spurts as the filtration system turned off and on.

The two Drucker men are returning to their ship, Viggo reported.

Good. Do you know if the others went back too?

The sirens and sounds of weapons fire had long ago faded, so she assumed the skirmish had ended. She hoped that none of the locals who had helped her had been hurt. Even though she'd paid them to pick a fight with the Druckers, she hadn't paid them *that* much. It had only worked because she'd chosen a station full of people who hated the pirate family.

My cameras can only see what's adjacent to the ship, but I am scanning the local news channels. I believe the Druckers still have a shuttle docked here. There was something about them being responsible for a fight that broke out, injuring people and damaging station structures, and the locals are attempting to impose a fine on them.

Any chance they've all been ordered back to that shuttle?

There's a chance. But I did not see anything in the news about their access to the station being denied.

Bonita nibbled on her lip. *We'll wait a while longer before heading back.*

Her stomach growled. She wished she'd brought snacks instead of extra ammo.

"Viggo says the two men guarding the ship just left," she said quietly, well aware that they were close to a wall that led out to the main concourse. Now and then, clunks and shouts drifted back to them. She didn't want their voices to be audible to someone walking past a vent. "Hopefully, the rest of the Druckers will leave."

A clunk sounded as Qin shifted her weight in the claustrophobic air passage. If Bonita hadn't been in combat armor, it would have seemed spacious, as far as ductwork went, but Qin was much taller and broader than she, even without armor.

"Thank you for taking that risk for me," Qin said. "Maybe you should go back to the ship and let me know when it's safe for me to sneak aboard."

"They might object to *me* walking back on too. I don't have any way of knowing if they believe I arranged all that, if I was haplessly caught in the middle, or something in between."

An alert flashed on her contact. A request for permission to send messages directly to her chip—from Johnny Twelve Toes.

She groaned.

"Problem?" Qin asked.

"I'm about to find out *exactly* what they think."

Unless she denied the request. But if she didn't have anything to hide, why wouldn't she accept the request? Johnny would be suspicious if she didn't.

She accepted the request and preemptively sent the first message. *What the hell was that, Toes? If you didn't want to pay me, you could have said so. Now we've all got the station militia on our asses.*

There was a long pause before he replied. Dare she hope some lucrative accounting business had called him across the system, and the pause represented lag?

Toes? That was all that came with the response at first.

Your nickname is too long.

Johnny would be sufficient. That reply came much more quickly, which sadly meant there was no lag. He wasn't on a ship heading for the gate. *Stallion is also acceptable. Or* mi rey, *if you prefer.*

I do not. Bonita couldn't believe he was still in the mood to flirt with her—and in her own language. She hoped he wasn't merely distracting her while his men tracked her down, drawing ever closer to her hiding spot. *What do you want? You going to tell me you had nothing to do with your people messing up the exchange and almost getting me killed?*

I was going to ask how much you *paid the locals to mess up the exchange, as you say.*

Bonita grimaced. She'd been afraid he would see through her ruse.

Where are you? he added.

At the spa and wax on Level 23, getting my leg hair removed.

In anticipation of meeting me later?

I'd be shot by the locals if I met you anywhere on this station. You've already deprived me of my crewmate and the money you agreed to give me for her. I want nothing else from you.

She withdrew her permission for him to contact her. She had an encrypted chip, so it shouldn't be easy for the government or anyone else to track her through it, but it was always possible the Druckers had some state-of-the-art technology that could outmaneuver it.

"Let's move somewhere else." Bonita patted Qin on the foot. "Another level. The Druckers are still here. I think we're going to have to hide on the station for a couple of days and hope they can't find us."

"Are they searching for us?" An audible whine came from Qin's stomach.

Her metabolism was faster than Bonita's, so she had to be even hungrier.

"I'm not sure, but Twelve Toes wanted to know where I was, and despite what he said, I don't think it's for the purpose of dating me. He suspects that I set all that up back there."

"Do they believe I'm dead?" Qin sounded painfully hopeful as she shuffled down the duct on her hands and knees.

"I didn't ask. I didn't want to draw any attention to you or your demise. I'm hoping the locals didn't give them the opportunity to investigate the remains of that freezer case."

"Maybe you should have left some steaks in it." Qin's stomach whined again, and she snorted. "Not for me to gnaw on while I was in there. But so there would be some realistic chunks of meat spattered on the walls."

"That's a little too macabre for my ruse-designing skills. Besides, if they analyzed the meat, they would have seen that it had come from a vat, not a Qin."

"The Druckers aren't big on forensics. I don't think there was a lab on any of the ships."

Bonita supposed Qin would know, but the fact that they had an accountant made her think they had more career niches filled on those ships than she would have guessed. "I'll remember that for the next time we need to stage our deaths around them."

The third time Qin's stomach made a pitiful noise, Bonita said, "Let's head to one of the lower levels. We can get a room and something to eat."

"It would be safer to stay in the ducts for a couple of days."

"Not if your stomach whines so loudly it leads the pirates to us."

Qin snorted again, but she found one of the perpendicular shafts that would take them to the lower levels. They found a quiet spot where she could force open one of the grates without anyone hearing the noise. They slipped out, and Bonita looked around, recognizing the area.

"Level 12. You can rent anything from inexpensive wall drawers to sleep in to posh hotel rooms, and also—"

Qin's nostrils twitched. "Food. Cochinita pibil… pemita with milanesa… pozole… huevos divorciados."

"Well, you can't technically rent those things. I'm impressed that you can identify so many foods from my culture."

"You've made them all at one time or another while I've been aboard. The slow-roasted pork is my favorite."

"Can you identify all things you've only had once?"

"I can identify all *things*." Qin grinned at her, fangs flashing. "All things with odors, anyway. But that's most things."

Bonita almost said that was probably the true reason the Druckers wanted her back, but she didn't want to bring them up, or the threat of them being captured. She hoped the pirates truly believed Qin to be dead, even if Johnny was suspicious of her. She could deal with their ire, ideally by working three systems away from now on; she just wanted to make sure Qin wasn't on their radar any longer.

They stuck to alleys and maintenance shafts behind buildings, angling toward a modest hotel where Bonita knew the owner and doubted he would rat on them. From there, they could order food. But the less they were out in public, the better.

"There's an entrance just around the corner." Bonita took the lead, pointing to where a flashing sign promised cheap rooms, free soap included.

Before they reached it, three figures in green combat armor rounded the corner and faced them. Bonita groaned. Even though Qin wore her helmet and galaxy suit, they would guess right away who she was.

They were all armed, but Qin charged them anyway. She looked like she would fire the Brockinger but must have thought better of drawing that much attention to herself.

A crackling yellow net of energy dropped down from above before she reached her targets.

"Look out!" Bonita blurted.

Qin sprang and tried to roll fast enough to evade it, but the net was huge, almost like a parachute, and it fell like a rock. It caught her in its clutches.

Bonita leaped back, hoping she could avoid it and help free Qin, but a second one appeared out of nowhere—she'd glanced up when the first one fell and swore a second hadn't been there. She wasn't nearly fast enough to avoid it. The strands wrapped around her, energy snapping and crackling like a wildfire, and it embraced her like an unwelcome lover. Whatever the net was, it was as strong as steel and sticky as a spiderweb. It soon smothered her, pressing her legs together and her arms to her sides. She couldn't move.

She could see through it well enough to tell that Qin was equally bound. Even with her great strength, she couldn't escape it.

Two of the men grabbed her, hefting her over their shoulders. The third man strode toward Bonita, and somehow, she knew who it was before he pushed his helmet back.

"Good evening, Laser," Johnny Twelve Toes said. "I apologize for apprehending you so, but I feared you would stand me up if I suggested a nicer place to meet for our date."

"Screw you."

"Are you sure? You haven't even seen all of my toes yet."

She spat a string of curses that he wouldn't likely understand, but she didn't care. She was frustrated with herself for walking into the trap. She'd known the man was dangerous—she'd sensed that right away—but she'd still gone through with her plan. Qin had been right. They should have stayed in the ducts until they were certain the Druckers had given up and left.

"I do like a lady who's not afraid to curse when appropriate." Johnny smiled at her, but he also slapped his rifle down into his palm and pointed it at her. "I'm afraid I must insist you come with me, Captain."

The men carrying Qin disappeared around the corner. Bonita wanted to fight, to continue to curse at Johnny, but she couldn't let Qin out of her sight. She didn't know what fate awaited them, but their odds would be better if they stuck together.

That didn't make it any less bitter when Johnny grabbed her around the waist and slung her over his shoulder. She still had her weapons, but it didn't matter. With her arms and legs pinned, she couldn't reach them. She couldn't do a damn thing.

Casmir stood in front of the console side by side with Secretary Nguyen while Asger paced behind them and Tork guarded the entrance. Casmir and Nguyen were staring at the scanner display, waiting for something to happen. He was worried because he didn't think the virus had taken this long to unpack itself when Tork had sent it to the *Osprey*. Was it possible he had messed something up when he'd added on his hastily constructed code? Or had the pirates seen it coming and neutralized it somehow?

It had taken a good programmer—Grunburg—with Tork standing by and sharing his insights about astroshamans to come up with the antivirus program. Were the pirates likely to have someone that good?

Nguyen glanced at him. "What did you say your name is?"

"Casmir Dabrowski."

"And you're a professor of robotics?"

"Yes."

"To answer your earlier question, I taught space archaeology for more than twenty years on Nabia before running for office here. I grew up and went to school here before moving away for better work opportunities. I was gone for more than twenty-five years, but then I married a man on Level 2 here—a second marriage—and thought to retire. But when I came back to live with him here, the people were divided, and there was so much more political tension than when I'd grown up here. President Bakas always seemed so beleaguered. I thought she needed another woman on her cabinet that she could lean on, and I somewhat naively thought I could help. Now she's gone, and I've been stuck dealing with…" She waved, either to encompass the station or indicate her frustration in general.

Casmir thought the word she'd left off was *assholes*. Or something like it.

"No good deed goes unpunished, eh?" he offered.

Nguyen grunted and checked the scanner again. No change. At least the pirates had stopped firing at the station. For the moment. What would happen when they realized the transmission code was bogus?

"Do you know a Dr. Erin Kelsey-Sato?" Casmir asked.

"Yes. I've known her for a long time."

"In both forms?"

Nguyen snorted. "Yes. I told her to pick a sexy female android body. She chose to be whimsical."

"Her daughter, Kim Sato, is my best friend. She's here on the station, too, looking for her colleague, a Scholar Chi." Casmir didn't mention Rache. He was tempted to check in on Kim, but if she was dealing with the same crap that he and Asger had dealt with on the way here, he didn't want to risk distracting her.

"Oh, she's spoken of her daughter."

Casmir raised his eyebrows. He always had the impression of Kim and Dr. Kelsey-Sato being very distant. Even though Kim had risked much to recover her mother's deactivated droid body from Skadi Moon, they'd barely spoken two words in Casmir's presence.

Nguyen must have read uncertainty on his face, for she added, "Good things. She's proud of the work Kim does."

"Huh, I'll let Kim know. I think she'll be pleased."

"Erin is a hard person to know well, and I've read between the lines that she finds her daughter equally challenging to relate to."

"Yeah. They must have difficult genes. I wouldn't know anything about that." Casmir's eye blinked, and he snorted. At least he didn't sneeze. The station didn't seem to be overflowing with allergens, despite the various trees he'd passed.

Nguyen eyed him sidelong. "Has anyone ever told you that you look like Admiral Mikita?"

"Yes. Nobody in the Kingdom though. The pictures there seem to have creatively evolved over the centuries. He's eight feet tall in them and dashing and handsome."

"Hm. Are you working with the Kingdom now? Or did you and your knight truly flee those ships?"

"*Your* knight?" Asger's pacing paused.

Nguyen had shifted to look straight into Casmir's eyes. The one that looked straight ahead, anyway. He felt compelled to honesty.

"It was a ruse. *I*—" Casmir pressed his hand to his chest, "—do not approve of everything Jager is doing, and I do not think we should be conquering anyone or tricking anyone into joining the Kingdom, but when the king says you're going on a mission, you go. I have family back on Odin, so I must be loyal to Jager."

Asger frowned. Maybe Casmir shouldn't have spoken so openly, but he sensed that he could make some headway with Nguyen, that she was curious about him and might be grateful for his help—*if* they got the better of the pirates.

"The people here who think they want the protection of the Kingdom," Nguyen said, "don't realize that one must be loyal and do what the king wishes, or they may not like the consequences."

"Has there been a lot of need for protection lately?"

Nguyen waved toward the pirate ships. "More than there used to be, yes. The pirate families are growing ever larger and more powerful. Some stations have started sending bribes—tributes, they call them—to the princes of the Miners' Union for protection. Others are increasing their military spending. We've never considered ourselves militant and haven't wanted to go that way, but… What are the options? Few, I fear."

"What if a deal could be made that allowed your station the freedom of expression and beliefs that it's always known but made you a satellite colony of the Kingdom?"

She arched her eyebrows. "You think you can arrange that?"

"I think…" Casmir wished he could say yes, that he had the power to do so. But who was he back home? A simple robotics professor.

"Their power went out." Asger pushed between them to the scanner and checked the other pirate ships. "*All* of their ships have lost power." He gripped Casmir's shoulder and grinned. "It worked."

"Good. Good." Nguyen pressed a hand to her chest, murmured something in her own language, then added, "How long will it last?"

"Until someone with a battery-operated tunnel-boring machine and the antivirus program shows up," Casmir said.

Nguyen gave him a strange look.

"It's a long story," he said.

Asger moved away, chin to chest and eyes glazed. He had to be talking to Ishii.

"*Is* there an antivirus program?" Nguyen asked.

"Yes. Tork has it. He has it and the original virus." Casmir waved at the android.

Nguyen's eyes sharpened, and he could almost see ideas churning in her mind.

"Is there a price at which you would sell these programs?" she asked. "Are they yours to sell?"

Casmir considered Tork, who was only online with his memory intact because of him. Neither Ishii nor anyone else on the warship had expressed any interest in the android or the virus. They'd all wanted both destroyed.

"I didn't make the original virus, but Tork is currently working for me. If he's amenable to it, I would be willing to let him stay here, so long as you were willing to provide him a telescope."

Nguyen's eyebrows rose again.

"He has an astronomy hobby, you see," Casmir said, "and I promised to help outfit him so he could work on it."

Tork watched them, blatantly interested in the conversation. "The schematics for Tiamat Station show an observatory with an excellent high-powered telescope on one end."

Casmir had worried Tork would reject the idea of being foisted off on someone else, but he sounded intrigued. A stationary position would be more ideal than a roving warship for observing the stars. It would definitely be superior to stargazing from Odin, where the atmosphere made observatories less effective than in space.

"That is true," Nguyen said. "If your android were to stay…"

"Tork is his own android and would have to be treated like a person with rights," Casmir said, "but I would consider leaving him here if I knew he was in good hands. I should warn you, however, that others would eventually figure out an antivirus program and learn not to accept transmissions from your station."

"Maybe, but that might take a while. It's not like the pirate families are buddies and share intelligence with each other freely. They compete ruthlessly with each other, from what I've observed." Her gaze locked onto Casmir again. "You didn't mention your price, other than telescope access."

Casmir looked down at the console. How much trouble would he get in for this? Grunburg probably still had a copy of the antivirus program on his tablet, so it wasn't as if Tiamat Station would be able to use the virus to keep Kingdom warships away. It would largely be helpful to them in deterring others from targeting their station.

He was inclined to give Tork to Nguyen to try to foster some goodwill between Tiamat and the Kingdom, even if that seemed vain when the warships had been so unwilling to help with the pirates. At the least, she would feel goodwill toward him, though he wasn't sure if that granted any advantage. Would he ever be this way again?

Maybe not, but did it matter? He hated bullies, and he loved giving people a means of fighting them.

Casmir met her gaze and stuck out his hand. "Free with the telescope, providing Tork agrees."

He and Nguyen looked at Tork together.

"I am reading the specifications for your telescope right now," Tork said. "It is *magnificent*. The largest and most powerful in System Hydra."

"It is," Nguyen said. "Astronomers and astrophysicists throughout the system come here to do research."

Casmir hoped it hadn't been damaged by the pirate strikes.

"I agree to stay, so long as Professor Dabrowski doesn't mind."

"Zee will miss you," Casmir said, "but I don't mind."

"Excellent."

Nguyen accepted his hand clasp. "Thank you, Professor."

In Kingdom style, he bowed over the handshake. "You're welcome, Secretary Nguyen."

"You can call me Linh."

"And you can call me Casmir."

A beep came from the console, and they both jumped.

"What happened?" Nguyen asked.

"The pirate ships still show dark." Casmir touched the display. "But the Kingdom's warships are moving. They're firing…"

"On us?"

"No," Asger said grimly from behind them. "On the pirates."

Casmir spun and stared at him. "But they don't have power. They're already hanging dead in space."

"I know."

"They're completely defenseless."

Asger's lip curled. "Hence why Ambassador Romano has decided to be opportunistic and wipe out one of the most notorious pirate families in the Twelve Systems."

The four warships blasted into the pirate ships, tearing them to pieces, annihilating them and all aboard. Casmir had a thought of sending them the antivirus, of trying to help them get their power back online so they could at least flee for the gate, but it was over too quickly. Target practice on a range at defenseless bales of hay that couldn't fire back.

Casmir's legs went weak, and he slumped down to the floor. This was horrific. Manslaughter. Even if those pirates had been criminals…

"It isn't right, Asger," he whispered. "You're supposed to capture criminals and rehabilitate them, not… murder them without a trial, without warning. Without anything."

"I know, Casmir. I don't disagree."

Casmir dropped his head into his hand. Asger's agreement wasn't enough.

CHAPTER 24

KIM LED RACHE AND ZEE—AND ALMOST A HUNDRED hostages—into a government building and through an open bookcase door. She'd gotten the directions, if very tersely, from Casmir. When she'd messaged him to ask if the pirates had been driven away, she'd gotten the word "Yeah" back, along with a map showing his location. That was it.

Kim wasn't sure what she expected when she walked down the long corridor, passing an open metal security door, and into a control room that looked like the bridge of a ship, but it wasn't for Casmir to be sitting on the floor with a fifty-something-year-old woman she'd never seen before resting a hand on his shoulder.

At first, he looked like he'd been drugged, with his chin slumped to his chest, so Kim was relieved to spot Tork and Asger. But Asger, with his arms crossed over his chest, radiated anger. Kim glanced toward a large display showing the stars outside, and she worried the pirate ships would be looming within spitting distance, but all she saw was a lot of wreckage floating around.

"I'm going to have to get out of here soon," Rache murmured.

Kim glanced at him. "Do you know what happened?"

"Yes, I just got an update from my men. The pirate ships all lost power at once, and the Kingdom ships destroyed them. I don't think they know the *Fedallah* is out there, but I need to take my shuttle and leave so it stays that way."

"Lost power?" Kim mouthed, then focused on her friend. "Casmir? The virus?"

He looked up at her for the first time, his eyes haunted.

"I didn't know the warships would attack," he whispered, the words so soft, so pained, that she almost missed them.

"Oh. I see." Kim saw, but she didn't know what to say. Her pragmatic side wanted to point out that Casmir wasn't to blame, but she knew him well enough to know it wouldn't matter. He would blame himself for playing a role, however inadvertently.

"He saved the station," the woman said firmly.

"Secretary Nguyen," one of the freed hostages blurted, rushing past Kim and Rache. The man gripped her shoulders. "I'm so glad you're all right."

"I'm glad you are too." She—Nguyen—patted the balding man. "You and I, Secretary of the Treasury Esposito, may have to put the station back together." Her eyes narrowed. "Will President Chronis fight us, do you think?"

"President Chronis is dead. Some of the hostages blamed him for everything and killed him the first night we were locked up together."

"Ah." Nguyen did not appear overly upset. Or maybe she was too numb to react.

Kim couldn't tell if she'd been aligned with the Bakas Vengers or not. And she didn't much care.

She walked forward and crouched on Casmir's other side. "You're not injured, are you?"

"No, I'm fine. Uninjured, anyway."

Kim rested a hand on his shoulder as Nguyen moved toward the control console. Zee came to stand in front of Casmir, his silent protector.

"Vice President Woods died in the initial fighting," Esposito added to Nguyen. "It truly is just the two of us, I think. Until we reestablish order and hold elections. We can't just assume to take their positions."

"No, but for now, we have to do their jobs."

"Does it even matter?" Esposito asked. "The Kingdom warships are out there. They must have come to take over the station, to impose their will on us."

Nguyen looked at Casmir. "We'll see about that."

She tapped a comm console, and a man's voice that Kim didn't recognize replied.

"This is Ambassador Romano, King Jager's representative in this system," the deep bass voice said. "We have annihilated the pirate threat for you and hope you are appropriately grateful. Is President Chronis yet available, and is he willing to speak about the possibility of Tiamat Station joining the Kingdom under our protection?"

"Chronis is dead. I'm Acting Vice President Linh Nguyen. Acting President Esposito is also with me here."

Esposito shook his head and waved his hands, clearly not wanting the job. Nguyen's expression said *too bad.*

"We're aware," Nguyen went on, "that you killed the pirates only after your rogue roboticist planted a virus on their ships that rendered them defenseless."

Kim thought Casmir would crack a joke or at least smile at the term *rogue roboticist*, but he didn't even lift his head.

"We are grateful to *him*," Nguyen added.

"Excellent," Ambassador Romano said. "He is not a rogue. He is a respected professor and civilian advisor from our home world."

This time, Casmir reacted, lifting his head, an incredulous expression on his face.

"Are you and your acting president willing to speak about the possibility of Tiamat Station joining the Kingdom under our protection?" Romano repeated, as if he wasn't fazed at all by Casmir being credited.

"We don't believe we *need* your protection in light of recent events." Nguyen nodded at Casmir, who nodded back, though his expression remained grave. "But we must look to the future, and—" she took a deep breath, "—it is possible that an alliance with the Kingdom might be worth considering. However, we will only negotiate with Professor Dabrowski."

Casmir's mouth drooped open in surprise.

"Dabrowski is a teacher, not a diplomat." Romano sounded irked for the first time. "He has no training in negotiations, nor any authority to represent the king."

"Perhaps you should go back home and see if you can get that authority granted to him, because he's the only one we're talking to."

Kim grimaced. How had Casmir gotten himself into this situation? Not only would this irk the ambassador, but she highly doubted Jager would be pleased about the development.

"He is busy advising on another mission right now," Romano said. "As are we all. We can't go home until that is completed."

"We'll wait," Nguyen said cheerfully.

Romano didn't respond, and Kim checked to see if the channel was still open. It was.

"It'll give us time to get our station back in order and hold elections," Nguyen added.

"At which point, someone *else* might win the position of president?" Romano sounded hopeful.

Esposito got over his fear for long enough to lean forward and say, "Acting Vice President Nguyen is very well liked here on the station. If she runs for president, I believe her victory will be assured."

Nguyen's lips twisted, as if she wasn't sure this endorsement was good for her future. But she didn't shy away from the statement or imply she wouldn't take the job if she got it.

"I see," Romano said. "I will pass along your demands to the king."

"Excellent. I look forward to hearing from him and to seeing Professor Dabrowski alive and well again, and here on Tiamat Station to negotiate a deal. We are very pleased with him for the role he's played in saving the station, and I must reiterate that we will *only* deal with him."

Now, Casmir's lips twisted. Kim assumed Nguyen was trying to make sure no assassin's blade found his back due to his work here or anything she'd said.

The channel closed without another remark from the ambassador.

Asger cleared his throat. "Ishii wants us to come back, Casmir." He nodded to include Kim. "We need to return to our original mission, especially since it's been rumored that there's some competition in the area." He looked blandly at Rache, which Kim assumed meant he'd reported Rache's presence on the station as soon as he'd shown up.

"I understand." Casmir pushed himself to his feet. "Sorry, Kim. I didn't ask. Did you find your colleague?"

"I did." Kim waved to the corridor, which was loaded with the curious hostages, all peering into the control room. "And we also found Dr. Peshlakai's parents."

"That's good. I'm glad something positive came of all this."

His expression remained bleak, and Kim was tempted to give him a hug, since she doubted anyone else here would. But she couldn't make her body do it with so many people around. She patted him on the shoulder again, hoping it was enough.

CROSSFIRE

"How are you feeling?" Yas asked his young patient.

He had treated Princess Tambora for a concussion and a sprained wrist, and he was tempted to ask if he could do a full exam of her legs, because he'd glimpsed swelling and numerous bruises before she'd settled in her float chair and draped her long dusty dress over them. But there was a limit to what he could do hunkered behind the reception desk in the bombed out building.

"It's been a while since the last jolt," Tambora whispered hopefully.

"Let's hope there won't be any more."

"And that the station hasn't been taken over by pirates. The Kingdom would be better than that. These people…" She shook her head, a few of her long braids spilling off her shoulders and down to her waist.

Yas bristled a little since *these people* were *his* people. "The Kingdom's culture is far too stifling for most of Tiamat Station's populace."

She rolled her eyes. "They could have accepted the offer of protection without giving up their culture. That's what negotiations are for. That's what my mother the queen is in talks with Jager about. Accept their protection, marry some Kingdom noble to cement it, but get it in writing—in blood—that you're allowed to keep your religion and culture and way of life. That's better than waiting for someone to conquer you. Those pirates out there aren't even the real dangerous guys. The Miners' Union and coalitions forming in System Cerberus—they're trouble. If they take your habitat by force, you don't get to keep any of your freedoms. You just become some slave in their system. Better to deal with the known enemy who's willing to make concessions than wait until you're usurped and have no choices at all."

Yas didn't know whether to argue with her or be surprised by the cogency of her words. He'd first thought the princess around eighteen, but he decided she might be older than that.

"I hope Abidugun and Ibironke are all right." She raised her float chair to peer over the reception counter. "The last I heard, they were pinned down by robots in Bay 3 and hadn't been able to figure out the code to get into the ship. I'm afraid Ibironke will get in trouble when we get back. For leaving me. I told her to go instead of hiding in the lab with me, but she's my bodyguard, so she's not supposed to leave. I'll try to defend her, but my mother the queen is so… difficult in these matters. In all matters."

"Maybe that's why she's able to make headway in negotiating with the Kingdom." Yas didn't think his own people had heard any hint of the concessions she mentioned.

"She is taller and scarier than King Jager." Tambora smiled, then pointed at something, and lowered her chair below the desk. "The people in black armor are your people? That was Tenebris Rache before, wasn't it?"

"Yes." He was surprised she'd figured that out—Yas didn't think he or Kim had said his name. He lifted his head as an armored man strode toward the building's front doors. Chaplain? As promised?

Doctor, a message came from Rache, *are your parents as arrogant and snooty as you are?*

They're urbane, well-educated people.

I'll take that as a yes. We've found them—and the rest of the hostages. Chaplain is coming to escort you and the princess to our shuttle bay. I'm sure you'll want to see your parents so you can give them hugs and kisses before we leave. Which needs to be soon. Now that the pirates have been destroyed, someone unfriendly may have time to notice our shuttle docked.

"The pirates are destroyed?" Yas blurted out loud before realizing it. Tambora stared at him. *The Kingdom ships attacked them?*

Eventually, yes. It's a long story.

Is there any chance— You know I'd hoped to clear my name.

Yes, I haven't forgotten. I asked Casmir to take care of it.

Casmir? Yas blinked in confusion. *Your, uhm—the roboticist?*

What did Rache's clone brother have to do with justice on Tiamat Station?

Yes, he's Secretary of Education Nguyen's new best friend. And apparently, she's most likely to become president after your people hold elections. Oh, did you hear that Chronis is dead?

I don't know what to say.

You can give Casmir hugs and kisses too.

Yas snorted, not fooled by Rache's indifferent sardonic comments anymore. Rache had left his men and risked himself to help Yas. Yas and Kim. Watching him flirt—if one could call it that—with Kim had been strange, but Yas decided it humanized Rache. When he wasn't around his subordinates, he was a lot less stiff.

Tambora poked him. "Doctor, tell me about the pirates. Nobody is doing news updates for this station now. I *checked*." She waved toward her embedded chip.

"They've been vanquished, and the Kingdom roboticist who made that announcement earlier played some role in it. He's made friends with what remains of our presidential cabinet."

"That guy was from the Kingdom? He sounded geeky."

"He is. The Kingdom has geeky people." The Kingdom was large enough that Yas was certain they had every type of person represented.

"Does it really? I know not everyone is a knight, but I thought that was what they all wanted to be. Sports celebrities and knights. Princess Oku always makes it sound like she's surrounded by those types that want to woo her. I'm not supposed to be envious, but I am. Men on Shango are supposed to be meek and let the women handle the fighting. Otherwise, they end up being asked to leave or work in the mines. Even the muscly ones are polite and avoid eye contact." She wrinkled her nose.

Yas didn't know how much of that was the culture that had developed at Shango Habitat over the centuries and how much was because Tambora was royalty. Yas would avoid looking into the eyes of royalty, too, at least royalty with bodyguards that had instructions to thump people who were too direct.

A black-helmeted head looked over the reception desk. "What's going on back there, Doc? You sexing it up with a cripple? *Kinky*."

Yas gaped at Chaplain in horror. The man hardly *ever* spoke, and now that he had something to say, *that* was what came out of his mouth?

"She is a *princess*, Corporal," Yas said, afraid and ashamed to look at Tambora's face.

"Yeah? Way to go, Doc." Chaplain gave him a thumbs-up. "I'll wait outside for you to finish up, but I got some people out here who want to see you, and the captain said not to dawdle. We got a mission to do and too many hostiles in the area."

The helmet disappeared, and Chaplain walked whistling back to the front door. He was in a better mood than usual. Yas wondered how many men he'd killed while collecting submarines for Rache. He also wondered what *people* might be with Chaplain who wanted to see him. Someone injured? Someone else with a dubious mole?

"I'm so sorry about him, Your Highness," Yas said, stepping out from behind the desk and offering her a hand.

When he risked looking at her face, hoping she was closer to amused than offended, he caught a pained expression there. Yas wanted to punch Chaplain for calling her a cripple. He wasn't positive that was the reason for the expression, but he wagered it was hard to be disabled in a habitat full of warrior women.

Tambora smoothed her face into a mask that didn't seem right on her—her eyes had been determined and lively when she'd been suggesting political tactics for dealing with the Kingdom. "It's not your fault, Doctor. Please have your man lead the way to the shuttle bay. I'm anxious to make sure my bodyguard and advisor weren't injured in the fighting."

"Understandable."

Fortunately, the streets and corridors were quiet when they stepped out of the building, where Chaplain waited with two people Yas hadn't expected to see, at least not so soon. Their stances were weary and beleaguered, both appearing to have aged ten years in the six months since he'd last seen them, and each had fresh gouges where their chips had been removed, which explained why he hadn't been able to get in touch.

"Mother!" Yas blurted. "Father!"

He rushed forward to hug his mother and, he hoped, get a customary handshake from his stoic father, but faltered, fearing they didn't know he was innocent of the president's assassination. But his mother crossed the distance and smothered him with a hug. His father came up and patted him on the shoulder.

"Look here, boy, why didn't you ever contact us?" he asked gruffly.

"I'm sorry." Yas felt like a kid again standing with his head bowed in his father's study as he listened to some lecture. His father turned the shoulder pat into a firm grip, and that took away some of the sting. "I didn't want you to be implicated in that mess, sir. That horrible crime. I didn't do it." Yas leaned back from his mother so he could look into their eyes, needing to see if they believed him.

"Of course you didn't," his mother said.

"We knew you wouldn't harm anyone," his father said, "and for those who were in doubt, it all came out when that mob tortured and hanged President Chronis. I didn't approve of that, of course, but after his own assassin outed him, it got ugly. And our guards didn't care if we fought amongst ourselves. They said they were kidnapping people for the good of the station, but they had their own agenda. Everyone did. Shortsighted ignoramuses." He shook his head.

Yas swallowed, relieved his parents hadn't doubted him. And even if it was selfish, he was relieved someone else had killed Chronis. For a while, he'd feared Rache would do it as part of Yas's request to have his name cleared. Then the man's death would have been on Yas's hands.

"But what is this about you working for mercenaries, dear?" his mother whispered, glancing at Chaplain, who was tapping his fingers against his rifle and shifting his weight impatiently.

"It's a long story." Yas wished he could explain it to them over dinner and help them get their home back in order, but it sounded like Rache wanted to leave right away. Yas hoped they would soon have surgeries done to replace their chips and heal those painful-looking gouges—fortunately, the failsafe sockets seemed to have prevented any obvious neural damage from the rough removals—so he would be able to contact them from anywhere in the system. "I'll try to sum it up on the way to the shuttle bay."

"About time," Chaplain grumbled, heading off down the street.

Tambora revved her float chair to pass him, probably eager to learn the fate of her bodyguard and advisor.

As Yas and his parents trailed them, some of the tension of the day—no, of the last six months—slowly unknotted from his shoulders. His mother and father were safe, and though the fate of the station might still be up in the air, the inhabitants were no longer fighting each other. If Secretary Nguyen, or whoever else ended up in charge, was willing to clear him of the crime he'd never committed… maybe that would be the start of feeling like a man again. Even if his word meant he had to continue serving Rache, he would do it as an employee, not a fugitive hiding among criminals.

CHAPTER 25

KIM ENCOUNTERED YAS ON THE WAY TO THE shuttle bay and talked with him for a few minutes, surprised he was heading back to the mercenary ship instead of staying and spending time with his parents. But he'd once mentioned a promise to serve Rache for five years. It looked like he intended to make good on that promise.

When they walked into the shuttle bay, he lifted a hand in farewell to her and walked toward the black-armored figure standing in front of an airlock farther down from Asger's shuttle. Kim knew right away that it was Rache, even though his helmet was up. And she also noticed that his shuttle was docked in a different slot than it had been before. How many times had it come and gone while she, Casmir, Asger, and Rache had been dealing with the chaotic situation on the station? Had his men found the submarines they'd wanted? Would the *Fedallah* beat the Kingdom warships to the gate?

Rache's helmet turned in her direction, and she realized she was standing near the door and staring at him.

She felt she should walk over and say something. Chi was safe, largely thanks to him, and even though Yas was Rache's man more than he was a friend of Kim's, she was pleased that Rache had helped his parents and made sure Casmir talked the secretary of education—would she truly become the new president?—into clearing his name.

A message popped up on her contact from Rache, and she jumped. She'd forgotten that she'd given him permission to contact her.

Are you gazing adoringly at me because you regret that we must now part ways? he asked. *Or did I smear crumbs from my ration bar on my armor?*

She walked across the bay toward him, not sure whether it would be appropriate to answer with snark or if she should be more serious, since she wanted to thank him.

He waited, facing her, not moving. Even though she didn't spend a lot of time gazing into people's eyes or studying their faces when they weren't looking, she wished she could see his. Casmir had implied that Royal Intelligence knew who Rache was, at least the higher-level officers. Would he ever decide it didn't matter if he let people see his face?

She stopped a couple of paces away from him. "Thank you for your assistance in retrieving Scholar Chi."

The words came out more stiff and formal than she intended.

Rache bowed. "You're welcome."

"I am also glad that Dr. Peshlakai's parents are safe and that he won't be considered a criminal any longer in his own home. Will you release him from his obligation to serve on your ship?"

"Not unless another surgeon falls in my lap. Or at my feet under the café table, as the case was. Good doctors are hard to find."

"Ah."

"Was that a note of disapproval? I believe it was a fair tradeoff, though I'll admit I took advantage of his desperate situation. As a mercenary captain who heads off into danger often, I find it hard to attract the interest of qualified medical professionals simply by putting want ads in the network news feeds."

"Perhaps you're not offering high enough pay."

"I give a higher-than-average salary and include combat bonuses."

"Perhaps you should change combat bonuses to bonuses for saving lives. The implication with combat is that your doctor will be required to march into battle with your troops. Doesn't Yas usually hang out in sickbay until you bring people back?"

"Usually. I'll consider your suggestion."

She looked at the dark mask inside his helmet and shook her head. "I feel ridiculous talking to someone without a face."

"And yet you're here. I'm honored." Rache bowed again. "I believe I did suggest a situation in which I'd be willing to unmask for you."

"The odds of us finding a way to have a private dinner date seem poor."

"Hm, unfortunate, but I suppose that is true, since neither you nor Casmir has decided to accept my job offer."

"If he keeps finding ways to irk Jager, he may yet need to seek off-planet employment."

"And you?"

"I don't want to be a mercenary."

"Are you sure you wouldn't like to see how large my combat bonuses are before dismissing the job offer?" He sounded amused, not offended.

Kim was certain he didn't expect her to sign on, so that was a relief. "I'm arrogant enough to believe that the work I'm doing is important and can be of benefit to large portions of humanity. It already *has* been to many space-faring people. I need to operate within the system so I can continue to do that work, ideally from my laboratory back on Odin. Which I miss a great deal."

"In that case, may I give you a brief tour of my airlock chamber before you depart?" Rache extended a hand into the compact space that was suitable for a couple of armored men to stand in while waiting for the air to cycle.

The word closet came to mind.

"*Just* the airlock chamber?" Kim raised her eyebrows.

"My men are in the shuttle proper. You don't want to tour them. Trust me." Rache stepped into the airlock chamber and closed the inner hatch, tapping a button that dropped a cover over the Glasnax porthole. He clasped his hands behind his back and gazed back at her, waiting to see if she would join him.

Kim looked over her shoulder, wondering if there were witnesses. Casmir had walked into the bay, but he was talking to Secretary Nguyen and Princess Tambora, who sat in her float chair, flanked by a dark-skinned man and woman. The missing bodyguard and advisor? Hopefully, their ship was intact, and Tambora wouldn't need Kim's or Casmir's help any longer. Kim didn't want to see her stuck on a Kingdom ship where she might end up being used as some pawn or bargaining chip.

Secretary Nguyen was gesturing animatedly, and Kim thought Casmir might be wrapped up in the conversation and wouldn't notice her slipping away for a few minutes, but he spotted her looking at them.

"What are you *doing*?" he mouthed, waving toward Rache's shuttle and then pointing three times at Asger's shuttle.

Kim held up a finger, trusting that he would be involved in that conversation for a few more minutes and that she wasn't delaying their departure. She stepped into the airlock with Rache, ignoring the incredulous gape that Casmir sent across the bay.

Rache pointed toward the small panel with the controls to close the outer hatch. Letting her decide if she was willing to lock herself in with him instead of presuming to do it himself?

For good or ill, she no longer worried that she had anything to fear from him on a personal level. She did worry about what might happen if he continued to fight against the Kingdom and she continued to get drawn into the Kingdom's military endeavors. But she doubted he would do or say anything inappropriate to her.

Kim hit the button, and the hatch swung shut. She hoped Casmir wouldn't race over and bang on it, demanding to know what insanity had ensnared her mind. He probably wouldn't with Tambora and Nguyen watching. She hoped.

A red light came on, so they weren't standing in the dark. Rache's helmet retracted, folding into its niche on the back of his armor, and she watched with a mixture of curiosity, anticipation, and wariness as he lifted a hand to remove his hood and mask.

Casmir had seen him without the mask a couple of times now, she reminded herself, and she was positive he would have mentioned if Rache was horribly maimed or had a bunch of astroshaman mods or tattoos or anything out of the ordinary.

And that was what the removal of the mask revealed. Rache wasn't exactly ordinary, but there was nothing strange about his face. His eyes were more intense and focused than Casmir's, and also more intense and focused than those of twenty-one-year-old David Lichtenburg from the race photos. His face was leaner than it had been then, making his cheekbones more prominent and his jaw chiseled and strong. He did have a few faint scars, but they were more the kind that would intrigue someone into asking what had happened than anything that detracted from his looks. She wasn't sure she would call him handsome—intense was the word that kept coming to mind—but he wasn't unappealing. If anything, she found herself looking more closely at him than she could remember ever looking at anyone else. And for some reason, she thought of the fact that he'd read the books she'd written without even knowing she was the author—or that the author was female.

"Are you comparing me to Casmir?" Rache asked, his typical dryness in his tone.

"A little, but more to the pictures we found of David Lichtenburg after winning air-bike races."

"Ah, you looked me up? I'm honored. I would bow, but in these close quarters, I fear I'd clunk you in the chest with my head, and you may consider that overly familiar." He raised his eyebrows, a hint of humor lessening the intensity in his eyes, though he was still watching her closely.

She had a feeling he wanted her to say she wouldn't mind chest-clunking. She was conflicted over whether she would or not.

She'd never wanted a man—or a woman—to touch her, her brief experimentations as a university student doing nothing to excite her, and she'd always assumed that her libido was as odd and atypical as the rest of her. Occasionally, she regretted that sexual interest seemed a prerequisite for romantic relationships, because it wasn't as if she always preferred to be alone. Sometimes she did, but sometimes she wondered what it would be like to have a life partner. For a lot of years, Casmir had somewhat filled that role, and she'd always been relieved that he hadn't seemed to care that she didn't want a physical relationship with him, but she knew he wanted to find a true romantic partner one day and to have children. And she knew she would be lonely when he departed, and she was left occupying a house by herself.

But was that a reason to pursue a physical relationship with someone, when she feared it would be far closer to enduring than enjoying? She didn't know.

"Yes," Kim said, realizing she'd been silent for a long time and Rache might be waiting for an answer. "I've told you my feelings on touching."

"You have," he agreed, a slight sad smile curving his lips.

Uhm. A message from Casmir popped up on her contact display. *Are you being kidnapped, Kim? Or did you accidentally walk into the wrong shuttle? The inside of Asger's airlock is painted royal purple, so I'm not sure how you could have made that mistake, but perhaps you're fatigued after the day's events.*

I'm not being kidnapped.

Well, Asger says we're ready to go, and Ishii is waiting for us. Probably that grumpy ambassador too. So if you're coming, you should probably join us soon. You are *coming, right? Or are you there because you plan to spy on Rache's dastardly plans and report his moves back to us?*

Kim snorted. *I'll be over there shortly.*

Rache raised his eyebrows.

"Our shuttle is ready to return to the warship," she said.

"And that was snort-inspiring?"

"No. Casmir wanted to know if I'd accidentally walked into the wrong shuttle. And then he suggested I go with you to spy on you and report back to the Fleet warships."

"You know, if you ever decide to have a romantic relationship with a man, you should plan to turn off input from the outside world when you're together. He would appreciate that."

"I'll keep that in mind. Pleasing men is always my number one goal."

The words came out a little harsher than she intended—she never liked having someone presume to correct her, even when she knew she was wrong and had failed to grasp some obvious social convention—but he dropped his head back and laughed. It was a nice laugh, not the maniacal laugh of a super villain, and she found it pleasant.

"Why did you stage your death?" Kim asked, the words burbling up before she could consider if this was the best time to ask. "What happened in the months you weren't racing? And when your fiancée was reported missing?"

His humor vanished, and the intensity returned to his eyes. Almost a ferocity, and she feared she'd misstepped and presumed too much.

She'd forgotten that Casmir had mentioned overhearing the information about his dead fiancée and that it wasn't something Rache had voluntarily shared. His enemy had brought it up, possibly to hurt him, to twist a knife that had never been pulled out.

"We were kidnapped by pirates that I eventually learned Jager had hired to capture us—to capture me. I happened to be with Thea when it happened, and they took her too." For the first time his gaze shifted from her, to a spot on the hull where his eyes grew very hard, very angry, and Kim was glad he wasn't looking at her. Ten years clearly hadn't dulled the pain that much. "Because she was beautiful, and they wanted to enjoy her beauty, even though she was unwilling. They didn't care, and Jager didn't care either. They checked apparently."

He clenched his fist so hard it looked like it would hurt.

"He wanted me to fight them, to be motivated to do so, to come up with some brilliant way to escape, even though there were hundreds of them. He wanted me to learn what a bad place the universe was so I would stop racing bikes and screwing around with my life, as he put it, and become the hardened military leader he'd invested so much in me becoming. And I did fight them. They tortured me, and they tortured her, and I did everything I could to escape and to kill as many of them as I could on the way out. I finally got my chance, and I almost died getting Thea out of there. But it had taken me too long, and they'd hurt her too much. She died before I could get us back to medical care. I was in a hospital for weeks myself when I got back, but I didn't care about that. I just cared that I'd lost her, and that because she'd known me, because she'd fallen in love with me, the end of her life was the worst possible end imaginable." He paused and swallowed, and there were tears in his eyes now. "Because Jager wanted to build my fucking character."

Kim didn't know what to say. *I'm sorry* would be ludicrously inadequate. She'd imagined something tragic must have happened to Rache—to David—to create his obsession with hurting Jager—and everyone who swore an oath to serve him—but she hadn't envisioned that.

She wiped moisture from her eyes, and he stirred, blinking and visibly pulling himself back together—putting the mask back on, the symbolic one, not the real one. The real one he still gripped in one hand, the mask he'd worn for ten years so Jager wouldn't know that David Lichtenburg had survived that crash and was coming after him. Or maybe, she realized, it had been to protect those back on Odin that he cared about. If his adoptive parents had been decent, or if he'd had friends he raced with and trained to be a knight with, he might have worried that Jager would use them to get to him.

"Tell Casmir to watch out for that man." Rache leaned over and hit the button to open the hatch back into the station. "And whatever else you want. I don't care."

No, he cared a *lot*. But not if his clone brother knew his past, apparently. Maybe he even wanted her to share it as a warning to Casmir. But she didn't think she would. They weren't her secrets to tell.

Light flooded in when the hatch opened, and even though there was nobody standing outside, the chamber lost its privacy. Its intimacy.

"I'm sorry, David," Kim said, even though she'd already decided the words were insipid and not enough. Maybe all words were like that. But to leave without saying anything to acknowledge his story would be worse than not saying enough.

She leaned close and kissed him on the cheek, then walked away without looking back, not wanting to see what his reaction was, not wanting to know if it was too little, too distant. Not wanting to be reminded how bad she was at people, at relationships.

Kim found Asger waiting in the pilot's pod and Casmir slumped in one of the rear passenger pods, his eyes glazed as he stared at a bulkhead. He didn't blink when she drew close to him. She sat in the closest pod and touched his arm.

"Are you all right?" she asked, knowing he could have a seizure that looked like he was just spacing out.

He blinked and focused on her. "Yes, sorry."

"You don't have to apologize for being tired." Kim realized that probably wasn't the problem. He'd given the order to share that computer virus, which had allowed the Kingdom ships to swoop in and destroy the pirates. Pirates or not, people had still died. A lot of people. "Or for being disturbed by the day you had," she added softly.

"I know. Sorry." He rolled his eyes at himself and waved away the second apology.

"Preparing for departure," Asger announced from the pilot's pod, not commenting that they'd chosen the back seats instead of sitting near him. "And to return us to Ishii's loving embrace."

"I'd prefer he not embrace me," Kim said. "Casmir probably wouldn't mind. He looks like he could use a hug."

This time, Casmir's hand wave seemed one of agreement.

"He may punch us," Asger said. "I'm not sure what the official stance will be on all of this. Or the unofficial one."

"I'm sorry, Asger." Casmir leaned his head back and closed his eyes. "I'd wanted… I thought that on this mission, maybe I could help you gain back the trust or honor that you lost in your superiors' eyes by helping me."

Asger glanced back. "That's not your fault. I chose to help you, because…" He stretched a hand out, fingers groping in the air. "You try to do the right thing. And sometimes it works spectacularly. The only problem is that Jager cares more about what's right for the Kingdom than what's right for humanity in general."

"Shouldn't we be concerned that those aren't the same thing?" Casmir asked.

"Yes."

The shuttle pulled out of its docking slot, and the sensation of weightlessness washed over Kim.

Casmir kept his eyes closed, and she decided to let him rest until they were back aboard the *Osprey*, even though her mind was whirling after her discussion with Rache, and she wanted someone to talk to about it. Less about the exact details—she wouldn't share those—and more about her own jumbled feelings. Casmir was the only one she could imagine opening up to, even if he would grimace at any hint that she wanted to have a relationship of some kind with Rache.

"Are *you* all right?" he asked, glancing at her.

"Yes. Better than you, I think."

"I should hope so, or something would be broken in the universe." He smiled briefly. "Was working with Rache… all right? Sorry, my vocabulary is lacking today. And I just apologized again."

"I'd rather sit next to someone who apologizes too often than someone who never does."

"Is that Rache? Or just random people in general that you sit next to?"

"He was fine. Actually, he was kind of amazing at getting the hostages out. Zee was great too. I barely did anything."

"Amazing? Damn, Rache got to be amazing, and I got to have a panic attack when a pirate commed me."

"I'm sure you didn't have a panic attack."

"I almost did. Did I mention it was a pirate admiral? Chaos Cutty."

"Nicely alliterative."

"I should have complimented him on it."

Kim smiled, glad he was able to joke, even if his eyes still had a haunted cast to them. It reminded her of when he'd padded out to the patio, admitting to that nightmare. That seemed ages ago. Had it truly been only a few weeks since then?

"Did you compliment Rache on being amazing?" Casmir asked.

"No."

"A man likes to hear that."

"Even a self-confident man who already *knows* he's amazing?"

"Probably so. I am doing the exercise of putting myself in someone else's shoes since I'm still working on building my own self-confidence. It's an ongoing project."

"Casmir…" Kim felt the urge to fidget, but the pod had her clasped on all sides to keep her from floating away. "What would a normal person do to let someone know they're not unappreciative of another person's help and not unaware of their… interest, but that they aren't good at feelings? Other people's or their own." She rolled her eyes at herself. That had been vague.

"You're asking me for advice on being normal?"

"Maybe I should have said emotionally accessible."

"I am that. I'll accept hugs from anyone. Even Ishii."

"What if it's a punch?"

"That has less appeal."

Casmir closed his eyes again while he considered his answer. Or maybe he was considering the stability of his stomach. So far, Kim found the ride very smooth—Asger didn't seem to be in a hurry to get back to the *Osprey*—but zero-g was zero-g.

"I don't have the best track record when it comes to relationships," Casmir finally said, speaking quietly so Asger wouldn't overhear, "so I'm probably not the best person to ask, but since I can't see you asking your brothers or father for advice on this—"

She drew back, horrified at the idea of talking about anything except dojo life with them.

"—I'll say that you should probably say *something*, if you're at all interested, to let him know, because we—men—aren't the best at reading between the lines. I mean, maybe someone who likes to decipher symbolism in literature is different, but women always seem to assume you know things, but we really need you to tell us the things we're supposed to know, because most of the time, we don't pick up on subtle."

"Yes, I've noticed that you don't grasp that I want you to tidy and sanitize your room when I leave cleaning supplies on your desk."

"Too subtle." He smiled. "But if you're not ready to make blunt statements to a man—not that I've noticed a lack of bluntness is one of your failings—then you can do things to let him know you're thinking of him and hope he's thinking of you." He lowered his voice even further. "I'm sending Oku little video clips of things that are important to me and that she may find endearing."

"Like what?" Kim assumed Casmir was, unlike Asger, wise enough not to send nude pictures of his anatomy.

"Last time, I sent a clip of Zee and Tork talking about me."

"Are you sure that was cute and not disturbing?"

"I found it cute."

"Hm. Robots don't talk about me, as far as I know."

"Do bacteria?"

"I don't think I can send a guy videos of petri dishes."

"If you did and he was still interested, you'd know he was a keeper."

Kim snorted. Maybe so. She decided she would read that book Rache had mentioned and that they could discuss it through messages or whenever they met again. Hopefully, not when their allies were trying to blow each other up over that damn gate.

"Casmir?"

"Yes?"

"Thank you for a serious answer—a semi-serious answer—instead of saying how horrifying you find the notion of me having any kind of interest in him."

"Well, I assumed you knew that already."

"Did I tell you that Princess Tambora knew who you were?" Kim asked. "Princess Oku had mentioned you."

"Really?" Casmir opened his eyes, some of their usual alert curiosity back. "Because of bee stuff?"

"Yes. Even if Oku wants to try bacteria before robots, you must have made an impression on her."

"Because she's telling other people she knows me instead of pretending she *doesn't* know me? That is a good sign when it comes to girls."

"She also messaged you to ask me about the bee project when she could have messaged me directly. It's not like I would have denied a contact request from royalty."

"Is that true? You're pretty particular about who you accept for chip-to-chip contact. Even when you accept people, sometimes you don't respond to them. You've occasionally taken *days* to answer my messages, and I'm your favorite person."

"That's only because I refuse to answer text messages when your room is down the hall from mine and you have legs."

"I really don't understand this fascination with exercise that you have, Kim."

Despite his rueful head shake, he looked a little less grim for the rest of the flight. Kim was glad. She had a feeling Casmir had set events in motion today that he would be inextricably linked to in the future, whether King Jager approved of them or not, and she suspected it would be important for him to have something else going on in his life that could provide him some pleasure. She hoped the robot videos were as endearing as he thought.

EPILOGUE

CASMIR WOKE FROM A NIGHTMARE, GASPING AS HE lurched up in bed. His heart slammed against his ribcage, and he stared at the rumpled bedspread underneath him, needing to focus on anything but the vivid memory of the dream.

It had been of Bernard again, that grenade blowing up and his head exploding, and then it had gotten worse, morphing into those pirate ships being annihilated. On the space station, Casmir hadn't seen the blood and the agonized faces of people dying, but in his dream, his treacherous subconscious mind had filled in the gruesome details.

He rubbed his face, his hand shaking, and checked the time, hoping it was morning so he wouldn't have to go back to sleep. But only a half hour had passed since he'd collapsed face-first on his bed without taking his boots off. He'd been so exhausted from the day's activities that he'd thought he would sleep like a dead man, not dream of dead men.

"Casmir Dabrowski," came Zee's voice from the shadows near the door. "Did you hear the chime?"

The soft bong of the door chime went off to punctuate his last question.

"I did this time." His voice was raspy, his mouth dry. "Thanks."

He levered himself off the bed, pausing to push his hands through his hair. It was sweaty and sticking up in all directions. That had been a rough half hour.

The lights came up partway as he waved at the sensor to open the door. Asger stood in the corridor, wearing gym togs instead of his usual liquid armor and cloak, and Casmir barely stifled a groan. The last thing he wanted was to be tortured in the gym.

"Ishii wants to see us."

Casmir didn't bother stifling the second groan.

Asger eyed him. "You look like hell. Did you have a seizure?"

"No, I took a nap."

"I don't think you did it right."

"I definitely did not." Casmir tried to muster a smile, but the nightmare still lurked near the surface. "Maybe I'll create an error-management protocol to help with troubleshooting future naps."

"Good idea. Come on. Leave the crusher."

Casmir had taken a step into the corridor, but he paused. "Is Ishii requiring that?"

"No, but he suggested it."

"Because he wants to beat me up?"

"My guess is because he doesn't want anyone—or anything—with recording capabilities in his quarters."

"His quarters?" Casmir had assumed that Ishii was summoning him to the bridge or his office.

"Yup. This way." Asger walked down the corridor, his gait a little stiffer than usual. He must have taken more of a battering on the station than Casmir realized. Maybe that was what he got for slinging women over his shoulder.

They didn't go far. Ishii's quarters were on the same level as the guest cabin.

Asger pushed the chime, and the door slid open.

"Found him, Captain," Asger said as he entered.

"Was it difficult?"

"Nah. I didn't have to battle his bodyguard to enter his lair, not like in the knights' quests of old."

"A lair?" Casmir stepped in a little warily, not sure whether he'd been invited for a friendly chat or a warning chat. "I thought only dragons got lairs. Princesses get towers. Kings and queens always have castles."

"What do roboticists have?" Asger asked.

"They never seem to feature in the knights' tales."

"And yet, here you are in my tale."

"Your tale? I was envisioning it as *my* tale, with you playing a small but significant role."

"*Small?*"

Ishii stepped into view, and Casmir held back his response. Ishii also wore casual clothing, as if he meant to head to bed soon.

Ishii squinted at him. "Did you have a seizure?"

"No, a nap."

The squint deepened.

Having no interest in confessing to his nightmare, Casmir said, "Asger suggested I create an error-management protocol to troubleshoot my sleep."

"Yes," Asger said. "That's just how I put it."

Asger flopped into one of two padded chairs angled toward a couch and coffee table. The room also held a desk, wall display, gaming unit, and a number of bookcases and cabinets, everything glassed in or contained by brackets to protect the contents if the ship lost gravity. An interior door led to a dimly lit bedroom. The perks of command, a cabin with more than one room.

"I'm sure." Ishii, instead of taking exception to Asger presuming to seat himself, waved Casmir to the other chair. He walked to a small cabinet built into the corner. "Sake, whiskey, or cabernet?"

"Sake," Asger said.

Ishii looked to Casmir. "Drink?"

Casmir rarely consumed alcohol, even though his doctor assured him it wasn't likely to interact with his seizure medication, but he was also rarely invited to sit and have a drink with a couple of men from the nobility. He didn't feel like celebrating, but this didn't look like a celebration. More like group commiseration over events that had gotten out of hand. If so, then alcohol seemed appropriate. Maybe it would help wash away the remnants of the nightmare.

"Yes." Casmir hesitated over the options. Red wine made him flush—Kim had mentioned it was a side effect of too much histamine that his body did a poor job of clearing—so he waved toward the sake bottle. "I'll try that."

Ishii carefully removed a trio of ceramic cups from protective holders in the cabinet, and he poured larger quantities than Casmir would have expected. He couldn't remember what the proof was for sake but assumed it was somewhat potent since he'd always had it mixed with soda. It was, in his opinion, best with lychee fizzop. Somehow, he doubted Ishii would bring out bottles of soda.

Once he handed them their cups, Ishii sank into the couch. "I am officially on Ambassador Romano's shit list."

"Why?" Asger sipped from his cup. "You did what he wished. You blew up the pirates."

Casmir tried to decide if there was censure in Asger's tone, or if he imagined it. On the station, Asger hadn't seemed any more pleased with how the pirates had been handled than Casmir.

"And it's possible Tiamat Station may accept Kingdom rule in the future," Asger added, "should the negotiations go well."

"It's unlikely there will *be* negotiations. Romano was spitting teeth when that woman said she would only deal with Casmir. He wanted to strangle him." Ishii shook his head at Casmir. "The king will never go for you as ambassador."

"It wasn't my idea." Casmir looked at his cup instead of meeting Ishii's eyes. "I'd once thought I might go into politics when this is all over and try to make a difference back home, but I wasn't thinking of *galactic* politics."

Ishii grunted, and Casmir couldn't tell if he believed him or not. Would *Jager* believe him? Or would he think this some attempt of Casmir's to bid for power? Jager might know all about his genes, but Casmir didn't think the man knew *him* at all.

He sipped from the cup, the cool liquid not as harsh sliding down his throat as he'd expected, but his left eye still blinked several times and watered. Strange that there were more allergens on this ship that bothered him than there had been on the station. He missed the *Stellar Dragon* and Viggo's excellent vacuums. And Bonita and Qin. He would have to send them a message and see how they were doing with the Druckers.

"It'll be interesting to hear what Jager says. It's hard to imagine him doing anything but using Casmir to his advantage to get the station." Asger sipped from his cup without any noticeable effect.

Casmir, not wanting to consider Jager using him further, wondered about how alcohol worked with Asger's precisely tailored diet. Did he have to calculate macronutrient ratios, or was something with so few carbohydrates a gimme?

"I'm just glad the station inhabitants have stopped trying to kill each other," Casmir murmured.

"I imagine the defender robots you left there will help with that," Asger said dryly.

Ishii raised his eyebrows.

"He turned the security robots into—I don't know what you would call it. He got on the speaker and told the whole station that all they had to do was run up to one, and it would protect them from anyone trying to perpetrate violence. And they *did.* I saw some of the videos."

Casmir smiled. He hadn't had time to look at videos, but he was glad the robots had worked.

"That seems like what they should do anyway," Ishii said.

"You'd think," Asger said, "but we first encountered them trying to blow a hole in my shuttle hatch. My superiors wouldn't have been pleased with that. It's bad enough a pod was blown up."

"I don't think either of our superiors will be pleased with any of this." Ishii leaned his head back against the couch.

Casmir thought the station inhabitants were pleased. Maybe it was wrong that that mattered more to him than what Jager wanted, but after seeing the dead bodies in the streets and the hostages that had been imprisoned for days, he was glad he'd helped someone in some way.

"It must have been nice to be a Fleet officer in the old days," Ishii said, "when everything was more black and white. When the king was noble and doing the right thing, and you were positive that *you* were doing the right thing in swearing an oath and serving under him. It's all murky these days, but you don't find out how murky until you're higher up the ranks, until you've committed yourself to a career, and your family's fortune and honor are all bound up in you serving the throne."

Asger eyed Ishii's cup, then raised his eyebrows toward Casmir.

Casmir suspected that was to imply that Ishii had started drinking before they arrived.

"It's not an easy time to be a knight either," Asger said quietly.

Casmir thought about saying the same thing of roboticists, but he'd been enjoying teaching and researching and his career in general, the crusher years aside, before all this started. Whatever life he was leading now, it had very little to do with the career he'd chosen.

Ishii drank deeply from his cup and cradled it in his hands instead of setting it down. "Sometimes, I wonder what it would have been like to be a military officer in those original days of expansion. I bet it was something to serve under Admiral Mikita."

Casmir had been in the middle of taking a drink, and he almost choked on it.

Asger gave him a knowing look.

"I'll wager he never asked his men to use morally offensive tactics to win his victories," Ishii said, not paying attention to them. "He was too smart. He didn't need to." He lowered his cup. "Or do you think that's true? Was he as good as the history books tell us? Or has he been shown in a more favorable light because it served the needs of the present?"

Ishii looked at Asger and Casmir, as if he truly wanted their opinions. Casmir's left eye blinked again.

"I'd guess he was an all right guy," he said carefully, though he couldn't truly know. Rache had been cloned from the same genes, and he was…

Casmir wasn't sure what Rache was. Maybe not as evil as he'd once believed but definitely not a good guy. Good guys didn't blow up refineries and shoot soldiers simply because they'd sworn oaths to the wrong king.

Asger smiled. "If you look at any of the histories, as told from the conquered systems, he was considered better to deal with than any of the Kingdom's other war leaders. I suspect he was at least fair."

Casmir slumped back in his chair and vowed to do something he'd been thinking about before—research Mikita more now that he was outside of the Kingdom and could, he hoped, get a more realistic picture of the man.

Asger and Ishii started talking about Xolas Moon and if the submarines they had rented from Tiamat Station would be enough to find the astroshaman base, and Casmir closed his eyes. He didn't want to go back to sleep—and his dreams—but the drink was making him drowsy.

An incoming message alert popped up on his contact, and he would have ignored it, but it was from Princess Oku.

A little flutter teased his insides. It had likely been sent days ago, waiting for a Fleet or courier ship to pass through the wormhole and deliver digital messages to the System Hydra network, so it wouldn't have anything to do with the events on Tiamat Station. Too bad. Part of him hoped that Tambora would mention him to Oku and say good things, such as that he'd been kind, helpful, and dashingly handsome as he'd reprogrammed the station's robots. Even if she'd met him only briefly at the end, after everything had been wrapped up.

Professor Dabrowski,

Thank you for finagling Scholar Sato's help with my bee project. She sent me a request for more information! I'm very excited. If we can get the bees to survive on Shango Habitat, then we can share them with the habitats in the other systems and help people increase food output and gain more independence from planetary agriculture consortiums.

Casmir smiled, wishing Oku were in charge of the Kingdom instead of Jager, though he suspected she would do her best to avoid such an onerous fate and was probably relieved her older brother was their father's heir. But Casmir could imagine her on diplomatic missions, winning allies for the Kingdom by handing out hives of bacterially enhanced bees.

Your robots are very cute, she added on a new line, and his first thought was that she meant the robot bees, but then he remembered the video about Tork and Zee chitchatting about him. *I have seen the file on the crusher project, and I would not have thought one could ever be considered cute or could be at all playful. But perhaps they are like hounds and only need the right handler to mellow their personalities?*

There was a video file attachment after that showing a short-haired gray-blue hound on its back in a dog bed in front of a fireplace, its forelegs crooked in the air and its head lolled to one side. *Her* head, Casmir decided, since the pose made it easy to tell.

A hand came into view, dangling a fluffy bird toy above the dog's head. She didn't move. The hand returned with a squishy ball that Casmir guessed squeaked—he would have to play this later on a system with speakers. The dog yawned, lolled her head to the other side, and didn't open her eyes. Finally, the hand returned with a dried fish. The dog sprang up, sat perkily, and thumped her gray tail. The hand delivered the fish, and the dog bounded out of view. The camera shifted from the fireplace, past a dark window, and to a large canopied bed where the dog was now lounging again, her head on the fluffy pillows.

That is Chasca. My brother breeds hunting dogs—well, he has someone breed them for him—and she was the runt of the litter and afraid of loud noises, so deemed unacceptable for hunting. I said I'd take her, and she goes with me on my travels now. And everywhere else.

Have a good journey, Casmir.

Casmir! She'd used his first name.

Maybe it had been an accident since she'd started the message more formally. He grinned and decided he didn't care. If she'd accidentally used it, that meant she was thinking of him by first name when she thought of him. That was excellent. He wasn't sure what to make of the implication that the dog slept in the bed—how did that work if she had human… visitors?—but he decided it was sweet that she'd sent the video. Her response to him sharing his robots.

"He looks more content than we do," Ishii observed.

"Perhaps sake mellows him out," Asger said. "I've never seen him go this long without talking."

Earlier, their voices had turned into a drone in the background, but now Casmir opened his eyes, realizing they were talking about him.

"Sorry," he said. "I was reading a message from… home."

"It must not have been from your mother," Asger said. "I've seen your expression when you're dealing with her."

"I get along well with my mother. That particular time, she was displaying unnecessary and excessive concern about the state of my underwear."

"You can see the quartermaster on the ship if that's still a problem," Ishii said dryly.

"It's not. She sent me a bunch when I was back on Odin. There was even enough to give some to—a friend."

Ishii grunted, having no idea who he was talking about. Asger, who had been there, looked disturbed at the identification of Rache as *a friend.*

"How far are we from Xolas Moon?" Casmir decided a topic change was in order. "Do we need to start planning how best to use your men and those submarines?"

"There's a briefing in the morning." Ishii finished his cup and went back for more sake. "I suggest we let ourselves relax for the night and worry about it tomorrow."

Casmir hoped he *could* relax and that the nightmare wouldn't return. He found himself wishing he were back home so he could visit his parents for dinner and spend a Sabbath speaking with his father about the decisions he'd made lately. About whether he was doing the right thing by getting involved.

Kim was logical and gave practical advice, but his father, even though he was a math teacher, always understood the conflicts of the heart better than anybody he knew. He would pull Casmir aside for Torah study, and ever so coincidentally find passages that applied to whatever Casmir was wrestling with. For a time, Casmir could sit back and allow himself to be the student again, with his father the teacher. Though he feared even his father would be daunted by what had been going on in Casmir's life lately.

Perhaps for now, with the future still a question mark that promised only danger, and the road home a long one, Casmir would try to focus on what pleasant thoughts he could find. Maybe he could talk Zee into doing something entertaining that he could record in preparation for the next time he came up with a reason to send a message to Oku. Would *he* sit up for a fish? Perhaps not. And Casmir found the idea of him lounging on the bed with his head on the pillows alarming.

He would think of something else. Something *cute*. Something that Oku would find endearing and that would take his mind off the worries he feared wouldn't end anytime soon.

THE END

Printed in Great Britain
by Amazon

46306154R00189